I0691981

Avalee's Gift

by

Linda Apple

Moonlight Mississippi Series, Book 2

This is a work of fiction. Names, characters, places, and incidents are either the product of the author's imagination or are used fictitiously, and any resemblance to actual persons living or dead, business establishments, events, or locales, is entirely coincidental.

Avalee's Gift

COPYRIGHT © 2017 by Linda Apple

All rights reserved. No part of this book may be used or reproduced in any manner whatsoever without written permission of the author or The Wild Rose Press, Inc. except in the case of brief quotations embodied in critical articles or reviews.
Contact Information: info@thewildrosepress.com

Cover Art by *RJ Morris*

The Wild Rose Press, Inc.
PO Box 708
Adams Basin, NY 14410-0708
Visit us at www.thewildrosepress.com

Publishing History
First Mainstream Women's Fiction Rose Edition, 2017
Print ISBN 978-1-5092-1307-8
Digital ISBN 978-1-5092-1308-5

Moonlight Mississippi Series, Book 2
Published in the United States of America

Occasionally, vivid red cardinals sang out, *cheer, cheer, cheer,* from evergreen boughs blanketed in white. When we walked through the gate, I marveled at the scene before me. The park looked enchanted. The swings, slides, and the grounds were sparkling and pristine. So much so, I hated marring the surface. We brushed off the seats and sat on the rubber slings. Rocking back and forth, I enjoyed the moment.

"Avalee?" Ty turned his swing around toward me. "Remember the morning I carried you across the swinging bridge over Moon Creek?"

"Remember? I still have nightmares." I didn't mention the other dreams of desire related to that particular day while suspended thirty feet in the air.

"Don't I know it? You nearly strangled me holding on so hard." Snow laced his beanie and caught on his ridiculously long lashes. I swear, Mother Nature did prefer her boys. No woman I knew had lashes like that unless they were fake. "But when I realized you actually were afraid of heights, I was sorry for putting you in that position. That's when I knew I wanted to protect you and care for you the rest of my life." He leaned forward and kissed my nose. "I already knew that I loved you."

"It was then I realized I had fallen in love with you, Tyler Jackson."

He reached into his pocket. "We aren't on the swinging bridge, so these swings will have to symbolize that day." Ty held up a small red satin box and opened it. Nestled in black velvet was a ring sparkling with diamonds.

Praise for Linda Apple

"Linda Apple's writing style is charming and down to earth. Her books are well written and heart touching."
~Jodi Thomas, New York Times and USA Today
Best Selling Author

Dedication

For my mother, Freddie Mae Diehl,
who taught me to be a southern lady
and whose personality inspired
many of the characters in my book.

Dear Readers,

After *Women of Washington Avenue* was published, many of you expressed the desire to know more about each of the women in my novel. Therefore, I decided to create the *Moonlight Mississippi Series.* Avalee, Lexi, Jema, and Molly Kate will each get their own book. But you won't miss out hearing from all the ladies in each book because, as we say in the south, they are always *up in each other's business*.

I had one reader comment, "There is a lot of eating and drinking in your book." My answer was simply, "Yep. That's what we do." You see, in the south, food is our elixir for everything. If you're sad, we will comfort you with food. Sick? We will feed you. Lonely? Food's on the way. Angry? Eat and you will feel better. Happy? Let's eat! Holiday or special event? Let's celebrate with food. And as far as drinking goes, well, we do enjoy our nip on the porch and with friends.

Many of you have requested recipes for the dishes mentioned in *Women of Washington Avenue.* Therefore, in the back of *Avalee's Gift* are the four most requested recipes from the book.

In *Avalee's Gift*, we pick up the week after Ty proposed to Avalee at Molly Kate and Stan's wedding reception. All the girls plan and pull off a quick and fabulous wedding for Jema. But when it is Avalee and Ty's turn, as the old saying goes, life has other plans.

I hope you enjoy *Avalee's Gift.* I love hearing from my readers and as you can see, I listen to you. Please feel free to email me at lindacapple@gmail.com.

Magnolia blooms, sweet tea, and porch swing blessings to you all!

~Linda

Prologue

Life is truly strange—both unfair and beyond generous.

~Avalee Preston

After Marc Jackson proposed, I wasted no time buying the perfect wedding gown.

I never wore that dress.

We set the date for the week after we graduated. I know, it was crazy to set the dates so close, but after a short—very short—honeymoon, Marc was to start medical school and I had to find a job.

We finished our final exams at Ole Miss and were preparing for our graduation ceremony and the wedding. Life was crazy-busy, but I kept up with the pace. That is, until my suspicions brought everything to a jolting halt.

I thought I was pregnant.

You have no idea how much I dreaded telling him. Sure, we wanted children, but not until he finished school and had a practice. Even so, I had to admit, when I thought about the possibility, I couldn't help but run my hand over my stomach and smile.

I planned to take a test the following morning and not say anything until I knew for sure. But when Marc came to my sorority house after his frat brothers threw him a bachelor party, I changed my mind. He was in such a good mood—and pretty inebriated—so I decided to take a chance at his understanding. Maybe, he might even be happy?

I led him to a private area in the sorority house common room. It was a walled off, quiet nook. My sorority sisters and I used the area to study when there was too much distraction in our suites.

"Marc," my voice barely registered a whisper, "I have something to tell you."

He flopped down in an overstuffed floral chintz chair and pulled me onto his lap. "What, doll?" The smell of whiskey on his breath hovered around my face like a fog.

"I think I'm pregnant."

He stared at me through bleary eyes, but soon the meaning of what I said registered. He smiled. He actually smiled. I drew in a deep breath of relief. That is, until he said, "No problem, babe. You can't be *that* pregnant. We'll take care of it when we get back from our honeymoon."

"Take *care* of it? What are you saying?" Of course, I had a pretty good idea.

"You know…get rid of it." He pressed his booze-pickled lips against my neck. He must have felt me stiffen because he pulled back and looked me in the eyes. "Hey, babe, we can have a kid, I promise. But later, when it's more convenient."

Get rid of *it?* Have a *kid? Convenient?* I glared at him noting the alcohol induced flush on his skin. For an instant, I despised him. "Absolutely not." I vaulted to my feet. "We won't get *rid* of *it*. A child is not a piece of trash."

Marc's mood turned from jovial to frustration in a

nanosecond. "Avalee, now isn't the time to be parents. I'll be in school, and you'll be working. You have to think about this logically. It wouldn't be fair to the kid. We'll be too busy."

"Then I suppose we will be too busy for each other, too?"

He furrowed his brow and stood rather unsteadily. His voice grew hard and loud by degrees. "Don't take that tone with me, A. You know what I meant."

There is no need to go into detail about the conversation from that point, only to say it deteriorated into a screaming match. My sorority sisters peeked around the corner then quickly shrank back. Thank goodness our housemother wasn't around. The argument came to an abrupt end when he blurted out, "Mother was right when she warned me about you. She said I should have never proposed, because you'd be nothing but a distraction. Now you're knocked up just when I'm about to start med school."

His confession shocked me silent. In a cold, calmer voice, he leveled his gaze at me. "We are through, Avalee."

Tears gathered in my eyes. This couldn't be happening. Marc speared the air with his finger. "One more thing. If you decide to keep it, don't expect anything out of me. I'll pay to get rid of it, but I'm not paying any kind of child support. Just try and say it's mine, I'll swear you are lying."

His words were like hot needles piercing my heart. How could he?

I tugged my ring. "Get out. Go home to your momma. Maybe she will stick this diamond pacifier in your mouth to suck when she tucks you in at night." I yanked the solitaire off my finger and threw it in his face.

He snatched it from the floor, stuck it in his pocket, and stormed out. I followed him as far as the door and watched him stumble to his car, yank the door open, then fall onto the front seat. His screeching tires sent up a plume of smoke as he sped away.

All night, I replayed our fight in my mind. He couldn't have meant what he had said. He was drunk. He was frightened. This had not been in his plans. It was something he couldn't control which made him angry. Surely, he'd sober up and think logically. He wasn't the kind of guy who would throw a life in the trash because it was inconvenient.

After hours of tossing in my bed, I threw the blankets off and went to the window. Wisps of dark clouds slipped by in front and behind the pearl moon. The thin thread of dawn divided earth from sky. I touched the pane with my fingers. "Oh, Marc. Call me and say you love me. Tell me how sorry you are and say we can keep our child, if there is one."

A soft rap sounded on my door. *Marc?* I threw it open only to see my housemother hugging her chenille robe.

"Avalee, honey, you have a call."

By her frown, I suspected it was Marc and she was none too happy to be getting a call at this hour of the morning.

"Who is it?"

Her frown smoothed into compassion. "Someone from the Jackson family."

"Marc?" I hurried past her, ran down two flights of stairs, and grabbed the receiver in the common room.

"Hello?"

"Avalee. This is Mr. Jackson, Marc's father." His voice was tight and low. "I'll get right to the point. Marc is dead."

"Wha…" I sank to the floor. "No." I glanced at my finger, still indented where my engagement ring had been just hours before. "No, no, no, no…" The room blurred and hot tears ran down my face. "What happened?"

"The officers said he missed a curve and ran into a tree at a high rate of speed." He paused. "I suppose you should come home as soon as it is…" His voice broke. "Convenient."

A click sounded, but I continued to hold the phone to my ear listening to the disconnect hum in stunned silence.

"Sugar?" The housemother took the phone from my hand. "I've called your parents. They will be here soon." She helped me to my feet. "Now go pack your things, honey."

The days before the funeral blurred into each other. Voices, faces, soft touches, filled my days. During the visitation, Marc's parents guarded his casket like sentinels. Whenever I came close, I picked up on their air of hostility, which confused me. Had he found a pay phone and told them about our argument, about my suspicions, before he wrecked his car? Tyler, Marc's little brother, sat alone on a pew. The Jacksons didn't even seem aware their youngest son was in the room. The loneliness and despair on that ten-year-old's face broke my heart and fed my guilt.

There was no baby.

None of this would have happened if I had kept my

mouth shut.

The morning of the service, I asked Pastor Dixon to unlock the church early so I could be alone with Marc without his parents' laser glares following my every move. I stood alone in the front of the sanctuary. The polished cherry wood casket glowed under the soft light. Thick silence enshrouded me as I crept forward. With trembling hands, I opened the lid. He appeared as if he were simply asleep. No cuts or bruises. I brushed my fingers across his cold, waxy face while hot tears ran down my cheeks and dripped onto his coat lapel.

"Marc," I swallowed and whispered. "I'm so, so sorry. I'm not pregnant after all. The doctor told me sometimes a woman's cycle is thrown off by stress. And Lord knows we were burning the candle at both ends."

I studied his still form before an emotional tsunami washed over me and my words rushed into each other. "Baby, you didn't have to die. This was all my fault. I should have waited until I knew for sure if I was pregnant before I spoke with you. I should have known better than to try to reason with you while you were drunk. If only I'd done things differently we would be getting married instead of having your funeral."

Clinging to the sides of the casket, I broke down. My legs grew weak and rubbery. I needed to sit. Before closing the lid, I kissed his unyielding cheek. "I'm so sorry. Please forgive me."

For a few moments, I sat on the pew and tried to gather myself. Today would be a long one. But I'd said my piece, for whatever good it did. Standing, I cast a last glance at the casket then left the church.

It seemed everyone from town showed up for his

funeral. Pastor Dixon conducted the service with compassion and hope. I felt better than I had in days. Afterward, at the graveside, I hoped to have one last private moment with Marc. The crowd lingered, much to my chagrin, but finally started to thin. Eventually only Marc's parents, his brother, and I remained. My impatience for them to leave, made me tense and on edge. Across the cemetery lawn, Mrs. Jackson turned her ice-blue gaze toward me. I felt pierced with white-hot anger. I wasn't the only one on edge. She strode toward me stopping just inches from my face and held up her pinky.

"Avalee Preston, why was this in his pocket?"

I had to step back to see what she had on it. My engagement ring? Guilt bled through me, and I stammered, "We had…words."

Seeing my ring brought back memories of that awful confrontation. I bit my bottom lip to hold back the surging grief threatening to explode.

Her expression steeled. "So, because of your childish tantrum, my son is dead?" She shook from the effort to control her rage.

Mr. Jackson eased up beside her and put his arm around her shoulders. "Come on. Let's go home." He glowered at me, shook his head, and nudged his wife to turn away.

"This thing is cursed." She flung my ring across the cemetery lawn. Stunned, I watched them walk toward the waiting limousine.

Tyler ran across the lawn. Soon he returned. "Avalee?" He held up my ring. "Momma didn't mean it. She's just sad."

I looked into his beautiful brown eyes fringed with

thick lashes. They were windows into his deep sorrow. "Thank you, sweetie."

"Are you sad, too?"

"Yes. Very sad."

He hung his head. "Me, too."

"Tyler Jackson." Mrs. Jackson stood beside the limo with clenched fists. "Get in this car."

"You better go, hon." I patted his shoulder. "Thank you for finding my ring."

"You're welcome."

"Tyler." Mrs. Jackson stabbed the open doorway with her finger. "Now."

He gave me a tiny wave and jogged toward his parents. I turned my back to them and waited until the sound of the car faded.

Slipping the ring back on my finger, I placed my left hand on the casket and rested my head on it. "Please, please, forgive me."

A warm breeze brushed my hair against my face causing it to cling to the dampness on my cheeks. I smoothed my hair away and stared off at the graves. It was so quiet—an anomaly—peaceful and yet sorrowful. In a nearby tree, a robin broke out in song. *Peek, peek, tut, tut, tut.* How odd for such a joyful song to be sung on such a mournful day. I kissed my finger and pressed it onto the cherry wood then turned to leave with the heaviness of knowing it was too late. Marc would never be able to forgive me. And I would never be able to forgive myself.

The following three days, I canceled all the wedding arrangements. Explaining the situation to venders over and over left me drained and depressed. There was no way I could endure a graduation ceremony. Instead, I sold my ring, packed my bags, and fled to New York City where I could get lost in the crowd and hopefully find a successful career. And that is exactly what happened. Having been raised by generations of florists, I started in floral design for high-end clients. This led to me writing books on floral arrangement, herbal creations, and landscape tips, which led to speaking opportunities at floral events all over the world.

I loved living in the city. Frankly, I never wanted to return to Moonlight, Mississippi and risk ever seeing Mrs. Jackson again. But I did miss my parents. So, instead of visiting my parents in my hometown, I flew them to New York, or wherever I happened to be in the world. I never married. There were several serious candidates, but the shadow of guilt that resided in my soul insinuated itself into every relationship I ventured to try.

But life is truly strange. It is both unfair and beyond generous. While it was unfair in my youth, it was generous in my waning years of middle age.

In a whiplash of events, I returned to Moonlight to help restore the struggling family floral business and met a ghost. Tyler Jackson, Marc's baby brother, had grown into his twin. After a ridiculously short amount of time, he professed he'd fallen in love with me. Of course, I resisted him. Not only was there a twelve-year age difference between us, the guilt that had kept me single all my life also stood in the way of my loving him. It didn't help that he looked enough like Marc to be his double.

Undaunted, Ty chipped away at my resistance with his playfulness, tenderness. His maddening crooked smile that pushed in his deep dimples also factored into my weakening. And those deep mahogany eyes. They were still windows into his soul. Somehow, he convinced me he truly preferred older women. But what really made my wall of defense fall was the tenderness and patience he showered on me. He honestly understood the true meaning of love.

Until Ty, I really hadn't understood love. I equated it with romance—bursts of heady feelings of exhilaration, desire, and passions. Like what I had with Marc. Not that those feelings weren't real. They were, but they were not love. I've come to think of them as a by-product of love. These ecstasies, like fireworks, burn out and the ashes fall cold to the ground. Ty valued, respected, and treasured me as a person, putting my needs above his.

Marc never treasured me, and in the end, he didn't value or respect me either. And if I were being honest, I didn't him either.

I love Ty—truly love him.

Because of this love, I must face what I ran away from over thirty years ago—his parents.

Tonight, at supper we plan to tell them of our engagement.

God give me strength.

Chapter One

Friends can blow away the darkest clouds, if only for a while.

~Avalee Preston

Morning broke in gray, rain-heavy clouds. I snuggled deeper under my comforter wishing the day were already over. The storm brewing in the atmosphere over Moonlight would be nothing compared to the one sure to erupt inside the Jackson home when Ty and I told them about our engagement.

Such a shame. There were so many things to be happy about. I hated having this cloak of dread draped over me. Molly Kate, my *forever sister-friend*, married her long-lost lover, Stan Montgomery. We had only three weeks to plan and pull off their wedding. And I must say, we did an excellent job. Christmas was in four days, *and* we had yet another whirlwind wedding to plan for another one of my *FSF*s, Jema and her fiancé Levi. Even with all these joyful events, I struggled with being glad about anything considering the gallows of condemnation awaiting me.

Pfff. "Snap out of it Avalee."

Great, now I'm talking to myself. Coffee. Strong and laced with real sugar and cream. The only thing powerful enough to coax me from my cocoon of blankets. The room felt unusually cold. Was it the weather or simply the transition from a warm bed to a cold room? I slipped on my robe and slippers then ambled down the stairs to the kitchen—and to the coffee.

Momma sat at her small drop-leaf table positioned against the wall where her little smiling plaster of Paris fruits and veggies hung. As tacky as these whimsical figures might appear to decorators, I liked them. They had greeted me every morning as a child. In fact, I wouldn't mind a few of my own for my kitchen after Ty and I married.

She looked up from her paper. "Morning, baby."

"Morning."

"Have an orange roll. Molly Kate brought some by as a thank you for feeding Gypsy and Kricket while she and Stan were on their honeymoon."

Tempting, but first thing's first. I grabbed a mug and filled it with dark roast. "Some honeymoon. Two nights in Memphis."

"Oh, they plan on a cruise in early summer." Momma held out her cup to me. "But what with it being Christmas and all, they'd rather be home."

After filling Mom's cup, I joined her at the table and stared longingly at the box of orange decadence. MK's rolls had taken over the town, which caused some pretty hard feelings. The baker at Magnolia Tea Room was the first to introduce the rolls, and he accused Molly Kate of copying his recipe. He even threatened to sue her although he'd done the same thing. Before the tearoom opened, he visited Molly Kate's cafe, *Taste of Heaven*, and bought several of her baked goods after asking her all kinds of questions. When the tearoom opened, sure enough, a few of her items appeared on his menu. In the end, the great orange roll drama only amounted to his kicking up dust, or should I say powdered sugar? Her recipe was clearly superior.

I put the coffee cup to my lips and tried to stop lusting after the pastries. "So, what are your plans today?"

"I hope to finish up my holiday baking, and then Felix is going to carry me in that old truck of his to make my deliveries."

Every year, Momma gave food gifts to everyone in the neighborhood, all her doctors and their staff, her bank tellers, and the church staff.

"So who gets what this year?"

She cocked her head, pursed her lips, and looked up through squinted eyes. "Let's see, I made turtle candies and orange glazed pecans for the neighbors. They always ask for those you know. For the doctors I made corn dip, haystacks, and the pecans. For the bank folks, I made a pan of fudge and corn dip. And I made several batches of cookies for the church office. That's what I'm finishing up this morning."

"Wow, that's a lot of work." Secretly, I hoped she saved back some corn dip for us. I could eat it with a spoon. Who needed corn chip dippers?

Momma smiled. "It sure is, but I love it. Making all this and delivering it is one of the things that makes Christmas for me." She reached across the table and patted my hand. "That and having you home this year."

Guilt rose inside me. I could count on one hand the times I came home the day before Christmas and left the day after. In my defense, I'd flown my parents to New York for Christmas many times, but I knew it wasn't the same for them.

"What are you doing today, sugar?"

I groaned. "Dreading tonight. I'm mentally preparing myself for an evening of passive-aggressive conversation."

"Oh honey, surely it won't be that bad."

"Fortunately, you didn't see her attack me after Marc's funeral." I snatched part of Mom's roll and popped it in my mouth. The tangy, buttery-sweet pastry made me forget everything except the next bite.

"Baby, back then she was hurting. We all were. Losing a child is the ultimate injury."

She put a roll on a plate and pushed it toward me. I didn't give myself time to think about the fat and calories I was about to consume. Mindlessly, I plucked out the tender center, smeared it with butter, nudged it into my mouth and savored the soft, melting, food of the gods.

Momma's words stirred deep within me the ghost of *what had never been*. Even at my age, the longing for a child had never died. However, my fifty-six-year-old body had given up trying to create a child and created Hell instead. Hot flashes and night sweats plagued me. "I suppose you're right. But it's hard. I was hurting then, too."

Momma stood and collected the dishes. "Hon, don't be chained to bitterness. Life is too short. Let it go and make room in your heart for peace."

Her reference to chains reminded me of two dogs I saw on one of my walks. They were all tangled up in the leads their owners used to tether them. Poor animals. They were miserable. Perhaps it would help to remember that pitiful image while at the Jacksons and hopefully keep from growing even more bitter.

Perhaps…

Mom went to the cupboard and pulled out a bright red tin with white and silver snowflakes scattered over the lid. "I made three different kinds of fudge for you to take tonight for Emma and Marcus: chocolate with pecans, peanut butter, and white chocolate macadamia. If nothing else, this should sweeten their mood."

"One can only hope." I finished my roll and pushed back from the table. "For now, I'm going to focus on the more pleasant aspects of the day."

"Oh? What's that?"

"Planning Jema and Levi's New Year's Eve wedding." I stood and stretched. "We are meeting at MK's this morning."

Momma plunged her hands in the sink of hot, soapy water. "I'm certainly glad Levi kept his name instead of going back to Matthew. I just couldn't wrap my mind around his first name after calling him by his middle name for so long."

"Me either."

I thought back to when Levi first entered our lives. My friend Jema befriended him at Life Source, the homeless shelter where she volunteered. He was a pitiful sight when she first saw him in the soup line. His long, matted hair, dirty fingernails, and tattered clothing would have given most people pause before they gave their heart away. But not our Jema. She immediately recognized his kind soul, and her compassionate heart connected with his, never expecting anything from him but his devotion. Turned out he was Matthew Levi Abrams, a billionaire from Canada who disguised himself as a man who had nothing in hopes of finding someone who would love him for himself and not his wealth. He found a gem in our Jema. When he decided to continue going by his middle name, Levi, he explained it this way, "I was reborn in Moonlight. I found true love and true friends. In Canada, I'm Matthew, the only heir to our family fortune where the focus is wealth and the accumulation of more wealth. But here I'm Levi, a man with purpose. A man who is loved for nothing more than himself."

"Well, all I can say is Jema isn't letting grass grow under her feet before she marries. New Year's Eve is in three weeks."

"True. Just like Molly Kate. Glad I'm not in a rush. Ty and I have months to plan." In my heart of hearts, I wished we were marrying earlier. But May would be beautiful, and I'd always wanted to be a May bride.

"Are Jema's girls coming to the wedding?"

"No, they will still be in Italy. This is such a hurry up deal they couldn't make arrangements, and besides, they didn't want to disappoint their hosts."

"I suppose they will see their mother in Italy then."

"I think that's the plan."

Momma dried her hands with the dishtowel draped over her shoulder. "I'd love to see Italy. Hey, why don't y'all honeymoon there? Mother's Day is in May." She poked my side with her elbow. "Hint, hint."

"I'll think on it." And I did for a hot second before deciding no one was going with me on my honeymoon but Ty.

The little yellow cuckoo bird slid out of its Swiss chalet clock and chirped eight times. I had to be at Molly's by eight-thirty.

"I'd better get ready Mom." I leaned over her five-foot frame and kissed her forehead before hurrying upstairs.

****

Every time I turn onto Leslie Lane and see the old Norton Mansion, I'm enchanted. Since childhood I'd dreamed of seeing the inside of the mansion and playing on the magnificent lawn under the enormous Magnolia trees. And now it belonged to one of my best friends in the world. Molly Kate and Stan were turning the majestic white antebellum into a B&B. They moved into the two-story house adjoined to the mansion by a sunroom breezeway. This house, I understood, was built as a mother-in-law home. The previous owner, Mr. Norton, must have thought a lot of his wife's mother. It is exquisite in its own right.

Molly suggested we meet at the mansion instead of her house since the wedding would be held there. She also offered to leave all decorations from her wedding from two weeks ago in place, which made my job easier. The fairy lights were already strung and the greenery in the arrangements would still be good. All I had to do was order fresh flowers to replace the faded ones.

A cold breeze blew across my face when I opened the car door. It smelled crisp and moist with a faint evergreen note. Could this be a harbinger of a rare snow? I hoped so. Hugging myself, I hurried up the brick walkway to the porch and rapped on the double cherry wood doors.

The moment Molly Kate answered my knock, their little Jack Russell, Kricket, rushed out gleefully barking her hello.

"Get yourself in here, girl. It's turned cold out." Molly Kate patted her knee. "You, too, Krickers."

The pup scampered inside and turned to see if we were following.

"Where's Gypsy?" I was pretty sure introducing a dog into the family had her kitty's nose out of joint.

"She's with Stan at the house. I brought Kricket with me to give Gyps a break. She doesn't appreciate puppy-enthusiasm." Molly took my coat and hung it on the hall tree. Marriage sure agreed with her. The expression in her jewel-green eyes and her broad smile evidenced her happiness. "Lordy, it is cold out."

"You can say that again. I sure hope you have…" I didn't have to finish my sentence because the heavy aroma of fresh ground coffee wafted over me. I lifted my nose to the fragrance and breathed deep. Nothing says, "Welcome. Have a seat. Relax and stay a while," like brewing French blend.

MK read my mind. "Coffee? It will be ready in a jiffy. We're still waiting on Lexi. Jema is in the kitchen sampling apple spice scones."

"Ooooh, sounds wicked. I'll have to try a pinch." Nothing, other than her orange rolls, tasted better than Molly Kate's scones.

"Oh, for heaven's sakes, eat a whole scone." Molly shook her head. "How will you ever be fabulous like me if you stay in that skinny body?"

Lexi pushed through the door and rushed in. "Sorry for barging in without knocking, but it is too bitter out there to be polite." A flaming red strand of hair fell from under her knit wool beanie.

"How does coffee sound?" Molly held her hand out for Lexi's soft gray hoodie.

"Like heaven." After tossing the hoodie to Molly Kate, Lexi danced around hugging herself, reminding me of an Irish sprite. "Why in heaven's name doesn't this place have a hot tub? It's got everything else."

"Good idea. I'll talk to Stan about that very thing." She nodded her head toward the kitchen. "But for now, we need to get a wedding planned."

When we tromped through the door, Jema looked up from her magazine and beamed revealing perfect teeth. I swear that girl could be a lipstick model, even at fifty-seven. "Hi y'all.

Lexi rushed the coffee pot and grabbed a mug. "Ready to get this planning party started?"

"More than ready." Jema folded the corner of her magazine and closed it.

A thrill rose up in me when I thought of how the next wedding we planned would be mine. Even though I stood at the threshold of qualifying for Social Security, I intended to go all out. Jema, bless her, promised to come and be a part of all my wedding plans even though she and Levi would still be in Italy. She now had more money than an oil sheik, so flying back and forth wouldn't be a problem. I could be jealous; the temptation was certainly there. But if anyone deserved this fairy-tale life, my precious friend certainly did.

After Lexi took a tentative sip from her mug, she cupped her hands around it and sighed. "Ahhhh, that's good."

We all chatted a few moments, then Lexi set her cup down, jumped up and announced, "All right everybody, it's time to go crazy. With all of Levi's money, this will be the wedding of the century!"

Jema grinned. "Welll…"

Lexi put her hands on her hips. "What?"

"You are not going to believe what I want. And the

wedding of the century isn't it."

I poured a second cup, sat at the table beside her, and reached for one of the pads and pens Molly set out for us to take notes. "So, tell us. What do you want?"

Jema glanced at each of us before she spoke. "I know y'all are going to think Levi and I are crazy, but we don't want a large wedding. Just the opposite, we want a small, intimate ceremony. During his masquerade as a homeless man, he learned firsthand about the hardships of not having the most basic things like food, clean water to bathe, and privacy. But he also found he enjoyed a quiet life.

"But honey," I could tell Lexi's ire was growing. "What about you? You've struggled *all your life*. You *deserve* extravagance."

Jema arched her eyebrow and gave a wry smile. "You don't have to have a large wedding bash to be *lavishly* elegant."

"Ooooh, I see." Lexi rubbed her hands together. "I feel better. Now let's get lavishly elegant."

Molly Kate moved the platter of apple-spice scones to the table. "Are y'all going to sell your house?"

"We decided to rent it. The plan is to tour Italy and decide where we would like to buy a villa, then after we purchase one, we plan to live in it for a year or so. Then move home and build a house on the lake."

"Sweet baby Jesus." Molly shook her head.

"Are you selling the villa after you leave Italy?" I reached for a scone and cut it in half, knowing full well I'd end up eating the whole thing.

"No, we will keep it for vacations and such. Levi can use it for business. *And* of course it will be available for my three closest friends."

Molly Kate and Lexi high-fived each other.

"Hmmmm, think y'all can find something by May? I wouldn't mind honeymooning in Italy." The scone tasted fabulous. I grabbed the other half.

"I promise you this, A, we will do our best."

"Okay girls, let's get down to business." Molly Kate sat back in her chair and poised her pen over a tablet. "What's the theme going to be?"

"Well, Levi and I chose New Year's Eve because It symbolizes saying goodbye to the old and hello to the new. That's what we are doing. Goodbye to our old lives and hello to our new life together. We want to throw a fabulous party, confetti, sparklers, fireworks, champagne—the works."

"Hey." Lexi leaned forward. "I'm liking this."

Jema put out her hands. "Wait till you hear this. The ceremony will be timed so that at the first stroke of midnight we will say 'I do' and then kiss in the New Year for the other eleven." She clapped her hands together and fisted them under her chin. "Isn't that the best thing ever?"

"Lord have mercy, I'll have to sleep all day to stay up that late." Molly Kate buttered her scone. "Stan and I are usually asleep by nine. But we are up by five."

"I have faith in you MK. You'll do just fine. Oh, one other thing. Would you mind keeping the Christmas tree in the library up? That's where Levi proposed to me and I'd like to be standing there when he first sees me in my wedding gown before we join the party."

"The party before the vows." Lexi patted her hands. "That's my kind of wedding."

"No problem, hon." Molly Kate made a note.

My mind went back to the night Ty proposed to me in that very room on the same night. I could still smell leather, lemon oil, dusty books, wood smoke, and cedar. Magical. In the dancing glow of firelight and twinkling LEDs on the Christmas tree, I confessed my secret shame about how I felt responsible for his brother's death. My confession didn't faze him. Instead, he asserted his love for me and asked me to be his wife. The thirty years of guilt that had held my heart in its grasp, released its hold, freeing me to love. "Ty proposed to me in that room, too."

"Hey," Molly bobbed her eyebrows. "When I advertise the B&B, I'll say the library has magical romantic powers."

"Great angle." I thought a minute. "Invent a romantic legend about the house. Maybe even a ghost."

"Great idea." Molly scribbled on her pad.

"Okay, back to business." I pointed at Jema with the last bite of my scone. "What kind of flowers do you want? I'll need to put the order in soon to make sure they arrive in time."

"White roses." Jema closed her eyes. "Lots and lots of white roses."

"What else would you like in your bouquet?"

"I love pearls and crystals."

Ideas began to build in my mind. "Great, I'll take it from here."

"You have plenty of bridesmaids." Lexi swirled her finger indicating all of us. "So, what about groomsmen?"

"Well, that's another thing I want to do differently." Jema put her hands up in surrender. "Now don't y'all get your panties in a twist, but there won't be a wedding march or a center aisle."

Lexi's eyebrows pulled together. "But…"

Jema patted the air. "Hear me out, now. Like I said earlier, we want the ceremony to be small and intimate, so we are only inviting close friends. No more than thirty people and a few dignitaries."

"Dignitaries?" Lexi's frown deepened.

"Some of the people from the city council and Mayor Campbell. Levi wants to be in their good graces for when we get back. He hopes to expand Life Source and we will need all the favors we can get."

Molly Kate crossed her arms over her chest and leaned back in her chair. "Now there's a sad story."

"Truer words were never spoken, bless his heart." Lexi slid off her stool and walked to the coffee pot.

"What?" I'd never heard this story.

"Well, Mayor Campbell, Sid, was married to this floozie who called herself Babs." Lexi smirked. "Her name was Barbara. She had illusions of Streisand. That girl was one of the most ungrateful, entitled, tacky, descendants of a female dog I've ever known. She always whined about how hard her life was because she had to work while raising her kids. That woman made Sid's life miserable. My ex, Toby, and I used to run around in the same circles. Never fail, but she'd get floor-lickin' drunk and flirt with Toby, because he was a doctor." Lexi took a swig of her coffee. "Heck, she flirted with every man in the room, except for Sid. He usually sat alone so I usually invited him to our table. Poor soul had to sit and endure her embarrassing behavior.

"Things went from bad to worse. She started putting the moves on a rich client and leaving Sid with the boys at night saying she had," Lexi made air quotes, "meetings." Then one day she and that man ran off together. She just up and left." Lexi lifted her arms. "Her kids even. What kind of mother does that?"

"That's terrible," I said. "Did she ever come back?"

Molly Kate joined in. "Nope. She hasn't been back. Sid tried for a solid year to find her. He hired private investigators, put ads in papers, co-operated with the police. But nothing. So he raised the boys by himself and has done a darned good job, I might add."

How had I missed this story? "Did he divorce her?"

"Nope." Jema held up her finger. "Sid Campbell is one fine man with a lot of integrity."

"So why didn't he divorce her?"

"Because he says he doesn't know if she's dead, alive, or injured. He doesn't feel right ending the marriage until he knows something for sure." Lexi plopped down on her stool. "A rare quality in men these days," Lexi added and grinned at Jema. "Levi excepted."

Molly Kate cleared her throat.

"And Stan." Lexi flipped her hand at me. "And Ty. Sheesh, y'all got the last good men on the planet. Thanks a lot."

Jema stood and placed a hand on Lexi's shoulder. "One day, Sid might just be available and as you implied, he is the last man with integrity left on the planet."

"Now don't you go there Jema Presley." Lexi brushed Jema's hand off her shoulder. "I like my bad-boy Nathan. We need to get back to planning your wedding."

The doorbell chimed in a rich Westminster tune, and the front door opened then shut. Molly Kate frowned. "Who could that be?"

"Anybody home?"

"It's Momma." I walked to the foyer to meet her. "Hey, I thought you were busy being Mrs. Santa."

"I was, but I finished early and thought I'd get in on the planning." She grinned. "And Molly Kate's scones."

"Well, follow me. I think MK is brewing a fresh pot of coffee."

"That sounds good. It's as cold as a well-digger's behind out there."

Jema's face lit up when she saw Momma. "Cladie Mae. Now my day is perfect."

"Hi, sugar. Excited?"

"Beyond excited."

Molly Kate held up the coffee pot. "Hey y'all, fresh coffee here."

Momma took the cup of coffee Jema handed her. "What have I missed?"

Jema pulled out a chair next to her. "I'll catch you up."

Lexi plopped down across from Momma. "She just told us there won't be a wedding processional."

"Now Lex, hear me out." Jema's eyes glistened as she spoke. "All of you have been such a source of strength and support, I'd rather y'all form a circle around Levi and me. I mean, that is what we do for each other, right? We circle the wagons so to speak." She patted Momma's hand. "You, too, Cladie."

"Well," Lexi shrugged, "I hate to admit it, but I kinda like that idea."

"And," Jema held up her finger, "I'm buying the bridesmaid dresses." She slid catalogues in front of each of us. "I've hired a designer to make them exclusive to your bodies. All you have to do is pick out the style you like."

"Will there be time?" My organized mind couldn't fathom this.

"Yes. Levi is flying the designer here day after tomorrow. He will spend the day taking your measurements, talking with you about your style choices, and then return to create the dresses. He has several seamstresses at his disposal. The only thing you don't have a choice in is the color and material. I'm having all of them made up in gold, but leaving it up to him about the fabrics. He will know what materials will work best for the dresses you all have selected."

Molly Kate lifted her eyebrows. "Wow, I'm lovin' this. What color are you wearing?"

"Silver."

Momma piped up. "Reminds me of a song we used to sing, 'Make new friends, but keep the old. One is silver and the other gold.'"

"That's nice," said Jema. "In my mind, gold symbolizes the value of our friendship. Silver symbolizes my new life with Levi."

"Love it." Molly Kate pointed to a dress with a plunging neckline. "And I love, love, love, this one."

"Now why am I not surprised?" Lexi crossed her arms. "Plenty of boobage exposure."

"I've got to show off my best assets. Oh, and Lexi, bring that cleavage make-up like what you used at my wedding."

"You've got it, Dolly. I've got enough for all of

us."

Momma wrinkled her nose. "Cleavage makeup?"

"Yeah." MK leaned forward. "It's like powder you brush on top of and between your breasts."

"Fathers." Mommy waved her hand. "I'm not studying on letting anyone paint on my tiddies. Sakes. The very idea."

Lexi glanced down at the dresses. "Lord, my nails could use a manicure." She studied her hand and then looked up. "Hey, mind if I ask Tryna to come and do our mani/pedis? It will be a lot more fun than us trying to do everything."

"And don't forget David for hair," Molly Kate added.

"Sure. Sounds great to me." Jema frowned. "You think they would? It will be on a holiday."

"Write them a fat check." Lexi flipped her hand. "Levi can afford it. Want me to call them?"

"That'd be great. Thanks."

"Girls, nobody gives a flying fig what we look like." Momma pushed the catalogue away. "Now let's get to the important stuff. What about food?"

"Levi and I talked about it and decided to go all out on the food since we are marrying on the night that most couples have their own New Year's Eve parties. The country club will cater and we will have an open bar. And for music we will hire an orchestra.

"Y'all know I have to be the voice of reason." Of course my mother was always the voice of reason. She crossed her arms across her chest. "If you have an open bar, what about the folks driving home?"

Mimicking Momma, Jema crossed her arms. "Well, Miss Thing, we thought of that too, as a matter of fact and we have a fabulous solution. Levi is hiring limos to pick up all the guests and take them home."

Lexi's mouth dropped open. "Sweet baby unicorns."

"I know! Right?" When the guests get in the limo, we will have chilled champagne in souvenir flutes waiting for them. Cool, huh?"

"Beyond cool." Lexi leaned forward. "Tell us more."

"Well, we thought we'd get the party started around ten, then around eleven thirty-ish, start the ceremony. Afterwards, we will dance the night away until people decide they want to leave. Then all they will have to do is get in the limo and go home."

Molly Kate slapped the table. "I love it."

I had to admit, I did, too.

"Dancing the night away?" Lexi arched an eyebrow. "That's exactly what I'd want to do on my honeymoon night."

"Oh, hush." Jema grinned. "I'm sure no one will miss us." With a wink, she changed the subject. "Now, let's talk reception. Since we are keeping the ceremony small, Levi and I thought we'd have a large reception on New Year's Day."

"Now you're talking," said Momma. "What can I fix to bring?"

"Nothing, Cladie. We want you to enjoy the party. We thought we'd have the country club cater a traditional New Year's meal. They have a great pork roast."

Momma held her hand up. "I'm telling you right now, *I'm* doing the greens. No one at that fancy country club knows diddle about how to cook a good pot of collards."

"Now don't get all riled up, Cladie Mae." Jema patted Momma's arm. "I just wanted to pamper you. After all, as far as I'm concerned, you are the mother of the bride."

Momma placed her hand over Jema's. "That's mighty sweet of you, sugar, but you know it's my joy to cook, especially for those I love."

Ideas swirled in my mind for a decorating theme. "What about decorations? I suggest using a color palette of gold, silver, white, and black with pops of red. We will already have some round tables set up. We could have more set up."

"I have plenty of black round table cloths with white toppers. I ordered them for when we host receptions at the B&B." MK thought a minute. "Also, I saw really cute ideas on Pinterest for New Year's table decorations such as clocks, pocket watches, numbers. Anything depicting time."

"Love it," I said. "And how about flower arrangements that have gold and silver sparkler decorations. Oh, and lots of gold and silver confetti in number shapes."

Picking up a note pad, Lexi jotted some things down. "Give me the guest list. I will take care of getting the invitations addressed and mailed. But I'll need it pretty soon."

Jema fisted her hands under her chin. "Perfect." Her demeanor turned a bit timid. She faced Molly Kate. "Would it be a problem if we invite some people from the tent community? Levi feels very connected with them."

"Heavens, no. Invite whomever you want. We've

got the room. Lord love them. They could use a good party to start their year out right."

"Thank you, hon." Jema shook her head. "Levi worries about them, especially the children since it has turned so cold and all. He ordered more cots and bedding for Life Source to help out."

"Good man." Lexi voiced my sentiments exactly. "I'm sure the showers he had installed have worked wonders for them, not to mention the laundromat."

"Oh, it has. I never realized how much I took for granted before Levi." Jema gave Molly a grateful smile. "Thank you so much. It means a lot to Levi and me for you to welcome our homeless friends. Not many people would."

"Oh pssh. I wish I could do more."

"Be careful what you wish for." Jema raised her eyebrows and lowered her chin. "I have your phone number."

I glanced at my watch. Past noon. I needed to get home and prepare for the evening, both physically and emotionally. "Well, girls, I've got to run. Tonight is *the* night."

"Oh, Lord." Lex rolled her eyes. "I don't envy you."

Jema hugged me and whispered, "I'll be praying all evening."

"Thanks, I'll need it." I left the warm embrace of B&B's kitchen and walked into the frigid wind outside.

The word *prophetic* came to mind.

Chapter Two

Bitterness magnifies past pain and blurs present healing.

~*Avalee Preston*

The doorbell rang just as the Grandfather clock struck seven. From upstairs, I heard Momma bustling toward the door. Knowing Ty was on the other side of the door always sent my heart into a girlish fit. But not tonight.

I took one last look in the mirror. The decision whether to dress conservative or stylishly younger dogged me all evening. Either way, I was screwed. Conservative emphasized the difference in our ages. Stylishly younger sent vibes of an older woman trying to recapture her youth, which, of course, would send his mother in convulsions over her baby boy being seduced by an older woman. In the end, I went with my old standby—black. Black leggings, black and white sweater dress, black boots, and pearl earrings. Conservative *and* stylishly younger. What was that Harry Truman said? If you can't convince them, confuse them?

I decided to go simple and let my hair fall around my shoulders instead of pinning it up. My stylist, the famous David, highlighted my dishwater blonde hair to perfection making it brighter, but still natural. Tryna, his new nail technician, did a fabulous job on my nails. She was such a hoot. Just what I needed to keep me from stressing over tonight.

Momma called from the foot of the stairs. "Avalee, honey. Tyler is here."

"I'll be right down." I stared in the mirror. *Deep breaths...Deep breaths.*

When I reached the top step, Ty looked up from speaking to Momma and flashed his sexy crooked smile, revealing dimples in his five o'clock shadow. One look from his heavy-lashed, dark, bedroom eyes dissolved my nervousness and filled me with craving. All I wanted in that moment was for him to pull me tight against his body and kiss me—long and melting.

"Now, Tyler, honey, here is the fudge for your parents." Momma held out the festive box.

"Thank you, Miss Cladie." He exhaled and held out his hand to me. "Well, are you ready to get this show on the road?"

"I'm ready to get this over with."

Momma patted my shoulder. "Now, baby, remember what we talked about."

"I know; hurting people hurt. But I still dread it."

Outside, Ty hurried me to the passenger side of his truck, but before he could open it, I stood on my tiptoes and pressed my mouth hard against his.

"Wow, what was that for?" He hugged me close. "Not that I'm complaining."

"Courage. It reminds me of why I'm going into the lion's den tonight."

He whispered against my neck, "And after we emerge from said lion's den, can we lick each other's wounds?"

I kissed him again, soft and lingering. "Absolutely."

Momma must have been watching from the kitchen window, because she called out the door, "You two love birds need to fly on outta here or Emma Jackson will have good reason to give you what for."

"All right, Momma." I slid onto the truck seat and watched Ty jog around to the driver's side. The idea for our post-supper, first aid plans comforted me— somewhat.

****

Memories of Ty's kisses sustained me on the way to his parent's home, but the second we turned into Nottingham Estates, my heart started to race. By the time we pulled onto the circular drive of the Jacksons' sprawling Georgian home, it pounded so hard I could hardly catch my breath.

Ty must have noticed. "Hey, babe, you all right? You look like you're going to be sick."

"Well, that's a fine way to start." I gave a weak smile. "Just nerves."

"Believe me, I get it. I guess I'm just used to their disapproval." He reached over and stroked my cheek. "But I will make you this promise. The minute they cross the line, we are outta there."

"Oh, Ty." My eyes began to sting. "I don't want us to be at odds with your parents. I want us to be family. You have children. I don't want to be the elephant in the room at family gatherings and ruin it for everybody."

"Trust me." He leaned over and brushed my lips with his. "You will never be the elephant. A tigress, yes. Never an elephant."

The interior of the cab suddenly illuminated. I glanced toward the house and there stood Emma Jackson in the doorway with light from inside the foyer spilling around her and onto the flagstone porch.

"Well, gird your loins, my love." Ty opened the door. "Showtime."

I tried to calm my nerves while he strode around to help me out. We climbed the steps and walked between the stone columns to the massive oak door where Ty's mom waited. She was still an elegantly attractive woman even though she was in her late seventies and a lung cancer survivor at that. But, I couldn't help noticing the deadness in her eyes. Like a stone statue in an ancient cemetery.

She held both hands out to Ty. "Tyler. I'm so glad to see you. Even though we live in the same town, I see so little of you as of late."

"Mother, please. I was here for supper a few weeks ago."

Completely ignoring him, she turned her attention to me. Molten steel replaced the deadness in her eyes. "And Avalee. You finally decided to come home to your poor mother."

I opened my mouth, but closed it. What could I say to that? Guilty as charged? Probably everyone in town held my thirty-year absence against me. Heck, I held it against myself. The few times I'd returned to Moonlight were in and out visits at best. I didn't want to see anyone but my parents, Molly Kate, and Lexi. And the reason for my avoiding home stood before me.

Ty put a protective arm around me. "Don't start, Mother, or we will leave now."

Did I see surprise register on her face? She held her

hand toward the door. "Come in. It's cold out."

Once inside, I remembered the box I clutched and stammered, "My mother sent this. It's fudge, one of her many specialties." I held out the package.

"Oh, how nice." Emma looked as if I had handed her a box of worms. "I'll have Doris put it out for guests to enjoy."

Nothing had changed. She was still as pretentious as when Marc and I were together. We followed her into the family room where a cozy fire danced in the hearth. She gestured toward the enormous corduroy and leather couch. "Have a seat. I'll get Marcus."

I gingerly moved the pile of gold and copper pillows for us to find a place to sit. Ty took my hand, but I pulled it away. "Not now."

Doctor Jackson entered the room, stoic as I remembered him. He had aged rather nicely. He still had a respectable amount of hair, which had turned white. His short-cropped beard gave him a dignified look. He peered at us through wire-rimmed glasses. "Good evening, Tyler. Avalee."

Ty bent forward to stand, but his father held up a hand. "Keep your seat, son." He eased down in a leather recliner across from where we sat. "Emma is instructing Doris to bring the wine." He turned his gaze on me and after appraising me for what seemed like minutes, but were in reality only seconds, said, "I must say, Avalee, time has been good to you these past..." He rubbed his beard and glanced up at the iron chandelier above us. "Thirty years is it?"

"Yes sir. Thank you, Doctor Jackson. Time has been kind to you as well."

He inclined his head, and then emotionally

disappeared in uncomfortable reserve. We had been in the house less than fifteen minutes, and it already seemed like hours. At long last, Doris brought wine, followed by Mrs. Jackson. She lowered onto a club chair next to her husband. My stomach felt in knots. If it were not for his parents sitting across from us, I would have grabbed the bottle and turned it up.

After Doris poured the wine and left the room, Mrs. Jackson spoke. "I have to say, Tyler, your call came as a surprise."

"In what way, Mother? I call all the time."

Her glacier glare slanted toward me. "I was surprised you had the nerve to bring Avalee here. After all, she has made it a point to avoid Marc's family all these years." Her mention of Marc briefly softened her lined face but soon hardened when she looked at me. "I'm extremely disappointed in you, Avalee."

Nettles and thistles sprang up in my soul at her words. Did she not remember our *last meeting?* How dare she? Everything inside me wanted to defend myself, but instead I said, "I'm sorry Mrs. Jackson. At the time, I felt the only way I could deal with losing Marc was to stay away."

Her short-cropped white hair accentuated her reddening face. Her voice seethed through tight lips. "For thirty years?"

I stared at my lap at a loss for words.

Ty took my hand. When I tried to pull it away, he held fast.

"Mother, that was a long time ago. She was Skye's age at that time. A kid." He released my hand, propped his arms on his thighs and leaned forward. "However, since you brought up my bringing Avalee, I want to tell

36

you why I brought her with me tonight. We—"

Marcus interrupted. "Your mother and I have no quarrels with Avalee. It was a senseless tragedy which hurt us all." He picked up his goblet and held it to his lips. Before he took a sip he said, "Isn't that true, Emma?"

She opened her mouth to speak, but he held up his hand to stop her. "You both were just two kids who made unfortunate decisions with disastrous results." Marcus picked up his glass. "Now let's enjoy our wine."

"No, Dad. Not yet." Ty glanced at me, took my hand again, and drew in a breath. "The reason I brought Avalee here is, well, last Sunday night I asked her to marry me."

Stunned silence gripped the room. Mrs. Jackson put her hand to her breast. Her mouth dropped into an O, then she drew her lips in and her brows down in silent protest. Mr. Jackson only stared—first at Ty, then me, and back at Ty. Finally, he spoke. "Son, I hope you will give this more thought. After all, you hardly know Avalee."

Ty's mother found her voice. "Not to mention, she is *twelve* years *older* than you." Bursting to her feet, she clenched her fists. *"Tyler Jackson*, what *are* you thinking? There are a lot of *younger* women who would love being your wife. You don't want to wind up playing *nursemaid* to," she thrust her finger in my direction, *"her."*

I wanted to die. Right then and there. Disappear. Run away—again.

"Oh?" Ty's voice grew hard. "Like Dad did for you?"

Mr. Jackson leaned forward. "Now see here, son—"

"—No. You see here. You took care of Mom when she was sick because you loved her. Well, I love Avalee, and if that means playing *nursemaid*, well, it would be my honor. You both are being incredibly rude and insensitive. If you two knew what your precious Marc had done to Avalee, you'd be ashamed of him and yourselves for the way you are acting. It's a good thing Avalee is too kind and too gracious to mar my brother's memory by keeping his disgusting behavior to herself."

I put my hand on Ty's. "Babe, let's go before this gets more out of control."

Ty stood. "Good idea."

Mr. Jackson rose. "Now son, let's all settle down and talk about this later. You just took us by surprise. You are not being fair to your mother and me."

"Fair?" Ty's glare pierced the distance across the coffee table. "You call that scene at the cemetery fair?" He nodded his head. "Uh, huh. I still remember Mother dissecting Avalee's heart. I'll remember the look on Ava's face for as long as I live." He shot his index finger toward his mother. "You are the reason she was gone for thirty years."

Mrs. Jackson paled. "Why, that's a horrible thing for you to say to your mother."

"It is a horrible thing you did to Avalee."

Emma Jackson's voice grew shrill. "It is a *horrible* thing that woman did to this family. She might as well had killed *my son—your brother*—with her own hands." Ty's mother narrowed her eyes at me. "What is it, Avalee Preston? Ruining one of my sons' lives isn't enough for you? Now you want the only one I have

38

left?"

The room grew distorted and her words sounded far away. Sparkles danced before my eyes. I felt myself sway, but Ty's strong arms enfolded me. *Breathe. Breathe.*

Mr. Jackson's voice boomed out. "Emma, that's enough."

Ty choked out in a whisper, "I can't believe you just said that."

His mother looked away and clamped her lips into a thin line.

Ty drew me close. "Come on, baby. We're leaving."

"Son, wait." Mrs. Jackson put out her hand.

Ignoring her, he gave me my purse, threw my coat over my shoulders, and led me to the truck. I watched the silhouettes of his parents watching from the window as we drove away. Ty gripped the steering wheel so hard his knuckles turned white. All of a sudden, I felt old. Very old. Guilt, my old nemesis, returned with a vengeance. Would I ever be able to forgive myself? I laid my head back and closed my eyes willing myself to stay strong.

****

The quiet in the truck's cab may as well have been a bullhorn in my head. I couldn't speak. Finally, Ty broke the airless silence.

"I'm sorry," he thumbed back in the direction of his parents' house, "for that back there. I had no idea they would—could—be so rude."

I swallowed to steady my voice. "I expected it. Listen, we need to talk."

Ty stomped the break, throwing me forward. He

pulled his truck to the curb and faced me, his voice low. "Avalee, don't you go crawdadding on me. You hear? Don't start back on that age thing again, or that you killed my brother. Got it?"

"Baby, I'm not," I lied. "But we do need to talk—I need to talk. Tonight made me realize there *are things* we need to consider."

"I don't like the sound of this, but all right." He pulled back onto the road. "How about a drink? And some food. I'm starving. Mockingbird Moon Pub is probably quiet tonight."

"I could go for a Guinness. Good idea."

Ty turned onto Silverlight Drive. Again, we rode in silence. Occasionally I glanced at him. In the darkness, I noticed him working his jaw, then noticed something else. A glint of a tear? My throat tightened. I hated seeing him hurt, and for the first time since we'd been together, so vulnerable.

The parking lot was surprisingly full for a Sunday night, but the table host found us a booth in a dark corner. Ty sat across from me, rested his elbows on the table, and looked me in the eyes. "Hey, are we okay?"

I wanted to make everything okay. I wanted to take him home with me. I wanted to elope. But he wasn't the problem. It was me. Not only did I have problems, I was the problem. I wasn't okay. "Yeah."

The waiter took our order for steak pies and Guinness. While the sound system played Van Morrison's *Tupelo Honey*, Ty and I sat lost in our thoughts. Soon the waiter brought our beers. Ty picked his up and murmured, "Marc's ghost has tormented me for as long as I can remember." He took a long draw from the thick frothy head and set the mug down with a thunk. "Don't get me wrong. I loved him. When my parents told me he was dead, I wanted to die. As time went on, everything and everyone close to me changed. Including you."

"Me?" I didn't like where this was going.

"You left. After my mom waylaid you at the funeral, I never saw you again. You know, I think I loved you even then, although some would have thought it was a childish infatuation." He raised his shoulders then let them fall. "And maybe it was. Maybe it was the way you toasted pound cake for me when you and Marc watched me while my parents were out." He gave the briefest of grins. "But as the years went by, I couldn't stop thinking about you. Wondering where you were. What you were doing. If I'd ever see you again." He took another deep drink and focused on the crescent moon salt and peppershakers. "A shadow fell on our lives after Marc died and never left. Holidays were the worst. Our forced cheerfulness left me exhausted. My parents canonized Marc and somehow it was decreed by acclamation that I would follow in his footsteps. It was also decided that I was not to get serious with anyone while in college or in residence." A contemptuous laugh escaped his lips. "No one ever asked *me* if I wanted to practice medicine."

The waiter brought our order. I thought I had no appetite until Ty stuck a fork into the flaky crust of his pie releasing fragrant steam. The aroma of baked onions and roasted beef made my stomach growl. "Did you tell them you didn't want to go into medicine?"

"I tried. They didn't accept it when I told them I wasn't interested being a doctor, they told me I was too young to decide that. Then I tried another tactic and

Linda Apple

argued I wasn't good enough in math and science. That's when they decided to send me to a community college so I could build confidence, then transfer to the university in my third year." He forked up a bite of steak, mashed potatoes and gravy. Before popping it in his mouth he smiled. "Best thing they ever did, cos that's where I met Max."

"Max?"

He nodded his head while he chewed, then swallowed. "My art prof."

"Oh." I pierced a piece of tender steak, a mushroom, and potato chunk for the perfect bite. It didn't disappoint. "What about him?"

"Max was an avid photographer, and since photography is art, he incorporated it into his curriculum. I picked up a cheap camera and gave it a try. Man, I really got into it, trying to reflect the raw emotions and the stories behind my subjects or the beauty of nature and art. One afternoon, Max called me in his office and told me I had an eye for photojournalism. Then he asked if he could enter some of my work in a statewide contest."

The waiter came to our table and asked if we wanted another Guinness. We both nodded our heads. The food and beer were just what the doctor ordered.

"Anyway, I won first place and five hundred dollars. Man, I was stoked. I had found my calling. Or so I thought. My parents were less than impressed. They weren't even interested in seeing the photograph. They viewed my passion as a hobby. When I won the Photographers Forum Award, which is a big deal I might add, I had the photo professionally framed for my parents. They looked at it, said, 'That's nice.' You know where it is?" He stabbed another piece of steak."

"No."

"Neither do I. It sure isn't anywhere in their house. I even looked in the attic."

"That's terrible."

He chewed and muttered around the steak in his mouth, "That's the way it is." After he washed his bite down with his beer, he glanced up at me. "That's the way it has always been."

I set my fork down and watched him eat. Ty Jackson was one of the most wonderful men I'd ever known. Why couldn't his parents see that? Why couldn't they accept him for who he was? It occurred to me that my fiancé's soul was sitting on empty and had been running on fumes for a long time.

Right then and there I made up my mind to dedicate my life to filling his soul with love and respect, no matter what the future held for us. Emma Jackson was right. I did want her other son, not to ruin him, but to make him realize his dream. I would do everything within my power and scope of influence to insure he was one of the most successful, appreciated photographers around.

I reached across the table, took both Ty's hands, and squeezed them. "I love you, baby."

He inclined his head quizzically then the heaviness fell from his expression. "Wow. We will eat steak pie and drink Guinness more often."

I picked up my mug. "To love."

He lifted his glass and clinked mine. "To love and you."

Ty didn't know about my epiphany. But he would soon enough.

****

There is a saying that friendship isn't one big thing, it is a million little things. Lexi, Molly, and Jema confirm the truth of that statement. How desperately I wanted to talk to one or all of them after Ty dropped me off at home. Emotionally, we were both drained. The passion we'd hoped to use in soothing our emotional wounds had dissipated into weariness. He kissed my forehead, whispered, "Night hon," and returned to his truck. I held my hand up and watched him pull out of the driveway, only dropping it as his taillights disappeared down Washington Avenue. Poor fellow. How could his mother have been so vicious? Ty deserved so much more.

Indignation welled up inside me. I wanted, no, I needed my friends. I glanced across the street. Jema's lights were off. Hugging myself, I walked to the corner and saw Lexi's lights on. It was late, but I didn't care. As I walked, I ruminated over the things Marc and Emma Jackson said. Angry tears spilled down my cheeks. By the time I reached the door, I'm sure I looked a fright with mascara tracks down my face. I tapped several times before Lexi swung the door open. Her smile disappeared into a frown. "Girl, what's wrong with you?" Concern registered on her face. "Is it Miss Cladie?"

"No." I stomped inside and plopped on the couch.

"Ty? Is it Ty? Are you two fighting?" She slammed the door. "Do I need to go and yank a knot in his tail?" Sinking beside me on the couch, she put her arm around my shoulders. "Because I will, you know."

I swiped at my face. "No, it's his parents, his mother mainly."

"Bad, huh?"

"Worse."

She patted my knee. "You sit right there and I'll grab us some wine." Before she left for the kitchen she pushed several tissues in my hand. "Here, you need these. You look like something from a punk rock band."

While Lex rattled around getting wine, I went to the powder room and washed my face. Emma Jackson would get no more tears out of me.

Lexi had just settled on the couch when I returned. "Here." She'd chosen a warm, rich, pinot noir. "Now, tell me what happened."

I fully expected a reaction out of Lexi as I told her about the evening's disaster. But not the volcanic eruption that ensued. She sat beside me, a proverbial calm before the storm. A mini torrent disturbed the wine in her glass as she listened. Before I could finish my tale of woe, she had heard enough. After slugging down her wine, she blew up. "Why that witch."

She paced back and forth in front of me throwing her hands in the air and slapping them down to her sides. The air was blue with her profanities. Finally, she exhausted her encyclopedia of cuss words and disappeared into the kitchen. This time she returned with the bottle.

"I need another glass. Hold out yours." While she poured, images of a redheaded Tinker Bell throwing a temper tantrum came to my mind and I got tickled. "Hold still, Avalee. You are going to make me spill this on my new rug." But I couldn't quit snickering. She eyed me. "What?"

"You." My giggles broke free.

The corners of her mouth began to twitch. "Me? Why?"

"Your Tinker Bell tantrum. My ears are on fire. Why, sailors would bow at your feet crying, "We are not worthy.""

Her mirth ignited and we both enjoyed the cleansing tears of laughter. When we finally caught our breath, she held up her goblet. "She's still a witch."

I clinked my glass against hers. "Yep. She is."

A cozy silence, best known by close friends, settled between us. After a while I asked, "So what do I do?"

"About the wicked witch of the south?"

"No, Ty."

"Marry him, of course."

"That's what I want more than anything, but am I being selfish?"

Lexi took my glass and sniffed it. "Did you drop something in here? You are talking like a crazy person."

"No, Lex. I'm being serious. Think of what this will do to his family—his kids. Every holiday or family gathering I will be the gorilla in the room making everyone uncomfortable." I sipped my wine and another disturbing thought came to me. "What if his kids hate me?" Another sip, then a gulp. "Oh, Lexi. That would be awful."

"Oh stop with the *what if's,* Ava."

"But…"

Lexi took my shoulders in her strong grip. "What if a frog didn't jump? He wouldn't bump his butt." She let go and fell back against the cushion. "But a frog's gotta jump to get to where he's going. He figured it out. Y'all will, too."

"I suppose."

"Now quit borrowing trouble. You are exhausted, that's what. Wanna sleep over?"

"No, I'd better go home."

"Come on. I'll walk you halfway." Lexi stuck her feet in slippers and wrapped a crocheted comforter around her shoulders. When we stepped outside the cold air nearly took my breath. Lexi's, too, by the sound of her gasp. Fog speech balloons floated from our mouths as we talked along the way. At the halfway point we hugged and then headed in opposite directions. I felt better. A lot better.

Chapter Three

Living in someone's shadow makes you invisible.
                                        ~Tyler Jackson

Ty pounded his pillow trying to make it comfortable enough to at least doze off. But the evening's fiasco still had him burning inside, making sleep impossible. Poor Avalee. She didn't deserve his mother's bitter attack. Emma's words still played in his mind and it was all he could do to keep from calling her and finishing what she had started. She'd opened old wounds. Not just Avalee's but his, too.

What had happened to his mother's mind when Marc died? It was like she'd mentally snapped and never recovered. Then, by some cruel genetic joke, he grew into the spitting image of his brother. And that's all it took for his mother to make it her goal to morph him into Marc. What was she thinking? That this would bring back her lost son? Even worse, if he did step into Marc's empty shoes and became like him, would she not miss Ty? Did she even know him?

The truth of that thought perturbed him. Neither his mother or father really knew him. When Marc died and they became a family of three, the days, weeks, months, and years were shrouded with mourning. His parents wanted him back. To hell with Tyler.

This wasn't the first time she'd caused such drama,

but up until tonight it had been for his eyes and ears alone. When he was in college, she discouraged him from dating because it interfered with his studies. "Wait until you have a profession. When you are a doctor you will be able to afford a wife and a family."

The problem? He never wanted to be in the medical profession. He wasn't sure what he wanted to do until he got behind the camera. That was when his mind came out of hibernation. Photography was sunlight, fresh air, and nourishment for his soul.

His parents simply refused to understand he couldn't be and never wanted to be like Marc. Especially after Avalee told him the circumstances surrounding their break-up. Frankly, Marc didn't deserve her. He never did. The urge to drive to his parent's home and tell them just what kind of son they had raised had him out of the bed, keys in hand, and almost to the door. He stopped. It wouldn't do any good. They'd just say she was lying. Impossible situation.

Ty tossed the keys on the counter and braced himself against it. Man, didn't anyone care he'd found the woman he wanted to spend the rest of his life loving?

He planned on taking Avalee to Oxford to meet his kids and tell them about the engagement, but the night's events changed his mind. Instead, he decided to go by himself to see if they were decent about his news. If they were, he would surprise Avalee by taking her to meet them. If they were as unfiltered, rude, and antagonistic as his mother had been, he would have to think of some way to soften their disapproval when he spoke with Ava.

Gracie, his ex, would be cool with it. She never liked his mother and for good reason. He had met Gracie at the community college and they dated for over a year. Oddly enough, in a way, history had repeated itself. Gracie told him she was pregnant. But unlike his brother, he manned up and married her. They kept the reason for the elopement a secret. But when his mother eyed Gracie's expanding girth, she understood and blamed Gracie for distracting her son and blamed her for his leaving college and taking the job of a *common photographer* to support his family.

After ten years, it became evident that he and Gracie would not grow old together. Between his mother's interference, low pay, and a certain blues crooner Gracie had met in a bar, the marriage fell apart. She walked out of his life and into the arms of Bo, big time musician in the small town of Moonlight. A legend in his own mind. Gracie was convinced he'd be famous one day. So they married and she worked day and night to fund his *imminent* discovery. Dreams of being in the spotlight by Bo's side blinded her to the truth—he was a small town boy who stayed drunk during the day and sang at night. Finally she'd had enough and left him, too. Gracie had hinted that she wanted to get back together, saying how good it would be for the kids. But fool him once…. She wound up marrying a professor at the University of Mississippi and as far as he knew, she was happy.

Ty straightened, placed his palms on the small of his back, and stretched. Maybe a hot shower would relax him and help him sleep. He lumbered to the bathroom and turned the shower lever. He drummed his fingers as he waited for the water to turn hot. A plan.

He needed a plan. He'd call his kids in the morning and see what their schedules looked like. Maybe take them out to eat.

Steam finally drifted from the stall and he stepped in. The pulsating jets of water felt good against his skin. Soon, he was in a better frame of mind. He had good kids. Open minded and fair. He turned the lever to off and reached for a towel. They would understand. Right? At least he hoped to God they would.

****

While waiting for his kids to arrive at the Pizza Factory, Ty rehearsed different approaches in telling them about his engagement to Avalee. First he'd say she returned from New York to help her mother and they were reacquainted. Maybe he should tell them he'd known her all his life. On the other hand, telling this bit of knowledge might lead to the fact he was in sixth grade while she was in college. The age difference might sound a little weird to them. Perhaps he should just say they met and he knew she was the one, pure and simple. If they wanted more information—and he hoped to high heaven they didn't—he'd answer honestly. Skye would be the one who'd question him. She prided herself on getting to the heart of any story, and she did it well, which is why she chose to study journalism.

Glen, on the other hand, was a laid back, *whateves*, kind of guy. He studied music and music business at the community college in Senatobia. Ty wasn't exactly sure what *music business* was, but his son was a talented musician and he trusted Glen's choices.

A jingle at the door alerted Ty of their arrival. He waved them over to the table and stood to hug them.

Before they could take a seat Skye started in with questions.

"Wow. Dad." She crossed her arms on the table and leaned forward causing her wavy brown hair to swing over her shoulders. "This is a surprise. You never come in the middle of the week. What gives?" Her green-eyes drilled him like the talk show hosts who made their guests cry.

"Gee, Skye, it's good to see you, too." Sometimes her approach just nettled him.

"Hey, Sis. Back off a little." Glen leaned back and tossed his head sweeping the bangs off his forehead. His hair looked as if it had grown six inches since Thanksgiving. "It's Christmas Eve. Chill."

Glen's mellow demeanor always had a relaxing effect on Ty. Everything about his son spoke 'calm' from his easy smile to how he draped his lanky frame on any place he sat. Thank goodness he was water to Skye's fire.

"But we are all going to be together at Grandmother's the day after Christmas, so why are we meeting today? Obviously Dad has something to tell us in private and it is too important to tell in an email or over the phone. She tilted her head. "Sooo?"

His daughter's astuteness amazed him. Before he could begin a cute little waitress with dark hair and coffee-brown eyes bopped up to their table. Pinned to her well-endowed chest was a nametag printed with the name *Regina*. She zeroed in on Glen. Ty shook his head. His boy was a chip off the old block—a chick magnet.

"Evening everyone, I'm Regina. How are y'all tonight?" Without waiting for an answer, she went on.

"Have you made up your minds about what you'd like, or do you still need time?"

Glen waggled his eyebrows. "I'll have the usual."

Regina grinned and color rose up in her cheeks.

Skye eyed her brother. "The *usual?*" She rolled her eyes. "I'll have the Thibideaux and a diet coke.

"One andouille sausage with swiss po-boy and one dc coming up. White or wheat?"

"Wheat."

After a quick glance at Glen, Regina turned to Ty. "And you sir?"

"The Peter Tosh on white." Ty put down his menu. "What do you have on draft?"

She named off the beers all the while watching Glen.

"I'll have a Bud Light."

"Got it. One Jamaican jerk chicken and swiss on white and one *why bother.*"

"Funny." Ty handed her the menu.

"Just sayin'." She winked and bounced off.

"So," Ty gave his most sarcastic smile. "You come here pretty often, eh?"

The dimples Ty had passed on to Glen deepened. "Hey, what can I say? The atmosphere is great."

"So. Dad." Skye fell back into birddogging. "What's up?"

Well, it was now or never. "I've met someone."

Glen beamed at his dad. "About time old man. That's great."

For the tiniest second, Skye was struck speechless. "Met someone? Who? Is it serious?"

Good thing Regina brought their drinks. It gave him time to gather his thoughts. When she left, Ty drew in a deep breath and let it go. "Her name is Avalee Preston and I guess you could say it is serious." Letting that sink in, Ty cleared his throat. "I've asked her to marry me."

"What? Wait. Did you say…" Skye lowered her brow and turned her head to the side as if to hear him better. "Marry?"

"Hey, Dad. That's awesome." Thank goodness for Glen. "Is she cute?"

"She's beautiful."

Skye held up her hands. "Hold on. Wasn't your brother engaged to an Avalee? The one Grandmother says is responsible for his death?"

Mother strikes again. Ty picked up his beer and took a long swallow to keep from snapping.

Her frown deepened. "Grandmother said for all practical purposes, she killed your brother."

Glen sat up. "Hey now, Sis, rein it in. Not good."

Fury raced through Ty, but he bit back his words. Hadn't he raised her better than that? He wanted to pound the table with his fist, but he restrained himself and instead shot a stern stare at his outspoken daughter.

She must have gotten the message, because she closed her mouth and sat back, arms folded across her chest. "I'm just repeating what grandmother said. Geeze."

When he could trust his voice, he spoke in quiet, measured, words. "I don't know what my mother has told you, but it isn't true. She knows nothing of what happened. Everything she believes about that day, she has conjured in her bitter-soaked mind. Avalee is a professional woman. Beautiful, loving, and kind. I've waited all my life for someone like her, and I plan to spend the rest of my life making her happy. Got it?"

He didn't normally take that tone with his daughter. However, it produced the desired result. She didn't say another word. She just nodded.

Regina brought their orders, but her smile faded. The weighted emotion must have been evident. She set their food in front of them and hurried away, then returned with fresh drinks. Even another Bud for Ty. "On the house, sir. You look like you could use it."

Ty managed a smile. "Thanks."

They ate in silence for a while, until Skye laid her fingers on her father's arm. "I'm sorry, Daddy. I know Grandmother can be a little overbearing."

A little? He wanted to break into a litany of what he thought about his mother, but held back. "Thanks, hon."

A thought came to him as he bit into his spicy jerk chicken sandwich. Since his daughter wanted to be a journalist, he'd do a little name-dropping. He set his sandwich down. "Have you ever heard of a man named Nathan Wolfe?"

"Who hasn't? He is a journalism god."

"Really now. Didn't know that. But I do know he's a good friend of Avalee's."

Skye's eyes widened and her mouth dropped open. "Shut up. Are you freakin' kidding me? Nathan Wolfe? *The* Nathan Wolfe? Can I meet him? Will he be at your wedding?" She fanned her face with her hands. "Oh my gosh. *Nathan Wolfe*? I can't believe it."

Bingo.

Ty noticed Glen had one bite of his muffuletta left. No wonder he'd been so quiet. Noshing for him had always been serious business. After pushing the last of his sandwich in his mouth, he looked up. "Who's Nathan Wolfe?"

Skye's voice went up a few octaves. "He's the best news journalist ever." She fanned herself again.

"Hey. Baby. Settle down and eat before your food is completely cold. I'm sure Avalee will be happy to introduce you to him." He couldn't resist having a little fun now. "He was in Moonlight a couple of weeks ago."

She seized Ty's arm. "No way. *No way.* Oh my gosh. *Oh my gosh.*" Her heart-shaped face turned angelic and earnest. "Daddy, when can I meet him?" Wow. What a transformation. Within minutes, his daughter had turned from hard-nosed journalist to a child sprinkled with pixie dust.

"Not sure. He does have a thing going with one of Avalee's friends, so I'm sure he will be in town sometime." He finished the last of his beer. "So, enough about me. What's going on in your lives?"

"You mean," Skye wiggled her fingers Glen's way, "besides cute waitresses?"

"Oh, stop." Glen tossed the crumpled up paper from his straw at her. "Why not tell Dad about your Mr. NFL wannabe?"

A brilliant smile broke across her face. "Oh, Dad. You will love him. His name is Duff."

"Duff, huh?" Bad enough his daughter was dating a football player, but Duff?

"Yes. It's Scottish. Anyway, we've been going together for a couple months now."

"Well, don't let this Duff guy distract you from your studies. I'd rather you not get serious with anyone until you graduate."

As if a bolt of lightning shot through his brain, he realized he'd just turned into his mother, using the same logic with his daughter as his mother had used with him and with Marc. Both sons had ignored her.

Skye arched her eyebrow. "You know who you sound like don't you?"

He lifted both hands in surrender. "Yeah, I know." Time to own up. "And to shock you even more, she was partially right. If Marc had listened to her, he might be alive today. Then again, he also liked to party hard and drove while drunk, so his death may have been inevitable. And for the record, it wasn't your mother who distracted me. It was my art teacher who introduced photography to me."

"Nice try, Dad," Skye smirked. Glen and I both know why you married Mom. Grandmother told us."

Yep, Emma Jackson had no filter at all. "You were not a distraction, hon. You were an unexpected bonus. If I had that part of my life to do over, I wouldn't change a thing because two of my most amazing achievements came from that union."

"Do you ever miss Mom?" Skye's expression begged him to say yes.

Okay, diplomacy needed stat. Ty thought a moment. "I guess you could say I miss what we could have been. But I'm happy she found her professor, and that he has been a great stepfather to both of you. So, you see? It all worked out."

Regina bounced over holding out the check. "Y'all done? How about dessert? Gotta have something sweet."

Ty took the check. "No, we're good." He pulled out his billfold, handed her enough money to cover the bill plus a generous tip. "And thanks for the free *why bother*."

"My pleasure, sir."

Skye propped her arm on the table, rested her face in her palm, and glanced up at Regina. "My brother would probably like something sweet, after you get off that is."

Regina's face flamed and Glen groaned. "Sis. Really?"

Not to be outdone, Regina mouthed at Glen, "I'm off at eleven."

Glen gave a slight nod. This, of course, was not missed by Ty.

Distractions. They happen.

****

Christmas morning dawned gunmetal gray. Ty watched the dark, pregnant clouds while he sipped his coffee and thought over the conversations he had with his kids the previous evening. Avalee would be thrilled when she heard his news. In fact, she'd probably be more excited about Skye and Glen's approval than any gift he purchased for her. She asked him to come over around ten for Christmas brunch with her and Miss Cladie, saying she wanted some private time with him before the big feast that evening.

He checked his watch. Five-thirty. While pouring his second cup of coffee, he debated about going to his parents' before going to the Prestons' for brunch. He had made up his mind to ignore them completely, not even inviting them to the wedding. But his little epiphany the night before when he had all but quoted his mother's words while admonishing his daughter about the NFL wannabe—Duff was it?—made him reconsider. Even though his mother came across as impossibly rude to Avalee, underneath, perhaps, there was honest concern. Maybe her fear sharpened her tone and exaggerated her imaginations. And while this was no excuse, it still helped him understand her a little better.

Yes, he should go and at least have a cup of coffee. He'd keep the conversation light then slip out to Ava's. Next decision. Should he give his parents the present he made for them? Lord knows how hard he worked on it. Months earlier, he insisted on taking a family portrait. His parents balked because, of course, Marc wasn't there to be in it. But Ty had a plan. When they finally consented, Ty set up his camera, moved furniture out of the way, and arranged two chairs in front of the fireplace. He had his parents sit, then he set the timer and stood behind them. First part of the plan finished. Then, for the second part. He needed a picture of his brother. Thursdays were his mother's beauty shop day and his dad's standing golf game. After they had left he went to the house and looked through pictures until he found the perfect one for his project.

He worked into the night photo-shopping Marc into the family portrait, placing him directly behind his mother. He aged Marc a bit to appear more authentic and manipulated the picture to make it appear as if Marc rested his hand on Emma's shoulder. When he finished he felt pleased with the results. Those who were not aware of the family's tragedy would have no idea that Marc hadn't been there standing for the portrait.

Ty rinsed out his coffee cup and set it in the sink. Yes, he'd take it to them. Perhaps the portrait would help his mother realize Ty understood her pain. He wished, more than believed, it would also help her understand the prison she'd built around her heart.

****

Emma and Marcus Jackson's home reflected the austerity of the morning—gloomy and frigid. No Christmas trees stood in the two picture windows on either side of the entryway as there had been when Marc was alive. Nor were there wreaths on the stately double doors.

What a shame. He shook his head while tapping the brass knocker against the strike plate. Doris, the housekeeper, answered his tapping.

"Good morning Tyler." She stepped aside for him to pass. "Come on in. You'll catch your death out there."

He frowned at the plump little woman. "What are you doing working on Christmas?" Had mother turned into Ebenezer Scrooge?

She angled her head up at him and grinned. "Now what would I be doing celebrating Christmas? Hanukkah, yes. Christmas…Well…." She spread her fingers and twisted her hand back and forth. "Only if the food is good."

"Oh, I forgot." How did he not know after all these years Doris was Jewish? "Well, at least it is good to know my parents haven't been swallowed up in a bah, humbug, frame of mind."

She ducked her head and murmured in a conspiratorial tone, "Your folks are not really happy with you at the moment." She placed her palm on Tyler's arm. "Now I'm not one for telling folks how to run their business, but I'd tread lightly if I were you."

"Doris?" His mother called from the living room. "Who is that at the door?"

"It's Tyler, ma'am." She gave him a firm grandmotherly look and held up her finger. "Lightly...."

His parents sat in their usual chairs drinking their morning coffee. Sections of the newspaper lay in their laps. Both remained silent as they watched him enter the room. Uncomfortable didn't begin to describe the atmosphere. However, he made the decision to come so he might as well take the plunge.

"I came by to wish you a Merry Christmas." Silence. He wasn't surprised. Christmas hadn't been merry since Marc's death. "And I brought you something."

He propped the eleven-by-fourteen package on the couch. "Mom. Dad. I'm sorry about the other night. I've had time to think and I honestly do not know what I'd do if either of my kids died. All I know is how it feels to be the brother who was left behind." These words eased the tension in the room and genuine interest shown in their faces. "I made this for you. I hope you like it."

Ty motioned for his mother to open it. She stood and stepped over to the couch. When she tore the paper free from the portrait, she slapped her hand against her mouth and gasped. His dad walked behind her and stared. "My god."

His parents studied the portrait in speechless bewilderment. After a long while, they tore their attention from the picture and focused on Ty with red, tear-filled eyes. He couldn't read their faces. Did they hate it? Had he taken too much liberty? Instead of healing, did he just rip open old wounds?

As if in answer to his wondering mind, his mother strode over, fell on him, and held him tight while sobbing on his shoulder. He noticed his father had removed his glasses and mopped his eyes with a handkerchief.

"Mom? Dad? Do you like it?"

His mother released her hold on him and joined his dad to admire the portrait. In a hoarse whisper his father said, "You've given us the greatest gift since the birth of you boys." He put his arm around his wife. "You've rekindled the light in this holiday."

"Thank you, son." His mother gently touched Marc's image. "You will never know what it means to me to see our family whole again."

For the first time, Ty noticed how frail his mother looked. Even more so since the cancer treatments.

"Coffee everyone." Doris carried a tray of cookies, a carafe, and cups. She arranged them on the coffee table, then straightened up and examined the picture. Crossing her arms, she nodded. "That's right nice, Tyler." She gave him a nod. "Really nice."

The next couple of hours were some of the most pleasant in memory. They reminisced past Christmases, even laughed. How long since they had laughed together? He checked his watch and saw he had five minutes to get to Avalee's. When he stood, his mother reached her hand to him. "Must you go? I could have Doris make us a nice lunch."

Man, he dreaded bringing up Avalee. "I'm going to Avalee's for brunch."

"Oh." She sat back and sighed. Weary resignation colored her voice. "I see."

His father cleared his throat and joined Ty. "Thank you again, son. Please send Avalee and her mother our regards."

"Thanks, Dad. I will." He side-hugged his dad and leaned over to kiss his mom's cheek. Her skin felt as thin as tissue paper. How had he missed this?

In an abrupt about-face, she turned her glare on him. "Your father may send regards, but I do not." Her mouth formed a hard pucker. She rose to her feet and stalked out of the room.

The lamb had turned back into a lion.

Chapter Four

Having myself a merry little Christmas.
                              ~Avalee Preston

I love Christmas. It really is the most wonderful time of the year. Especially this year. The yellow cuckoo bird slid out of his chalet and chirped ten times. Ty would arrive at any minute. I wanted to surprise him with his favorite breakfast treat, toasted pound cake. Earlier I had slathered thick slices of pound cake with butter and arranged them on the tray. Now all I had to do was slide it in and switch on the toaster.

Sounds of chairs scraping and flatware clattering came from the dining room. Momma was in her element setting the table for a holiday feast. She had invited our handyman Felix, Pearly Armstrong from across the street, Jema and Levi, Lexi, Molly Kate and Stan, as well as MK's daughter and granddaughters. But Molly had a change of plans. Seems Stan's brood had decided to visit. This put a momentary damper on Mother's holiday enthusiasm, but she recovered and seeing how she hated empty spaces at her table, she now busied herself rearranging to accommodate eight instead of thirteen. Poor woman. She cooked enough for thirty. Then again, no food ever went to waste. Leftovers were sent home with guests and also given to Life Source.

"Baby?" Mom pushed through the swinging door separating the kitchen from the dining room. "What time is Ty supposed to be here? The breakfast casserole will be ready soon, and you know how I hate serving cold food."

Before I could answer, Ty pulled into the driveway. I lifted my palm toward the kitchen window. "There you go, Momma. Your word is his command."

"Good boy, that one. Now you hop on outta here while I finish up. Did you set up the tables in the front room?"

"Yes ma'am. Everything is ready."

"All right then."

The doorbell rang. "Why doesn't that boy come to the kitchen door? He's good as family now." Momma nodded her head in the general direction of the front door. "Don't keep him waiting. It's colder than a polar bear's toenails out there. If I didn't know better, I'd swear it was fixing to snow; I don't care what the weatherman says."

Snow in the south was a very rare happening, especially on Christmas day. Normally, snow held no fascination for me after living in New York for so long. But on this particular day, it did. I had to admit, it really did look like snow. But here in the south, winter weather usually wound up being ice.

When I opened the door, Ty stepped in, grabbed me, and swung me around before pulling me into a deep kiss.

"Wow." I had to catch my breath. "Merry Christmas to you, too."

He closed the door and shrugged of his coat. "I have good news for a nice change."

"Really?" I took his coat and hung it on the hall tree. "What?"

"Let's go in the family room first."

"How about a mimosa?"

"Sounds great." He sniffed the air. "Is that your momma's breakfast casserole?"

"Sure is."

"Oh man, I can't wait. Where is Miss Cladie? I gotta kiss that little lady." Once again, my mother proved the clichéd wisdom about the way to a man's heart.

"Tyler Jackson." Momma swung through the door with her arms held open wide. "Get over here and give your future mother-in-love a hug."

While my fiancé and Momma cuddled, I slid the pound cake into the toaster and switched it on before starting the mimosas. Soon the aroma of vanilla and toasted brown butter filled the air. Ty opened his eyes wide, and he looked down at Mom. "Toasted pound cake?"

"Hey." I punched him on the shoulder. "That was my idea. You need to give me some of that foodie love."

He wrapped his arm around my waist and pulled me close. "No problem."

"All right, you two. I'm going to leave you to your sparking and pull out that cake before it burns. Brunch will be ready in two shakes."

Ty took my hand and led me to the couch in the family room where we settled and watched the fire in the hearth. Red, green, blue, and yellow lights twinkled in the tree as Bing Crosby crooned carols on the CD player. Holiday perfection. We clinked our glasses and sipped our drinks. Leaning against him I marveled at how this man loved me. Me. Avalee Preston, spinster, twelve years his senior. This tall, dark-eyed, incredibly handsome, fun, talented, man loved me. "So, what's your good news?"

"I had supper with Skye and Glen last night. I told them about us."

"And?"

A smile broke across his face. "They are happy for us."

Oh, the relief. "They are?"

"Well, at first, Skye was concerned. Mother told Skye her version of what happened and of course, you were the villain."

I slunk back into the cushions. "Great."

He slipped his arm around my shoulders and nudged close. "Babe, don't worry. I set her straight. And…."

The guilty look on his face bothered me. "And?"

"Well, I did a little name dropping. I hope you won't be angry. But I knew this would open an avenue to you both being friends for life."

"Whose name?"

"Nathan Wolfe. Skye is a journalism student and I knew this would be a game changer."

"I don't mind at all."

"Until she floods you with questions."

"She'll have the opportunity to ask him herself soon, seeing how he invited himself to Jema's wedding, just so he could be with Lex."

"Lexi is really gone over him, too, isn't she? Because if she isn't, you might want to tell him to back off." Ty had a brotherly-type of protectiveness when it came to Lex.

"Looks like it. But I get the feeling it is more him than her. She isn't like any woman he's been with that I remember. Most fawn over him because of his fame. But not Lex. She's determined to bring him down several notches, and he likes it."

"She's the woman to do it."

"Nate wanted her to come to New York for New Year's Eve, and she turned him down. Which shocked him, I'm sure. No woman turns Nathan Wolfe down for anything. I mean, a date in the city for New Year's, all expenses paid?" I tapped my empty mimosa glass. "But she did because it was Jema's wedding."

Ty caught my hint and rose to make us another. Funny how things happen. Levi was the reason for Nathan's first visit to Moonlight. He came to investigate the Matthew Abrams kidnapping after being told large purchases of commercial washers and dryers had been made by Abrams' company and delivered to Life Source. When Nathan met Levi, a mysterious homeless man, he immediately suspected him as the kidnapper and in turn made everyone else suspicious as well. Everyone, that is, except for Jema and Mother. And their instincts about Levi were right. He was an excellent man. But none of us expected him to be a billionaire trying to find life and love outside of his wealth.

Ty returned and said, "Our drinks are on the table. The food is ready and I'm starved. Let's eat."

"Me too. Let's."

I followed him to the kitchen where Momma handed us each a plate and said, "Get it while it's hot."

"Yes, ma'am. You don't have to ask me twice." He

scooped egg, sausage, asparagus and mushroom casserole on his plate, piled on pan-fried potatoes and onions, took several pieces of bacon, sliced open two biscuits and smothered them with sausage gravy, then took two wedges of pound cake. Momma's euphoric expression attested to the satisfaction she received when someone enjoyed her cooking.

I couldn't produce the same level of pleasure as Ty, but I filled my plate for the first huge meal of the day.

****

Brunch left me *food drunk.* It was like a thick fog had rolled over my brain. As usual, Momma refused our offers to help her clean up, so we dragged ourselves to the couch. Thank goodness supper wasn't until seven, which gave us plenty of time to recover for the next round of Olympic eating.

The room had grown dark even though it was late morning. The twinkling lights on the tree and the fire's dancing flames shown brilliant in the shadowy room.

"How about some Frank Sinatra?" The comfort of a full tummy and a warm fire intensified my holiday spirit.

"Nobody can sing Christmas like him."

"Except for Bing."

"Except for Bing."

While selecting a CD, I glanced out the window. Was that? "Ty. Hurry. Come see."

He jumped up and hurried to the window. "What?" His gaze followed mine. "Oh, wow."

Huge snowflakes fell, blanketing the brown grass and frosting the tree branches. Mom must have seen the snow from the kitchen window while washing dishes.

She strode into the room, wiping her hands on a towel. "Mercy Lord, have you ever seen such a sight? Her elven-blue eyes danced. "And on Christmas day at that."

"Let's go out in it." Ty grabbed his coat.

A little girl squeal escaped my lips. I couldn't help it. "Okay. Let's. How about you, Momma?"

She shook her head. "I like watching it from here." Slapping the towel over her shoulder, she said, "But I'll have hot cocoa waiting on you to thaw you out when you come in."

I grabbed my black quilted coat from the hall closet. I never thought I would need it here in the South and was glad I kept it. I threw it on and ran outside like a sixth grader. The frosty air nipped my nose as I held my face to the sky catching snowflakes on my tongue, feeling twelve again.

"Heads up." A snowball burst against my chest. Ty's triumphant grin was testosterone at its finest.

I gathered snow on the sly from a birdbath and held the ball behind me. "How about a snow kiss?"

"I'm up for that anytime." Ty bounded to me and took me in his arms. He closed his eyes and lowered his mouth to mine only to have it filled with snow as I pushed my hidden weapon into his face. Startled he let me go and spit snow. "Why you little…."

I took off, but he caught me and pulled me down to the ground. Laughing, we rolled onto our backs and made snow angels. Snow in the city was never this fun. I sat up. "Hey, I have an idea."

Ty turned his head to look at me. "What's that?"

"Let's go get Lexi."

"I have a better idea. Let's go to the park and

swing." He sprang to his feet. I couldn't remember the last time I was able to do that. But it didn't matter. He grabbed my hand and pulled me into a warm, snow-melting kiss. "Now isn't that better than cramming snow down my throat?"

"Mmm-hmm." I pulled his face down for another. I could get real used to this.

We strolled hand-in-hand down Washington Avenue admiring the Christmas trees shining from living room picture windows in homes along the street. A peaceful quiet settled in with the drifts. The only sound was a crystalline ping as if tiny fairies toasted the day with minuscule goblets. Occasionally, vivid red cardinals sang out, *cheer, cheer, cheer,* from evergreen boughs blanketed in white. When we walked though the gate I marveled at the scene before me. The park looked enchanted. The swings, slides and the grounds were sparkling and pristine. So much so, I hated marring the surface. We brushed off the seats and sat on the rubber slings. Rocking back and forth, I enjoyed the moment.

"Avalee?" Ty turned his swing around toward me. "Remember the morning I carried you across the swinging bridge over Moon Creek?"

"Remember? I still have nightmares." I didn't mention the other dreams of desire related to that particular day while suspended thirty feet in the air.

"Don't I know it? You nearly strangled me holding on so hard." Snow laced his beanie and caught on his ridiculously long lashes. I swear, Mother Nature did prefer her boys. No woman I knew had lashes like that unless they were fake. "But when I realized you actually were afraid of heights, I was sorry for putting you in that position. That's when I knew I wanted to protect you and care for you the rest of my life." He leaned forward and kissed my nose. "I already knew that I loved you."

"It was then I realized I had fallen in love with you, Tyler Jackson."

He reached into his pocket. "We aren't on the swinging bridge, so these swings will have to symbolize that day." Ty held up a small red satin box and opened it. Nestled in black velvet was a ring sparkling with diamonds.

"Oh, babe." I looked closer. It looked like a blooming rose. Petals set with diamonds surrounded a large solitaire. The delicate platinum band had diamond encrusted leaves on either side. The pave-set wedding band was simple and elegant. "I love it."

"Merry Christmas." He took the engagement ring and slipped it on my finger. "When I saw this rose, I couldn't pass it up."

I opened my mouth, but he put his finger to my lips.

"It is none of your concern about what it cost or how I paid for it."

"How did you know the size?"

"Miss Cladie did some sleuthing. She found a ring you wear and traced the band."

"It's gorgeous." I tore my gaze off the ring long enough to kiss him.

"Just do me a favor." He smiled at me with his impish grin that pushed his dimples deep.

"What's that?"

"Never take it off." He held up his hand like a boy scout. "And I promise I will never give you cause to throw it at me."

I studied his face. "No, I don't think you ever will."

He took my hand and kissed it. "Come on. Let's go show Momma Cladie and warm up with that cocoa."

"Let's." As we walked home, I noticed the snow had covered the tracks we made on our way to the playground. It felt like a good omen to me. Past mistakes erased, a fresh beginning.

****

By seven-thirty, the snow tapered off. Good thing everyone lived within walking distance because when it snows in the south, people go crazy. They drive with their foot on the brakes, slamming it to the floor as they creep along. Before the first flake hits the ground, the grocery shelves are empty. My friends in New York always made fun of me. I soon learned the drill. Snow? No big deal. Just order takeout or hail a taxi.

Mom had everything set up. In the foyer by the family room entrance, she had two bowls of eggnog on the sideboard. One marked 'naughty', meaning it had bourbon in it. The other said 'nice', no alcohol, only nutmeg. Just inside the family room were long tables against the wall that adjoined the foyer wall. There she set up a bar with different liquors and mixers, wines and an assortment of beers. On the other tables, she had heavy, and I mean *heavy,* appetizers. I don't know how after meat canapés, five different varieties of cheeses, breads, jams, and fruit that anyone could eat a meal. But we always managed. Some may think we southerners do a lot of eating and drinking. Well, we do. Food, wine, laughter—a lot of laughter—and even more love, what could be better?

Lexi arrived first. Her voice, bigger than her five-foot-two frame, sang out, "Merry Christmas everyone."

Momma pointed to the punch bowls. "Naughty or nice?"

"You have to ask?" Lexi twisted her mouth in a smile. "Why, naughty of course." She planted a kiss on Mom's cheek and handed her a bottle of wine. "Now don't you go and serve this to everyone, you hear? This is a special bottle of Muscadine, the kind you like."

"Thank you, sugar. I'll hide it right now." Just as Momma disappeared to put up her special wine, a soft rap sounded on the door.

I called out, "I'll get it."

Jema and Levi stood on the porch stamping the snow off their shoes. He looked up and smiled. "Happy Christmas." Then he offered his arm to someone behind him. "We dropped by to help Mrs. Armstrong across the street."

Mom came bustling back into the room. "Hey Jema. Thank you, Levi. I was going to send Felix to get her." She reached for Pearly. "Get yourself inside before you catch your death."

Jema followed Pearly to help steady her and Levi closed the door behind him. Mom pointed to the eggnog. "Choose your poison."

Jema pointed to the Naughty bowl. "Levi, we want this one." He lifted an eyebrow, and Jema smiled. "You will understand when you taste it."

Momma held out a glass to Pearly. "Here you go Pearl. Nice as usual."

Pearly's faded blue eyes fixed on Mom. "I haven't played in snow since Moses was a baby in the bulrushes. Makes a body feel young and spry again." She nodded at the glass. "I think I'll take naughty tonight."

Mom raised her eyebrows. "Lord a'mercy Pearly Armstrong. I never thought I'd see the day."

"And you're likely never to see it again. So get a good look." She tapped Momma's leg with her cane as she hobbled to the hors d'oeuvre table. The poor old soul had outlived all her relatives. She told me a while back she had no plans to die. I was beginning to believe her.

Jema strolled over to where Mom and I stood. She held out a blue box with gold ribbon. "Merry Christmas, Cladie Mae."

"Why, thank you, honey." Momma took it and hugged her.

Jema patted her hands together in anxious anticipation. "Open it."

"All right." Mom slid off the gold ribbon and opened the lid. She gasped and put her hand to her mouth. "Good gracious."

Jema broke into a huge smile. "It is a Faberge-inspired egg ornament."

"Faberge?" Momma took the delicate ornament from the box and held it by its gold satin ribbon. Emeralds were set on the golden egg in a holly bush design, with rubies as the berries. The ornament was beyond breathtaking.

"Yes, and those are real stones." Jema patted her hands together again. "Isn't it lovely?"

"Heaven help me child. This is too—"

Jema held up her hand. "Don't even use the 'E' word. You deserve so much more than this. Hang it on the tree and remember your worth is far above jewels."

Levi wrapped his arm around Mom. "You saw something in me that only my Jema saw. In all my experiences and dealings with people throughout my life, your generosity is unmatched. He looked lovingly at Jema. "I can never repay you for the happiness you helped me find."

"Well," said Lexi, "I guess y'all are going to give me a bag of coal." Lexi had been so enamored with Nathan when he was here investigating, she inadvertently helped him spread suspicion about Levi. Something she now guiltily regretted.

Jema strolled to Lex and hugged her. "You only acted in love trying to protect me and I love you for it."

The doorbell rang and Felix let himself in. Before Mom could ask he said, "Naughty."

Pearly lifted her glass. "I guess we are a naughty bunch this year. Got any more of this stuff?"

At suppertime, we sat in our places at the table. Felix rubbed his hands together. "Miss Cladie, you shore put the big pot in the little 'un."

I had to admit, she had outdone herself this Christmas. We feasted on prime rib beef roast with horseradish cream, garlic mashed potatoes, sautéed green beans and almonds, candied yams and pecans, and her luscious twenty-four-hour salad made with pineapple bits, white cherries, mandarin oranges, and mini-marshmallows all folded into custard, with a whipped cream base. It should have been a dessert, but we ate it as if it were a vegetable salad and didn't feel guilty at all.

Speaking of desserts, there were a plethora of choices that gave plenty of reasons for feeling guilty. Such as her specialty, a four-layer coconut cream cake. She also made several pecan pies and a rum raisin bread pudding with chocolate bourbon sauce. *Have mercy on us, Jesus.*

After supper, we all lumbered into the family room and found a place around the fire to veg and sip Alka-Seltzer. Full stomachs and the warmth from the hypnotic flames had me nodding off until Lexi piped up.

"I have news." She grinned at Levi and Jema. "Guess who is coming to your wedding?"

Ty opened his mouth to say Nathan, but I squeezed his hand. I was pledged to silence and I had let it slip when he told me about Skye's fascination with him.

Jema tilted her head. "Who?"

Never one to miss a dramatic pause, Lexi looked each of us in the eye before announcing, "Nathan!"

She was answered with mute bewilderment. Finally, Levi cleared his throat. "He is welcome to come of course, but why would he *want* to come?"

Lex waved her hand as if she were shooing a fly. "Don't you worry. He has an idea to make special amends for his little error." She shrugged and grinned. "Besides, it all turned out, right?"

"Yes." Levi took Jema's hand and kissed it. "Yes, it did."

I glanced at Ty. "When are you telling Skye? She will be over the moon about this."

He shook his head. "You have no idea." Grinning at Lexi he said, "Get ready for some competition with my daughter for Nathan's attention."

Lexi arched her brows. "Don't worry, Tyler Jackson. I have my ways."

Momma crossed her arms. "Humph. I don't know that I like the sound of that, missy."

A rosy blush burned Lex's cheeks. "Now, Miss

Cladie, you know me better than that."

Momma murmured under her breath. "That's the problem."

Ty burst out laughing, and Lexi threw a pillow at him. "Oh, shut up."

Poor Lex. We all caught Ty's hysterics and held our poor strained stomachs as we howled at her expense. Even she had to join in. Like I said earlier, for southerners hilarity is the perfect digestif to end a day of feasting and friends.

****

When everyone had gone home, Momma went to her room to watch her favorite Christmas movie, *It's a Wonderful Life*. Ty and I stretched out on the family room floor in a nest of pillows. I rolled on my side and propped up on my arm. "This has been an amazing Christmas. I don't think there will ever be one to match it."

Ty faced me. "It certainly has been the best one of my life."

This was the perfect time to give him my gift. I held up my finger. "Just a sec." He watched me under furrowed eyebrows while I pulled an envelope from the tree's branches. "Merry Christmas."

"Thank you." He took the envelope and slipped his thumb under the flap. Inside were a handful of business cards. He read each one and peered up at me clearly confused. "Who are these people?"

"These are the movers and shakers for the top magazines in the nation. Scott, Nathan, and I have connections with them." I laid my hand on his. "Ty, I believe in your dream. You tell stories in your photos as well as any novelist. I want to see you succeed. I am going to email them about you. So get your portfolio ready."

He shuffled through the pile of cards. "Wow. Conde Nast? National Geographic? The New Yorker?" A little boy gleam excited his eyes. "I don't know what to say. No one has ever shared my vision."

"Well, I do." Scooching close to his side, I touched the side of his face. "I love you."

The cards fell to the floor as he laid me back. I closed my eyes and sank into the pillows aware only of the heat from his lips and his heart beating against mine. Yes, this was a perfect end to a perfect day.

When the Grandfather clock chimed one, Ty whispered against my neck, "It's getting late. I'd better go."

"Must you?" Evenings like these made me long for the time when we would be together in our own home.

"Skye and Glen are coming tomorrow if the roads are clear. I need to get up early and make a place for them at the apartment."

"They won't stay at your parents?"

"No and I can't blame them. A little Emma Jackson goes a long way."

"Well, if she starts turning them against me, use our little ace in the hole."

"What's that?"

"You mean, *who's* that? Nathan."

Ty stood and pulled me into his arms. "We don't need no stinkin Nathan Wolfe."

"Maybe not." I stretched toward his lips. "But it's nice to have an little advantage,, right?"

Lost in our kiss, Ty mumbled, "Right."

Chapter Five

When you want to pout, play instead.
                                        ~Tyler Jackson

Ty knew he should clean his place and make up beds for the kids, but he couldn't keep from looking at the business cards Avalee had given him. He read and re-read each one, then ran his fingers over the embossed names. Was it possible the fruition of his dreams were literally at his fingertips? Finally, someone who believed in him—Tyler Jackson. He may be nothing more than a tiny speck on the planet, but hey, tiny specks accomplish big things all the time, right?

The cell phone interrupted his thoughts. The screen read, *Her Highness*. "Morning, Mother."

"Good morning, Tyler. Skye and Glen have just arrived. Will you be joining us for brunch or do you have other plans?"

He checked his watch. Eight-thirty. *Sheesh*. He'd never known his children to be out of bed before ten. "I'll be there in an hour."

"Will you be bringing *her* with you?"

"No. I won't do that to *her* again. She deserves better."

"Don't we all." She paused for a melodramatic interlude in order for that last stab to sink in. "Very well then. I'll be expecting you in an hour."

Ty clicked off his phone and shook his head. No telling what garbage his mother was spewing to his kids. He didn't worry about Glen. But Skye? Thank God for Nathan Wolfe.

****

While waiting for Doris to answer his parent's door, Ty thought about how weird this formality felt. When he was a child, he walked through the front doors anytime he wanted. After all, it was his home. But after moving out, his mother thought it necessary and proper for him to be treated as any other guest. He couldn't imagine Miss Cladie ever requiring Avalee to ring or knock after she moved out.

Doris opened the door and beamed up at him. He couldn't help it; he adored this woman. If he had to describe her in two words, it would be 'friendly mischief'. She could hear a mouse cross the road while she vacuumed the sitting room on the third floor. Nothing said or done in the Jackson home escaped her notice.

"Good morning, Mr. Jackson."

He put his hand up. "I wish you wouldn't do that 'Mr. Jackson' bit."

Her brown eyes sparkled and she muttered from the side of her mouth. "I've got to keep your momma happy. Christmas bonus time you know."

"But you're Jewish."

"Your mother insists." Doris shrugged her shoulders. "Who am I to argue?"

She stepped out of the way and examined his feet for snow. After she closed the door, she nudged his side with her elbow. He stopped and started to ask what she wanted, but she motioned for him to act like they weren't talking. Instead, she took a rag from her apron pocket and pretended to polish a vase on the hall table. While she worked, she said in a low voice, "I'm not one to stick my nose in someone else's business, but if I were you, I'd prepare myself for trouble."

He slipped off his coat and hung it in the hall closet. "Why? What has Mother done now?"

Doris busied herself re-arranging the flowers in the vase. "She's been showing your children photos of your brother since he was a baby and filling their heads with her version of why he died."

Oh great. That was just great. "Thanks for the warning, Doris."

"You didn't hear anything from me. I mind my own business."

"Right. Got it."

Just as Doris had warned, pictures lay scattered on the coffee table in the library. His daughter and his mother sat bent over them. Skye looked up. "Hi, Dad."

He couldn't read her expression. "Hey. Whatcha got going there?"

His mother straightened. "I'm showing her pictures of your brother. I'm sure she doesn't hear about him from you."

Ty threw his hands in the air. "For crying out loud, Mother. He was ten when I was born. He left for college when I was eight. I was in sixth grade when he died. And when he was home, he didn't have time for a little brother. Hell, I hardly knew him. What do you want me to do? Make things up about him like you do?"

His father entered the room and laid a hand on Ty's shoulder. "Tyler, calm down. Let's try and have a pleasant meal this time."

If it were not for the kids, he would have left and never returned. He'd had enough. "Where's Glen?"

"Oh, he got tired of looking at photos." Skye flipped her hand toward the window. "He went outside to," she made air quotes, "play in the snow."

"Good idea. Think I'll join him." Perfect for cooling off.

His mother tore her gaze from the photo album. "Don't be out too long. Brunch will be served soon."

"Just send your servant to fetch me." *Geez.*

Sunlight glinted off the blue-white yard. In a few hours, the magic that had made everything seem fresh and new would melt into ugly muddy puddles. Somewhere in this image was a story. He took his phone and shot a few pictures, wishing he'd brought his camera.

"Hi, Dad." Glen worked at finishing up a miniature snowman on the patio table.

"Hey, son. Building a snowman?"

"Yeah, I had to get out of there. Grandmother is such a downer."

"Yes, I'm very aware. She's been like that for as long as I can remember."

"She sure hates your Avalee."

Needle pricks stung Ty's neck. *Stay calm. Be in control.* "What did she say?"

"That Marc was so upset when she broke up with him that he sped home, and because he was crying so hard he ran off the road into the only tree along the highway."

Oh, if Glen only knew the truth. "Do you believe that?"

"I don't know. Should I?"

"No." Now wasn't the time to resurrect the family skeleton. "Nothing she said is the truth. Maybe I'll tell you one day."

"Okay. That's cool."

Wasn't that just like Glen? He was a pool of water. Reflective and refreshing. And when someone caused ripples on the surface, he remained calm down deep.

Skye stuck her head out the door. "Come eat."

Ty turned and headed toward the house when a barrage of snowballs beat against his back.

"Hey." In one swoop, he scooped up snow, formed a ball and nailed Glen in the chest. His son shot one off Ty's shoulder. There was nothing to do but…Ty charged Glen and tackled him in the snow. They rolled and wrestled while laughing with deep, cleansing, guffaws.

"Boys, get up from there." Ty's mother stood at the door with her hand on her chest. "Your clothes will be soaked and you will ruin Doris' floor."

Her Royal Highness had burst his and Glen's magical moment. But he wouldn't let her ruin his day. He stood and helped Glen to his feet. They brushed snow off their clothes, wrapped their arms around each other's shoulders, and tromped inside. No, she couldn't ruin his day now.

****

Shortly after a brunch of Clams Casino, Eggs Benedict, cheese strata, and fruit tarts, Ty made his excuses and left. If he had to listen to another word from his mother about the importance of a high-paying profession, obviously aimed at Glen who had chosen the same path in the arts as he had done, or his father's political rants, he would have exploded. He wished he could go straight to Avalee's and drink coffee in Miss Cladie's kitchen while sitting at her little table beside the wall decorated with smiling plaster of Paris fruits. Maybe enjoy the simplicity of toasted pound cake. There he could relax, laugh, and feel at home. However, the plan was to meet the kids at his place within the hour. He had just enough time to put clean sheets on the guest bed and the futon.

While he worked, he wondered how to approach Skye about the tales his mother had told her. Should he tell her what really happened? Or should he trust her journalistic instincts to be able to ferret out the truth? He decided to trust her instincts. Maybe she'd recognize what he already suspected, that his mother had an obsession. Almost like a mental illness. That thought brought Ty up short. Did his mother have a mental illness? Or was it depression? Could depression last that long? Perhaps he should try—once again—to be more patient, more understanding. A resolution, he knew, that would most likely disappear like cotton candy in the rain as soon as Skye arrived spouting off all his mother had said.

When Skye and Glen sauntered through the door, Glen plopped in a chair. "Wow, am I glad that's over."

Skye lowered one eyebrow and squinted her eyes. "You sure didn't mind the thousand dollar check she handed you."

He stretched. "You're right on that score. Small price to pay."

"Hey Dad," Skye scooted onto a barstool. "I saw that picture you made for Grandmother. That was cool how you added Uncle Marc. She actually cries when she looks at it."

"Yeah, I thought it might help her somewhat. But I may have made things worse. She hasn't brought those albums out in years."

Skye propped her elbow on the bar and rested her chin on her hand. "You know as well as me why she did that. She knows we are going to meet Avalee."

The moment of truth had arrived earlier than expected. "And?"

"And she is a bitter woman. I feel sorry for her."

"You believe her?"

"Some of it." Skye dropped her hand and leaned forward. "I've thought a lot about this since you told us about your engagement. So, what if everything Grandmother said was true? It doesn't mean it was Avalee's fault. Uncle Mark made poor choices. People live and die by them all the time. In his case, well," she held her palms up, "he died." Shrugging she added, "If I broke up with Duff and he drove like a bat out of hell and hit a tree, I'd hate to be blamed for it."

Ty was glad he trusted her instincts. One day he would tell her the truth. "Well, are you ready to go to the Prestons'?"

"Will there be food?" Glen stood. "I hear Mrs. Preston is a great cook."

Skye rolled her eyes. "You've already eaten, you Neanderthal."

"I didn't eat. I just pushed that crap around my plate."

"Oh." She popped her brother on the shoulder. "I guess you only eat food served by a certain cute waitress?"

Glen shrugged. "I only eat real food. Not some ladi-da food eaten with special forks while we stick our pinkies out."

"Believe me," Ty shrugged on his coat, "you will get real food at Miss Cladie's, and lots of it."

"Great." He strode to the door. "I'm in."

Skye tied a scarf around her neck. "Wonder if Avalee has talked to Nathan Wolfe lately?"

"Do me a favor, Skye."

"What, Dad?"

"Get to know her a little before you start plying her with questions about Wolfe."

"For heaven's sake, Dad. You raised me with better manners than that."

"Yeah, yeah. Get in the truck." He knew all about her manners. Manners that were quickly incinerated by her enthusiastic fire personality. Ty pulled his phone from his pocket and texted Avalee.

—Ready or not, here we come.—

Chapter Six

Love made me young at heart.

~Jema Presley

Jema couldn't help it. She just had to try on her wedding gown one more time. After slipping it on, she twisted this way and that while viewing herself in the full-length mirror. The dress she chose was nothing near as flashy as Molly Kate's figure-hugging dress with the thigh-high slit. Jema wished she were more like Molly Kate, who had a good sixty pounds on her, but was so comfortable in her own skin she thought nothing of the crimson, sequined, strapless dress that showed her every curve and bump. Still, the dress Jema chose suited her perfectly.

The stunning off-the-shoulder silver sheath dress shimmered under the overlay of sheer silver chiffon. The fitted bodice dazzled with crystal-encrusted appliqués giving the gown a perfect touch of elegance. She swayed back and forth watching the hem billow at her feet like a crystal cloud, reminding her of the gowns Ginger Rogers wore while dancing with Fred Astaire.

She stepped over to the dresser and lifted the diamond and pearl necklace Levi had given her for a wedding present and held it against her neck. Glancing down at the matching earrings, she smiled. She never told him she loved pearls and crystals. And yet, he somehow knew, only instead of crystals he showered her with diamonds.

Jema returned to the mirror and began swaying once more while humming "Young at Heart" then singing, "Fairy tales have come true, they have happened to me now I'm young at heart."

Truer words had never been sung, at least for her. Even at fifty-seven she was living a fairy tale. Who would have thought her mysterious, homeless friend was looking for love for all the right reasons, hoping to find someone who didn't love him for the billion reasons he had in the bank. They both found treasure of the richest kind, which had nothing to do with money. Even so, money was a wonderful bonus. Ever since she watched *Roman Holiday,* she'd dreamed of going to Italy. Now, Levi planned on buying her a villa there. What could she say? Fairy tales.

A knock at her door made her jump. Levi? He couldn't see her in her wedding dress. Then Avalee called, "Anybody home? I hope so because the door is open."

Relieved, Jema answered, "I'm in the bedroom."

Avalee sashayed in with a bottle of wine and two glasses, but stopped short when she saw Jema in her dress. "Oh my word, Jema, that is one of the most beautiful dresses I've ever seen."

Jema twirled making the hem of her dress flow and dance around her ankles. "It is, isn't it? When I saw this one, I knew it was the right dress for me."

"You look like a princess." A troubled look shadowed Avalee's eyes.

Jema noticed and stood still. "Ava? Honey? What's wrong?"

Avalee held up the bottle. "I know it is only noon, but I need to talk and relax before this afternoon."

"Never too early for wine. Let me get this off, and I'll meet you in the kitchen. Pull out some crackers and cheese and we will call it lunch."

"Sounds good."

Everything was ready when Jema strolled into the room. Avalee sat at the small table nestled in the kitchen's bay window sipping wine and watching something outside. Jema's wine was poured and a cheese platter ready. She sat and propped her elbows on the polished oak. "Spill."

Avalee turned her attention from whatever she found so interesting beyond the window to Jema. "I probably shouldn't have come. I hate to be a downer on your special week, but I just had to talk to somebody with a level head."

"Then you are at the right place. What's up?"

"I'm meeting Ty's kids today. Even though he says they are happy about us, I get this bad feeling. Maybe Emma has infiltrated their minds. She has the power. And if our meeting is anything like when we were at his parents…." Avalee drained her glass. "Well, I don't know if I can take it." Tears filled her eyes, and she fingered them away.

"Bad scene at his folks, I take it?"

"Beyond bad. It's as if I'm a curse on the Jacksons. What do I do if his kids feel the same about me as his parents? I would be the reason for Ty's complete alienation from his entire family. How could I do that to him?" She swiped more tears as she rambled on in a breaking voice. "How can I marry him under those conditions?"

Jema didn't answer right away, but weighed her words as she refilled Avalee's glass. "Do you love him?"

"Yes, of course. That's the problem. He has had enough things happen in his life to hold him back. I don't want to be one of them."

"Can you imagine your life without him?"

Avalee turned her attention back to the window. After a sip of wine she nodded. "Yes. I can. And it would be awful." She laid her head back and ran her hands through her hair, then huffed a sigh. "Oh, I don't know, Jem. I've been like a silly teenager with all this wedding stuff. I'm buying bride's magazines, planning flowers and the ceremony. For heaven's sake, I'm fifty-six, not twenty-six. I feel so foolish and selfish right now."

Jema hurt for her. Here she was getting married for the second time, and Molly Kate had just married for the second time. Avalee deserved a magnificent, over-the-moon wedding at the very least. "I get what you are saying about Ty's family. But you aren't giving him much credit, are you?"

Avalee frowned and tipped her head. "What do you mean?"

"He knows what he wants, and he is aware of the cost. Obviously, he has made his choice. Sugar, you are simply borrowing trouble." Jema tilted her glass on her lips. "I have no doubts his children will see in you what he sees in you—a beautiful woman with a loving soul."

Avalee reached across the table and took her friend's hand. "Jema, I'm so glad you are in my life. You are like the sister I never had."

"I'm the one who is glad. I knew you were special

that first day you came into the Piggly Wiggly to buy something for your headache, and you told me you were Cladie Mae's daughter. I loved you immediately, because, after all, we kinda share a mother. She's been that for me for years since my own mother passed."

Avalee smiled at Jema over the rim of her goblet. "Yes, we do." She set her glass down and rested her arms on the table. "Enough about me. Let's talk about you. You say your girls won't be coming to the wedding?"

"No, they will still be in Italy with their sorority sister's family and by the time we arrive they will be flying back to school."

"That's a shame. I know they would have liked to be a part, and I'm sure they are curious about Levi."

Jema ran her finger around the rim of her glass. "Actually, they have no idea who he really is and we aren't saying anything for now."

"Really?"

"No. Of course, I know we won't always be able to keep his identity a secret."

"When he buys you a villa, won't that clue them in their stepfather is loaded?"

Jema swirled her wine. "Yes, they will know he has money. Just not how much."

"I get that." A text message chimed on Avalee's phone. She glanced at it and said, "They are on their way. I'd better get home." She rose and picked up the glasses and cheese plate, carried them to the counter, and then headed toward the door. "Thanks for letting me bend your ear. I'm full of liquid courage, and now I'm ready to face the lions."

Jema stood and followed her to the door, then

gathered Avalee into a tight hug. "Just remember, Ty is the lion tamer. Besides, they will love you. I just know it."

Ava put her hand on the knob. "And if they don't, can I run away to Italy with you?"

"Your room is ready." Jema closed the door and walked to the window to watch Avalee hurry across the street. She put her hand on the glass pane and spoke in a low voice. "And I'm not kidding. I'll always have your back."

Chapter Seven

Sometimes families are created, not born.
                                    ~Avalee Preston

I bent over the couch to straighten the pillows for the sixth time while mom polished the coffee table—again. Our nerves were jitterbugging and we had to do something to break up the party.

"Well, Momma, you are about to meet your future grandchildren. How do you feel about that?"

"To tell the truth, I'd always thought they'd come one at a time and wrapped in a pink or blue blanket." She took my hands and angled her head peering up at me. "Sugar, now don't you worry about those kids. They are going to love you, if they have a lick of sense."

Dread plundered my brain. "I can't help it. There is no telling what Ty's mother has filled their minds with."

"Oh pshaw. If Tyler's children believe Emma Jackson's smoke, then they don't have the brains God gave a goose."

From the dining room, I saw a flash of Ty's truck. "Oh Lord. They're here. Showtime."

"I'll get the coffee and hot chocolate on."

Bless that little mother of mine. She worked her magic through food. Today we needed nothing short of

Divine intervention. Footfalls sounded on the porch. I drew in a breath. The bell rang. I let it out and stepped to the door, forced a smile, and swung it open. Two beautiful adults stood beside Ty. I don't know what I had expected. Kids in knickers? Ty stepped inside and pecked my cheek. "Hi, Babe."

"Hi." I smiled at his kids. Y'all come in." A faint whiff of men's cologne reached my nose as Glen passed by. I couldn't identify it. However, I recognized Skye's fragrance when she handed me her coat. It was the same as I wore, Chanel's *Chance Eau Fraiche*. Good sign?

Ty began with the introductions. "Avalee," he gestured toward his son. "I'd like you to meet Glen." I looked for Ty in the young man's gentle face. He had the dimples and the brown eyes, but not his thick eyelashes or dreamy look. Glen's were kind and playful. He was taller than Ty, long and lanky. He had tied his dark hair in a ponytail at the nape of his neck, but had trouble with his bangs which kept falling over his brow. He tossed his head to move them as he stuck out his hand. "Pleased to meet you, ma'am."

Ma'am. Bless him for his manners, but they sure did make me feel old. I rested my palm in his. "It's good to finally meet you."

Ty slipped his arm around his daughter. "And this is Skye."

I don't know who was checking out who the hardest. She was a lovely girl. Shorter than me, around five-four, I guessed. Her long brown hair framed her heart-shaped face and her eyes—oh, those eyes—were a luminous green. Mesmerizing and penetrating. She had a great sense of style. Skinny jeans, black boots, a white tee under a cropped black leather jacket and a patterned scarf. In a straightforward business manner, she shot out a hand. "Pleased to meet you, Avalee. I've heard a lot about you."

Well, isn't that just great? I took her hand, not sure if she'd shake it or flip me on my back. "Likewise, Skye." My plastered smile grew a little stiffer, but I trudged forward trying to keep my voice upbeat.

"I'll bet you all are freezing. Momma has coffee and hot chocolate to thaw you out."

Ty rubbed his hands together. "Sounds great."

"Why don't you take them in the family room, and I'll help Mom."

He led the way, and I hurried to the kitchen and found Mom loading a cart with chocolate chip cookies, two carafes—one of coffee the other hot chocolate—and all the fixings. She glanced up. "Well?"

"Introductions went okay, I think."

Mom put her hand on the cart's handle. "Now it is my turn. Let's go." She charged into the room where they sat and called out, "Well, here you two are at last." All three stood up. Ty spoke first. "Hi, Momma Cladie. These are my kids, Skye and Glen. Kids, this is Miss Cladie."

Skye held out her hand, but Momma wasn't having anything to do with that. She pulled her into a big bear hug. I would have given a hundred dollars if I could have caught Skye's shocked expression on film. Then Mom turned to Glen and hugged him, only Glen enjoyed her embrace.

"Hey, what about me? Don't I get a hug?"

Momma swiped the air. "I was saving the best for last. Get yourself over here." When she wrapped her arms around Ty, I saw him visibly relax. Perhaps this was the mother's touch he longed for.

"Okay, kids, what'll it be? Chocolate or coffee?"

Skye took coffee, black. No surprise there. Glen, on the other hand, looked like a kid with his nose pressed against the candy counter. "Are those chocolate chunk cookies?"

"Yep, my special recipe. Eat all you want."

Glen took one and shoved it in his mouth. He looked toward the ceiling and moaned. "Oh, man. Miss Cladie. I think I've died and gone to cookie heaven."

That's all it took. Mother was in love with the boy. "Baby, eat every last one if you want. I can always make more. Now, coffee or hot chocolate?"

"Hot chocolate. Do you have marshmallows?"

Momma stuck her hands on her hips. "Of course I do. Can't have hot chocolate without marshmallows." She lifted the lid off what I thought was a sugar bowl. It was full of miniature marshmallows.

Glen rubbed his hands together. "Great. I'm starved."

Momma frowned. "You're hungry? Child, follow me. I have some leftovers I can heat up for you in a jiffy."

Like a puppy, Glen followed close at Momma's heels into the kitchen. In no time at all, they returned. Momma's expression attested to the satisfaction she felt at Glen's dinner plate full to overflowing.

Over the next hour, Momma carried the conversation asking questions and making all of us laugh. Well, everyone but Skye. She nibbled on a cookie, smiled occasionally, but mostly she observed with those keen eyes of hers. I'd seen that intense expression before, the kind that makes you want to admit to doing something when you really didn't. *Who had that same look?* Then it came to me. Nathan Wolfe. The girl seemed a natural. No doubt she'd go far.

When it was time to leave, Skye rose and thanked us. Glen, however, hugged mom. "Thanks Miss Cladie for those rockin' cookies and the awesome food."

"Why you are welcomed, grandboy."

He snapped his fingers. "Hey, that's right. What should I call you?"

Momma thought about Glen's question. "Well you have a *grand* mother. And truth be told, I'm not so grand."

Ty hugged her to his side. "You are too, Momma Cladie."

Mom thought a minute. "I called my grandmother Big Momma. How about that?"

Glen nodded. "Perfect. You've got something my grandmother seems to have lost. You've got a *big* heart."

Momma patted her hips. "And the name fits my hips as well as my heart."

Glen waved her off. "Don't even go there. You are beautiful in my eyes." He hugged her again, kissed my cheek, and then wrapped his arm around Skye's shoulder. "Let's go, sis."

She glanced back and waved as he led her out. When they had walked outside, Ty heaved a sigh. "Well, that went okay, right? At least with Glen."

"Actually, it did." I laid my hand on Momma's shoulder. "Thanks to you."

"One down." She lifted her index finger. "And one to go. Won't be no time till Skye fits right in."

"Thanks *Big Momma*. See you tomorrow." Ty wrapped her in a grateful embrace then held her at arms' length. "And just for the record, you are the grandest lady I know besides your daughter."

"Why thank you, son."

Ty gave me a quick kiss. "See you at Molly Kate's tomorrow to discuss photos for the wedding?"

"Tomorrow." I waggled my fingers. "I love you."

"Love you back."

I watched him jog to the truck and thought about Skye. She never mentioned Nathan. But she wanted to—bad. That probably explained her restraint. I was glad I didn't have to pull the Nate card. I wanted to forge a relationship with her on my own, and only had a week to do it seeing how he was arriving next week. It would take a miracle, but Momma says miracles slap us in the face every day.

I needed a good slap.

Chapter Eight

Everyone has a story. The happily ever after depends on our attitude.

~*Avalee Preston*

A soft tapping on the door drew me from the fog of sleep. "Avalee? Honey? Be waking up. We are supposed to be at Molly Kate's at ten."

I pushed the hair out of my face and peeked through one eye at the clock. Nine? What the heck? I hadn't slept that late in years. "Okay, I'm getting up." I lied. I continued to luxuriate under the soft mountain of puffy duvet deliciousness. The stress of yesterday must have really taken its toll on me.

At long last, I threw the covers back, stretched, and swung my legs over the edge of the bed. If it were not for the aroma of coffee wafting up the stairs, I would have fallen back. Instead, I slipped on my robe and slippers and lumbered down the stairs.

"Morning, sleepyhead." My sainted mother poured a cup of dark roast and pushed it in my hands.

Through a yawn I managed to say, "Morning."

"Hungry?"

"No, my stomach is still in bed." After several sips of my morning elixir, its magical, mental-mist clearing properties kicked in gear. "Besides, I'm sure MK has quite a spread ready and waiting."

"I'm sure she will."

"It's hard to believe little Jema will be married in only five days." Nostalgia tinged Mom's voice. "And there is so much to do."

"Not really. Jema and Levi are planning a very small wedding, thank the Lord."

"Are any of his people coming?"

"No. Jema told me that he really doesn't have any people left except for a sister who disowned the family years ago."

"What on earth for?"

"She didn't like being known for her wealth any more than Levi. So, she took her part of the inheritance, changed her name, and disappeared. No one knows where she is or even who she is now."

"She doesn't even keep up with her own brother?"

"Doesn't appear to. I seem to remember Jema saying something about her being resentful that Levi was the heir just because he was the oldest and a male."

"So, in other words, she picked up her marbles and left the game."

"Exactly."

Momma peered into her mug. "I need a refill. How about you?"

"Please." While she filled our cups, I thought about Skye. Nathan would arrive in three days. I wanted to at least see if I could start a relationship with her on my own. "I'm thinking of texting Skye and see if she wants to meet for lunch."

"I think that's a good idea. Here." She held out my cup and sat at the table. Running her hand over the butter-yellow tablecloth Mom said, "She's a hard one to read all right, and I usually have good instincts about people."

"Frankly, she behaved better than I expected after the evening I spent with Emma Jackson." I wrinkled up my nose. "Bleh."

"Baby, let me tell you a little about Emma."

"Do I want to hear this?" I propped my chin on my hand and looked into mother's solemn face.

"Yes. Maybe if you understand a little about her past, it would help you to consider the source and realize you are not the reason for her misery, only the target."

"Oh, well, I feel better already, being a target and all."

Mom tucked her chin and gave me *the look*. "Anyway, Emma was raised across the tracks—literally."

"Shanty Town?" Wow. This *was* news.

"Yes. I was a couple of grades ahead of her, but we all knew each other. Her mother, Lola, was a single parent. Emma's father was an immigrant worker passing through. He probably never even knew he had a child. When she was born, she and her mother lived with the grandparents. Of course, they were dirt poor. If a trip around the world cost a dollar, they couldn't have made it to the state line. They ate from the garden and what Lola's daddy shot or caught. They had a milk cow, and chickens, so they didn't starve by any means. Her clothes were homemade, which wasn't unusual when I was growing up. All our mothers sewed. But Emma's dresses were made from the material taken from her grandmother's worn out dresses or from flour sacks."

Momma stared off. "I can still see young Emma at

school in a rag-tag dress, the product of an unwed mother which in those days was unheard of, carrying her lunch in a tow-sack." Momma returned her gaze to me. "If I had to describe her life as a child in one word, it would have been *shame*. No one, and as ashamed as I am to admit it, me included, had anything to do with her. And even if we were inclined to try and befriend her, our parents forbade it."

Shame. While mother spoke, it occurred to me that Emma Jackson and I struggled with the same thing.

Momma kept on with her story. "When she was sixteen, Emma got a job at the Piggly Wiggly. It was brand spanking new. The first self-serve grocer. Up until then we went to Hanson's, gave them our list and they bagged our order up for us. Emma worked hard. She learned how to use make-up, bought new clothes and had her hair styled. That girl turned out to be a right pretty thing. Marcus Jackson sure thought so. He stopped into Pigg's for groceries, they met, and the rest was history."

"They met? Didn't he already know about her?"

"No, he'd just moved from Illinois to set up a family practice in Moonlight. They married and Emma began to enjoy life as a respected lady, and when the money came rolling in, she let it go to her head. Then, when little Marcus Jr. came along Emma was obsessed with him, vowing he'd never suffer the shame she had."

"Why wasn't she as obsessed with Ty?"

"Ty didn't come along until years later. She loved him, of course, but I think from the start she lived vicariously through Marc. He was a bright lad, as you well know." Momma tilted her head to the side. "I guess you could say he restored her pride. Anytime she met her old school mates, including me, she made sure to let us know her son out-shined all of our kids."

"But not Ty?"

"He just came along a little too late. And when he was old enough to follow in his dad's footsteps as Marc had, he refused, which bitterly disappointed Emma, as you well know."

"Isn't it odd? In a way, she is doing the same to Ty as her classmates had done to her."

Momma sighed. "That's the sad truth." She rose and took our cups. "But my reason for telling you her story is so you might find it in your heart to give her grace."

"Does Ty know about his mother?"

"I don't know. I doubt it. Emma has wiped out that time of life like one wipes chalk off a blackboard." The cuckoo bird chirped nine-thirty. "Lord a'mercy, we better get a move on." Momma yanked off her apron.

"I'll be ready in a jiff." I rose and climbed the stairs. As I dressed, I thought about what Mom had told me. Sad story, but a lot of people had sad childhoods. That wasn't an excuse for being mean as a junkyard dog was it? I mean, she had a choice, right?

Chapter Nine

Forever friends, plans, and Martini Mondays. Life is good.

~Avalee Preston

Just as I predicted, Molly Kate had a huge spread of food, including our traditional celebration mimosas, of which Jema and Lexi were already partaking. Lexi held hers up. "Hi y'all. We waited on you like one dog waits on another."

Jema turned from the dining room buffet and hurried over to us. She looked fabulous. The air about her seemed as if she might burst out in hilarious laughter at any minute. Her eyes danced behind her gold wire-rimmed glasses. I noticed her hair was highlighted too and cut in a short shaggy style. Very flattering. No doubt this was David's handiwork.

After Lexi handed us our mimosa, she lifted hers, "Girls, I propose a toast. Here's to our forever friend, Jema. May she and Levi live long and love fully."

We lifted our glasses and cheered, "Here, here."

Jema's eyes glistened as she lifted her glass again. "And here's to you. My friends whom I love as dearly as sisters." She looked in Mom's direction. "And as a mother. May nothing keep us apart."

"Here, here, and amen." Momma took a sip of her drink. "Whoa, who mixed these things?"

Molly Kate jerked her head toward Lexi. "Really? Need you ask, Miss Cladie?"

"Oh pssh." Lexi nodded at Momma. "Keep drinking. You'll get used to it."

"Okay girls, let's get this show on the road." Molly Kate wandered to the dining room table. How about a progress report."

"I'll start." I pulled sketches from my portfolio. "I've ordered dozens of white roses, and I plan to enhance some with crystal bits. In the bouquet, I'll add lacy fern and drape the handle with strands of white pearls."

Jema drew in a breath. "Oh, that is so beautiful."

"I've also ordered enough flowers to refresh the arrangements from MK's wedding, so we are good to go there." Counting on my fingers, I ticked off all the other things that were on my list. "I picked up gold candles to put in the glass vases we already have, ordered indoor sparklers, loads of confetti, gold and silver party poppers, gold and black party horns...oh, and are you ready for this? A balloon drop!"

Lexi frowned. "Say what?"

"This is going to be so fabulous. Wherever Jema and Levi decide they are standing, and all through the room, I will have netting hanging from the ceiling filled with gold, silver, pearl, and black balloons. So, when Jema and Levi say 'I do,' the first balloon drop will fall over them. Then with each stroke of midnight, the others will fall as we kiss the New Year in. Isn't that the coolest thing ever?"

"Well," said Momma. "What about those of us who don't have anyone to kiss?"

"Y'all can play with the balloons." Lexi reached

for a piece of banana bread.

Jema clapped her hands like a little girl. "I love it."

"Heck, that makes a gal want do-overs," said Molly Kate. "I'm jealous."

"Sorry MK, but Ty and I are next. Besides, none of us will beat your fabulousness in that crimson Mae West dress."

Molly Kate stood and struck her best Mae West pose. "You have a point."

"Anyway, that's it for me. Who's next?"

"Me." MK pulled pictures from her folder. "Okay, here are some sketches of cakes I'm thinking about. I've designed a small cake for the wedding and a large one for the reception on New Year's Day. I'm thinking a three-tiered white cake. The bottom tier will have gold scrolls, the middle will have pearls, and the top will have crystal sugar."

Momma piped up. "You aren't using that nasty fondant are you?"

Molly squinched up her nose and pursed her lips like she'd just smelled rotten cabbage. "Heaven's no. That stuff tastes like the play dough I tried to eat as a kid, only sweeter. No matter how pretty it may make the cake look, it still isn't enough reason for serving nasty. Besides, I can make buttercream look as smooth."

Momma nodded. "Good. I had a lady once tell me the fondant was supposed to be peeled off to get to the buttercream underneath, but who wants an extra step between slicing and eating cake? Besides, it would be rude to lick the frosting off the *fondough*."

"Oh, MK, that is amazing!" Jema's delight felt palpable. "How many will the reception cake serve?"

"Around fifty depending on how it is cut. But I'll also have a groom's cake and cupcakes." Molly snapped her fingers. "Which reminds me. What should I put on Levi's cake? Something Canadian?"

"How about a Canadian goose?" Lexi sniggered at her own pseudo-cleverness.

"Cute Lex." Jema thought about the cake. "Well, he likes anything chocolate, loves Guinness beer, sports, and nature."

Molly's creativity went into full swing. "How about a moose wearing Levi's favorite sports team's logo, holding a Guinness?"

"Perfect! He will love it. I'll check to see who his favorite team is."

Lexi raised her hand. "Need a buttercream tester? I'm available." She slapped her rear. "Seeing how I'm the *only* one not getting married. Doesn't matter how big my butt gets."

"Now, Lex," I said. "You never know. Nate may come through."

"Naw. He isn't the marrying kind. I can tell. Neither am I really." She lifted her shoulders and let them fall. "*Que sera, sera.*"

"I don't know. Neither Jema or I expected to get married and now look." This thought never ceased to amaze me. I was going to be married in May. *Wow.*

Molly faced me. "And you are going to keep with tradition and have your ceremony in the mansion, right?"

"I thought you'd never suggest it, but I'm warning you it is going to be big and traditional. Even though I'm an old lady now, this will still be my first wedding."

"Finally," Momma added.

"Okay, let's talk the day of the wedding. But first," Lexi held up a finger and looked at Molly Kate. "Are there anymore mimosa makings?"

"Are you a bottle-redhead?"

Lexi smacked Molly on the arm. "Oh, hush up. I'll be right back."

While we waited, Jema perused the sketches and plans. "Five days. Just five days and I'll be Mrs. Abrams. It is almost too much to take in."

"Well, this will help you." Lexi carried a tray of fresh drinks. After we'd all been served, Lex commenced. "I talked to Tryna and David about doing our mani/pedis and hair. And they both agreed." She turned to Jema. "I hope you don't mind, but I promised them *big* bonuses seeing how they are working on a holiday."

Jema grinned. "You're better at spending Levi's money than me, and that's saying something."

"Well, *it is* for a good cause—us. We've got to look fabulous in the wedding photos. Besides, Tryna makes killer margaritas."

"Did you invite them to the wedding? Levi and I would love to have them."

"Yes, but they both had plans. But they will be at the reception. David even offered to fix our hair again. He's such a great guy."

"I just hope he and Tryna aren't worn out from fixing me by the time they get to you girls." Momma gave her slyest grin.

"Don't worry, Miss Cladie," said Lexi. "David is an artist. I'll bet a solid quarter you won't darken the door of the Beauty Box ever again."

"Okay girls, the final thing on my list, the honeymoon suite. And while it won't be as nice as it was for Stan and me since Scott won't be here to fix it up, I promise I'll do my best to make it romantic."

"Are we dressing in the pool house again?" I sure hoped not. It had gone from a nice sixty degrees to low forties in three weeks.

"No, I think we should get ready in one of the suites upstairs in the mansion. I'll put the guys in the pool house seeing how they are supposed to be tough and all." Molly glanced around the room. "Anything else?"

"It all sounds so unbelievably amazing." Jema rose and walked to me. Taking my hands in hers she said, "And if we can do all of this in just a couple weeks, think of what we will all do for you."

With her beautiful words in my ears, we all got ready to leave. Full of hope and good cheer, I texted Ty.

—Think Skye'd want 2 join me for lunch 2day?—

He texted back.

—She said sure. Where 2 meet?—

—Magnolia Tea Room. On my way.—

I dropped Mom off at the house and headed to the tearoom. On the way, I tried to think of things to talk about. What if she just stared at me with her intense eyes? I'd probably turn into a blathering fool.

Maybe lunch wasn't such a good idea.

****

During my youth, dreams of my wedding did not include my fiancé's twenty-something daughter. While waiting in an inconspicuous table in the tearoom my nerves shimmied in my stomach. I felt ridiculous. After all, I'm a grown woman in love with a grown man. We didn't need anyone's permission. Right? I nodded my head to no one. *Right.*

The bells on the door jingled. Skye stepped in and looked around. She had a relaxed expression, thank the Lord. I waved and caught her attention just as my favorite waitress, Birdie, approached her. If *Gone With the Wind* were remade and they needed an actress to play Aunt Pity Pat, Birdie would be their gal. Her ample figure, wild blonde hair, and rosy cheeks, fit the character perfectly. Skye waved back, smiled at Birdie, pointed at me and then strolled to the table.

"Hi." She shrugged off her coat before sliding into the booth.

"Hi. Glad you could make it."

Birdie ambled over and gave us the tearoom's fan-shaped menus. "Lordy, it's as cold as an ex-husband's heart out there. How 'bout some tea? Coffee? Hot chocolate?"

"Hot chocolate for me." Skye glanced at me.

"I'll have English Breakfast with cream."

"All righty y'all. While I'm getting your drinks, take a gander at the menu. All the soups are to die for, and the Parker house rolls just went into the oven."

When she walked away, Skye and I watched each other across the table with fixed smiles. Even with all my rehearsing on the way, I didn't know where to begin. I know where I wished to begin. I wanted to tell her Emma Jackson was an outright liar. My expression must have shown it because Skye angled her head and quizzed me with her eyes. Thank goodness Birdie returned.

"Here y'all are." She set our drinks in front of us. "Now, what can I bring you to eat?"

"I'll have the loaded potato soup in the bread bowl." Skye handed Birdie the menu.

Youth and carbs, I remember those days, now long gone, darn it. "I'll have the roasted butternut soup."

Birdie didn't look up while scribbling our orders on a pad. "You want yours in a bread bowl, sugar?"

Yes. "No, but I'd like a roll, please."

"All righty then. I'll be back in two shakes." She wagged her finger. "Don't forget to save room for dessert."

When Birdie was out of sight, I decided it was time to just say what was on my mind. "Skye, I asked you to lunch because I know your grandmother has told you things about me, and I'm sure you have questions. I will be happy to answer them as best I can."

There, I said it. The only thing I could do now was to wait for the barrage of accusations.

Skye lowered her gaze and stared at her hot chocolate, then said in a low voice, "Dad warned me to not deluge you with questions, and I've really tried to hold my tongue, but…are you *really* good friends with Nathan Wolfe?"

Nathan Wolfe? That's the reason she's been so silent. She wanted to know about Nate?

"Why, yes. I am."

She met my gaze. "Wow."

Wow?

"I watch him on every news show I can find; I even search him on YouTube. I study him because I want to be like him someday."

I relaxed. "I will tell him when he gets here. He'll be flattered."

"When he…? Wait. When he gets here?" She put

112

her hand to her chest. "As in…he's coming *here*?"

"Yep. Next week."

She gasped and covered her mouth with her hands. "Oh my gosh. Really? Oh my gosh—*oh my gosh*"

"I'll introduce you to him at Jema's wedding."

Fluttering her hands, she squealed. "I can't believe this."

As happy as I was for this meeting to turn out so positive, there were things we needed to talk about, and I needed to walk this conversation back to my original reason for lunch.

"We can talk about Nate—"

"—Nate? You call him Nate?"

I nodded. "Yes, sometimes. But, as I was saying, let's talk about him later. Right now, I'm wondering if you have questions about your father and me?"

She shrugged her shoulders and took a sip of hot chocolate. "Not really. Dad has dated a lot over the years. Nothing serious. So I felt pretty confident when he proposed that you were the one. I mean, he ought to know. I'm cool with it."

"What about the things your grandmother told you about me?"

"As if." She waved her hand and shook her head. "I never pay attention to her when she talks like that. I never knew Dad's brother, but I know I wouldn't have liked him."

"Why is that?"

"Because Grandmother acts as if Dad doesn't exist. I don't know what I'd do if my mother always compared me to my brother."

Suddenly, I felt the need to defend Marc. "Marc wasn't a bad guy. Just sorta immature. But he was also exceptionally smart. Emma had high hopes for him, and I'm sure if he'd lived, she would have been just as proud of your dad. But after Marc's death, I guess she kinda got lost."

"You think?" She rolled her eyes. "Lost and crazy."

A smile demanded to be set free on my face, but I bit my lips. Birdie brought our lunches and suddenly I was famished. "Birdie, would you bring me a bacon grilled cheese, too?"

"Sure thing. I'll have it to you in a jiffy." She hurried back to the kitchen calling, "Hey Tom, one BGC."

I tore my roll and dipped it in the thick, orange, soup. "So, you don't have anything to say about me being nearly twelve years older than your dad or that I've only been back five months before he proposed and I accepted?"

She held her spoon to her mouth and blew. "Nope. I have a friend whose parents knew each other a week before they eloped. They've been together for over forty years."

"And the age thing?"

"No biggie." She smiled. "We all live till we die, right? Take Marc for example. I say we love and be loved when we can."

Wow. Such wisdom from one so young. "And if I was not friends with *the* Nathan Wolfe, would your answers be the same?"

She put her finger to her cheek and looked up. "Umm, let me think on that a bit." After a second, she looked me straight in the eyes. "Absolutely."

"One more question and I'll stop."

"Good. My soup is getting cold."

"Wanna split an orange roll?"

"Nope." A mischievous grin commandeered her face. "I want one all to myself."

When Skye said that, I knew we were going to be good friends.

****

Martini Monday. It seemed like years instead of months since we first instituted this get together. It was our way to combat the dreaded first working day of the week by giving us something to look forward to. All evening, we'd drink martinis, eat fattening food, and just plain laugh till our sides ached, the best medicine ever. This evening would be the last one for a long time.

So much had changed. We began as four friends with no hope of romance, but cupid showered his arrows and just like that we all found love. Well, all except for Lexi. I think she just found lust. Soon Jema would be gone, leaving our number at three. Sorta bittersweet.

Momma stuck her head in my room. "Hon, your martini munchies are all packed up in the kitchen."

"Thanks, Mom. Why don't you come?"

"I'm tuckered out, baby. I'm going to my chair to watch Wheel, and then go to bed."

"Good. You worked yourself to exhaustion this Christmas."

"I'll allow, I do love the holidays. But this year it wore me out. I'm gettin' old, baby."

She did look tired—more than tired. Her sparkle seemed snuffed out. I tucked that worry back in my mind to dwell on the next day. "Oh poo, mom. Age is just a number. Isn't that what you always say? Now let's get you settled before I leave."

I followed her downstairs to her sitting room, or what she called her *front* room, and helped her settle in her chair. After I tucked her Christmas throw around her, and turned on *Wheel of Fortune* I asked, "Can I get you anything before I leave?"

"I'd love a big glass of sweet tea. I just can't seem to quench my thirst lately."

"Okay, be back in a sec." While I poured her tea, I wondered if she needed to get checked out by Doctor Derrick. Of course, if I suggested it to her she'd probably brush me off. But a little niggle in the back of my mind warned me she needed to see a doctor. After Jema's wedding, I decided to put my foot down and do what it took to get her there. No if's, ands, or buts.

I returned to the front room and set the tea on the table beside her chair. "Here you go."

"Thank you, hon." She flipped her hand in the air. "Now run along. I'll be fine." Right then Pat Sajak's smiling face appeared on the screen. From that moment on, no one else was in the room but her, Pat, and Vanna. I kissed the top of her head and left to load the little red wagon I'd had as a girl. That wagon used to carry my puppies, kittens, and dolls for miles during my youth. Now that I'm grown, it follows me to my friends' homes laden with adult beverages and snacks.

I bundled up and hurried to Lexi's. The savory aroma of her spicy and deliciously greasy sausage balls reached me before I set foot on her porch. She made them every Martini Monday. No doubt she had also concocted one of her exquisite chocolate martini recipes. She had several, all of them amazing and chocked full of calories. Which was a problem because none of us could drink just one.

I gathered my vodka, Momma's cheese balls, corn dip, Fritos scoopers, and pita chips from the wagon, climbed the steps and walked inside. "Knock, knock."

"Come on in." Lexi grabbed the vodka and chips from my arms. "Jema's here and we are one martini ahead of you."

"Am I late?" I set the cheese balls on the table and arranged pita chips around them.

"No," said Jema. "We're just ready to get this party started." She poured my Gray Goose over ice and started shaking it. "MK should be here any minute. She's been bad about being on time since she married. I wonder why?" With a wink, she thrust a perfect martini in my hand—cold and dry.

"The same reason you will be in four days." I held my glass up. "Cheers."

She tapped her glass against mine. "And you will have the same reason in five months."

"Oh stop it, you two." Lexi stuck out her tongue. "Y'all make me want to throw up, not to mention incredibly jealous."

Molly Kate strolled into the room holding a platter of what I hoped were chocolate chunk cookies. "Hey y'all. Sorry I'm late."

"Late and one martini behind." Lexi took the platter from her and peeked. "You read my mind, Mrs. Montgomery." She took the foil off the pile of indescribable yumminess.

"For your information, Stan and I had one before I left."

"Which," Lexi lifted a cookie to her mouth,

"explains why you are late."

"Oh stop." A flush rose up Molly's neck. "So what's tonight's entertainment besides me?"

"Well, it just so happens Jema is our entertainment." Lexi pointed to a basket filled with small wrapped packages.

"Me?" Jema put her hand to her chest. We all stood around her like grinning emojis. She glanced around. "What?"

"This," said Lexi, "is a honeymoon basket." The air was abuzz with hilarious energy bursting to be free. "And *you* my dear, are our entertainment."

"However," I held up my glass, "not until we've had another one of these."

We filled our plates and refreshed our drinks, then formed a semi-circle around Jema in evil anticipation. We had shopped at an adult entertainment outside of town. With each gift her blush evolved from rosé to merlot. You've heard of *Fifty Shades of Gray*? Well, our Jema turned at least fifty shades of red. Her comments had us rolling. "You do *what* with this?"…"This goes *where*?"…"Y'all actually expect me to fit in that?"…"Levi puts this on his…?"…"You gotta be kidding me."

By the time she opened the last gift, we were all weak from laughter. Wads of gift paper were strewn about the room.

Lexi stood and stretched. "Girl, if you don't have a fine time on your honeymoon, it won't be for lack of supplies."

"All I can say is," Jema held up a pair of edible panties, "y'all are Levi's new best friends."

"I gotta get me a pair of those." Molly squinted at

the package. "How many calories are in those things?"

"Oh, Lord help me." Lexi walked to the bar. "Okay everyone, prepare to be amazed. I have a new chocolate martini recipe. Perfect for MK's chocolate chip cookies." She mixed several things together, shook them with ice, then poured the contents into her fanciest glasses. Holding it up, she announced, "Chocolate Espresso Martinis."

We helped ourselves to martinis and cookies. As usual, Molly Kate's baking never disappointed. Crisp and buttery cookies held treasures of creamy semi-sweet chocolate chunks. The strong espresso and crème de cacao in the martinis made the perfect complement. Out of body experience? You betcha.

"Oh my." Jema grabbed Lexi's arm. "I want these waiting in my room honeymoon night."

"Consider it done." Lexi was clearly pleased.

Later in the evening, yawning replaced laughter. "Well, girls, we'd better call it a night." Jema bent over and started picking up paper off the floor.

"Don't you pick up another thing." Lexi grabbed the paper from Jema's hands. "I'll do this."

Jema started to protest, but then stopped. Instead, she looked deep into Lex's eyes, then Molly's, then mine. We all stared at each other, unmoving, as if we were stuck in some kind of emotional inertia. So much had happened in such a short amount of time. We wove our arms around each other and held on tight.

Jema sighed and murmured, "Lord, I love you girls."

After a long hug, we began gathering our things to leave. I stayed behind to help Lexi straighten up. Neither of us said what I'm sure we both were thinking.

Tonight a page had been turned in our lives and in our friendship. But while it would never be the same, I hoped—no—I knew it would grow into something better.

****

The next morning, memories of the previous evening ran pleasantly through my mind as I finished my third cup of coffee. While debating on if I should have a fourth, the phone rang. I hoped it wasn't Ty wanting to go to breakfast because I looked horrible. I checked the screen. Good. It was only Nate. I chuckled to myself at the thought of Skye's reaction if she ever heard me say 'it's only Nate.'

"Hi handsome."

"Hi gorgeous."

"Where are you?" I checked the clock. Nine-thirty.

"Just arrived in Memphis. I'm renting a car and should there in about three hours."

"Get a GPS this time."

"Don't worry. I learned my lesson. *And* I won't be stopping for grits in Tupelo either. So I hope Miss Cladie has something to eat."

"Oh, don't you worry about that." I swept the kitchen with a glance. Chicken stewed in the pot for chicken and dumplings. Purple hull peas simmered on the stove, a sausage and squash casserole baked in the oven and her English pea salad was *marrying* with the onions, mayo and spices in the fridge. A four-layer chocolate cake sat next to a caramel apple pie. All there was left to do was to make fried corn bread. "I think we will be able to scrounge something up."

"Great. Hey, my GPS is bugging me to talk to you. Just a sec."

"It's bugging you to do what?"

"Giiiirrrlll, I've missed you. How long has it been? Two weeks?"

"Ohmigosh! Scott?"

"Yep, me and Nathan seem to have a bro'mance thing going on. Every time he travels to Moonlight, he invites me."

In the background, I heard Nate say, "Sorry dude, but you're not my kind."

"Aww, Nate, give me a chance." Scott turned his attention back to me, finally. "Anyway, Avalee, you tell that sweet mother of yours we are going to talk serious about our book, *Southern Soiree.*"

Mom put her hand on my arm. "Is that Scott? Our Scott? What's he want?"

"He's with Nate and he wants to talk about that book he suggested y'all write."

"He was serious?"

Scott must have heard her. "You tell her, 'yes I was serious.' I've already run it by my publisher, and she loves the idea."

"That's fantastic." I held up my finger to Mom who stood there with questions dying to be asked.

"And if it is all right, I plan on coming back and staying a few weeks to work on it with her. Is Molly Kate's place open for business yet?"

"Not yet, but even if it was you'd be staying here anyway. And don't even bother to argue. Momma and I wouldn't have it any other way."

"You'll get no argument out of me. See you in a few."

Nate came back on the phone. "See ya, babe. Oh, and in case she hasn't said anything, I'm staying with

Lexi."

"I figured as much. But you better plan on eating here or you will starve to death."

"Got it. Thanks."

After we hung up, I took Momma by the hands. "Scott is dead serious about that book. He even has a publisher on board. So he said he's coming back to Moonlight and staying a few weeks so y'all can discuss it and lay it out."

"Merciful heavens. My recipes will be in a cookbook? Published in New York City? Will my name be on it, too?"

"Name, face, stories, the whole nine yards."

"Move over Julia Childs, Big Momma is coming to town." The oven timer went off, and Momma grabbed her oven mitts. "Since Scott is coming, do you think I should make a few more dishes?"

"Seriously, Mother?"

"Well, you know how I hate not having enough." She checked the pantry. "How about a pear salad?"

All I could do was shake my head. Even though we had enough to feed everyone on Washington Avenue, I said, "Sounds good, Momma."

Three hours later, the doorbell rang. The way I hurried to the door one would have thought I hadn't seen the boys in years instead of two weeks. I threw the door open and wrapped Scott in a bear hug then flung my arms around Nate. As they handed me their coats they sniffed the air appreciatively.

Scott rubbed his hands together. "Something smells good."

"That's the truth." Nate put his arm around my shoulder. "I'm starved."

"Where's my Miss Cladie?" Scott knew the way to the kitchen. I could tell he still had those ten pounds he'd gained his first visit here. Probably what convinced the publisher Momma's cooking was *that* good. Scott hadn't gained that much since I'd known him the past thirty years.

Nate, on the other hand, was as handsome as ever in his tight jeans and black sweater. Not bad for a guy who was sixty-something. Ty's daughter would freak.

Momma pushed through the swinging door and met Scott on his way to the kitchen. "Come here, Scotty boy, and give me a big ol' hug." When she wrapped Nate up in her arms, this time he hugged back. Some of the reserve was wearing down. "Good to see you boys back so soon."

Scott nudged Nate. "She called us boys. Another reason I like coming here."

"I hope you're hungry cause lunch is ready."

Both guys grinned and said, "Yes ma'am."

Well. If that don't beat all. Darned if my mother didn't make them Southern boys after all.

Chapter Ten

I walk the fine line of love and lust.

~Lexi Lowe

Lexi checked her mirror one last time. Nate would arrive at any second, and she had to look fabulous. But, she also had a job to do. She closed her compact and tried to concentrate on getting her column finished and sent to her editor, Vince, before Nate arrived. Her topic for this week was self-image. Did women accept themselves? Who or what defined them? She wrote about this because she, herself, was buried under negative self-image issues and, as any writer knows, they usually covertly write about themselves.

She was just about to hit *send* when Vince came sliding into her office, his chest heaving. "He's here again. He's actually here." Vince jackhammered his finger toward the floor. "Here. In this building."

"Who is here?"

He looked at the ceiling and spoke to her in a slow, deliberate, measure as if she didn't understand English. "Nathan Wolfe is here in this building."

"Already?"

"You knew he was coming, and you didn't tell me? I could have dressed nicer. I would have made reservations at the club for lunch…"

She held up her hand. "He is here for Jema and

Levi's wedding. Besides, he will be busy with me." She tilted the screen of her new Apple computer; a large purchase order approved by Vince at the suggestion of Nate, clicked on Photo Booth and checked her hair. In the background, she watched Vince pace behind her chair worrying his hands together. Sighing, she closed photo booth and twirled around in her chair. "You look fine. We will stop in your office before we leave."

"Maybe I have a fresh shirt in my closet. I'll go check." Without waiting for an answer, he hurried out. Thank goodness. She didn't want to delay the lip-lock she'd been planning since the moment Nathan had called to say he was coming.

It wasn't long until he showed at her door and leaned against the frame. He looked even sexier than she remembered. Every nerve in her body trembled. Without a word, she strode over, took his arm and pulled him into the room, kicking the door shut with her foot. The cologne he wore was from the gods. He pulled her tight against him and they instantly lost themselves in the other's kiss. She ran her hands along his back wanting to be closer even though an atom couldn't fit between them. He lifted her up and kissed her deeper and deeper until they both had a fine sheen of perspiration on their foreheads.

Lexi opened her eyes and gazed at Nathan. "Have mercy, I've missed you."

He cupped her face with his hands. "Not as much as I have you. I can't concentrate on anything but getting back here."

She stepped back and admired his tight jeans. Getting the right fit was something most sixty-two-year-old men had no clue about. The men at the office wore baggy jeans pulled up to the middle of their waists and cinched with a belt.

"Are you finished here?" A lock of salt and pepper hair fell across his forehead and he raked it back in place.

"Almost. I need to shoot Vince my column." She sat in her chair scanned it one more time before hitting send.

Nathan read over her shoulder. His warm breath on her neck made it hard to concentrate. "Baby, you have no reason for self-image issues." A shiver shimmied through her as she hit send. In one fluid movement, she rose and ran her fingers through the graying hair on his temples and pulled him down into another marathon kiss. Nate finally pulled away. "Ready to go to your place?"

"Yes, but we have to pay homage to Vince."

His intense blue eyes deepened. "And then?"

She grabbed his hand and pulled him out of the office. "Hurry, let's get this thing over with."

In mere seconds, she and Nate popped in and out of Vince's office and raced home to Washington Avenue.

Chapter Eleven

My New Year, my new life.

~Jema Presley Abrams

Jema stared out the window in the upstairs lounge at Molly Kate's B&B and marveled. Today was her wedding day—her *wedding day*. If someone at Molly Kate's wedding had told her that in three weeks she'd be getting married on New Year's Eve, Jema would have said that person had one too many flutes of champagne. But here she sat waiting with the girls for the beauty miracle workers David and Tryna to arrive. Soon a clamor of voices filled the stairwell, followed by heavy steps. Lexi strode into the room with a bowl of corn dip and chips. "They're here. Margarita time."

Tryna made it to the top of the stairs and leaned against the rail. "Whew, Lordy. What a climb." Her arms were loaded down with plastic grocery bags. "Here are the margarita things." She dropped them to the floor. "Where do you want them? Molly Kate told me to bring everything upstairs."

Avalee picked up a couple of the bags. "They have a kitchenette up here for guests to get drinks and snacks when they want them. Molly Kate and Momma are in there now getting the food ready. Follow me."

They passed David who had just walked in the room. "Man, it's cold out there. It has to be thirty degrees." He pulled off his coat and called after Tryna, "Now don't start drinking, Tryna. You've got work to do."

Tryna retorted, "Pfff. I'm a professional no matter how many margaritas I've had."

David leaned close to Jema. "We are in big trouble. Make sure she does you first."

Jema laughed. "Never fear. Miss Cladie brought ham biscuits and my very fave thing, corn dip. Between her and Molly Kate, we should be fine and fairly sober."

"Corn dip?" David pursed his lips up. "Yuck."

Lexi sashayed over with a dollop of corn dip on a Frito chip. "Don't knock it till you've tried it."

He stepped back, but opened his mouth to keep Lexi from shoving the chip up his nose. As he chewed, his grimace relaxed into pleasant surprise. "Wow, that is really good."

"Told ya. I thought you'd love it." Lexi consulted the wall clock. "It is seven o'clock." She raised her voice. "We can all have a margarita, that is except for David and Tryna 'cause they will be slaving over us."

From the kitchen, Tryna hollered. "Hey, I don't like the sound of that."

Lexi called out, "Sorry girl, but you'll be too busy to drink."

Avalee, Cladie Mae, Molly Kate, and Tryna walked into the room carrying food and drinks. Tryna lifted her chin at Lexi. "You'd be surprised at what I can do. I'm a multi-tasker." She set her tray on the snack table, turned to Lexi and pretended offense. "And if you want my secret recipe, you'd better play nice."

David lowered his head and looked at Tryna. "Play

nice? I have two words to say to you, *big bonus.*"

"Tilting her head in mock thought, Tryna said, "All right." She motioned at Lexi. "Follow me to the kitchen and I'll show you how to make them. The secret ingredient is beer."

While Lexi followed Tryna, she looked over her shoulder and mouthed, *"Beer?"*

"I think I'll go supervise," said David. "You never know about Tryna, or for that matter, Lexi either."

In no time, David sauntered back with something looking much like an adult beverage. Jema lifted an eyebrow. He put on his little boy grin, the one the girls at the salon swore helped him get away with murder. "It's okay. I'll sip."

Momma clapped her hands. "Okay kids, it's time to get down to business. Who's first?"

Tryna took Jema by the hand. "I'll start with the bride."

"Okay, I'll start with Miss Cladie." David flipped his hand toward Molly Kate, Avalee, and Lexi. "And y'all talk amongst yourselves."

"No problem." Lexi took a drink and began doing what she did best, telling tales, thoroughly entertaining everyone. Time flew by.

When Jema's manicure was finished, she went to David's chair and handed him a box. "Would you open this, I don't want to mess up my nails. It's a comb I picked out to wear in my hair after I purchased my gown."

David opened the box and stared at the diamond and pearl comb nestled in a pillow of black velvet. "Wow. That's amazing."

Everyone stopped what they were doing and

walked over to see what David was talking about.

He pulled it from the box and looked at the jewels. "Are they real?"

Tryna popped him on the arm. "David, that's just rude. You aren't supposed to ask something like that." She leaned closer for a better look then asked, "Well, are they?"

Lexi blurted out. "Well of course they are—" Avalee and Molly Kate shot her a look warning her to keep her mouth shut. "—n't.

"Sure looks real." David held the comb on the right side of Jema's head. "I was thinking about giving you a lot of soft curls and we can pull your hair up just above your ear, like this." He lifted her hair and slid the comb in.

"I like that." Jema sipped her margarita. "Tryna, these are really tasty."

Tryna took Molly Kate's hand and began filing her nails. "I know, right? And the more you drink, the better they taste."

"But," David tapped Jema's head with his comb, "you want to walk down the aisle, not stagger."

Avalee inspected the colors of polish Tryna had brought and said without looking up, "There isn't going to be an aisle."

Tryna looked over at Jema. "No aisle? What are you going to do then?"

"Everyone is going to stand around us, you know, sorta be a part of the ceremony."

David looked dubious. "But doesn't that kind of take away from Levi seeing you for the first time? From the hundreds of wedding parties I've done hair for, the groom not seeing the bride before the ceremony seems to be a big deal."

"It is. But we've figured something out. When I get dressed, I'll go to the library, where he proposed. Cladie Mae will position me to the best advantage, then go to Levi and bring him to me."

"And then his mouth will drop open." Molly Kate hugged herself. "I love it."

Tryna pointed at MK. "Careful, you'll mess up your polish."

The ensuing two hours David curled, teased, and sprayed while Tryna filed, buffed and polished. When everyone was magazine perfect, thanks to the combined talents of David and Tryna, the girls went in the bedroom to help Jema dress. Just as she slipped into her gown someone knocked at her door. She threw a worried look at Avalee.

"Step over there and I'll see who it is." Ava peeked through the crack and opened it all the way. "Surprise, Jema."

"Giiirrrlll, you look stunning."

Jema's face brightened and she clasped her hand to her chest. "Scott. I didn't know you were coming."

"You mean Lexi kept a secret? I didn't feel the earth roll or anything."

"Oh shut up." Lexi stuck out her tongue.

He took Jema's hand and twirled her around causing her dress to billow out. "I'm going to start calling your Ginger. That dress is gorgeous."

"Thank you. Levi is an excellent dancer, so I'm sure I'll feel like Ginger Rogers when we dance tonight."

Molly Kate moseyed over next to Scott and said in a sing-songy voice, "We have a surprise for you." She smiled up at Scott and then beamed at Jema. "Wait until you see the honeymoon suite. Scott has worked his magic again."

Scott pumped his eyebrows up and down. "You're going to love it."

"Oh, Scott. Thank you." Jema fanned her eyes. "Darned leaky eyes."

David waved. "Hey everybody, we gotta be going." He side-hugged Jema. "I'll be back tomorrow to fix hair again."

"Thanks, hon." She tucked a white envelope in his pocket and another in Tryna's purse, quietly giggling to herself at the thought of what their faces would look like when they saw their bonus.

Cladie Mae eased over to Jema and said, "Sugar, it's time to get you ready for Levi."

"Okay, but first…" Jema held her arms out and all the girls embraced her in an affectionate hug. "I love y'all so much."

Avalee pulled away, walked to the kitchen, and came out with Jema's bouquet. "We'll see you in the ballroom."

Jema held the roses to her face and breathed deep of the sweet fragrance. Downstairs the grandfather clock sounded the quarter hour. Like a scene from the pages of Cinderella, Jema's fairy godmother, Cladie Mae, took her hand. "It's time." Tears trickled out of the old woman's eyes. "Your destiny awaits."

****

The mansion's library was discreetly tucked behind the grand staircase. It was said this was old Mr. Norton's favorite room. It was comfortable and even more important it was private. Jema loved it, too, not just because Levi had proposed there, but also because of its coziness. The mahogany paneling gleamed in the glow of the dancing flames in the fireplace and the white lights twinkled in the Christmas tree. Two deep leather chairs and a love seat were arranged around a low table, perfect for propping up one's feet and relaxing while reading.

While Jema admired the ambiance and remembered back to the first time she stood in the room, Cladie fussed over where Jema should stand to create the best effect for when Levi took his first look at his bride. She moved the leather chair and had Jema stand in front of the Christmas tree and just close enough to the fireplace to cast a radiant light over her dress. Stepping back, Cladie put her finger to her lips and studied Jema.

"Yes, that's nice. Now stand still." She fussed over Jema's hem and made sure it flared out just right. "Now. I think this will do." Her eyes filled as she handed Jema her white rose bouquet. "You are so beautiful, my dear."

Jema felt the warmth of tears threaten. "Now don't you start, Cladie. I have hours to go before I mess up my makeup."

Cladie pulled her hanky from her sleeve, where she always kept one hidden. "Here." The white linen square was hemmed with delicate lace. In one corner were seed pearls and the initials JA were embroidered in silver thread. "I finished it last night." Cladie wiped her eyes with the back of her hand. "I've hoped for this day for the longest time. Since Ray passed, I've watched you struggle, but you've always been so brave. And you have always been there for others. Especially me."

"Oh, Cladie. This is beautiful. I love it." At the mention of her first husband who had died in a work accident many years ago, she lost her battle to keep her eyes dry. "Cladie, I think Ray would be happy about this? Don't you?"

"Tickled to death." She slapped her hand across her mouth. "Lord have mercy, what a thing to say."

Jema didn't know if it was her nerves or Cladie's owl-round eyes, but she erupted in laughter. Waving Cladie off, she said through a fit of giggles, "Go tell my prince I'm waiting for him."

Cladie dabbed Jema's eyes. "I love you, precious girl."

"I love you more."

"I don't think that is possible." She patted Jema's hand and quietly left.

Alone in the enchanted feel of the room, Jema closed her eyes and gave herself up to the mystical moment. While she meditated, she became aware of a whiff of pipe tobacco and peppermint. She opened her eyes and looked around the room. No one was there. Nothing had changed. That was odd.

The sound of footsteps coming toward the library caught her attention, and all thoughts of the strange occurrence were forgotten. She straightened, breathed in and let it out slowly, then smiled just as the door opened spilling light in the room.

Levi stepped in, locked his gaze on her, and whispered, "My god." He never took his gaze off her as he approached, seized by wonder. "You are exquisite."

Jema fixed her eyes on him. Never had he looked so handsome. His salt and pepper curls had been tamed into waves and brushed away from his face. His dark, gentle eyes, like windows into his soul, mesmerized her. He took her bouquet and laid it on a nearby table before taking her in his arms and kissing her with wedding night ardor. All thoughts of make-up and hair were lost in their fervor.

"Hey." She pulled back and traced his jaw with her fingertip. "We better stop now or we will miss the wedding."

He collapsed on the chair and pulled her onto his lap. "Remember that night last October when we almost gave in to our passion, and I told you that we'd have to be strong?"

"How well I remember."

He kissed her neck and whispered, "We won't have to be strong much longer."

****

Just as Levi and Jema had hoped, their guests entered the ballroom with brilliant, delighted smiles, exclaiming what a fabulous experience it was to ride in a limo while sipping champagne.

Levi held his hand out to Jema. "Care to dance?"

"Love to." She took his hand and he twirled her around the dance floor to the orchestra's big band music—"In the Mood," "String of Pearls," and "Stardust." Servers milled among the guests with trays of champagne, wine and canapés. Around the perimeter of the room, round tables were draped with black skirts, white toppers sprinkled with gold confetti. Silver candlesticks with white candles were placed in the center of some of the tables. Others had tall crystal vases with feathery green ferns and white roses, which were sugared with crystal glitter.

Attached to the ceiling all over the room were

twelve black nets full of gold, silver, black, and pearl white balloons. One by one, they would be opened with each stroke of midnight. The one over the spot where Jema and Levi were to stand would be the first one to drop. Jema could hardly wait.

Eleven-thirty finally rolled around and the orchestra's vocalist sang Etta James' "At Last". This was the signal for everyone to form a circle around the bride and groom. Avalee, Lexi, Molly Kate, and Cladie stood around Jema. These women, her kindred spirits, looked beautiful in their varying designs of gold charmeuse gowns. Each wore the diamond and pearl necklace with matching earrings, or earbobs as Cladie called them, that Jema and Levi had given them for presents.

After the vocalist sang the last verse, which fittingly declared they were in heaven because they were each other's at last, Pastor Dixon walked over and stood in front of them. "Jema. Levi. Please join hands."

Jema placed hers in Levi's and gazed at him while listening intently to the pastor. She wanted to remember this moment clearly. They spoke their vows, rings were exchanged, and charges given. Then, at the first stroke of midnight, Pastor Dixon enthusiastically pronounced Jema and Levi as husband and wife. As they kissed and the balloons fell. With each stroke of the clock one by one the other nets were opened all over the room. Jema caught a glimpse of Scott kissing Cladie Mae on the cheek. Then Felix kissed her other cheek. She got her kisses after all.

While everyone cheered and kissed in the New Year, the balloons fell around them, bounced on the floor, and floated up. The guests had a grand time kicking them in the air and batting them back and forth.

The band struck up "Let's Dance", and Levi led Jema back to the ballroom. People stood along the sides and cheered. Then, when the first stanza finished, everyone joined the couple. After the dance was over, the bandleader announced a toast. Fresh flutes of champagne were served and toasts were made to the bride and groom. Then came the cutting of the cake.

When the formalities were finished, Levi clasped Jema's hand and led her to the stage where the bandleader handed him the microphone. Levi first looked at his new bride and then at their guests. "Jema and I thank you for coming to witness and celebrate one of the most wonderful moments in our lives." He turned his gaze back to Jema. "Actually, it is *the* most wonderful moment in mine." Turning his attention back to the audience, he smiled. "The bar is open, there is plenty of food, so as they say, 'eat, drink, and be merry.' Your limos will be here to pick you when you are ready to go home. Again, thank you all for joining us."

Everyone clapped and yelled congratulations as the band started playing again. Across the room, Jema spied Nathan and Lexi moving toward them. *Oh please, Lord, don't let him spoil tonight.*

Lex wrapped her arm around Nathan's. "Hey, y'all, Nate has something he wants to say to you both."

"I do." Nathan spoke to Levi. "The last time we met, it wasn't on good terms. This is not an excuse; however, I was there on an assignment. I was working. Still, while at Miss Cladie's and in front of your friends, was not the time to investigate or interrogate or to give rise to suspicion. I want to apologize for the pain I caused you."

"Thank you, Nathan; we'll let bygones be bygones." Levi held out his hand, and Nathan shook it.

Nathan wasn't finished. "As a wedding gift, until you return to Moonlight, I will join you and do a worldwide story on Life Source and bring whatever attention you need or want to the homeless situation, emphasizing the need for support."

Jema couldn't believe what she was hearing. "Nathan, how wonderful. Thank you."

Clearly pleased, Levi shook Nathan's hand again. "That's fantastic. Thank you."

Nathan held up his hands. "Hey, it is the least I can do. After all, what can you buy for one of the richest men in the world? Nothing. But I can use what I have and make a difference."

"Oh, Nathan, you've made our night complete." Jema hugged him and then Lexi. "I love you sister-friend."

"Love you, too, Jems."

While watching Lexi and Nathan walk to the bar, Levi stood behind Jema with his arms around her waist. She smiled up at him. "Tonight has been wonderful, hasn't it?"

He leaned over and kissed her temple. "Yes, my love. It has." He turned her to face him. "Come with me, and I will show you an even more wonderful night than you can imagine."

Her heart pounded in anticipation. She squeezed his hand and they disappeared from the crowd.

****

At first light, Jema stretched and then snuggled closer to her husband. He had promised her something more wonderful than she could imagine, and he came through with his promise. Scott's romantic touches turned the room into one that defined romantic, if not a touch kinky. Candles of all sizes were scattered on the furniture, the floor, and shelves. The room glowed and danced. Soft music played and an assortment of her honeymoon gifts from the girls were strewn about the bed. But the most unexpected addition were the mirrors above the bed. She blushed at the memory of how much she enjoyed watching Levi and how badly she wanted a repeat performance. If it weren't for all the invitations sent and trouble gone to for the New Year's Day reception, she would have called everything off and honeymooned all day.

Molly Kate had a buffet cabinet in the room with a coffee pot, mugs, cream, and sugar. She had a cake stand full of various pastries covered. The small refrigerator had fruit and several kinds of juice. But Jema wasn't hungry, at least for food. She did the logistics in her head; reception was to begin at noon. David said he'd arrive at ten. That gave her four glorious hours to luxuriate in Levi's lovemaking. And that is exactly what they did.

Afterwards, she dozed on and off when the alarm chimed. It was time to get ready. Reluctantly she slipped out and showered. When she walked into the bedroom with a towel wrapped around her, Levi met her with a kiss and a cup of coffee.

"Mmm, I could get used to this." She held the coffee up to her lips and took a delicious sip.

"Get used to it, then." He tugged at the towel and it fell to her feet. "I wish we had time to give it another go."

She set her cup down and slipped her arms beneath his robe. "No more than I do. But David will be here soon." Jema sighed. "And then we have our reception. We wouldn't want to miss our New Year's meal. That would be bad luck." She pulled on her robe and picked up her cup.

Levi returned to the buffet for his coffee. "So tell me. What is this New Year's Day good luck meal?"

"Well," she sat on a chair by the window. "We eat pork, black-eyed peas, and some kind of greens. Cladie is cooking collards."

He brought a plate with pastries and set it on a table. "Why are those considered lucky?"

"Pork is lucky because pigs root forward, unlike cows that stand still and hens that scratch backward."

"So, moving forward in the new year. Okay, I get that." He bit into a cinnamon scone. "These are great."

Jema reached for one and buttered it. "Peas are considered lucky because they sustained the confederate soldiers through the winter after Sherman's raids. Apparently, the Yankee soldiers didn't appreciate good food, thinking black-eyed peas were for the cows. And the greens represent prosperity."

"I see."

A knock sounded on the door. It was Molly Kate. "Sorry to bother you in there, but David's here."

Levi finished his scone. "I'll shower while you get your hair fixed." He leaned over and kissed her. "Till tonight?"

A dreamy feeling tingled all over her. "Tonight."

Jema hurried to the door and opened it. "Morning, Molly Kate."

"Morning, glory. Hope I didn't *interrupt* anything."

Jema felt the heat of a blush. "You're bad, you know that?"

Molly laughed. "Really, I'm sorry to bother you, but it's time. David is setting up where he was last night."

"Tell him I'll be right there. It won't take me long to dress."

"Will do Mrs. Abrams." Molly Kate turned to leave but snapped her fingers and said, "Oh, Levi's assistant called to verify he had all your bags on the jet."

"Thanks, I'll tell Levi. He sent them on before the wedding. He said it was one last thing to think about and all I needed to bring with me after the reception were my toiletries."

"Yeah, I don't envy you flying all night. But at least you will be in a private jet. Should be more comfortable."

Jema grinned. "Girl, Levi's jet has a bedroom in it."

Molly Kate put her hand to her mouth. "You mean you will be a member of the *mile high club?*"

"Darned straight." Again, the temptation to skip the reception plagued her.

"Okay, I'm just going to say it. I'm officially iridescent-green with envy."

"Hey, don't be. I will make sure that all of you will get to be part of *the club*."

"Whoo-hoo!" Molly Kate hugged Jema. It's good to have rich friends." She stepped back in the hall. "Now you better hurry. David is probably finished and waiting."

"Okay, take him some coffee and tell him I'll be

there in a jiffy." Jema hurried to dress in the cashmere dress and leggings she purchased for the casual reception. She thought about the helicopter that waited on a pad not too far away to fly them to Memphis where they'd board his private jet and fly to Florence, Italy. *Italy.* This was just too much happiness for one person. As she walked down the hall, she promised herself she'd dedicate her life to helping others realize the dreams they never thought possible.

Kindness without expectations had produced for her the most unexpected treasure. And the treasure wasn't the money. It was Levi's love.

****

Jema held Levi's hand as they strolled to the ballroom to see if they could help with setting up the reception. Of course, in Molly Kate style, everything was ready. The white table toppers had been replaced with fresh ones and gold confetti re-strewn. The detonated party-poppers had been replaced with indoor sparklers. She had the crystal vases of flowers moved to the buffet table. Where the small wedding cake had been the night before now stood a towering wedding cake, and beside it was the Guinness imbibing moose groom's cake.

Levi stopped to admire it. "She summed me up pretty good, eh? Fantastic cake."

Jema nudged him. "She had help, you know."

He drew her close. "I figured as much."

The jazz band hired for the reception started their warm up playing "Route 66". Jema couldn't refrain from tapping her toes. Even Cladie and the girls started shuffling their feet while arranging gift bags of essentials for the homeless guests and toys for their children.

She placed her hand on Levi's arm. "Molly Kate is such an angel for so readily agreeing to invite the tent town people."

"Yes, she is." Levi watched with satisfaction. "So many people are frightened by them. I'll admit while I lived among them, there were a couple of bad characters. But isn't that true anywhere there are people?"

"Sad, but true. Even in our churches." She squeezed his hand. "Let's go help them."

Around eleven-thirty, the kitchen staff brought chafing dishes full of roasted pork loin, black-eyed peas, and Cladie's collard greens with bits of ham, to the buffet table. Baskets of corn muffins were placed in the middle of each table. A beverage station had been set up close to the buffet line with choices of various sodas, water, beverage servers filled with tea—sweet and unsweet—carafes of coffee, and drink boxes of juice or individual cartons of milk for the little ones.

Promptly at noon, the guests began to arrive. Levi was elated to see his friends from tent town. While she watched his former tribe crowd around him pumping his hand and slapping his back, she remembered the first time she laid eyes on him in the food line at Life Source. She was drawn to his warm regard for those who stood close, chatting, and laughing with them. He was friendly with everyone, but one small family captured his heart: a single father named AJ and his little daughter, Junie. Over supper one evening, AJ told Levi his story. He once lived with his wife and their daughter in Chicago. He thought they were happy, but his wife grew increasingly discontented and finally decided to leave her family and go to Los Angeles to find herself.

After their divorce, his wife's mother wanted custody of Junie and kept dragging him to court. Soon, all his savings were spent fighting for his child. Even though he won every case, he knew his ex-mother-in-law would never give up. The only answer was to leave Chicago without his ex-wife's family's knowledge. He settled accounts and took what money he had left, packed two suitcases and left with Junie late one night. He had distant family in New Orleans, so he planned to move there. But his small amount of savings ran out in Moonlight. He and Junie were told about Life Source and went there for food. While eating, he met a family who lived in a tent outside of town. In fact, several families and individuals lived there. They called it tent town. Later in the day, AJ purchased a tent and settled down. He worked odd jobs and tried to save enough money to get them to New Orleans, but jobs were few. What he was most grateful for, however, was the daycare at Life Source. At least he didn't have to worry about his little daughter on the days he did have an opportunity to work.

A sweet little voice roused Jema from her musings. "Weebi! Weebi!"

Jema knew that voice anywhere. Junie's large brown eyes rounded with delight as she ran toward Levi. She wore pink sweats and stained sneakers. Someone had taken the time to braid her hair in neat cornrows. AJ followed wearing jeans and a sweater. His clothes were ragged and faded, but they were clean thanks to Levi's gift of commercial washers and dryers to the shelter. Plus, there was no charge to use them or for the laundry supplies.

Levi swooped Junie up on his hip and she clung to his neck as she surveyed the room.

"Webi? You wib here now?"

"No Junie, but my friend does."

Her little pink mouth formed a tiny 'o'. "Ooooh. She's so wucky."

Levi bit his lip and waited to answer until he could gain control of his voice. "Not nearly as lucky as I am to have you and your daddy for my friends."

AJ grinned and shook his head. "I guess you could say we are all lucky."

"Speaking of luck, have you found a job yet?" Jema hoped with all her being he had. It would be so easy to give him money, but both she and Levi knew he wouldn't take what he considered charity.

AJ crammed his hands in his pockets and sighed. "No ma'am. But, as they say, tomorrow is always another day." He grinned at his daughter and tugged at her foot. "Ain't that right, Junebug?"

"Yes, sur, another day." Junie pointed at Cladie Mae. "Who's that wady by all them toys?"

"That, Junie, is one of the nicest ladies you will ever meet." Something stirred in Levi's expression. Jema knew him well enough to know a plan had begun formulating in his mind. "Would you like to meet her?"

The little girl bobbed her head enthusiastically.

Levi set her down and led her to where Cladie worked. "Miss Cladie, I have some folks here who I would like you to meet."

Cladie knelt before Junie. "Why, if you aren't as cute as a bug's ear. What's your name sugar?"

"Junie." She clasped her dark little hands behind

her and swayed back and forth.

"Well, I'm pleased to meet you sweetie."

Junie pointed at AJ. "That's my daddy."

Cladie pushed herself to a standing position and groaned. "I remember a time when standing wasn't such a chore." She smiled up at AJ. "Pleased to meet you, too, AJ."

"My pleasure, ma'am."

Levi placed his arm around Cladie's shoulders. "AJ is looking for work, Miss Cladie. Any ideas or suggestions?"

"I certainly do." Cladie looked at AJ and thumbed back at Levi. "A former employee of mine left with no notice at all and poor Felix is working himself to an early grave." She faced Levi. "Can you vouch for this young man? Is he a hard worker?"

"I can and I do."

"Well," Cladie put her hand on AJ's arm, "Levi's word is as good as gold with me. If you want work, you're hired."

AJ's jaw fell open. He looked from Cladie to Levi then back to Cladie. "Thank you, ma'am." He ran his hand over his head and blinked back tears. "*Thank you.*"

Levi lifted Junie in the air over his head. "Did you hear that, little lady? Your daddy has a job."

Jema couldn't help it. The joy at seeing such hope in a deserving family made her vision go all misty. Now they could get an apartment or maybe even rent a house. *A house?* Wait. She had a house that would be empty for well over a year. Maybe two. Cladie and Felix had promised to look out for it. But…. She tapped Levi on the shoulder and whispered something in his ear. He set Junie down and faced her. "Are you sure you want to do this?"

She nodded vigorously. "Yes, more than anything."

Levi faced AJ. "My amazing wife has just offered you a place to live, rent free, if you want it."

"I…I don't understand?"

"You can live in her house, for as long as you want."

Jema knelt down and smiled at Junie. "Would you like that?"

Junie turned pleading eyes on AJ. "Can we daddy? And can we get a puppy?"

AJ was too overcome to speak. He only nodded. When he found his voice, he looked from Levi to Jema, then Cladie. "Man, I can't believe this is happening. To me…" He reached for Junie. "To us. There are no words…thank you doesn't seem enough."

Cladie crossed her arms. "Let's see what you say when you've worked so hard you fall in bed with your clothes on."

"I like hard work, Miss Cladie. You'll see."

"Good. Maybe I'll get back on Felix's good side. He's been such a crank since Levi left. Now come over Monday morning for breakfast, say around seven, and we will talk particulars."

"Yes, ma'am. I'll do that."

"Felix is here somewhere. Let's go find him, and I'll introduce you."

AJ smiled at his daughter. "Junebug, it's just like I always told you, isn't it? Tomorrow is another day to hope. Well, baby girl, tomorrow has come. Daddy has a job, and we have a home."

"Can we have a puppy, pweese?"

"Well, I don't know if Mrs. Jema wants a puppy in her home."

"Of course you can have a puppy. Any kind you want. That will be Mr. Levi's and my present to you." Jema turned AJ. "Find a puppy, any breed, and we will buy it."

"Aw, that's not necessary. I think we will go to a pound and find a puppy there. After all, we've been given hope and a home. We can do the same for a little shelter dog."

Cladie patted AJ. "Good man. I like the way you think. Now, let's find Felix. Junie, while your daddy and Mr. Felix are talking, I have some toys to show you."

Jema watched as Cladie led AJ to meet Felix when she noticed Lexi snooping around the closed bar. She and Levi had made the decision the only alcohol served at the reception would be champagne for a toast. She held her finger up and said to Levi, "I'll be back in a moment."

"Take your time. I see the mayor over there, and I'm going to ask him to give the invocation."

"Good idea."

With kitten feet, Jema approached Lexi from behind. She tapped her shoulder and said, "What'cha doing there, Lex?"

Lexi whirled around with her hand to her throat. "Lord in heaven, you scared the cats out of me. But now that you ask, I'm looking for vodka. I have this nice glass of tomato juice and it needs something."

"Go in the kitchen. I think you'll find something there. And while you are at it. I could use some orange juice." Jema bobbed her eyebrows. "If you get my drift."

Lexi pointed her finger and clicked her tongue. "Gotcha."

In no time, she returned from the kitchen and handed Jema her drink.

"Thanks. By the way, where's Nathan?"

"He stayed at the house." She tilted her glass to her lips and drank. "Um, that is good. Hair of the dog, you know."

"Why didn't he come?"

"He said it was your day, and if he came someone," Lexi wiggled her fingers with her free hand, "even in this little town might recognize him."

"I know of one fan who will be sorely disappointed."

"Skye? No, she won't. She's coming with Ava and Ty to my place for drinks this evening."

"I hope he can handle her."

"Hey, no problem; he handles me." Lexi frowned. "What's Sid and Levi doing over there?"

"Sid is going to pray over the meal."

Levi had the mic and lifted his hand in the air. "Everybody hungry?"

The crowd answered with a resounding, "Yes."

"Good. Before we eat, Mayor Campbell has consented to give the invocation."

Sid peered at the gathering through his John Lennon glasses. He looked like an aging hippy with his snow-white curly hair tied in a ponytail. His smile was genuine and pleasant. Jema hoped to know him better one day.

He smiled and said, "Let's pray. God, we are so grateful for Levi and Jema. For everyone in this room.

For the abundant food we are about to enjoy and for the hands that prepared it. Thank you for the peace we have in this momentous day and may we be the purveyors of this peace when we leave this room. Amen."

In about two beats, Cladie said, "Amen and let's eat. Come on y'all. Don't be shy."

While the line formed at the buffet table, Jema watched with deep satisfaction. The rich mingled with the poor, all smiling and laughing together. The professional conversing with the homeless. A prayer rose in her heart that this *rooting forward* would be the cornerstone for everyone's year.

Ty drew her attention as he inconspicuously moved among the people with his camera taking candids. Avalee joined Jema and admired her fiancé'. "He's wonderful, isn't he?"

"Yes, hon. You did good." Jema smiled and said to Avalee, "And so did he."

"Molly Kate told me you were about to become a member of the Mile High Club."

"Yes, ma'am. Tonight will be a first for me."

"I'm jealous."

"Don't be. I'll make sure Levi's jet is part of your honeymoon package."

"Oh goodie, I was hoping you'd offer." Ava side-hugged Jema. "By the way, you'd better eat something if you plan on having the strength to rock the heavens."

"I'm not hungry, but I guess I'd better eat a little something what with it being good luck and all. Come on, let's fix us a plate."

When most were finished eating, Jema and Levi stood on the platform with the jazz band. All chatting quit and everyone watched as Levi approached the microphone. "Jema and I want to express our deepest heartfelt thanks for all of you, for coming to share with us the first day of the New Year and the first day of our lives as husband and wife."

Applause and cheers broke out. After the clamor subsided, Levi continued. "The waiters are serving champagne, or sparkling grape juice if you so prefer, for a toast to your health and happiness." When all were served, Levi lifted his glass and fixed his gaze on Jema making her feel weak with love and desire. "To my bride," he looked up, "and to all of you. May this year be the best year of your lives."

The guests raised their glasses and shouted, "Hear, hear!"

Lexi called out, "Okay, let's cut that cake, and make mine extra thick."

Jema laughed as she took Levi's hand and led him to the cake. Just as they had the night before, they cut a slice and fed a piece to each other. It was delicious, especially when Levi kissed her with buttercream frosting on his lips. One would have thought they were on the red carpet from the spontaneous applause and camera flashes. While all this was going on, the band struck up a rousing rendition of "Blue Skies".

Jema hummed along wishing she were in those blue skies. When four o'clock finally came around, she was anxious to say goodbye. Molly Kate had everyone grab a sparkler and put on their coats to form a line for Jema and Levi to walk through to the waiting limousine. When the line was formed and the sparklers lit, that is when it happened. *Snow.* It had snowed, not one time, but twice in Moonlight, Mississippi. The children squealed with delight. Large flakes swirled among the glittering sparkles. The perfect touch for enchanted memories.

As the limo pulled away, Jema rolled down her window to wave. Children ran across the lawn trying to catch flakes on their tongues. The adults waved then hurried back inside. All except Avalee, Cladie, Lexi, and Molly Kate. They watched with their arms intertwined. Jema waved once more then closed the window and laid her head against her husband's chest. It was time to hit those blue skies to Italy.

Chapter Twelve

Dreams ebb and flow with life.

~*Avalee Preston*

Snow. What a perfect way to end Jema's wedding celebrations. My throat tightened as I waved goodbye to my friend and watched the limo drive away. In the short time I'd gotten to know her, I knew I'd miss her terribly. By the time they were out of sight, the snow stopped. It was a dazzling kiss from heaven.

When the party wound down, and as the guests left, I stood by the door passing out the gift bags Jema and Levi had put together. Most of the bags contained a thank you note, a gift certificate for two at the country club restaurant, another for Preston Gardens secured to a pack of seeds, and one for A Taste of Heaven secured to a box of Molly Kate's delicious truffles. Those in the tent town received more practical items. Their bags also contained a thank you note and a box of truffles, however their certificates came from Walmart, Lowe's, and Home Depot. Jema also thought to include some from local movie theaters with a note that if there were not enough certificates for everyone in the family to let Ricci at Life Source know and more would be provided.

Junie and AJ were the last to leave. The little girl skipped past us and took her father's hand. "Daddy? When can we see our new house?"

"I don't know, honey."

Momma leaned over and shook the house keys. "How about now, little one?"

Junie jumped up and down while clapping her hands. "Can we, Daddy? Can we? Pweeze?"

AJ nodded. "If Miss Cladie says we can, I guess we can."

"We can." Cladie took Junie's hand and waved at the shuttle driver. "They are going with us." She handed the keys to AJ. "Felix has the truck all warmed up, so how about he take you to get your things first and then bring you to your new home?

"Sounds good. Thank you Miss Cladie."

"Fine. Oh, and I'll have supper on my table at six-thirty. I expect you and little Junie to be there along with Felix. We won't discuss business tonight. Let's just take some time getting to know each other."

AJ picked Junie up and nodded his head. "All right, then. And thank you, again."

Junie blew a kiss. "Mr. Webi told me you were nice. But you are nicer than nice. You're nice as…as…Santa Claus."

As I watched this New Year's miracle unfold, I had never been as proud of my momma as I was at that moment. Her name should appear in the dictionary as the definition of altruism. I thought about Mrs. Armstrong, the person who embodied the exact opposite of my mother. Having a black family move into the neighborhood was sure to give her heartburn. Thank the Lord times have changed, but change comes hard for some old timers. On the other hand, I felt sure Junie would win her over. How could all that preciousness not melt the most stubborn of hearts?

Molly Kate strolled over with her cat-child in her arms. "Let's call it a day. I'm slap tuckered out."

Momma looked around. "Sugar, we can't leave you with this mess."

"Yes, you most certainly can." Molly stroked Gypsy's black fur. "The caterers are cleaning their mess, and I have a crew coming in tomorrow. Go on now."

"All right then. But I need to find Ty first."

"He's in the kitchen with Stan."

"See ya, Gyps." I reached over and scratched under Gypsy's chin. She stared at me contentedly through green slitted eyes and murmured, "Merrowr."

"Okay ladies." Ty sauntered toward us. "Your chariot awaits, all warmed up and ready to go."

Kricket scampered toward us, all wags and wiggles. Stan followed her and slipped his arm around Molly Kate's waist. "Krickers wanted to say goodbye, too."

"Sure she does." I rubbed the puppy's head. "There is more to your wanting us to leave than your claim to being tired, I'll bet."

"Shoot." MK winked at Stan. "They figured us out."

"Happy honeymooning." I blew them a kiss and hurried to Ty's warm truck wishing it were already May.

****

Before Ty, Skye, and I went to Lexi's we dropped mom off at the house. While Skye and I waited for him to return from helping Momma inside with all her dishes, the girl nearly drove me crazy. She sat behind me jiggling her legs. The constant bounce made me

155

want to scream. She leaned forward and gripped my headrest. "I'm so nervous; I think I'm going to be sick."

"Oh pfff. He's just a guy." I turned to face her. "And don't let him hurt your feelings. He has a pretty dry wit. Lexi learned that the hard way."

Skye fell back fanning her face with her hands. "Oh god, oh god."

Ty opened the truck door and slid onto the seat. "What's up with you, baby girl?"

Her voice soared four octaves. "I can't believe this. I'm actually meeting Nathan Wolfe."

"Oh, brother." Ty rolled his eyes, put the truck in reverse, and backed out. "Don't make yourself a pest, okay?"

That comment set her on fire. She gripped my headrest again. "Avalee, don't let me be a screw up. Don't let me totally fangirl him. Give me a sign or something."

Ty said, "I know, how about if I stick my finger down my throat."

Skye hit the back of his seat. "Funny, dad."

"How about if I fan my face?" I thought that was a pretty good idea.

"Perfect."

Skye sat still a full second and then started fidgeting again. The two blocks to Lexi's house felt more like two miles. We should have walked no matter how cold it was so she could have worked off all her nervous energy.

When we made our way to the door, she held onto my hand as if she were hanging from a cliff. By the time we were inside, my fingers had gone totally numb. Nathan and Scott sat on the couch talking. He stood when we entered the room, and she squeezed even harder. Eager to be released from her vise-grip, I hurried to make introductions.

"Skye, this is Nathan."

"I...I, I mean, I'm *very* pleased to meet you Mr. Wolfe." Thank God in heaven she let go of my hand in order to shake his. I should have warned him to be careful.

Rubbing my fingers to get the circulation going again, I said, "And this is Scott Allen."

Her eyes never left Nathan. "Nice to meet you."

Scott lifted his eyebrows, then shook his head and grinned at me.

Lexi walked between Skye and Nathan. "Hello Skye. Sugar, the last time I saw you, you were in diapers. My, how you've grown."

Skye frowned. "I'm sorry, your name is?"

"I'm Lexi. I work with your dad." She cocked her head. "Are you old enough for a glass of wine dear?"

"I'm twenty-two." Fire ignited in her eyes. "And yes, I'd love some."

"Nate? Another salty dog?" Lexi was actually acting jealous. I glanced at Ty and could tell this little interaction hadn't missed his notice.

When Lex left to make the drinks, Skye gushed. "Mr. Wolfe, I have to say your investigative reporting on human trafficking in Bangladesh was brilliant. I mean, you are so balanced. When you report on political issues, I can't tell which way you lean, conservative or liberal. You are one of the most objective reporters I've ever studied."

I believe the man was actually flattered. He straightened and said, "Studied? Why, thank you, Skye.

By the way, call me Nate."

Up went the voice. "Really?" I fanned my face and she backed off. "Nate, it is then."

He sat and patted the cushion beside him. "By your comment about your studying me, I assume you are into journalism?"

"Yes. And I have so many things to ask you." From that point on, Skye and Nate were totally engrossed in conversation to the exclusion of everyone else in the room. Skye hardly acknowledged Lexi when she handed her the wine.

Ty strolled to the bar and grabbed a long neck. "Hey, Lex. I'll tell her to back off if you want."

"No." She flourished with her hand. "Let him enjoy his little fan."

Scott, obviously tired of the nonstop conversation between Nate and Skye stood and joined us. "His groupies get younger and younger."

Ty took a long drink of his beer. "Probably because he is getting older and older."

Lexi snorted. "Now Ty, that's funny right there." She fixed another bourbon and Coke Zero.

The evening passed without a let up between Skye and Nate who sat huddled on the couch. Lexi tried to pretend it didn't bother her, but she watched them and ate everything in sight.

"Hey." I tapped her shoulder. "We are leaving and taking Skye with us so you can have Nate back."

Lexi sighed. "I'm okay. Well, no, I'm not, but it isn't her. It's me. Watching them makes me realize I need to know more than I do. Shoot, I don't even know where Bangladesh is, and I have the vocabulary of a sixth grader. And even though I know he is a news god,

I certainly haven't *studied* him."

"Oh, poo. That's silly talk. You are an amazing woman."

She waved me off. "Pssh."

Ty helped me slip on my coat and called to Skye. "Come on kiddo time to let these folks get some rest."

Stricken wouldn't begin to describe her expression. In a brave effort to keep from appearing juvenile, she graciously held her hand out to Nathan. "It has been wonderful talking with you, *Nate.*"

He rose and shook her hand. "Here's my card. Anytime you need input, feel free to contact me."

With the adoring eyes of a green-eyed golden retriever, she breathlessly whispered, "Thank you so much."

Lexi strode to Nathan's side. "It's been real nice, sugar. Night, night, now."

Startled out of her worshipful trance, Skye glanced at Lexi. "Yes. Right. Thank you for inviting me tonight."

"Hey, Scott, need a ride home?" Ty tossed Skye her coat. "Pretty cold out there."

"Sure, thanks."

Skye turned to her dad. "What about Nathan? I'm sure he'd like a ride."

Lexi put her arm around Nathan's waist. "He is staying here, hon."

A crimson blush burned Skye's cheeks. "Oh, well, goodbye."

Nathan nodded and Lexi fluttered her fingers. "Bye y'all."

The ride home was quiet. *Lord, what have we started?*

****

In the darkness before dawn, Momma and I nursed our first cup of coffee when Nathan gently tapped on the kitchen door window.

"It's Nate." My brain hadn't absorbed enough caffeine jolts to clear out my slumber smog. Momma, on the other hand, had coffee poured and handed it to him before he could step inside. "Morning. You look like you could use this."

"Bless you dear, dear, woman." He took a long sip. "Scott ready?"

"Ready." Scott bustled through the door with his bag. "I smell coffee. Please tell me you have coffee."

"Here 'tis." Momma handed him a to-go cup and poured another for Nathan. "Y'all need to be alert for that long drive to Memphis."

Nate hugged her. "Thanks again. I'll take good care of Scotty boy for you."

"You do that." She hugged Scott. "And I'll get right to work on that list you gave me."

"Good. I'll be back for the wedding. We'll put it together then. Plan on me staying a few weeks."

"I look forward to it, hon." Momma handed him a sack. "Something for y'all to snack on."

Scott picked me up in a big hug. "Love you girl."

I held onto him. "I love you, too. See you in May." When Scott put me down, I turned to Nathan. "You, too, right? You're planning on coming to the wedding?"

"Wouldn't miss it. And I hope to talk with Skye again. It's refreshing to speak with someone who keeps current."

Scott looked at the ceiling then back at Nate.

"What you really mean is, it's refreshing to speak with someone who keeps current on you."

"Exactly. She's a smart girl." Nathan waved and walked outside. Scott followed him and called over his shoulder, "Bye *y'all*."

Momma laughed. "There's hope for you yet, Scotty-boy." When she closed the door she asked, "Now what's this about Ty's daughter and that Wolfe fellow?"

"Mutual admiration, that's about it." At least I hoped that was all it was.

****

My mental fog refused to lift. Coffee clearly wasn't helping me wake up. I supposed two last-minute whirlwind weddings in one month and the emotional baggage handed to me by one Emma Jackson had taken their toll.

"Momma, I think I'll go back to bed for a while."

"You do that sugar. I'm going to whip up a batch of cookies for Junie and AJ. Then I might rest my eyes, too. Seems lately my get up and go has petered out."

"I'll be at Ty's this evening, so don't worry about making me any supper. Just rest, okay."

"All right, hon."

While I trudged up the stairs, I thought about what Mom said. She really needed to see Doctor Derrick and ask him to do some blood work. Maybe she was low on iron, or had some kind of vitamin D deficiency. Or maybe she was just as tired as I was from all the holiday celebrations. I'd think about all that later. For now, I just needed to crawl under my comforter and crash.

Hours later, I woke with a clear mind and energy to

spare. I checked the time—two o'clock. I had an hour and a half to get ready before I left for Ty's. Tonight we would dream and plan *our* wedding. This called for a hot bubble bath and a cold glass of chardonnay. I ran my bath before going downstairs for wine. On the way, I checked to see if Mom was in her chair. She wasn't. She wasn't in the kitchen either. But the plate of cookies was gone which meant she was probably playing with Junie. I wished I could have given her a grandchild. That thought was just enough for guilt to raise its head, which I quickly quenched. "Oh no. Not now. Not tonight."

Upstairs, I slipped out of my clothes and into the exquisite mango-pear scented bubbles. While soaking, I sipped my wine and imagined what my wedding might look like. What would be blooming in May? What style dress should I wear being an older, first-time bride? Did I want an outdoor ceremony or have it in the mansion? Who would give me away?

My throat tightened. I missed Dad. How he would have loved to see me finally happy and married. I pictured us walking down the aisle smiling at each other, arm-in-arm. But he was gone. I stared at the faucet. A drip formed on the edge then fell into the bubbles while another formed. Gone? Perhaps from my sight, but he was still present, and I knew I would see him again. I stopped the drips with my toe and leaned back until the water grew tepid.

Reluctantly, I climbed out of the tub. After wrapping myself in a soft, oversized towel, I slathered myself with shea butter and hummed the tunes from Jema's reception, which made me wonder, what kind of music should I have? So much to discuss. Smiling, I hurried to get dressed.

Mom still wasn't home when I left the house. Could she still be at AJ's? I had to set my mind at ease so I jogged across the street and up the steps to the porch then tapped on the door. AJ answered. "Hello, Ms. Preston. Come in."

"Hi AJ. And please, call me Avalee." I noticed Momma on the rocking chair with Junie on her lap. Telling one of her stories no doubt. I turned to AJ. "I came over looking for Momma and I see my instincts were right on target."

He smiled in their direction. "She's a fine woman." Glancing around the house, he shook his head. "All of you are fine women. I still cannot believe all of…"—he gesticulated with his arms—"…of this."

"You are an answer to our prayers, AJ. Momma and Felix need help, and Jema needed someone to stay in her house while she is gone. And I hope when she returns, you will have decided to stay in Moonlight."

He palmed his eyes. "You folks are a blessing for sure."

"Well," I crossed my arms. "There is one little requirement to living here and it needs to be attended to as soon as possible."

His rich brown eyes held such gratitude. "Anything. Just tell me."

I pointed to Junie. "Get that girl a puppy."

Laughing, he nodded. "I'll do that. We will go to the pound tomorrow."

Waving at mom, I called. "I'll be at Ty's."

"Okay, sugar. Take your time. Felix, AJ, and my little *junebug* here are coming over for supper."

Not surprised. Not surprised at all. How I loved my

little momma.

****

Ty met me at the door before I could even knock and pulled me into his embrace. While he kissed me, he shut the door with his foot. That kiss led to another, and then another. Plans? What plans? All I wanted was him.

When at last we caught our breaths and cleared our minds, Ty poured two glasses of Shiraz. "Before we talk about our wedding, I want to show you something."

"Sure." The Shiraz's essences of spice and fruit warmed my tongue and throat. "What is it?"

He sat beside me with his laptop. "These are the pictures I took at the reception. I tried to contrast the two dichotomies." He pointed to the picture on his screen of a homeless woman standing against the ballroom's heavy brocade curtains as if trying to hide her clothes while staring longingly at Lexi's dress. "Here we have Lexi totally unaware of this woman. The woman from the tent town is very aware of her surroundings. But Lexi isn't. Mainly because she has a home, a pantry full of food and a closet full of clothes. This is her normal. She truly doesn't realize how good she has it."

"But," I felt I needed to defend my friend, "Lexi is very generous and—"

Ty held up his hand. "That's not what I'm wanting to point out. What I tried to portray is how we take things for granted because they are commonplace. We don't know what we have until it's gone. Like this woman. She hasn't always been homeless." He enlarged the picture. "Look at her eyes. It feels as if she is remembering a time when she could walk into her closet and choose from several dresses. Now, she has to either wear everything she owns to keep them from being stolen, or perhaps she only has that one dress."

Ty's photo and his words struck my very soul. I wanted to take everything in my closet and give it all to that woman. I felt sure his picture preached a better sermon than any that were given last Sunday in Moonlight's churches.

"We all take things for granted. For instance, did you bathe last night?"

Where was he going with this? "Yes, and today before I came. Why?"

"Did you stop to think you were bathing in warm, drinking-quality water?"

"No. I didn't." But I knew I would from now on.

"One billion people in this world do not have clean water to drink, much less bathe in." He put his arm around me. "This is why I'm so passionate about photography. I can make a visual connection for people and motivate them. I believe I can make a positive difference. I just feel it deep inside me."

I touched his lips with my finger and gazed at his beautiful face. "I know you can. I have no doubts. I love your heart, Tyler Jackson. I believe in you, my love." And I did, so deeply. So passionately.

He continued to scroll through the other photos. I set my wine down and leaned forward squinting at the other images. He caught AJ being told he had a house, his dumfounded expression, the tiny tear coursing its way down the side of his face. Junie's unmitigated joy when she was told she could have a puppy. Photo after photo told stories of hopelessness and dashed dreams to hope of new beginnings and brighter futures.

I wiped my cheeks. "These are so incredible and so heartbreaking.

"I know." He closed the lid of his computer.

An idea formed in my mind. "Would you send these to me? I want to show them to Mom."

"Sure." Ty refilled our glasses. "Now, let's talk wedding."

Two hours later, we had everything planned. The ceremony would be held by the lake at twilight. I made a mental note to break this news to Molly Kate. Pastor Dixon would officiate. There would be hundreds of candles. For our flowers, I decided on all varieties of tulips, one of my favorite flowers. I had chosen them for Marc's and my wedding, too. I have to admit I struggled against being a bit superstitious about them but told myself I was being silly. We would hold the reception either at the Country Club, or maybe at Molly Kate's. Of course, we knew who my bridesmaids would be, but for groomsmen he chose Stan, Levi, and his best man would be Glen, of course. We still didn't know who to ask to escort Lexi. I just didn't know about Nate. I decided I wanted Felix to give me away. I had known him all my life. He'd worked side-by-side with my dad, making him the natural choice.

The only sticking-point were his parents. Should we invite them? I suggested we should and give them the choice of accepting or declining.

Ty shook his head. "No. I don't want to invite them. Even if they don't say a word, I don't want to see their sour faces." So, at this impasse we decided to take a wait and see approach.

As I prepared to leave, I had a wild hair idea. "Ty? Do you think Skye would want to be a bridesmaid?"

"I think she would love it."

"Okay, I'll ask her." Asking her just seemed right. Right now, everything seemed right.

Chapter Thirteen

Dreams do not always just happen, sometimes you have to give them a nudge.

~*Avalee Preston*

January eased into a cold slumber. Perfect for sitting by the fire with coffee and a pile of gardening catalogs. It was time to put my plan for saving Preston Gardens from going under into action. After all, this was my original reason for leaving my home in New York and returning to Moonlight in the first place. I never expected to fall in love with Ty. What a wonderful surprise.

I had come up with the idea of creating a combined flower and farmer's market open every Saturday. The first Saturday of the month would be a festival with activities for children, all sorts of demonstrations such as floral arranging, landscaping, and cooking unique veggies, even edible flowers. We would also have plants, bushes, and trees of such unusual varieties that no other farm store, big box stores, hardware stores, or greenhouses in the south would be able to match us.

Mom and I decided to call our event *Moonlight Market—Treasures from the Earth.* We felt this would give us more flexibility and give us the option to include the arts. I had my business plan ready for when we met with Mayor Campbell and the city planners about our idea and get that pesky zoning law out of the way. The town square was too small to hold this event and we had plenty of space on our property. Besides, as host, Preston Gardens would benefit from all the business generated. I had a killer pitch ready and knowing the mayor's passion for putting Moonlight on the map as a prime tourist spot, I had no worries. Easy peasy.

I lifted my mug to my lips. Empty. Also the flames in the hearth had succumbed to glowing coals. Time for a refill of both wood and gingerbread latte. After I had the fire roaring again and a steaming cup in my hands, I turned on my laptop and noticed a file from Ty. The pictures I asked him to send. It was time to put my idea into action and email Scott. Settling on the couch, I began my note:

Hi Handsome!

How is everything in NYC? Cold? As Momma would say, it is so cold here dogs are sticking to the hydrants. Before you can ask, the answer is yes. I'm getting my southern on quite well, thank you.

The reason I'm writing is to ask a favor. Attached are a few pictures Ty took at Jema's reception. Remember how I told you Ty tells stories with his photos? I've sent some superb examples. As you know, because of the friendships Levi made while living in the homeless community, he asked many of them to the reception. He was especially close to two from that community, AJ Mayfield and his little daughter, Junie. You may remember Jema offered them her home, rent free, for as long as she lives in Italy, which will be well over a year, and that Mom gave AJ a job. The pictures I'm sending were taken when AJ found out he was getting a home and a job. Also one of Junie when she was promised a puppy. Others are of contrasts, but I won't say any more about the story Ty tried to tell. I want to see if you can guess what he was trying to portray.

So, here's the deal. If you agree with me that Ty has exceptional talent, would you show these to the right people? It would be beyond awesome if he received national recognition for his work if for no other reason than to prove to his parents that he has amazing talent and could be successful in his own right. I'd love to see him moved from under Marc's shadow. Since I know you will agree with me—I know you that well—thank you in advance. :)

I owe you…again.

"Hi baby."

I looked up as Momma shuffled through the family room door. Something about her didn't look right. "Hey. You feel okay?"

She flipped her hand. "I'm fine. Just tired. Your momma's getting old. I just can't seem to get my ducks in a row since Christmas."

A wave of worry crossed my mind. This didn't look tired. It looked like something much worse. It had been coming on so gradually, but now, whatever was wrong with her, had come to fruition with a vengeance.

"Here." I jumped up and dragged a chair close to the fire. "Sit down and rest a bit. Can I get you anything?"

"I'd love a big glass of ice water. I just can't seem to quench my thirst these days." She sank down in the chair. "And of course that means I have to go to the bathroom. Lordy, half my day and most my night is

170

spent sitting on the pot."

"I'll be right back." Thirsty and tired. I'd read about these symptoms but couldn't remember what caused them. Whatever it was, I sensed the urgency of it.

When I returned, I gave Mom her water. "Momma, why don't you make an appointment with Doctor Derrick?"

She waved me off. "Oh pshaw. He can't do nothing about old age."

I watched while she gulped down the water. "But what if it isn't old age?"

"Mercy, child. You worry too much." She pointed to my Mac. "Now get on with what you were doing. I think I'll just rest my eyes a bit."

"Yes ma'am."

By the time I finished my email, Momma was sound asleep. Her head sagged to her shoulder. She'd surely get a crick in her neck if she stayed in that position. I tucked a small pillow between her neck and ear, then propped her feet on a stool and covered her with a throw. She didn't flinch. Her purring snores were even and deep. I watched her a while. Whether she liked it or not she would soon have an appointment with Doctor Derrick if I had any say in it.

****

The next morning, much to my relief, Momma seemed pert as always. She was dressed and ready for the town council meeting. "Morning, sugar. Coffee?"

"Please."

She brought my cup to me. "You look mighty pretty. All spiffied up in that suit."

Before I answered her, I fortified myself with a

deep sip. "I think our proposal for the flower market is in the bag, but it never hurts to look professional."

Momma carried a plate of sliced cinnamon loaf to the table and sat in a chair. "This is the last of the Christmas goodies. Best they not go to waste."

I reached for a piece and pointed to my stomach. "Oh, they will go to waist all right."

"Oh, poo. You look better than you have in months." She nibbled at the corner of her slice. "You were so skinny when you came home, you had to stand up twice to make a shadow."

I sighed. Those days were long gone. I'd turned into Jema, a surrender eater. When the cuckoo bird chirped the time, I finished my coffee and stood. "Well, Momma. Time to slay the dragon."

She rose and carried our cups to the sink. "I need to get my pocketbook and go to the bathroom before we leave. Would you grab me a couple bottles of water out of the fridge? Grab yourself one, too."

Drinking water is good. Right? But Momma suddenly drinking water gave me weird vibes.

We reached Sid's office in plenty of time. His secretary asked us to have a seat before she picked up the phone to let him know we'd arrived.

"I'm nervous as a turkey at Thanksgiving." Momma daubed at her neck with a hanky.

"Don't worry. Sid's a nice guy. Besides, our plan is right in line with his vision for the town."

Sid strolled into the reception room. "Good morning, Avalee, Miss Cladie."

"Morning Mayor." I stuck out my hand. "Are you ready for this?"

"Yes. We shouldn't have a problem. Well, maybe a

little pushback by Jim Fleming. But he just likes to flex his small man authority when he can."

Momma piped up. "How are the boys, Sid?"

A pleased expression crossed his face. "Great. I'm going to be a grandpa."

"Oh, Sid. How wonderful." Momma didn't waste any time adding. "I'm going to be a grandma, too."

He cocked his eyebrow and looked at me. "Oh?"

"Well," I stammered. "Actually, she means Ty's kids."

He lifted his chin in understanding. "Skye and Glen. Fine kids." He pushed his shoulder toward the door to the boardroom. "Why don't we go on in? Everyone should be here shortly. I wish I had coffee to offer you but—"

"Did someone say coffee?" Lexi strode into the room with a drink carrier holding four cups. "I thought y'all would need some fortification."

Sid grinned. "Which is the fortification? You or the coffee?"

"Both." She handed him a cup. "That old coot, Fleming, is such a stickler. I swear he lives with a reindeer up his butt."

"Oh, Lord." Momma wiped her forehead again.

I patted her hand. "It's all right, Momma."

Sid agreed. "He won't give us any trouble Lexi can't handle, Miss Cladie."

"Shoot. I'm not worried about him." Lexi handed me a coffee. "If leather were brains, he wouldn't have enough to saddle a June bug."

Momma smiled. Then frowned. "Sid Campbell? What have you done to yourself? I can't make it out. You still have that long straggly hair, but something is different."

"Momma! Really?" I felt a blush heating my face.

Lexi scrutinized him. "You aren't wearing your glasses."

"Nope. I got lazered."

"Well, good." Lexi bumped him with her hip. "Now we can see those baby blues even better." She turned and winked at me.

What was going on? That girl was out and out flirting. And Sid didn't mind a bit.

Shortly after we were seated in the conference room, eight members of the city council meandered in. Jim Fleming, aka, the troublemaker, brought up the rear. How appropriate.

When they were all seated, Sid stood. "Good morning everybody. I called this informal meeting to discuss and hopefully come to an agreement on Miss Preston's proposal, which I believe will be a considerable draw to our town. I am now turning the floor over to Avalee Preston of Preston Gardens to present her proposition. Please hear her out, and afterwards we will open the floor to questions and discussion." Sid turned to me. "Miss Preston?"

I cleared my throat and stood. "As you all know, my mother is the owner of Preston Gardens. This company has been in the Washington Avenue location for three generations. A few months ago, all of you were gracious in allowing her business to be grandfathered in as a rural district. Well, today I am coming to you again for a very special favor. However, this time I believe it will be good for our town as well."

A glance around the room confirmed I had their attention and maybe even interest. This gave my confidence a little spark.

"We would like to begin a farmer's market of sorts and call it the Moonlight Market, Treasures from the Earth. We propose holding it every Saturday morning beginning in late spring and ending late fall."

Jim Fleming, a man of considerable bulk, folded his arms on the table and leaned forward. His tortoise shell aviator glasses slid down his bulbous nose. He peered over the rims and asked, "With all due respect, Miss Preston, exactly how will a farmer's market draw tourists? There's nothing special about farmer's markets. Even if we had one, why would tourist come? What need do they have of fruits and vegetables on vacation? Seems to me you and your mother will be the greatest benefactors here."

Lexi sighed, rolled her eyes, leaned over to Momma and murmured, "If his brains were dynamite, he couldn't blow his nose."

"That's a fair question Mr. Fleming." I shot a look at Lex. "But this won't be just a farmer's market. The first Saturday of the month will be a festival and our focus will be on local art that is taken from or inspired by the earth. This could include pottery, jewelry, paintings, and such. We will also hold demonstrations on floral arranging, cooking, and crafts, landscaping tips, and fun things for children. There will be food tents, too. The other three Saturdays we will feature unique plants, trees, and shrubs that cannot be found in the big box stores or local greenhouses. These offerings will draw people from miles around. And if it is the success I think it will be, word will get out to surrounding states. It will be a destination event. We will also invite local gardeners to sell their vegetables and flowers. I also hope local restaurants will join us and give demonstrations and food samples."

Jim sat back in his seat and rubbed his chin. I hoped, no, I prayed to God above, the man was pacified. I turned my attention back to the group. "I would also like to set up an information booth about Moonlight for visitors with pamphlets to take home with them." Actually, that idea had just popped in my head. It might be the nudge I needed to tip the scales in our favor.

Ruby Greer, the quintessential of a southern genteel matron, raised her hand. "Honey, what about parking and such? I am sure tha neighbors won't be too tickled to have cars blocking their drives."

"I'm sure they would not like it, Mrs. Greer. I wouldn't either. We have five acres of land behind our house between Moonvine Road and Whispering Pines. The market will be set up there and we will rope off an area for parking along the Whispering Pines side, which is adjacent to the National Forrest, so there will be no private residences inconvenienced. Inside the folders in front of you, you will find a rendering of the parking plans, plus documentations of inspections, zoning, insurance, and permissions."

Fleming flipped through the folder, closed it, and leaned back in his chair. "I'm not buying it. I just don't see this little *plant circus* amounting to anything. In my opinion, this is a bunch of falderal."

I felt heat burn my cheeks, but before I could open my mouth, Lexi slammed her palm on the table.

"That's it." She stood and pointed at him. "Where have you been, Jim Fleming? Under a rock?" She put her hand to her cheek. "Oh wait, you probably *have* been under a rock." Slinging her finger toward me she said, "Avalee Preston is known *worldwide*. Do you know what that means Fleming? She has contacts, all—over—the—world." To emphasize her point, Lexi drew a circle in the air. "All she has to do is put the word out to her colleagues, and Moonlight will be put on the map like," she snapped her fingers, "that."

"Thank you, Lexi." I smiled at Fleming. "I hope this helps alleviate your concerns. I also forgot to mention the information before you contains revenue projections the city might expect."

Sid stood. "Personally, I think this is an excellent plan." He faced me. "Thank you, Miss Preston." Facing the council he said, "I'm requesting the council members to remain after the Prestons," he tried to hide his smile, "and Miss Lowe leave. I would like us to discuss their proposal and take a vote on it. Miss Preston, I will call you after the vote."

"Thank you, I will look forward to your call." I picked up my things and walked to the door with Momma and Lexi following me.

As Lexi passed by Fleming, she drilled a glare at him. "I think I might just write about this meeting and its outcome for the community news." When she got to the door she called back over her shoulder, "Don't forget," She drew a circle in the air. "*Worldwide*, y'all."

****

On our way home from the town council meeting, Momma pointed and said, "Avalee, honey, stop over at Pigg's. I'm out of bottled water. I like to have some with me when I leave the house."

Something wasn't right. I could feel it. Taking water with her was a new thing. But instead of questioning her, I pulled onto the parking lot. "Want to come in?"

"No, I'll wait."

"Want anything else?"

"No, baby." She fished out a twenty-dollar-bill from her pocketbook. "And get that thirty-six pack."

"Okay. Be right back." Thirty-six? It would take her six months to drink that much. But, oh well.

When we got home, I lugged the water to the pantry while Momma made coffee. After that meeting, bourbon would have been my choice. However, when the rich aroma filled the kitchen and drifted through the house, I decided coffee would be perfect on such a cold day. Nothing says *home sweet home* like brewing coffee.

After I filled my mug, I grabbed my laptop to check emails and sat in front of the fire. Scrolling down, I saw an answer from Scott. Anticipation radiated through me. Did he like Ty's photos? I clicked on his email and eagerly read.

Hi there, sweetie,

You're killing me hon. Me and some buddies were at the Blind Tiger for a cocktail meeting. Remember those? Drinks and decisions? Anyway, we were on our second round when your pictures came through my email. I checked my phone and I couldn't quit staring at the images. It must have obvious I had dropped out of the conversation because Taige elbowed me and said, "Hey man. Answer the question."

I looked up and realized I'd totally ignored everyone. I didn't have a clue what anyone was talking about. I apologized then said, "You guys have to see these. I passed my phone around and asked them what they thought. I wanted their objective opinion. I could be a little biased and I sorta knew the story behind the shots.

When they had all seen the photos they asked me who the people were, and I just threw questions out for discussion. "Who do you think they are, and what do you think the photographer was trying to get across?"

Of course, my question started an animated discussion which lasted through a third round. All in all, the guys pretty much had it right. So, I think Ty accomplished what he'd hoped. The consensus was that the photographer's goal was to contrast two groups: those who were obviously poor and those who were not. They also pointed out how those who had plenty did not notice what they had and took the opulence around them for granted. While the poor appeared to notice, admire, and desire everything around them. Especially that haunted look in the woman standing by the curtains eyeing Lexi's dress. They also loved the unabashed joy of Junie and her father and speculated their happiness was from some sort of relief.

I'm telling you, Ava, Ty has a gift. When I told the guys what you'd said in your email, Taige asked me to send the pictures to him. He has friends at the New Yorker, so who knows? This could be Ty's moment. I hope so.

Tell Momma Cladie I'm working on an outline for the book. I'll get it to her ASAP so she can start dreaming up recipes.

I'll let you know when (not if) something develops for Ty. Love you to the moon and back,

Scott

Momma Cladie? I grinned. Oh well, I've always

wanted a brother. Mom would appreciate Scott's email, so I picked up my MacBook and toted it to the kitchen. No momma. Then I went to her sitting room and found her fast asleep in the recliner. A thirty ounce tumbler sat empty on the end table beside her. That was odd. My mother rarely took naps. But lately she took one almost every day. And what was with the water? I resolved to make an appointment as soon as possible and she would go, even if I had to get Felix to carry her.

An hour had passed since our meeting with the town council when my phone rang. Sid's name showed on the screen.

"Hello? Sid? How did it go?"

"You're in business."

"Oh, that's great news! Did Fleming give you any push back?"

"He wanted to, but I think Lexi's mention of writing an article for the paper gave him reason for pause. Wouldn't look good for his future political hopes."

"I will work hard to make this a success. I promise. I'll have to. Lexi set the bar high with her *worldwide* mantra."

"That girl is something else, for dang sure." Sid chuckled. "Congratulations and if I can be of any help, let me know."

"Thanks Sid. Bye now." As soon as I tapped disconnect, I gave a little squeal.

Momma called from her chair. "What's wrong? Are you okay?"

I strode to her room and suck my head in the door. "The mayor. We are in business."

She clapped her hands together. "Well, glory be.

That is good news."

"Time to start calling in favors." I hurried to the family room and foraged through my computer bag for the list I'd started.

Momma ambled toward me rubbing sleep from her eyes. "Seems you call in a lot of favors. You must have really been something in New York."

"Let's just say, I paid my dues. Now it is my turn." I ran my finger down the list. "We need to get word out about the market fast. Details can come in a few weeks."

While I punched numbers on my phone, Momma asked, "It's about lunch time. Are you hungry? I have some shepherd's pie left over."

"Sounds good."

"All right, then. I'll call you when it's hot."

The first call I made was to Lex. It didn't even get a full ring out before she picked up. "Hey, what's the word?"

"They voted yes, largely thanks to your thinly veiled threat of blackmail."

"Hey, works every time. Sometimes it actually pays to be a writer. Now what?"

"Advertising, talking to vendors and calling in orders for everything we need. The most immediate thing is to start taking bids on a parking lot."

"Wow."

"There is a lot to do. I've been planning this for months. Now that we have the green light, it's time to start pushing buttons."

"I'll help, too. Can I call Molly Kate with the good news?"

"Yep, and tell her to get ready. The guests are

going to start pouring in."

"Will do. Love you, sweetie."

"Love ya back."

"Avalee?" Momma called from the kitchen. "Dinner's ready, hon."

My stomach grumbled its gratitude. The savory blast of hearty beef drew me like the Pied Piper's song. Momma had mounded the tender beef and vegetable pie on my plate. The mashed potato and cheese topping swam in rich brown gravy. She warmed up potato rolls and set spun honey on the table. Way too much food, as usual. But, of course, I would eat every bite. Yep. Momma cast her spell on me like she did everyone else who put their feet under her table.

She sat across from me. "Is Ty coming over tonight?"

"No, we're going to Oxford to visit his kids later this afternoon and take them out to eat." The savory gravy and creamy potatoes were like a lullaby in my mouth. I closed my eyes and gave in to the moment.

"That's nice, hon."

"Want to come? I'm sure they would love to see their *Big Momma.* Especially Glen."

"No, baby. I think I'll go through my recipe box and pull out my favorites for when Scott sends me that list. Besides, I just can't seem to hit on all cylinders lately. All I want to do is lay around." While Mom talked she broke open a roll and slathered it with butter and spun honey. "All this nonsense better stop before we open the market."

My golden opportunity dropped out of the clear blue right onto my lap. "Why not visit Doctor Derrick then? Just for a checkup."

"No need. I'm fine as frog's hair, just done in by the holidays." She pointed my direction with her roll. "Your momma is getting old, that's all. So stop your worrying."

I wanted to remind her that in the few months I'd been home, her energy level had drastically dropped. But it wouldn't do any good.

After dinner, I helped her clean up then went to work making calls. After a couple hours had passed, I'd gotten a lot done and it felt good. I hadn't lost my business mojo. The fire in the hearth had died down, and I needed to stretch. I stood, grabbed my coat and hat to fetch some wood off the stack outside. It was then I noticed Mom. She came out of the kitchen with a sandwich, slice of pie, and a glass of iced tea.

"Momma? We just ate a little while ago."

"I know, but I'm hungry again. Now get on with your rat-killing, and I'll get on with mine." She moseyed on to her sitting room and shut the door.

She had turned into a regular curmudgeon on me.

****

While waiting for Ty to swing by and pick me up on the way to Oxford, I checked my email again hoping to hear more from Scott. No word from him, but one from Jema. Yay!

Hey girl, or should I say ciao girl?

So far I know ten words in Italian. It is a good thing Levi speaks the language, or we'd be in trouble. My southern accent keeps standing in the way of me ever pronouncing anything correctly here. Fortunately, most everyone I've come across in Italy speaks English. I keep thinking of that joke, What do you call someone who only speaks one language? North American. I sure wish I had paid more attention in my foreign language classes in high school or realized the importance of learning at least a second language while I still could. I know I can now, but it is harder for this old dog.

Italy is as wonderful as I thought it would be. It is a wonderland of history, architecture, art, delicious food, opulent gardens, and landscapes. Every place we have visited has amazing statues and buildings. My mind is numb from all the beauty. I love every city and village we have visited, especially Rome. I guess the villa we decide to purchase will determine which town where we will live. The Italian people are delightful and animated. They also drive like maniacs in the narrow streets, especially those on scooters, but never seem to have accidents. Oh, I could live here so easily if it were not for my friends in Moonlight. I miss you all so much. As soon as we find a place, I want you all to come. We hope to have a villa secured before your wedding so you can come here for your honeymoon. That is, if you want to come here. How about your first night on our jet? Okay, I know that is a bribe, and I'm the first to admit it!

How is Cladie Mae? I miss her so much. She has to come with you. Not on your honeymoon, of course, but when all you girls come. We will eat, drink, and dance our way across the country. Talk to Ty, ok? And if he is hesitant, just mention the 'mile high club' membership!

I love you. Write soon!

Jema

A smile relaxed on my face. I missed that dear girl. Wouldn't it be a kick to have a Martini Monday in Italy? Ty and I hadn't discussed honeymoon plans, well, at least where to have it. I liked Jema's suggestion, and I knew Ty didn't care where the room was just as long as there was a bed.

Someone knocked on the door. I closed my laptop and walked over to answer it. The second I saw Ty's face I knew something was wrong. I held my arms out and he walked into them burying his face in my hair.

"Baby, what's wrong?"

He didn't say anything. He just held me. Finally he murmured, "Same old thing. Same old ghost."

I pulled back and held his gaze. It was still so unbelievable to me that this man loved me. I put my arms around his neck and drew his lips to mine. I wanted to kiss away the sadness shadowing his gentle brown eyes.

He nuzzled my ear. "Mmm, Miss soon-to-be Mrs. That certainly helps." He pulled me in for another kiss, which I gladly obliged. One kiss promised another. In this case, time was our chaperone.

"Baby, we gotta get going."

"One more." His body felt hot against mine.

"Hon, it is after three." He slipped his hand down to the small of my back and pressed me closer to him. My only resistance was in my words. "Baby, we have to go."

He grinned down at me. "Must you always be so punctual?"

"It's a curse." I drew in a deep breath to calm all the sensations exploding in my body. "Want something to drink on the way? Tea?"

"Yeah, extra ice." He followed me to the kitchen. "Where's Miss Cladie?"

"In her sitting room." I grabbed two plastic cups with lids from the cabinet.

"Think she'd mind if I stuck my head in to say hi?"

"No, go ahead. I'll be a minute or two here."

Moments later he strolled into the kitchen. "She was napping, but she woke up when I walked in." He took the tea and added, "She was pretty out of it. Maybe she's just groggy from her nap."

"I'd better check on her before we leave." When I peeked in, she was asleep again. Momma never slept this much. Maybe she needed Vitamin B shots? I decided to ask the pharmacist at the Piggly Wiggly sooner than later. Once Ty and I were on the road I asked, "So, what was wrong with you when you came to the house?"

"My parents." He paused. "Actually, my mother."

"I kinda figured. What was her deal this time?"

"I stopped by their house to see if they had anything they wanted to send to the kids. They usually do. Mother didn't waste any time telling me she'd been doing some research and how Oxford had *wonderful* programs for people my age and how it wasn't too late to make something of myself. Then she went on and on about how good it would be for my children if I lived closer to them."

"She just won't give up will she?" Did that woman actually think I wouldn't move to Oxford with him?

"Nope." Ty spoke in a high voice mimicking his mother's. "Ty, dear, photography is a *luvly* hobby, I'm sure. And ah'll admit you are pretty good at it."

A slow burn ignited in my chest. "Big of her."

"Oh wait, I'm not finished." He continued in his mother's voice, "But taking pictures isn't much of a career like being a doctor or a lawyer. You don't want to live hand to mouth for the rest of your life do you?"

And now the kicker. "Why don't you invite Gracie and that professor husband of hers to supper with Skye and Glen? Ah'm sure he'd have some good suggestions." Ty took his eyes off the road for a sec and glanced at me. "Can you believe that? Ask my ex-wife and her husband to eat with us?"

"What did you say to that?"

"I flatly refused. Then, of course, she insisted on knowing why. I told her you were going and it would be too awkward.

Now we were getting to the real reason for his mood when he came over. "I'll bet it hit the fan then."

He blew out. "Did it ever."

"What did she say?" Part of me wanted to know and part of me didn't. The part that wanted to know won out.

Ty's face flushed. "I'm not repeating it. More of the same she said at Christmas. Let's just leave it at that."

"Will she ever accept me?" Why did I care so much?

"Baby, it isn't you. It's Marc. You are a convenient target for her to express her pain and anger. The sad thing is the bitterness she hurls does not defeat the Goliath of bitterness in her life. It just wears her out and isolates her from her son who is still alive."

As we drove, I laid my head back on the seat. What was it going to take for his mother to respect him? He deserved it and so much more.

****

We arrived early to Oxford. Ty pulled into a parking space on the square in front of Bouré, one of my favorite restaurants in the entire state. He jumped out and strode around to open my door. Always the gentleman.

"Thank you, kind sir."

"Anything for my lady." He glanced at his watch. "We're a little early. How about a beer while we wait?"

"Sounds good." I looked up toward the outdoor seating on the second floor terrace. "Too bad it's so chilly. I love sitting outside and watching people on the square."

"Oh, I'd keep you warm." He pumped his eyebrows up and down.

"Oh, I'm sure the kids would love that." I grabbed his hand. "It's cold. Let's get inside."

The cozy dark wood interior made me forget any disappointment I might have had for not getting to sit on the terrace. Our waitress pranced to our table. "Welcome to Bouré, what can I bring you to drink?"

"Two Dos Equis, amber. And bring us a basket of fried crawfish tails."

"Got it. Two beers and fried mudbugs coming up."

While we waited, we talked over more wedding plans. "What about music? Anything you prefer?

The waitress brought our beers and tails. "Can I get you anything thing else?" She hesitated in front of Ty and watched him through sultry eyes.

"Not at the moment." Was it in my imagination or was our waitress giving my fiancé the once over? I cleared my throat. "But we will have two others join us. We'll order when they arrive."

"All right then, I'll check on y'all later." With one last lingering look, she walked off. I supposed this was something I'd have to get used to.

Ty took a long drink of his beer. "Back to what we

were talking about. "I like easy jazz, blues." He grabbed a crawfish and dipped it into the sweet chili sauce. "Oh, man, I love these."

Not being a condiment-type person, I popped one in my mouth and savored the sweet meat mingled with the saltiness of the crunchy batter. I reached for another and noticed Ty's kids walking toward us.

"Hey, there." I wagged a crawdad at Glen. "Still hot and crispy."

He rubbed his hands together and sat next to me. "I could eat that entire basket."

Skye slid next to her dad. "Just one basket? Try two or three."

"I'd better order more." Ty looked around and hailed our waitress. She sauntered over and locked eyes with Glen. By the expression on her face, Ty was history. "Hi there, handsome."

"Hey, Ruthie."

Ruthie tapped her pencil on her chin. "I'm guessing you'll have your own basket of mudbugs and a Pabst?"

"Right as always."

She turned her gaze on Skye. "What would you like?"

"Diet coke and black-eyed pea hummus."

"Right. BRB."

Skye frowned at Glen. "What? You have a waitress in every restaurant in the town?"

Ty poked another tail in his mouth. "At least he won't go hungry. Say? What's BRB"

Glen reached over and grabbed a few for himself. "Be right back. And yes, sis, I do. Like Dad said, I'm not going hungry."

Skye rolled her eyes then leaned over the table.

"So, Avalee, have you heard from him?"

"Geeze, sis. Give it a rest." Glen turned to me. "It's good to see you, Avalee." He reached across the table and chuffed his dad on the arm. "Good to see you, too, old man."

Skye colored. "I'm sorry. I just get so wound up."

"Here y'all are." Ruthie served the drinks and appetizers. "Are you ready to order yet?"

Ty looked around. "I know what I want. How about y'all?"

We all nodded our heads. After we gave our orders, the conversation eased into a comfortable discussion about school, lively banters about current love interests. While we ate, I caught Skye up on Nathan. Glen told us about his gig in a local dive, and he asked Ty if he'd come and shoot some pictures for his portfolio. I felt at ease and somehow connected with both of Ty's kids. I didn't want the evening to end. They didn't either, so even though we were just south of being miserable from our meals, we ordered bananas foster bread pudding.

"Okay." Skye held her hand up. "Question. Have any of you read O Henry's *The Gift of the Magi*?"

"Yep." Ty spooned up his pudding. "But I liked the movie better."

"Oh, Dad." She looked at me. "Have you read it?"

"Yes, it's been years though. It was one of my favorite stories at Christmas. Why do you ask?"

"My lit teacher wants us to examine how the principle of self-sacrifice in this story is practiced in society today and give examples. I feel like I have a limited scope on this and wondered, with all your travels and all, if you'd meet up with me so we could discuss it?"

"I'd like that. Sorta like a book club, only with a short story?"

"Yeah, something like that." She turned to Ty. "Dad, mind if I come and stay with you next week?"

"Sure, my house needs cleaning."

Glen tore his attention away from his dessert. "Good luck with that."

"Oh, shut up, lover boy, or I'll tell Ruthie about Regina at the Pizza Factory."

He held his hands up. "Okay, okay. Don't do that, or I'll starve." He nudged Ty. "I'll come, too. I want to see Big Momma."

"She'll be thrilled." And I knew she would, too. "I'll tell her to set three extra places at the table."

When we all stood to leave, I put my arm around Skye's shoulder. "I've been meaning to ask, would you be one of my bridesmaids at the wedding?"

"Sure, as long as the dress you choose for me to wear isn't a candidate for *The Ugliest Bridesmaid Dress* on a Pinterest board."

"Deal."

We all waddled out of Bouré, miserably contented and said our goodbyes. Ty and I listened to Nat King Cole on the way home. Neither of us felt the need to talk, which was just as well. Dreams and thoughts of our wedding day swirled in my mind, and I didn't want them interrupted.

****

Morning's light glowed against the sheers on my window. Something wasn't right. It was too quiet. No coffee aromas drifting up the stairs. I sat up with a start. *Momma.*

I threw the covers back, pushed off the bed, and shot to her room across the hall. With my heart pounding, I eased her door open and peeked in. Light filtered in through her curtains just enough for me to see the rise and fall of the nine-patch quilt covering her. She was still asleep? I couldn't remember a time she ever slept past five in the morning, unless she was sick. Hot tears of relief filled my eyes. I pulled the door closed and plodded to the kitchen. I needed coffee.

While I filled the pot, all kinds of scenarios tormented me. Finding her paralyzed, finding her on the floor with a broken hip. Finding her dead. I slammed my hand on the counter. This couldn't go on. I had to do something.

While the coffee brewed, I hurried upstairs and dressed. Hugh, our pharmacist for as long as I could remember, had moved to Piggly Wiggly when they added a pharmacy to their store. I'd talk to him first. And, if need be, then Doctor Derrick.

The morning was brisk, but not too cold. I decided to walk the four blocks and clear my head. I poured coffee in a travel mug and jotted a note for Mom and left. The sidewalk along Washington Avenue was treacherous to say the least. After years of people walking on it, trikes and bikes, racing up and down, plus tree roots growing beneath, it was cracked and uneven. Still, many memories of my childhood were forged on this path of concrete.

Piggly Wiggly came into view and I smiled at the friendly pig in the red-and-white striped shirt waving at me from the roof. I needed that bit of levity. In the back of the store, Hugh stood behind the pharmacy window concentrating on something. I hated to disturb him, but as I approached, he glanced at me over his glasses and waved.

While pushing his spectacles up his nose, he welcomed me with a gentle smile. "Good morning, Avalee. You're up and out early this fine morning."

"Morning, Hugh."

"How can I help you today?"

"Well, I need some advice. Momma seems off lately. I've seen a dramatic change in the past month. When I returned to Moonlight, she was a bundle of energy. Now she is run down and lethargic. She's hungry all the time and drinks water by the gallons. I'm getting worried."

Hugh nodded. "Seems she is up to her old tricks again."

"Tricks?"

"Yeah, not checking her glucose levels and shooting insulin anytime she eats sugar instead of staying on a regular schedule and watching her diet."

What was he talking about? "I'm not following you, Hugh."

"Her diabetes. She did this last spring. Both Doctor Derrick and I have had long talks with her. But, stubborn woman that she is, she won't listen. She insisted it was too much trouble to alter her diet. But when she got word you were coming that little lady straightened right up. She checked her levels religiously and got on a regular insulin schedule." He scratched his head and frowned. "Frankly, I'm surprised she's gone back to her old ways, seeing how much better she felt and all."

"Wait." I put my hand up and closed my eyes. "Are you saying my mother is diabetic?"

He stared at me through his large black frame glasses. "Didn't you know?"

"No. I had no idea. How long has it been since she was diagnosed?"

"It's been about ten years now."

"Ten years?" How could I have not known? The voice of guilt answered me, "Because you haven't been there for her." Well, I'm here now and it is time for a come-to-Jesus meeting with my mother. I nodded. "Thanks, Hugh. I'll take care of this."

"I hope you do. She's asking for trouble one of these days."

For the first time in months, I jogged. All four blocks. By the time I reached the kitchen door, my heart thundered against my chest. Momma sat at the table reading the paper. I strode through the doorway and snatched the paper from her hands. "Why didn't you tell me?"

Her eyebrows arched like startled cats. "Tell you what?"

"That you are diabetic."

She crossed her arms over her chest and sat back. "Who told you?"

"Hugh. He thought I knew."

"Well, I swaney! He's as bad as an old biddy for gossiping."

"Mother." I tried to moderate my voice, but it was a struggle. "You are killing yourself. He said both he and Doctor Derrick have warned you."

"Oh pssh." She dismissed my concern with her hand. "Both of those old fogies need to retire." She pointed her finger at me. "I know my body. I know when my sugar goes up, and I take care of it. Bessie

Clark is diabetic, and I'm in a lot better shape than she is and she's religious about checking her sugar levels."

"Mother, you can't compare yourself to others to determine how you treat your condition. That's crazy thinking."

Momma stood. "Now see here, Avalee. I don't want to hear another word about this. I can take care of myself. I've done it for ten years. You hear me?"

I was taken aback by her aggressiveness. "Mother…?"

"No." She shoved her palm in front of her as if she were stopping traffic. "This conversation is finished." With that, she turned on her heel and left the room.

My sweet little momma had just tied my hands. She had willingly put herself in a dangerous position and refused to acknowledge it. Well, we will see about that. She may think she is sacking up kittens, but she just found herself a wildcat.

Chapter Fourteen

What a difference a phone call can make.
                              ~Tyler Jackson

Ty tried to concentrate on the best angle to shoot the new façade of Moonlight's Chamber of Commerce, but someone kept blowing up his phone making it impossible to focus. "Geez people, some guys have to work for a living."

He reached in his pocket and checked the screen. Three calls from Scott. Six from Avalee? The hairs on his arms pricked. What had happened? Something bad. The phone rang again. It was Scott.

"Hello? Scott? What's wrong? What's happened?"

"Well, thank God you finally decided to answer."

"What is all this about?" His anxiousness turned into irritation.

"Settle down, sweetie."

"Scott. Don't call me sweetie."

"Sorry. Listen. I have big news. *Big* news. *The New Yorker* wants to buy your photos."

"Photos? I'm not following you."

"Avalee sent me the photos you took at Jema's reception. The ones of the Life Source folks. My friend, Taige, sent them to a colleague who works at the magazine and the guy thought they were fantastic. He wants to buy them, and he also has some assignments he'd like to give you." Scott stopped long enough to take a breath and then blurted out. "Do you know what this means?"

Dazed, Ty shook his head as if Scott could see him.

"It means you are on your way to the big time if you keep taking pics like those."

Ty looked at his camera on the stand posed to take a shot of a building façade. A façade for crying out loud. *Finally. A real job. A real career. Finally....*

"Hey, Ty. You there?"

"Uh, yeah. Sorry. I'm just so blown away."

"You ought to be. Now listen. Be expecting a call from my guy, Taige. He will get you in contact with the *New Yorker* people." Scott paused and then said in his most sarcastic voice. "And answer your phone, okay, fella?"

Ty let the *fella* reference slide. This was big. Bigger than big. He was light-headed with the enormity of the news. "Will do. And, hey, thanks."

"Anything for a friend. Doesn't hurt you are so good-looking."

"Oh stop already."

"Kidding. Now call Avalee. She's worried about you."

"Calling now. Thanks again."

As soon as he hung up he called Ava. She answered before the first ring had finished. "Have you talked to Scott?"

"Yes, can you believe it?"

"Of course I can. You are brilliant. That's why I sent them. I just knew someone would snatch them up."

"But what about getting release forms? Don't I need people to sign them and what if I can't find them?

What if they won't sign?"

"All is good. Since it was a private event you don't need them." She paused. "I had called you about something completely different the first time."

"What about?"

"My mother. Ty, you aren't going to believe this. She's diabetic and she has been hiding it from me."

"Seriously? She's smarter than that."

"Apparently not." An impatient sigh sounded over the receiver. "When I try to talk to her about it, she just shuts down."

"Maybe she's frightened, or maybe even resents not being able to live like she always has before diabetes."

"Well, those kinds of feelings will either land her as an invalid in a nursing home or six-feet under."

Another call showed on Ty's screen. "I'm getting a call from area code 917?"

"Hang up and take it. Bye."

Ty hit 'answer'. "Hello, this is Tyler Jackson."

"Hello Tyler. I'm Taige…."

Chapter Fifteen

Life can be so complicated.

~Avalee Preston

By noon, it was as if Mom and I had never had our little confrontation. She was cheery as always, fussing over what we should have for lunch. I already made an appointment with Doctor Derrick for a consultation about her, but I wasn't about to tell her. I just needed to understand what was going on in her mind. Perhaps, by knowing what her thought processes might be, I could approach the subject of diabetes in a more delicate and convincing manner.

Momma had her head stuck in the fridge, calling out lunch choices. "We have left over meat loaf. That'd make nice sandwiches. We can have BLTs, I have bacon and some of Pigg's cardboard-tasting tomatoes." She squinted at me and stuck out her tongue. "I sure do miss the fresh tomatoes from my garden." She went back to rummaging. "I have enough chicken pot pie soup to make a respectable lunch."

"Soup sounds good."

"I was hoping you'd say that." She pulled out the bowl and emptied it into a pot. "And I'll whip up a pan of cornbread."

Once again, my mother was in her happy place. Cooking. Perhaps this is the reason she resisted the fact she had diabetes. This realization gave me a new perspective and a new compassion. I looked on as she dolloped a spoonful of bacon fat in her iron skillet and slipped it into the oven to heat. Then she mixed white cornmeal, flour, baking powder, a pinch of salt, milk and egg together in a bowl. When the grease in the pan melted, she pulled the frying pan out of the oven, dumped the grease in the corn meal mixture, gave it a stir, poured it back into the hot skillet where it sizzled and promised a brown, crunchy, crust. With one deft movement, she snatched up the cast iron skillet and stuck it in the oven. Watching her, I remembered how dad used to sit in the kitchen and watch her cook. One time while he watched her make cornbread, he turned to me and said, "You see how she handles that cast iron skillet, sis?"

"Yes, sir."

"That's why I don't give her any flack."

A smile involuntarily spread across my face. I missed him. And I couldn't lose my mom. Not now. Not for a long time.

"Baby? Want some tea while we wait on the cornbread?"

I could tell she was trying hard to erase any hard feelings after our fuss earlier in the morning.

"Sure." While she poured, I thought about Ty's news. That might help us over this awkward patch. "Guess what? The *New Yorker* wants to buy some of Ty's photos he took at Jema's reception."

"Shut up your mouth. Really?"

"Really. In fact, while Ty and I were speaking on the phone, someone called him from New York. I'm dying to know who it was and what they said."

"How did they get ahold of Ty's pictures?"

"I sent them to Scott and he worked his magic."

"I'd say Ty worked the magic."

"He did." I held my finger up. "Just a sec." I left to get my laptop and brought it to the kitchen. "Here they are, take a look."

She scrolled through the photos and occasionally murmured, "God love them. Poor souls." When she finished, she wiped her face with the tail of her apron. "The boy is gifted, I'll vow."

The timer went off and Momma rose, grabbed her hot pads, and pulled the skillet from the oven. We chatted as we always do over lunch and I felt pretty good about everything until she served herself a bowl of banana pudding. When she finished eating she headed straight to the bathroom. Only this time I felt I knew why. She was giving herself an insulin shot to ward off the sugar she'd just eaten. Lord knows how many shots she gave herself in a day.

My phone rang and dragged me away from my worried thoughts. It was Ty. I punched 'answer'. "Hey, was the call about your photographs?"

"Yes. I'm stoked. I can't believe this. Thank you baby for believing in me."

"Who called, what did they say?"

"A guy named Taige. They are not only buying my photos, they want to fly me to New York City day after tomorrow to meet with someone who is shooting a documentary. They didn't say who, but I don't care. An all-expenses paid trip to the Big Apple, just think!"

"That's wonderful, baby." I longed for the city and would have given my right arm to go with him.

As if reading my mind he said, "Would you come

with me?"

"I'd love to, but…" I turned around to make sure Momma was out of earshot. "I'm meeting with Doctor Derrick in a few. It depends on what he says. How about drinks tonight? We can talk about it then."

"My place? I'll even cook supper."

"Fabulous. Congratulations, sweetheart. No one deserves this more."

"Love you, hon."

"Love you, too. See you tonight."

After I disconnected the call, a satisfying image filled my mind—the surprised look on his parents' faces when they saw his photos in *The New Yorker Magazine*.

****

Doctor Derrick's wife and receptionist, Maud, glanced up when I stepped into the empty waiting room. It was good of them to stay over after hours in order for me to speak with him. "Hey, Avalee. Dan is in his office. Just go on in, honey."

"Thanks, Maud. How are you today?"

"Fair to middling." She stared at me through coke bottle lenses. Not getting any younger, you know. How about you?"

"Well, I've been better. I'm worried about Momma."

"Is Cladie sick?"

"I'm not sure, actually."

"Oh dear. We can't have anything wrong with our Cladie. Go on in now and talk with Dan. I'll be praying for her."

I nodded and walked down the hall familiar to me as my own home. The aseptic smell of isopropyl alcohol competed with the odor of the old building's ancient vinyl floors and layers of paint. This man brought me into the world and he helped ease my father out of it. He was probably as close to retirement as Hugh. I hated the idea of either of them retiring, but they had certainly earned it.

Doctor Derrick sat at his desk. A man in his seventies but still had a head full of unruly white hair. "Avalee." He rose and walked over to me when I entered his office. Wrapping his arm around my shoulder, he pulled me into a side-hug. "Hello, darlin'."

"Hi, Doctor Derrick."

He gestured to the seat across from his desk, moved to his, and sat. "I'm glad you've come home. We've missed you."

"I missed y'all, too. I'd almost forgotten my southern roots in the big city of New York. But I'm back to saying 'y'all' so I don't think too much damage was done."

His laugh was deep and pleasant. "So, my dear, what brings you to me today?"

"It's Momma. Doctor Derrick, I had no idea she was diabetic. She has hidden it from me all these years and the only way I know now is because Hugh told me. I had gone to him to talk about some sort of supplement because I'd seen such a change. In the past month, she's turned old before my eyes. When I came home last summer, she was spry and lively. Now she is dragging and grumpy to boot."

The doctor nodded but didn't say anything.

"And she gets angry when I try to talk to her about it."

"Yes, I know. That is what I come up against when

I speak to her about her condition."

"So what's up with that? Why does she resist so?"

"She's in denial. It is her defense mechanism."

"Defense? I don't understand."

"Several things factor into a person wanting to put up a defense. Fear, frustration. Cladie doesn't want to deal with or change her lifestyle. Last summer I suggested she see a psychotherapist, but she refused."

"Why a psychotherapist?"

"To help her with her fears. To put them in perspective. But she equated that with me saying she was crazy." He grinned. "She puffed up like a toad and left."

"So what can I do?"

"Nothing. She is going to have to do this for herself."

I nodded. "You're right, of course. But what will it take to wake her up?"

He opened his mouth to speak, but then closed it. Instead, he laid his hand on my shoulder. "Maybe one day she'll wake up and decide to take charge of her health."

"Here's hoping." I hugged the dear old man. "Thank you. I appreciate you seeing me after hours."

"My pleasure, hon. Have a good evening."

"You, too." I hurried out the door to my good evening—Ty, wine, and our bright future, that is, if I could quiet the nagging fears haunting me.

****

All the way to Ty's home, I kept reminding myself, *do not be a downer when you get there*. His moment had finally come, and I was determined to celebrate him and not whine about my mother. Still, the conversation with her, Hugh, and Doctor Derrick kept playing in my head and before I knew it, I was gripping the steering wheel until my hands went numb.

Relax. It is about Ty this evening.

At least I had the presence of mind to stop for champagne on the way. When I pulled onto his driveway, Ty walked outside. I threw the car in park, jumped out, and ran into his arms.

"We did it, baby." He lifted me up. "You did it."

Taking his face in my hands, I took in every detail of his joyful expression. His broad smile was contagious. His eyes held so much joy that even his eyelashes couldn't obscure his dark brown eyes. "You did it. This is all because of your talent, not mine."

Setting me on my feet, he leaned his forehead against mine. "It would never have happened if not for you. I love you."

"And I love you even more."

He touched my nose with his finger. "Not even possible."

"I have champagne. Let's go inside to celebrate."

Inside his place, the spice aroma of curry excited my nose. I took a deep whiff. "Oh, yum."

"Don't be impressed. It's take out." He opened the champagne, poured two glasses and handed me one.

"No problem." I put on my best-worried look. "I'm afraid there will be a lot of take-out in our future. I'm not much of a cook, even though my mom is a culinary goddess."

"I see a lot of visits to Miss Cladie's in our future."

Worry nudged my mind. I hoped she would be around for our future. Pushing the troublesome thoughts back, I lifted my glass. "To Tyler Glen Jackson. May you achieve success far beyond your wildest dreams."

He clinked his glass against mine. "That, my love, has already happened."

I stopped mid-sip and tipped my head. "How so?"

"When you said yes." He leaned in and caressed his lips against mine before gently kissing my upper lip, then the bottom, then completely covering my mouth with his. So warm, so tender.

Lord I loved this man.

"So," he refilled my glass even though it wasn't empty. "Will you go with me to New York? It'll be a quick trip, two nights tops."

My mind went back to Mom. I'm not sure what sort of face I made but he interjected, "You will get to see Scott." This, most likely, was his way of tilting my decision in a favorable direction.

"I want to go; I'm just concerned about Mom."

"Felix will keep an eye on her. Lexi and Molly Kate can drop in on her."

Of course he was right. It was only a couple of days and Felix was with her every day. Why not? "Okay, I'll go. When do we leave?"

"Day after tomorrow."

"Perfect. Where are they putting you up?"

"The Ritz." He took a drink and wiggled his eyebrows. "Where else."

"Where else indeed. That is fabulous." Going back to New York made me dizzy with excitement and without a doubt, the second glass of champagne could have had something to do with my giddiness. "Hey, let's eat. I'm starved."

"Me, too, but not for food." He drew me hard against him.

"Down, boy."

Ty gave me his best little boy pout. I could have eaten him with a spoon right then and there, but settled for the curried lamb instead—for the time being. One day….

****

On my drive home from Ty's, I thought about what a rollercoaster the day had been with extreme highs and lows. Thankfully, it ended on a high. At least I hoped it had. No telling what I'd find when I arrived home.

Lights shined from the kitchen window as I drove up our driveway. Momma stood at the sink. A sure sign of normalcy, thank the Lord. I walked into the house. Momma dried her hands and said, "Baby, we need to talk a minute."

Every muscle in my body tensed. Dread robbed me of my voice. I lowered onto the kitchen chair.

Momma sat catty-cornered from me. "Sugar, I owe you an apology. My snapping at you was uncalled for. Would you forgive your old momma?"

Relief rushed over me, leaving me weak in its wake. "There's nothing to forgive. I was just surprised; shocked would be a better word. And I was frightened. But that didn't give me the right to come at you like a freight train."

Momma laced her fingers together and stared at her hands. "It's just that I don't like feeling different or dependent. I don't like having to change the way I've eaten for over seventy years for heaven's sake. I hate the idea of having to check my blood and giving myself shots." She locked her gaze with mine. "Why, I've never been reliant on anything. Matter of factly, that is the reason I never took up smoking. When I was young, it was the thing to do, looking like movie stars and all. But I didn't want to fool with them, having to have them close by, always stopping what I was doing to smoke because I was hooked. I was smart enough to know that when you were hooked, you didn't smoke to look cool, you smoked to feel normal. Shoot. I already felt normal, so I figured, why start smoking and then have to pay to feel normal? Anyway, I'll try to do better."

I stood and bent over her, wrapping my arms around her neck. "You have so many who love and depend on you. Especially me. I'm here for you, too. I know I wasn't when Daddy died—"

"—Now baby, don't you go feeling bad about that. You were building your career."

"That may be, but I don't know that I will ever be able to forgive myself for leaving you when you needed me the most. It won't happen again."

I went back to my seat. "On a happier note, guess what?"

"What?"

"Some guy named Taige is flying Ty to New York City to talk to him about a photography job."

"Well, ain't that exciting?"

"Yes. He leaves day after tomorrow and will be gone two nights. I'm thinking of going with him, if you think you'll be all right."

"Don't you worry about me, I'll be fine. Besides, Felix checks in several times a day. And I'll be good. I'll check my levels faithfully every day."

"I really appreciate that, Mom. By the way, how are Felix and AJ working out?"

"Like peanut butter and jelly. They've bonded.

Why, you'd think AJ was Felix's son."

The Grandfather clock's low bongs and the high-pitched cuckoo clock both sounded ten o'clock. I stood and stretched. "Well, I think I'll go to bed." I leaned over and kissed her. "I love happy endings. Night."

She patted me. "I do too, baby. I do too. Night, night."

I climbed the stairs thinking how good the day had ended up and how good my bed was going to feel.

****

The next morning I scanned my closet. One would have thought this was my first trip to New York. I packed and repacked four times. Since it was cold there, I settled on slacks, two sweaters, a cocktail dress, boots, dress shoes, a coat, two scarves, and a knit hat. When I finished packing for the fifth time I was pretty proud of myself. I fit it all in a carryon, even my toiletries.

Footsteps thumped up the steps and Lexi called at my door, "Cover up. I'm coming in."

"I'm decent. Enter."

"So." She flopped on my bed like she used to when we were kids. "You are going to the big city again? I thought you just escaped from there."

"I never escaped. I loved it there, remember? It was Moonlight I escaped from and honestly? I thought I'd only be here a few months and then escape again. But…."

"But?"

"But I found my soul. Something I thought I'd lost."

"Your soul being Ty?"

"My soul being southern." I flopped down beside

her. "You ought to come with us."

She rolled over and stared at the ceiling. "I'd love to, but I can't on short notice, darned it all. However," she rolled back to her stomach, "I am going in March. Nate is flying me there to accompany him to some doodah. I get to meet his," she crunched her first two fingers up and down, "people."

"What's the occasion?"

"Not sure. I'll ask again before I leave just so I'll know what to wear." She nudged her shoulder against mine. "You'll help me, right?"

"Of course. Hey. Would you do me a favor?"

"Sure, what?"

I told Lexi about Hugh spilling the beans about Momma's diabetes, my talk with Doctor Derrick, my confrontation with her, and our discussion the previous evening. "Would you look in on her?"

"Good Lord." Lexi sat up and pulled her leg under her. "What a mess. Sure, I'll look in on her. I'll be on her like white on rice."

"Thanks. She promises to do better."

Lexi snorted.

"What?"

"Being better as in having one piece of pie instead of two? Or better yet, not eating a piece at all but not telling how many times she tasted the filling while making it?"

I had to admit, Lexi knew my mom pretty well. That was exactly something she'd do.

"Exactly. So, just pop in on her and talk with her a bit. See if she's energetic or lethargic which is a sure sign she is misbehaving. And call me if she's lethargic."

"Nothing doing, baby girl. You enjoy yourself with your man. I'll handle things on this end. Besides, you'll only be gone a couple of days."

"You're right. I just worry. She's been abusing her body—popping herself with insulin willy-nilly. I'm afraid for her. No telling what damage she's already done to herself."

Lexi stood. "Girl, don't you worry. I've got it all under control. Now, how about a white chocolate mocha at Molly Kate's?"

"Sounds amazing." I grabbed my purse. "And a chocolate chip scone? We can share one."

Lexi's eyes widened. "Share one? Pfff."

I slapped her arm and did my Elvis eyebrow lift. "I was hoping you'd say that."

We jogged downstairs, arm in arm, like we did as teens. Gratitude filled me.

Lord, I love my friends.

Chapter Sixteen

The ebb of our plans is the flow for Ty's future.
                                    ~Avalee Preston

The fellow who had first contacted Ty, Taige somebody, had a limo waiting for us at JFK making the forty-five minute trip from the airport to Manhattan more tolerable. I had never given much thought to how New York City might look through the eyes of someone who'd never been there. The old familiar sights were suddenly fresh and new. Ty didn't say much except to exclaim, "Look at that. What's that over there?"

No doubt, his photographer's creative wheels turned in his head; I sat back and enjoyed his excitement. My phone rang and the screen showed Scott and me making snow angels in Central Park. "Hi Scott."

"Hey, Girl. Where are you? I'm at the Ritz lounge with Taige waiting on you."

"Almost there. Can't wait!"

"Are you close enough for me to order your drinks?"

"Yes. I'll have my usual." I nudged Ty. "Baby, what do you want from the bar?"

He tore his gaze from the window. "Do they have beer in New York?"

Grinning, I nodded. "Ty'll have a beer. Get him something regional."

"Okay, one Mediterranean Martini and one Bluepoint, since, if my memory serves me correctly, he doesn't like hoppy beer. I'll put the order in, say, ten minutes?"

"Perfect. See you in a few."

"Counting the seconds, darling."

A few moments later, the limo pulled in front of the Ritz and Ty got that 'child seeing Santa on his rooftop' look. The Ritz was a stunning sight. And Central Park, only steps away, gave New York a more pastoral appearance than it was in reality.

We checked in and gave our luggage to the bellhop, then I texted Scott an exclamation point, our signal to each other whenever we arrived somewhere. He met us in the Star Lounge with open arms. Standing beside him was the man I assumed to be Taige, a tall handsome fellow with seriously blue eyes. He appeared to be in his late thirties dressed in dark jeans, black V neck tee, and a black leather jacket. Smartly understated.

Scott made the introductions and gestured to Taige. "This is Taige Stanford. Taige, this is my sweetie, Avalee Preston and the amazing, talented Ty Jackson, who also happens to be engaged to Avalee."

Taige's smile was warm and confident. "So glad to meet you guys. Scott's talked about you both so much I feel I've known you a long time." He motioned toward a table. "Your drinks are ready. I imagine after the ride from the airport you could use them.

"Oh, it could have been worse. I remember those Nascar taxi rides. Thanks for the limo." I sipped the best martini I'd had since leaving New York. Maybe I could talk Jema into hosting a Martini Monday in Manhattan.

"Yeah, thanks man." Ty tilted his beer toward Taige. "Thanks for everything. I have to admit, I'm still blown away by all of this."

Scott grinned. "Oh, just you wait." He nodded at Taige. "Why don't you tell Ty why he's here."

"Think he's ready? He hasn't finished his first beer yet. This is pretty big news to take in before he has, say, a third beer?"

This mysterious banter had me gulping my martini. I hit Scott's arm. "For pity's sake, what?"

Scott laughed. "Ahhh, my little southern belle. How the vodka does thicken your accent. Charming."

Ty grinned one of his devilish smiles, "How about another one of those?"

Scott sighed and looked longingly at Taige. "See, I told you he was drop-dead gorgeous."

Taige's smile was as million-dollar as Jema's. "Can't have them all." He raised his shoulders and let them fall. "How about a second round?"

"Second for them." Scott jingled the ice in his glass. "Fourth for us."

"Whatever." Taige signaled the waiter and gave our orders. When they arrived, he raised his glass. "To Ty Jackson and his future career. May he not have a heart attack when I make him my offer."

As we clinked glasses, my mind raced. What could this opportunity be?

"Okay. Let's get down to business." Taige set his glass down. "I'm sure you've heard of Cadence Terry?"

Ty lifted his beer to his mouth. "Who doesn't know

her?"

Who indeed? Cadence Terry was an actress extraordinaire, powerhouse vocalist, and stunningly beautiful. She'd won every award there was to win as an actress and vocalist. Even my mother knew of her.

Scott continued. "She is my client and a great philanthropist. Some time ago, she was asked by a friend to join him on a humanitarian trip. He was part of a clean water group that travels to third-world countries and drills wells in villages. This trip opened her eyes to a real problem and she wants to use her star-power to raise awareness for this cause. So, she is planning to make a documentary showing her visiting some of these places. She has a film crew but also wants a photographer. I've interviewed several, but none of them tells a story like you do. I showed her your photographs and she wants me to hire you."

Ty set his beer down with a thunk. "Shut up. Seriously?"

"Very serious. She plans on flying to Ethiopia and finishing in Sudan." He watched Ty over the rim of his Manhattan as he sipped. "So this might be something that interests you?"

I stared at Ty and he stared back. *What an opportunity.* He managed to answer Taige. "Interested? I've waited my whole professional life for something like this."

"I hoped that would be your answer." Taige leaned back in his chair. "Cadence will be thrilled to hear you agreed."

Finally. Finally. Finally. I wanted to dance on the table—and not because of the two powerhouse martinis. Ty's time had come and in a much grander way than I could have possibly imagined. If his mother or father could ignore this, they were beyond hope.

"All the details are being worked out, but just so you can get this on your calendar, you will be leaving from JFK the last of April and returning around June thirtieth. Cadence is having supper with us tonight and she will fill you in on things you need to bring on your trip."

Ty and I both stared at Taige like we'd been hit with a stun gun. He looked from Ty to me to Ty again. "Is there a problem?"

Ty's *yes* collided with my *no*. I put my hand on his. "No, that will work just fine."

Ty turned to me and opened his mouth, but I put my finger to his lips. "We will talk it over in our room." There was no way Ty was going to miss this opportunity. My love for him overrode the sinking disappointment in my heart. I forced a smile for Scott. "I think Ty and I should go to our room and rest up a bit before supper."

Scott knew me well and wasn't oblivious to the situation. He sent me a text with a question mark and an exclamation point. I glanced at him and barely shook my head. Then I took Ty's hand and squeezed it three times—*I love you.* He squeezed back four times—*I love you, too.*

Taige on the other hand was clueless. He patted the table. "Excellent idea. I'll call Cadence right away." When we stood to leave, I remembered my discussions with Skye about O Henry's *The Gift of the Magi.* I wanted to do this for Ty. After all, isn't love doing what is best for others? And there was nothing magic about May. We could marry in August. I leaned into Ty and whispered, "It's all right. I have ideas. We'll talk later. For now, enjoy this, baby. It is your hour."

He touched his lips to mine. "We'll talk."

****

I don't know if it was the two martinis, the flight, or both, but all of a sudden, I felt exhausted. We had six hours until our meeting with Cadence Terry. That gave us plenty of time for a nap and for me to take a long, hot soak. Taige had gotten us connecting rooms with fabulous views of Central Park. While staring out my window, I regretted not having enough time to show Ty the city.

"Ava?" Ty stood at my door. "Can we talk now?"

"Sure." We went to the living room adjoining our rooms and sat on the couch. For a man who had just been given his life's dream on a golden platter, he looked sober. Troubled. I traced his lips with my finger. "What's wrong, babe?"

"Our wedding. Putting it off. I don't like it."

"Sugar, this is an opportunity of a lifetime. You simply cannot miss it." I sat up and faced him. "We can marry the first of August. That is just a little over two months later than our original date."

His frown softened as he thought my suggestion over. "Well, I don't like it, but you're right." He kissed my ear, then down my jaw. A million tiny tingles pulsed through my body. I turned to meet his lips. It was going to be hard waiting two more months. So many emotions transferred through our kisses—love, excitement, disappointment, need. If we kept this up, I knew we wouldn't wait for our honeymoon. It was important to me, to both of us, to wait.

I pulled away. "We'd better stop this."

He groaned and pulled me closer. "Let's get married. Right now. Here."

"No way, mister. I'm going to have a romantic wedding if it kills me. Not one driven by hormones."

"Then, I need a shower."

"Take one. I'm taking a hot soak. The marble bathrooms in this hotel are amazing."

"Want company?" He lowered his brows and grinned. "I could wash your back, among other things."

I popped his arm. "Nope. My bath is my sanctuary. Then, I'm taking a long nap before getting ready. I need my rest. I don't want to look like my mother next to the young, beautiful, multi-talented Cadence. You might just change your mind."

"No way. I love your spirit, your soul, and your body. No woman can match what you are to me." He ran his fingers through my hair. "I love you. *You.*"

My vision blurred as I studied his face. How did I get so lucky? After all these years, the old adage proved true. Good things really did come to those who wait.

****

A long soak and two-hour nap made me feel as if I could take on Miss Cadence—thirty-six-year-old— Terry. But one look in the mirror quelled such lofty thoughts. Good thing Ty loved me for more than my looks. I was way overdue for Botox. Staring in the mirror at my crow's feet and drooping cheeks, I blew out a breath. "Avalee, girl, you are going to have to stop this nonsense. Accept who you are. There is more to you than what you see in the mirror."

Heartened by my *I am woman hear me roar* pep talk, I pulled the makeup out of my cosmetics bag to, as my mother put it, *paint the barn.* Unfortunately, as I applied foundation, it became evident to me that the barn needed more painting than when I first left New York. *Accept yourself...Accept yourself....*

At seven, we met Scott and Taige in the lobby. Even though they dressed casually, they still looked as if they belonged on a GQ magazine cover. Scott wore a gray wool coat, dark jeans, wingtip boots, and a phenomenal gray scarf. Taige wore a three-toned sweater under a blue coat, tight black jeans, and boots. Thank goodness Ty let me dress him, or else he would have worn his best worn-out jeans and lumberjack shirt. Before we left for New York, I went shopping and chose a wool camel coat, a brown cashmere sweater, dark jeans, boots, and a tartan scarf in several shades of brown. I loved how his skin and eyes looked in these colors.

While getting ready, I encouraged him not to shave, but to wear that sexy shadow. He never wore product in his hair, but submitted to me using pomade and combing it back into thick waves. Of course he grumbled, but I told him he looked just right for a night on the city.

I chose an outfit that coordinated with Ty's, a long, slim-fitting olive green dress with a wide brown belt, a faux-fur jacket, and dark brown boots. I felt pretty good about myself. That is until we walked into the lobby. One look at Ty and both Scott's and Taige's jaws went slack. On one hand, I felt good about dressing him so well. But on the other it really doesn't do much of a gal's ego when men ogle her fiancé.

"Avalee? Guess where we are taking you tonight." Scott had that gleam in his eye.

I knew right away. "Carbons?" My absolute

favorite Italian place.

"The very place." He swung his hand toward the door. "Ready?"

We slid onto the seat of the waiting sedan and soon merged into the crush of motor vehicles speeding down the road, stopping with a lot of jerks then starting again. All around us, horns blew and fists shook out of windows as we sped onward. Ty leaned over and whispered, "I feel like I'm on a roller coaster ride at Six Flags."

I never thought of New York traffic in such endearing terms. Crazy, yes. Wild, absolutely. But not fun. We arrived at Thompson Street, and the driver let us off in front of the restaurant. Oh, how I loved this place. Not just for the great food but also for the warm, cozy, feel.

"Hi everyone." Cadence stood and waved. To say she was stunning, even ravishing, would be a pathetic description. I don't think words have been invented to describe her beauty. I lost my appetite. "Over here."

I glanced at Ty. Her loveliness hadn't escaped him. How could it? Her blonde hair cascaded over her tight black sweater. She hardly wore a smidgen of make-up on her smooth face. *Note to self, beg the dermatologist to work me in tomorrow before leaving.* Her eyes were huge and dark blue. She only had a swipe of sparkly gloss on her perfect, full lips. Ugh. I'd forgotten how easily intimidated I always felt in this city.

Cadence held out her perfectly manicured hands to Ty. "You must be the storyteller."

Ty managed to keep his eyes on hers even though the sweater's straining fibers over her chest made it hard for any red-blooded man to avoid staring.

"Storyteller?"

Her laugh was musical. "Sorry, I'm Cadence." As if we didn't know. "And I was referring to your beautiful photographs."

Ty flushed. "I'm glad you liked them."

"They are amazing. When Taige showed them to me, I knew you were the photographer I needed." She glanced at Scott and Taige. "You guys did a fantastic job finding him."

"We aim to please." Taige winked at Scott.

Hello? I'm also in this group. You know, the south-side of fifty-something, woman in the room. Now I understood what Jema had referred to during one of our Whine Wednesdays about how, after turning fifty, she suddenly felt invisible. That was exactly how I felt while standing next to Ty.

At long last, Taige put his hand on the small of my back. "And this is Ty's fiancée, Avalee Preston."

Cadence's eyes widened. "Avalee Preston who wrote *The Feng Shui of Floral Design?* That's my decorating Bible. Who knew fresh flowers made such a difference in a home. And it is such a beautiful book. It is sitting on my coffee table this very minute."

"Thank you." Okay, so she wasn't so bad after all. At least she had great taste in books.

The evening turned out to be delightful and informative. Cadence told us about the event that had galvanized her to become involved with clean water projects.

"We came to a village which was like all the others. The people bathed in and drank from the same filthy, muddy stream as the livestock used. Disease had ravaged many of the children. After the drill hit water

221

and the well was set, we pumped clean water into a container. There was this one little boy who watched, still with such wonder, as the crystal clear water splashed into the bucket. I don't think his eyes could have gotten any bigger. He pointed at it and through our interpreter asked if he could touch it."

Tears spilled from Cadence's eyes as she described stooping down, cupping her hands and bringing the water to his lips. "I said, 'Drink little one.' He looked at the interpreter who told him what I'd said. He took a sip and stared at me in awe. I asked our interpreter to tell him to drink all he wanted. The little fellow didn't waste any time cupping his little brown hands and drinking great gulps of clean water. Then all the children who'd shied back while watching the brave little boy ran to the bucket. We just kept pumping container after container of cool, clear, sparkling clean water. Soon all the adults scrambled to find containers. It was a joyous sight."

We were all transfixed by her story. I had no doubt Ty fit this job perfectly. His time had come. He would be a part of a world-changing event.

****

Ty and I arrived home to Moonlight early afternoon the next day. The minute we walked through the door, Momma smiled and gave each of us a big hug. "Now y'all get some rest because this evening we are going to Molly Kate's for supper. All of us want to hear about Ty's new job.

"But Momma. We're so tired." I glanced at Ty, who didn't look tired at all.

"Land sakes, y'all will have plenty of time to rest. Oh, and we are picking Lexi up on the way."

"Sounds like a plan." Ty grinned. I supposed he was ready to brag, and the good Lord knows he had earned that right.

Momma studied my face. "Where did you get those bruises around your eyes and your mouth?"

Ty grinned. "Don't ask."

I touched my face. "I told you I was just tired. I'll be better after a little nap." And makeup. Okay, so I begged my old dermatologist to see me and got a few units of Botox. Accepting myself takes time. Little by little.

After a short nap, I reapplied my make-up to cover all signs of telltale Botox bruises and left with Momma and Ty to pick up Lexi and head to Molly Kate's. When we turned off Leslie Lane onto Nightingale and passed in front of the mansion, I noticed several trucks on the mansion's circular drive. Probably contractors. Molly mentioned how feverishly she and Stan were working to get the place ready for spring tourists. They had a parking lot built on the north side of the property on the corner of Nightingale and Moonflower Way, giving two entrances to the mansion; the circular drive off Nightingale or Molly Kate's private drive off Moonflower. This entrance was also to their personal house. Since their home connected to the mansion by a sunroom, they had a small foyer and hall added which bypassed their personal space and gave access to the mansion, which was handicap accessible and could be used on rainy days.

The Montgomery welcoming committee of one, Kricket, greeted us with joyful barks that converted into full body wags and attempts at wet kisses. Molly Kate looked down at the pup. "Hmmph, some watchdog you are. Gypsy does better than you do."

Stan walked up behind her. "Now don't go besmirching my dog." He grasped Molly Kate's hand, twirled her around, and planted a big kiss on her lips. She giggled and wrapped her arms around his neck then glanced at us with a mischievous grin. "And you wonder why you haven't seen much of us?"

Lexi joined us just in time to hear MK. "Oh puleeze. Y'all come on into the living room. Molly and Stan have laid out a spread, and I'm dying to hear Ty's news."

We followed her to the living room. Lexi was not exaggerating. With all the snacks laid out, why bother with supper? Stan manned the bar smiling and chatting all the while. His gentle expression had a touch of humor behind it. I could tell he would be a big part of their bed and breakfast success.

While we visited, Gypsy padded into the room and made a beeline to the only non-cat person in the group, that being Lexi, and rubbed up against her leg. "What's with this cat? Do I smell like tuna or something?" She bent over and scratched behind Gypsy's ears. "There. Does that do it for you?"

"Merrrow"

"Good. Now leave me alone."

I was happy for this distraction. After watching Molly and Stan's marital bliss, regret had gripped me. Putting off our wedding was the right thing to do, I knew that, but my resolve weakened by the minute. Judging by the expression in Ty's face, he struggled with the same feelings.

Lexi had Stan refresh her drink, then she returned to the sectional sofa and stretched out. This obviously appeared to be an invitation because Gypsy bounded onto her lap and started kneading Lex's stomach. "Good heavens, cat. What are you trying to tell me?"

Momma patted her lap and spoke in a child-soothing voice. "Come here, baby, I'll love on you."

Gypsy pivoted her head toward my mother, blinked, and then went back to kneading and purring like a motorboat. Lexi looked to the ceiling then back to the black feline. "You are a pest. You know that, cat?" I noticed she didn't push her off.

Molly Kate settled across from us on the love seat. "Okay, Ty, tell us your exciting news."

He looked at me as if to say, *which news do we tell them first?*

I spoke up. "Well, to begin with, you will never know who he will be working for and alongside."

Lexi held a mozzarella and prosciutto stuffed mushroom to her mouth. "Who?"

Ty picked up on my direction for the conversation. "None other than *the Cadence Terry.*"

Lexi's eyebrows shot to her hairline. "Shut up. Really?."

"Yep. And she's really a nice gal." Ty did not mention the fact she was as gorgeous in person as in film.

"You actually met her?" Molly Kate leaned forward. "In person?"

"We had supper with her." Which was the reason for me falling off the *accept yourself* wagon and into the arms of a doctor wielding a needle full of Botox. But of course I wasn't about to admit that little bit of information. "And besides being stunning, I have to say she has a beautiful spirit."

"So what will you be doing?" Stan didn't seem the least bit impressed. He only had eyes for Molly Kate. Lucky gal.

Ty shared all of what we had been told at the supper meeting, and then came the question we both dreaded.

Momma picked up Kricket and ran her hand along the pup's back. "When do you leave, and how long will you be gone?"

Ty shot a desperate plea my way. I nodded and breathed in. "He leaves May first and returns at the end of June."

Confusion registered on everyone's faces. No one spoke. You would have thought I'd just announced I was pregnant with sextuplets.

As usual, Lexi was the first to break the silence. "But you are getting married then."

"Change of plans." I glanced at Ty. "We've moved the date to August. Just a couple of months. If he turned this down, we both would always wonder what might have been. This can only enhance our plans."

"This change is Avalee's idea. I just want to make that clear." Taking my hand, Ty kissed my fingers. "I was ready to refuse."

"You would have been a fool." The no-nonsense side of Molly Kate materialized. "The time will pass like nobody's business."

"Yeah," Lexi pushed Gypsy to the floor. "Like you would know, *Miss married in ten seconds.*"

Molly threw a wadded up napkin at her. "Oh, hush up."

Stan stood. "Well, I think congratulations are in order." He held up his Scotch glass. "To Tyler Jackson, a man who has met his destiny. May his success exceed his wildest dreams."

We all raised our glasses and cheered, "To Ty." This helped strengthen my resolve. Everything had fallen into place, as it should. The thought of sacrificing my desires for his good was the balm my heart needed. Tyler Jackson deserved this opportunity and more. Stan's toast became my prayer: *May Ty's success exceed his wildest dreams.*

Chapter Seventeen

Ignoring that still, small, voice may one day lead to silence.

~*Avalee Preston*

Spring burst upon our little town making me even more excited about our first Moonlight Market. The sweet scent of lilacs and the herbal fragrance of fresh mown grass perfumed the balmy breeze, delighting my senses. The warm weather had brought a boom of tourists with it. Molly Kate and Stan's B&B stayed filled.

Momma's acreage had undergone quite a renovation. The parking lot took up a large corner of the property and was an eyesore to my way of thinking. Right away I went to work to rectify this problem by lining it with landscape rocks and half-whisky barrels filled with red and white geraniums. Darned rocks cost enough. But the effect was worth it. A flagstone path led to the close-cropped lawn. White event tents dotted the landscape where vendors arranged their offerings of art, and crafts. The large food tent had chairs set up inside for the cooking demos. Another large tent had tables set up for the children to learn and create a variety of crafts. We also splurged and bought several different types of inflatable bounce houses and slides for the kids. My tent was not as large as the demo tents, but it was a good size. I had a split-rail fence built around the plot of land in front of it where I could have outdoor seating while demonstrating flower arranging and teaching landscaping tips. Inside my tent were unique and unusual plants for sale. This month I highlighted olive trees, coffee plants grown in decorative pots, and black pepper plants.

Mayor Campbell, arrived early with Lexi to dedicate this new tourist venture. Those two were together a lot lately. When I asked her about their relationship, she just shrugged and said it was simply business. His push for publicity and her working at the paper just kept throwing them together. According to her, she and Nate were still a hot item. I didn't doubt that for a minute.

Promptly at eight o'clock the market opened. The citizens of Moonlight, tourists, local television and newspaper reporters, all crowded the reception area where a ribbon roped off the entrance. As the mayor spoke briefly and praised Moonlight's newest attraction, Ty shot photos. When the mayor and Momma cut the ribbon, Ty took several so Momma could choose the one she wanted to go into the paper.

The crowd surged onto the grounds and a bluegrass band began to play. The scenario in front of me gave an incredible sense of reward. People enjoyed the festive spirit enlivened by the music and delicious aromas of savory and sweet. Laughing children ran about in the lush grass. Vendors proudly showed their art. Fantastic. When I noticed people crowding in my tent, I tore myself from the festive scene and went to work. What a wonderful day.

****

Around ten, Momma ambled toward me. She seemed to stagger a bit.

"Baby, I'm feeling sorta cotton-headed. I think I'll go lie down a bit."

Immediately concerned, I took her hand. "Are you sick? Do you need me to go with you?"

"No, sugar. I'm fine. I'll come back after a little nap."

"I'm coming with you."

"I vow, Avalee, your hovering will wear a body out." She dismissively flipped her hand. "I said I'm fine."

Against my better judgment, I relented. "All right then. But I'm checking on you in a couple of hours."

She nodded and turned to walk home, but stopped and said, "Oh, I almost forgot. Molly Kate is going to do my cooking demonstration on how to properly fry green tomatoes. The Yankees in the group will really like that. I picked several bushels this morning in the green house, which is probably what is wrong with me. I've been up since four-thirty. Anyway, there are plenty for you to sell."

Three hours later, Momma still hadn't returned. I tried to call, but she didn't pick up. Was she still asleep? Worry worked its way back inside my head. The Preston Gardens tent was full of customers, and I hated to leave. I noticed Felix across the way showing a fellow the diagram of our hydroponic system. Waving, I caught his attention. He broke into his killer smile, his golden tooth gleaming in the spring sunshine.

Felix patted the gentleman on the shoulder and pointed at me before strolling over. "Mighty fine event, Avalee. You did yourself proud."

"Thank you, Felix. Listen, would you watch the tent for me? I want to check on Momma."

"No need. I'll go check. You stay here, and I'll be back directly."

What an angel God had sent to us in Felix. "Thanks. And tell her not to worry. To stay there and rest. We are fine here."

"Will do." He trotted to his truck and drove away. Ten minutes later a text came through.

—Come quick! 911!!—

"Oh God." Panic seized me. I flagged down Lexi. "Take over here would you?"

"Lord, girl, what's wrong?"

I sprinted to my car yelling over my shoulder. "It's Momma."

When I got to the house, the ambulance was already there. She lay unconscious on the gurney. I squeaked out, "What happened?"

An EMT answered, "We don't know for sure, but it appears to be a stroke. We won't know until we get her to the hospital."

"A stroke? Oh God." Once again, I wasn't there when she needed me. The ambulance sped off with the sirens and lights going full tilt.

Felix walked over, his cheeks wet and eyes red. I fell into his arms crying. He held me and patted my back. "I'll drive you to the hospital." I nodded and let him lead me to the truck. The cab smelled of fuel and cigarette smoke with a hint of Juicy Fruit gum. Probably to hide the fact from my mother he'd been smoking. Of course we all knew he smoked by the lingering odor on his clothes. The gears groaned when he shifted into first. The truck lurched, throwing me forward, causing the seatbelt to press against my chest. I grabbed it and held it away from my body. We both stared out the windshield while Felix ground through all the gears.

When we were finally speeding down the road I asked, "What happened?"

Tears dripped off his chin. "Well, I knocked on the door, but Miss Cladie didn't answer. I tried the knob, but it was locked. So I found me a wooden bucket and put it under the kitchen window to see if I could jimmy it open. And that's when I saw her. Sprawled on the floor."

"On the floor?" I pushed my face in my hands. "Oh God help her"

He sleeved his eyes with a shaky arm. "I thought she'd passed. I threw that wooden bucket through the glass on the kitchen door and let myself in. I checked her pulse and found she was still alive, thank the good Lord. Then I called 911 and texted you." He sniffed. "I can't tell you how relieved I was to find a pulse."

Ty. I needed to tell him. I punched in a message and sent it. The truck jerked to a stop in front of the ER. "You get out, Avalee. I'll park the truck."

"Thanks, Felix." I jumped out, ran through the doors to the triage, and breathlessly asked to see my mother. The sympathetic nurse shook her head. "You can't go in, honey. The doctor is with her now. I'll get you as soon as he is finished."

Before I could protest, she walked behind the doors separating me from my mother. An eerie chill worked its way through my body. Would today be the last time I would see her alive?

****

The hum of florescent lighting vibrated in my ears while I paced back and forth on polished white tiles. Felix sat slumped in a chrome-and-black vinyl chair. Every phone ring or bell chime jolted us to attention, only to be disappointed. How long had we been there? I glanced at the wall clock. Only fifteen minutes? It seemed like hours.

The automatic doors to the ER waiting room slid open and Ty ran to me and took me in his arms. "Is she all right?"

I shook my head. "I don't know."

Soon Molly Kate and Lexi were in the room. They huddled around me like we had Stan just four short months earlier in this very room when we thought Molly Kate had suffered a heart attack. Ty walked over to Felix and sat beside him, consoling our dear old friend. I appreciated Ty's sensitivity. Felix loved my mother as deeply as he would a sister, and she loved him just as much.

MK pulled a tissue from her purse and handed it to me. "Honey, what happened?"

I blew my nose. "It looks like she had a stroke."

Lexi covered her mouth. "Oh Lord. No."

"Felix can tell you more than I can." I looked over at him to see him rocking back and forth weeping while talking with Ty. "Oh, honey." I strode over and knelt beside him.

"Law, what will I do without my Miss Cladie?" He stared at me through red-rimmed eyes. "What will I do? She's the best friend I've ever had. She and your daddy."

I took his hand. "Let's pray we won't have to cross that bridge. Let's hope and pray."

Lexi and Molly Kate scooted chairs close to Felix and began fussing over him, cooing, and patting. When he regained his composure, he retold how he'd found Mom. I returned to pacing. Finally, the large doors to the ER opened and Dr. Derrick walked out. I froze and studied his face for clues.

"Avalee." He regarded me over his glasses. I didn't like the tone of his voice. My insides quaked so hard it felt as if my ribs might break. The good doctor must have read my face. He put his hand out and rested it on my arm. "She's resting comfortably. But we need to talk."

Ty came to stand beside me and circled his arm around my waist. "May I come, too?"

"I'd like him to if that's okay, Doctor."

"That's fine. Follow me."

I glanced back at Felix and the girls. "I'll be back as soon as I can with news."

Felix nodded. Lexi hugged him. "We'll take care of Felix. Don't you worry now."

Grateful, I bobbed my head and turned to follow the doctor. He found an empty room and motioned for us to sit, then leaned against an examination table.

"We dodged a bullet this time." He crossed his arms over his chest. "She's going to be fine. I don't think she will have any pronounced side effects, just some weakening on her left side. But with therapy, she should regain her strength and control."

I slumped in the chair and let my head fall back. "Thank you, Lord."

"Don't get me wrong. We are still on tenterhooks here. Cladie's blood pressure and diabetes are a lethal combination. Both damage the blood vessel walls. She is overweight and she eats what she wants. Even though she shoots herself with insulin every time she has a piece of pie, her blood sugar levels are all over the place. This could happen again, and we might not be so lucky next time."

"I tried to reason with her about that, and she told me she knew her body and could tell when her sugar was high."

Doctor Derrick shook his head. "That woman. By the time she feels it, the damage is done. She is going to have to be on a regular schedule with her testing and her meds, and stay on a low carbohydrate diet. She needs to exercise regularly, too. I know she works hard in her garden, but that isn't consistent enough to raise her heart rate."

I ran my hands through my hair and blew out. "How will I ever get her to do that? She keeps promising me she will do better, but I can't be sure she does."

"Do you remember when you asked me in my office what it would take to get her to see the light?"

"Yes."

He stood straight and rested his hands in his jacket pockets. "I started to say a stroke or heart attack, but thought better of it at the time. Today I think the message came through loud and clear."

"I hope so, Doctor."

Ty took my hand. "Doc, when can she go home?"

The doctor scrubbed his chin with his thumb and thought. "I'd like to keep her here a couple of days and watch her. Run more tests. Then I want to send her to rehabilitation for a couple of weeks. At that time, we can gauge how she is going to get along."

"Whatever you say, Doctor. Thank you." I stood. "May I see her?"

"Yes. She is in a room now."

Ty pushed up from the chair. "I'll update the others."

"Thanks, hon. And tell them to run on home. I'd like to be alone with Momma for a while."

"Sure thing." Ty stuck out his hand to Doctor Derrick. "Thanks, Doc."

"You are welcome." He turned to me. "Let's go see your mother."

****

Momma turned her head toward me when I walked into her room. A soft ray from the setting sun shone between the curtains, creating a play of shadow and light along her still form under the blankets. I sat beside her and took her right hand. "How are you feeling?"

She squeezed my fingers.

"Doctor Derrick says you need to stay here a couple of days." I decided to keep the rehabilitation part to myself for the time being. No need to work her up.

She closed her eyes, then opened them. I took that as an *okay.*

"We will get you through this." My eyes began to sting, and I blinked hard to keep the tears from coming. "You'll be right as rain, you hear?"

She squeezed my hand again.

"Try and get some rest. I'll be right here."

Her hand relaxed. I sat back and watched her sleep. I had plenty of time to think in the dim room. Would she have been in this shape, if I hadn't left Moonlight in the first place? I should have come home more. Anger at myself dominated my regret. I had been such a coward.

The familiar trespasser in my soul, namely guilt, weaseled its way into my consciousness. But this time, I made a resolution to banish all negative thoughts. I was home now and I would stay here and make sure my mother overcame this. I'd be to her what Scott had been to me. She'd get on that treadmill, like it or not. She'd eat better, too. No more ten-layer coconut cakes or sweet tea. I'd make sure of it. She'd be on a regular schedule with her testing and meds.

The room grew dark. Behind me, light glowed from the door when the nurse walked in to change Momma's IV. She advised me to go home and get some rest. At first, I felt reluctant, but the nurse assured me Momma would sleep all night, so I decided to go. Leaning over, I kissed her cheek. "I love you, Momma."

I slipped out the door into the blinding hallway light. It took me a bit to focus as I walked toward the elevators. When I passed the waiting room, I noticed Felix in a chair. He shot to his feet when I approached him.

"How is Miss Cladie?"

"Sleeping." I gathered him in a hug. Poor old fellow, he had suffered so today. "She is comfortable. You can go home now."

"Would you mind terribly if I sat with her a spell?"

"Not at all. I'll tell the nurse."

"Thank ya, I'm obliged."

We found a nurse and explained his relationship with our family and how he had my permission to sit with my mother. The nurse looked at him skeptically. This flew all over me. I had hoped we were finally over this racial thing, for heaven's sake. I took Felix's hand. "He is like a second father to me, in fact, he is giving me away at my wedding."

Felix raised his eyebrows and looked at me while squeezing my fingers.

"All right." She glared up at him. "But be quiet. She needs her rest."

"Yes'm, no tap dancing, I understand."

The nurse frowned, shook her head, and walked down the hall. I gazed up at Felix's dear face framed with tight gray curls and into his kind eyes. "I'm so sorry."

"Honey, I'm at an age where I finally realize ignorance in others is not my problem. I don't let it upset me." He touched my nose and winked. "You need to learn that lesson now. You'll be a lot more peace-like when you get old like me, 'sides, we have a lot to be happy about don't we? Miss Cladie pulled through." He hugged me. "Now you go on and get some rest. I'll be here watching over your momma." He pulled a book from his jacket. "I read most nights anyways. Might as well read here as at home."

"I love you, Felix. Thanks for saving Momma."

"Love you, too, sugar. Miss Cladie and your daddy have saved me many a time. Run on now."

When I arrived home, I walked through the front door. The house felt so empty. So quiet. The kitchen was a mess. I needed a good distraction and cleaning up was just the ticket. A canister lay on the floor. Momma must have been getting something from it when she had her seizure. I picked it up and a funny feeling came over me. *What was in there?* I unscrewed the top and peeked in. *Miniature chocolate bars?* What else was she hiding? On an impulse I dug through the trash can. Stuffed under all the other trash were snack-cake wrappers. A lot of them. *Really, Momma?* Had she eaten these since she promised me she wouldn't? She had to have. The trash pickup was two days ago.

I stomped upstairs to her room and searched every inch. In the last place I looked—the bottom drawer of her nightstand—was a bag full of peanut butter cups. *For crying out loud.*

Yep, I was going to be on that woman like hair on soap. There was no way on God's green earth I would ever leave her now.

Chapter Eighteen

O. Henry's, The Gift of the Magi, keeps calling to me.

~Avalee Preston

Spring is said to be the season of new life, or resurrection, of new hopes. And it is. Watching my mother struggle to walk, talk, and gain control over her emotions was hard, but with each baby step our hope grew. Doctor Derrick's prediction came true. Momma was finally a believer in taking care of her health. She made great strides during her two months in therapy. She was one of the lucky ones, and she knew it.

But this year, spring also represented dashed hopes and death of long awaited dreams. Every time Ty and I were together, it took all my emotional strength to keep from telling him I'd changed my mind. I kept reminding myself how my decision was for love. It was for Ty's best. With those thoughts, I focused on Ty, our new wedding plans, and the Moonlight Market. Scott made arrangements to fly to Moonlight even though there wasn't going to be a wedding. He said his reason was to work with Momma on their book, but I knew he wanted to be there for me because his flight arrived the day Ty left. I knew he wanted to see me through those first weeks of Ty being gone. Bless him.

On a brighter note, my relationship with Skye had

grown closer. We had several deep discussions over O. Henry's *The Gift of the Magi*. The more wine we drank, the more our discussions went deeper, like how incredible it was for a short story written in a tavern to have such a strong and enduring effect on culture. This was a springboard to talking about other ways to influence our culture. Afterward, Skye called to say she got a perfect mark on her paper, and that her professor asked permission to use it in future classes as an example. Wow. I received major stepmother points for my help. However, Skye wasn't the only one to benefit from our conversations. I did, too, because they reinforced my decision to put off my wedding for Ty.

My cell phone interrupted my musings. Ty's face appeared on my screen. "Hi babe. I was just thinking about you."

"Lady, I'm always thinking about you."

"Yeah, more like your big adventure with luscious Cadence."

"Oh, stop it. You know you are the only one for me. Cadence is strictly for the camera."

I believed him, as crazy as it seemed. Ty was different. "What's up, babe?"

"Well, since I leave tomorrow, I thought it might be nice to invite the kids and—now, I know this is asking a lot—but also my parents to join us for supper at the country club."

Ugh. "Anything for you, hon. Even your parents."

My respect for them had sunk to new lows. When Ty returned from New York, he'd gone to them and told his wonderful news thinking they'd finally understand and support him. But when he told them about the New Yorker, his father simply said he'd never read that magazine. When he told them about Africa, his mother worried about parasites, and his father only wanted to know about Cadence. Neither grasped the magnitude of Ty's talent and where it had taken him.

"Thanks, hon. I know it probably won't be pleasant for either of us, but you never know. Life doesn't promise us a tomorrow, and I'd like to leave them on a positive note. I'll make a *rezzi* as Taige says."

Ty's reference to Taige's rezzie bothered me a bit. Would this venture change him? *Get a grip, Avalee.* I'd never make it to August sane if I started worrying over such small things now.

"Sounds good, hon. Just let me know when."

"I'm pretty sure this will be an ordeal for both of us, so when we are finished how about wine at my place and a proper send off?"

His reference to "send off" sent me sinking into myself. I swallowed to strengthen my voice. "Absolutely, babe. Bye now."

"Bye. Love you, too."

When the line went dead, I held my phone to my chest and stared off at nothing.

****

When Avalee said, "I love you," it took all of Ty's mental will to hang up the phone. He knew he should be soaring because of this opportunity, beyond thrilled for the recognition, but he wasn't, and all this pretending wore him out. He was grateful and cognizant of the honor and he couldn't—he wouldn't—let her down. She'd worked a miracle for him and he'd make her proud. He knew it sounded crazy; it would have to him, too, had this happened this time last year, but he wanted nothing more than Avalee. If only she'd go with him, or if only they could marry before he left, then he'd be delirious with joy about it all. Even so, for now he had to focus on the positive side of things. He and Avalee would marry in August. His parents just might find it in their hearts to respect him. And there would be more money and opportunity to travel with the love of his life. Buoyed by that thought, he made the reservations, called the kids, and then his parents.

When he hung up the phone, he checked and rechecked his tickets, bags, and equipment. Everything was ready. Done. Now all he had to do was wait. He hated waiting. All his life he had waited. Waited for opportunity. Waited for his parents' respect. Waited for love. He wandered to the bookshelf and stared at Avalee's photo. With care, he lifted the silver frame and carried it to the couch where he flopped down. Yes, above everything else, she was all he truly wanted. The only part of his life he could not live without. When he returned from Africa, he didn't care what she said; he would never leave her again.

Chapter Nineteen

I hear you O. Henry. It is time to cut my hair.
                                        ~Avalee Preston

Ty and I arrived early to the country club in order to fortify ourselves before the others showed up. The *maître d'* showed us to a table overlooking Moonlight Lake. I leaned into Ty. "You got us one of the most romantic tables in the club."

"Yeah." He drew me in close. "Too bad we are wasting it on family."

"Well, at least we have time to enjoy it, just the two of us, for a while."

The waiter cleared his throat, reminding us we were not alone. We stepped apart and allowed him to seat us. "Could I interest you in anything to drink while you wait for the rest of your party?"

"I'll have a double Gray Goose vodka martini, dry."

Ty cocked his eyebrow and smiled. "You go, girl." He said to the waiter, "Double bourbon, Four Roses, on the rocks."

After the waiter left, Ty scooted his chair close to mine. We watched the glimmering moonlight reflecting off the rippling waters. When I was with Ty, I was home. Our waiter returned with our drinks, bowed, then left. Ty lifted his glass and stared deep into my eyes.

"To August, to us, forever."

"And ever." I tapped my glass against his then softly kissed his amazing lips. He leaned in for more, but I quickly took a sip of my drink. The cold vodka warmed my throat. "Not here, not now. Later."

"I'll take that as a promise." He put his arm around my shoulder and we enjoyed each other's presence while sipping our drinks and watching the soothing undulation of the lake's surface.

"Wow, what a great spot." Skye's voice startled us. I suppose we were so lost in our own private thoughts, we had forgotten the evening's plans. "Good job, Dad."

Ty pinched his nose and then stood. "Hi, baby." He pulled her chair out for her on his other side. "Glad you came." Ty looked around. "Where's Glen?"

"He's with the grandparents. We met them on the way in."

And so it begins. I finished off my martini. From across the room, Emma's voice assailed every diner's ears with complaints about her table being clear across the restaurant. Glen took the seat next to mine, creating a buffer between his grandmother and me for which I was truly grateful. The waiter returned for their drink orders. Glen ordered his usual, beer, Skye, white wine, Marcus, scotch on the rocks, and Emma, decaf coffee. Ty and I waggled our glasses at the waiter. It was going to be a long supper. We might as well be anesthetized.

Thank goodness for Skye's enthusiasm. She carried the conversation with questions about Ty's job. "Have you thought of a theme for your photographs about clean water? Where all will you travel?"

Before Ty could answer, his mother broke in. "Tyler, this will be the first time you've not been home for Mother's Day. Did you even consider this when you agreed to this little escapade of yours?"

Escapade? Little? I took another gulp.

To his credit, Ty held it together. "I'll send you a card if I can, Mother." He frowned into his glass before taking a slug of his drink.

Glen looked from his father to his grandmother and then back to his father. He tried to steer the conversation in another direction. "Dad, tell us about Cadence Terry." He punched Ty's arm. "Major dad bonus points if I get to meet her."

"She's nice. Not shallow like we expect in a women like her. She has a deep compassion for the poor. And yes, I'll make sure and earn those bonus points."

"Now there's a woman worth pursuing, son." Marcus straightened. "Can you imagine being married to her?"

What? What did he just say? I sat stunned. Those words swarmed inside my chest like stinging bees. All I could do was stare at him. Skye put her hand to her mouth and gaped at him.

"Dad?" Ty was just as stunned. "I can't believe you just said that."

Glen was equally appalled. "Grandfather? Seriously?" He shook his head. "Not cool."

Of course this pleased Emma. The witch.

Marcus lifted his palms. "I don't mean anything by it, but you have to admit, she will be quite a catch for someone." He gave me a decisive nod. "No offense to you Avalee."

I wanted to say, "None taken," but I couldn't. That son of a basset hound meant every word he had said. I needed a moment. I stood and said, "Excuse me, but I need to call my mother and check on her."

Ty jumped up so fast he knocked his chair to the floor. "Wait up, baby." He threw his napkin on the table and shot a look at his parents. "We're leaving."

Marcus pursed his lips. "Now, son…."

The waiter strode over. "Sir, is everything all right?"

"Miss Preston and I have to leave. Take their orders and put it on my bill. Be sure and give yourself a twenty-five percent tip."

Emma put her hand to her breast. "Twenty-five percent?"

Ty shook his head while picking up his chair. His voice softened when he spoke to his children. "Sorry, guys, but I'm sure you realize we have to leave. I can't put Avalee through an evening of barbs. Call me when you get home."

"I'm not very hungry." Skye stood. "I think I'll go to your house, Dad."

"Me neither." Glen joined her. "Mind if I come along?"

Ty glanced at me, and I nodded. "Sure." He slid his hand in his pocket, took out his keys, and pulled off the one that went to his house. "I'll be back later."

"Well, I nevah." Emma poked her husband. "Marcus, do something."

"Oh, for god's sake, Tyler." His father rose from his chair. "Stop making a scene."

Without looking back, Ty put his arm around me and said, "Come on, let's go."

When we got into the car, Ty turned to me. "Hungry?"

"I may be when my nerves calm down."

"I have an idea." He pulled onto the road and drove to the Thai Grill. "Wait right here."

"Okay?" While he was gone, I checked on Mom. Soon he returned to the car with a large bag. "What'cha got there?"

"You'll see." He got in and pulled back on the road.

"Did you get enough for the kids?"

"Not going home. And don't even bother to ask where we are going."

When he turned into the Moonlight Park entrance, I knew exactly where we were going—the swinging bridge. The path and the bridge were luminous under the moon's glow. Ty was careful to keep the bridge from swinging while I inched my way to the middle. Below us, the creek's hymn bubbled in exhilaration. I dared not look down. Maybe when I sat, I'd be brave enough and try to see the glints of light the water carried along its path..

Ty lowered himself beside me and leaned against the tight roping along the sides of the bridge, while I set out our small white boxes of food and bottled water. After we finished eating he pulled me against his chest and kissed my forehead, then my nose, then my lips. "Sometimes things work out for the best. This seemed to me to be the perfect place to spend our last night together for a while."

"It is. I love you for thinking of it." It was perfect. The bridge, the food, the velvety dark of the night, the music of the water below us, and the warmth of Ty's body so close to mine, made what started out as one of the worst nights to actually become one of the best nights I'd enjoyed in a long time. Nothing his parents had said bothered me any longer. I ran my fingers through his hair and pulled his face to mine. One kiss led to many. His hands explored my body as eagerly as mine did his. We were almost there, to the point of no return. I pulled back, pushed my hair from my face, and took a shuddering breath.

Ty reached for me. "Baby, I know we had an agreement…." He blew out a breath. "I mean, we are engaged after all. We *will* marry."

I felt his frustration. Most people would say we were being silly and unrealistic this day and age, to wait till we were married to make love. But I wanted to wait, and up till now so did he.

"I know. But even as romantic as it might sound, making love on this bridge isn't as intimate as I would like it to be for our first time."

"And the kids are at the house." He glanced up at the winking stars. "Seems we had a little help keeping our resolution."

He stood and pulled me to my feet. "So we will wait." He pressed his body hard against mine and covered my mouth with his. "But can we marry in July?"

When he pulled onto Mom's driveway, we both stared at the house. Neither of us wanted to leave the other. He took my hand and kissed each fingertip. "My plane leaves at five in the morning. I have to be in Memphis at three. I only have time to go home, grab my things and leave. So I guess this is goodbye until I come back home."

"But, you are exhausted. You can't drive until you've had some rest. Let me go with you to keep you awake."

"I'll be fine. All I have to do is think about that swinging bridge." He lowered his head and stared up at me. "I'll probably get a speeding ticket."

I studied his face, burning his image in my mind. "I love you. Be safe and come home to me."

"Nothing will keep me from you, Avalee. I promise."

Our parting kiss was soft, longing, and wistful. I climbed out of the truck and watched his taillights all the way down Washington Avenue. When I could no longer see them, I crumbled onto the driveway and wept.

****

May, and June flew by much to my surprise. With Ty gone, I thought the time would drag. But the Market, rehabilitating Mom, and spending time with Ty's children filled my days. Skye and Glen were frequent overnight visitors at our home, and Momma reveled in her soon-to-be grandchildren. Glen often helped Felix and AJ. Skye asked Mom to teach her to cook. This did wonders for my mother. I'd never made that request and now I regretted it. The only dish I could fix was macaroni and cheese from a box. Even Scott got in on the cooking lessons. All was good.

Ty texted and emailed when he could, but it wasn't often. His messages about what he'd seen were deeply felt and at times heart-wrenching. He wrote about the wretched conditions he witnessed in the villages and the villagers' ecstatic reactions when they saw the clean water, and how they broke out in joyous dancing, just as Cadence had described to us in New York. I was sure of one thing; Tyler Jackson would never be the same.

Who could after seeing such poverty?

As the weeks passed, he wrote about how well he and Cadence worked together. In the evenings, they brainstormed ideas about the story they wanted to tell. The next day, he'd figure out how to tell that story with his camera. I was so proud of my man. He was realizing his dream.

The day after he left, I started revamping our wedding plans. We decided on the first Saturday in August. I scratched through the original plans in my notebook including the idea of an outdoor wedding. Between the heat, humidity, and mosquitoes, I couldn't think of anything more miserable. Molly Kate penciled us in to marry at the mansion. I changed the date with the caterers, musicians, and changed my flower orders.

One morning, I took the girls on a road trip. Lexi, Molly Kate, and I went wedding dress shopping in Jackson. It was a real hoot. The sales women kept trying to guide me to the mother of the bride dresses before I explained, "No, I'm the bride, and I want a bride's dress."

Young brides with their mothers in the shops tried to conceal their curiosity about the old woman in white while Lexi and Molly Kate oohed and aahed their delight. But I didn't care. Let them stare. It was finally my turn, unlike the first gown I purchased when Marc and I were supposed to marry, I planned on wearing *this* wedding gown. We decided on an antique white one-shouldered silk charmeuse dress. The fabric at the bodice gathered into tiny folds. At the waist, larger folds made my waist look tiny. The low cut back added elegance, reminiscent of old Hollywood. In fact, Molly Kate told me I looked like Veronica Lake. The sparkly beads encrusting the shoulder strap gave me just enough bling. I decided against a veil. David would do something fabulous with my hair, so I really didn't need one.

When we returned, I hung it on the outside of my closet door as a reminder that soon I would be Mrs. Tyler Jackson. Perhaps it also served as a visual to ward off any fears of the marriage never taking place. After all, I'd been this close before.

With all the wedding plans revamped and my dress purchased, all I had to do was wait. I had plenty of things to keep me busy, which helped pass the time. Like today for instance, I was exhausted after helping Momma pick butterbeans, shelling them, and putting them up in the freezer, which is quite a process. First, you have to blanch them, which isn't any fun in a hot kitchen. Then, you have to plunge them in ice water, dry them off, and pack them in freezer bags.

At dusk, the evening beckoned me to enjoy a glass of wine and listen to the summer's night song being sung outside my window. Momma, who had been up since four-thirty, went to bed. Now that she was healthy again, I had a hard time keeping up with her. Scott turned in early as well.

I poured my wine and went to the porch swing. The air, perfumed by magnolia blooms, felt soft on my skin. Moving the swing back and forth with my toe, I laid my head back and listened to the cacophony of tree frogs, crickets, and katydids. Occasionally, a mocking bird or an owl would join the fray. The stars glittered in the inky heavens. Was Ty somewhere looking at the same stars? I checked my watch. Ten o'clock. It would be five o'clock for him. He was probably asleep in a tent or some run-down hotel. As if he had read my mind, a text from him pinged on my phone. I smiled as I lifted the wine glass against my lips and drank. But as I read, my smile faded.

—Hey baby. Hope you are still awake. I've struggled all night about writing you because I know what I have to say will upset you. So, I'll get right to the point. It looks like I won't be home until mid-September. Things are going so great here. Cadence has been sending my pictures to different magazines and newspapers and they all want more. When I get to a place with a signal strong enough to check my email, my inbox is filled with requests and job offers. The documentary hasn't even been aired yet, but the buzz is so strong companies are already investing in the cause. The response is astounding. Cadence and I spoke last night, and we both feel to stop now would be premature.

I agreed to stay on because I knew you would encourage me to do so. But even knowing you would understand doesn't make this any easier. So, how do you feel about a fall wedding? That is your favorite time of year, and we could make it a true fall festival celebration. I will make you this promise. When I come home, I will never leave again without you.

I'm so happy Momma Cladie is back to her old self, no, her better self. Tell Scott hello for me and to take care of my lady. I love you with all my heart. You are my first thought in the morning and my last at night.

All my love,

Ty—

My head hummed while I stared at my phone. His words blurred. I wiped my cheeks with my fingers.

Silly of me, I know. He was absolutely right in assuming I'd understand and agree. I did understand, and I did agree. Still, the disappointment was crushing. The night no longer held me in its magic. I turned up my wine glass then went to my room. My notebook of wedding plans lay on my dresser. All my May plans had been scratched out and updated to August plans. I made a note to email Jema—again—and then scratched through my plans—again.

****

August arrived in Moonlight with a vengeance. We had been spoiled by a mild summer. Combine the heat with the humidity and you have yourself a Dutch oven. Bees labored in flight from blossom to blossom as if they carried heavy loads on their backs. Flies moved in slow motion. Everyone, everything, wore the soggy blanket of mugginess.

The back door slammed and Momma strolled into the family room. "Mercy, but its hot out there." She mopped her face with the kitchen towel that never left her shoulder all summer.

"Sugar, cut on that fan over yonder for me?"

"Sure." I flipped the switch on the old black rotary fan. "What are you doing outside anyway?"

"Watering the garden." She walked over to the fan and stood in front of it while holding her blouse away from her body.

"Well, why didn't you water early like you usually do?"

"I've been cooking all morning. Scott said he'd be here around five."

Scott had made a quick trip to New York City to meet with the publisher. He'd only been gone three weeks but it seemed like months. I'd gotten used to his being around.

"I can't wait." Scott was exactly what I needed right now. He knew just what to say and do to make me feel better. It had gotten lonely around here lately. Lexi was always working with Sid. He'd appointed her the goodwill ambassador for Moonlight's tourist industry. When she wasn't visiting nearby states, she was meeting with Nathan somewhere. Frankly, I didn't know how she kept her job at the paper. Suffice it to say I rarely saw her. Molly Kate and Stan were still star-struck lovers and uber busy with the B & B. Jema, of course, was in Italy. My, what a difference a year makes. This time last year, we were all up in each other's business. Now we barely wave at each other on Facebook. Even Skye's visits had slacked off since her relationship with her football hero boyfriend, Duff, had grown more serious.

"Avalee, honey? You okay?" Momma's upturned face darkened with concern.

"I'm fine. Just thinking."

"How about some tea? The heat has us all panting like a fish stranded on dirt."

"That would hit the spot. It isn't sweet tea, is it?"

"No, I'm using that stevia stuff." She made a face. "I'm trying real hard to get used to it."

I followed her to the kitchen and true to her word, she had been cooking all morning. Every eye on the stove had a pot or pan on it. Both ovens were on. By now, I didn't even bother to ask if anyone else was coming. She cooked the same for one person as she did for ten. She handed me a sweating glass of ice-cold tea.

"Thanks." I rubbed the glass across my forehead

and took a deep swallow.

"Go look on the sideboard in the dining room. I wanted Scott to sample them and see if he could use any of them for the book."

"Okay." I pushed through the swinging door and gasped. Cakes and pies lined the sideboard's surface. When had she made all of this? Had she tasted them while she made them? I went into immediate worry mode and strode back into the kitchen trying hard to fix my face with a nonjudgmental expression.

"Wow, Mom. What time did you make all of those?"

"I got up around four. That's why I didn't get to the watering."

Trying to appear as nonchalant as possible, I stared at my nails. "Did you taste any of them?"

"Absolutely and they are delicious." She put her hands on the counter and sighed. "You know, it sure is hard to eat all that diabetic food and the foods I love, too. Why, I'm as full as a tick all day."

I jerked my head up so fast it popped my neck. "Momma?"

A sly grin pushed up one corner of her mouth. "Don't get your panties in a twist. I'm just kidding."

"Not funny." I had to admit, she got me with that one.

"I've cooked these recipes for so long, I don't have to taste." Sighing she conceded, "But it is hard. Having diabetes makes me feel about as lucky as a housefly in a white room filled with swatters."

"You are lucky, Momma. You are alive."

"That I am, sugar baby. That I am. And I'm grateful. Now skedaddle on out of here." She walked to a sink full of dishes and started rinsing them.

Yes, she was a fortunate woman to have survived her health crisis and I was blessed to still have her.

****

As far as I was concerned, Scott couldn't arrive fast enough. I waited on the front porch swing and watched the road like my mother had when I arrived home last summer. He finally pulled onto the driveway and I sprang up and ran to him. "Oh, Scott. I've missed you."

"Hi, Sweetie. I've missed you, too." He wrapped his arms around me and squeezed.

The screen door to the kitchen slammed and Momma strutted toward the car with her arms out. "Sugar, I thought you'd never get here."

"Hey, Momma C." I stepped back and surrendered Scott to my mom. He picked her up in a big hug and then set her down. "You look fantastic now. You look like you have lost more weight since the three weeks I've been gone?"

"Oh a few." She turned about. "You know? I feel like a kid again. That is until I try to get up from kneeling in my garden."

Scott turned his attention back to me with an appraising stare. "And how much weight have you lost?"

"Not sure, maybe a pound or two." Missing Ty was better than any diet plan on the market.

Momma clapped her hands. "All this weight loss talk makes me hungry. Come on y'all. Supper's ready."

Rubbing his hands together, Scott asked, "What's on the menu for tonight?"

"Fried chicken, fried green tomatoes, purple hull

peas, mashed potatoes, and white gravy. And for dessert, seven-layer butter cake with chocolate frosting."

"Oh, man. I'm ready. Let's go."

While Scott washed up in the bathroom, I helped Mom bring the food to the table. "Momma? If you eat all this, you'll go into a coma."

"Oh pssh, I have my plate already made and in the warming tray." She picked up the platter of chicken. "Now, come on. That boy is hungry."

As usual, Momma swooned watching Scott eat. People enjoying her food was definitely her love language. She seemed to enjoy her baked chicken, steamed broccoli, and sautéed okra. All good food, but by her standards, I knew how hard it was for her to eat healthy and appreciated the cheery front she put up.

After we finished eating and Mom had everything clean and put away she said, "Welp, y'all enjoy your visit. It's time for me to get in my PJs and watch Wheel."

Scott kissed the top of her head. "Night."

I hugged her. "I'm proud of you."

Momma cocked her head. "Why's that?"

"I know how hard this diet is on you. That's all."

"Oh pfft. I'm learning to eat to live. Not live to eat." She patted my arm. "But thanks baby."

When she left the kitchen I took two glasses from the hutch. "Wine on the porch?"

"Sounds divine. I haven't heard quiet since the last time I visited."

We settled on the porch rockers. The fans above stirred the night air, still heavy with humidity, and gave pleasant relief. The night bugs and tree frogs were in full voice and lightning bugs glowed on and off like earthbound stars.

Scott chuckled in the darkness. "Did I say something about quiet? Nature is roaring tonight."

"But, it is a good kind of noise."

"The best." He tasted his wine and laid his head back on the cushion. "Have you heard from Ty today?" His tone made me think he had.

"Early this morning. He texted to say he loved and missed me. Have you?"

"Yes. I'm surprised he didn't say anything to you. He got some incredible news today."

I sat up and turned to Scott. "What?" My feelings were on the edge of being hurt.

"*National Geographic* wants him."

"Are you serious?"

"As a heart attack. They reached out to him and want to discuss story ideas with him. But he is reluctant. Which is crazy, but I know his reason."

"What is it?"

"You. They want him this fall. He's a stand-up guy and he loves you. So much so, he is willing to turn down the chance of a lifetime. You've got a good man there, sweetheart."

I sat back and drank my wine while disturbing decisions formulated in my head.

"Don't let him know I told you. He may have wanted to tell you."

"Don't worry, hon. You did the right thing." I stood. "More wine?"

He held up his glass. "Sure. Thanks."

My emotions melted like a puddle around my heart. It was never meant to be, Ty and me. There was a reason for me to come into his life, but it wasn't marriage. It was for him to realize his dream. As I poured the wine, the phrase came into my mind, *others may, you cannot.* Marriage was simply not intended for me. On the way back to the porch, I made my decision. Like the heroine in O. Henry's book, it was time to cut my hair.

****

All night, I tossed in my bed struggling with my decision. I would always love him, but I could not stand in his way. He needed to explore all the possibilities and if, by some chance, he still loved me in my sixties? That thought nauseated even me. It was better this way. Better for him. His parents would be deliriously happy. And he might even get with Cadence. Another nauseating thought. I didn't want to think of him in her arms. Her beautiful, firm, smooth-skinned arms. How was I going to pull this off and make him believe me?

My answer came later the next afternoon when I received an email from him about the *National Geographic* assignment.

Hey Baby,

You are never, NEVER, going to believe this. I have assignments (note the plural form of that word) with National Geographic! It is even hard for me to believe. I'm still processing this and I owe it all to you.

There is one problem. I am going to have to stay out of the country. So here are my thoughts, I'll come home for a couple days in October, we will get married, then you will come with me and we can honeymoon all over Africa and Europe. Wouldn't that be incredible? What do you say? Why yes, of course! :)

Sorry to rush, but I gotta get this sent before I lose

my signal. Love you, babe, and miss you like crazy,

Ty

P.S. Cadence says to tell you hi. She may follow us while I shoot for National Geographic so she can make new contacts for her foundation. You two might end up good friends. Can you imagine that? Having her as a best friend like the other girls? Counting the days, sweetheart.

Well, talk about being handed my 'out' on a silver platter. It was too early to leave Mom, and I certainly did not want Cadence to join us on our honeymoon. Shades of Princess Diana and Camilla.

My hands shook as I touched the keyboard and my mind rebelled, refusing to give me the words I needed to type. I closed my eyes and willed my fingers to work. I didn't want to come across as jealous or cold. I had to be loving and reasonable.

Dear Ty,

My eyes filled and again my mind shut down. I looked at the ceiling and just typed from my heart without looking at the screen.

I am so proud of you. There will be no end to your footprint on the lives of people all over the world. And because of the magnitude of this opportunity for you to share your gift with the world, we have come to an impasse. You cannot live in Moonlight, and I cannot leave my mother at this point in her life. Therefore, after much thought and tears, I am ending our engagement. I love you too much to hold you back. That said, I would be lying, my love, if I said this decision was an easy one. Truth is, this is the hardest thing I've ever done. But true love is doing what is good for the other, after all. Therefore, I must let you go.

Please do not answer this email or try to contact me. I will not be talked out of my decision. Go, my love, and change the world. And should life bring you another woman to love, do not hesitate to accept that gift.

I love you with all my heart and soul,

Avalee

Fifteen minutes after I hit send, my phone rang. It was Ty. Writing the email took all my strength. I couldn't talk to him. Not now. Not for a while. I turned my phone off. I dreaded telling Momma and my friends about this. But I'd have to and soon. For now, all I wanted was a long, hot soak in the tub.

****

Twenty minutes into my soak, a knock sounded on the bathroom door. Sweet mother of pearl, couldn't a girl have some privacy?

"I'm in the bathtub." I made sure irritation fringed my voice.

"Well, then," Scott said from the other side as he jiggled the doorknob, which was unlocked. "Close the shower curtain, because you and I are going to have a little chat."

"Oh, for heaven's sake, can't it wait?"

He walked in giving me a nanosecond to jerk the shower curtain closed. "No." He reached through the curtain and set a glass of chardonnay on the tub's edge, then sat on the toilet. This simple gesture had me blubbering in an instant.

When my emotional storm had passed he said, "Why? Because of our conversation last night? Please tell me it isn't."

After a gulp of wine, I answered. "Partially, but his

email today was all the confirmation I needed to…" I took another drink "…end it."

"Avalee, honey, you're killing him. He is frantic. I'll bet he's called everyone in Moonlight."

If Scott had stuck me in the heart with a butter knife, it couldn't have hurt any worse. I stuck my hand out. "Would you hand me my towel?"

"Here."

I stood and wrapped the towel around me before pulling the curtain back. When I stepped out of the tub, I had to admit I was thankful for the comic relief at seeing Scott on the toilet. I held my glass out. "Be a good boy and get me another. I'll be down after I dress."

To my chagrin, when I walked into the family room, there sat Lexi, Scott, Molly Kate, and Momma waiting like a jury wanting an explanation. I sure didn't want to have to face them while it was all so fresh and painful, but maybe it was best to get it over with.

Scott handed me my glass and said, "He called them all."

Of course, Lexi was the first to speak. "Have you lost your ever-loving mind?"

Molly Kate stood and crossed the room. Kneeling beside me she asked, "Honey? What happened?"

How to explain this? I had joined in with Ty's dream and it was happening. By experience, I also knew what it took to make it in this world and the fewer commitments the better. I couldn't go with him until I was absolutely positive Mom's health was strong. I took the plunge and explained my reasoning. I finished by reminding them of my strong conviction how love isn't always convenient and it often involves sacrifice for the other's good.

No one said anything until I finished. Then Lexi daubed her eyes. "That's beautiful, Avalee."

"Would y'all help me with Ty?" I looked each person in the eyes. "Help him to understand. I can't talk to him. Not now."

Scott put his hand on my shoulder.

I looked up at him. "Would you help Ty?"

"Sure, hon." He patted me and walked to a nearby chair. Mom just looked away without saying a word. I felt positive I'd get an earful from her when everyone left.

"Well, y'all," I slapped my lap and stood. "I need to write Jema and tell her. And then I'm calling Skye and Glen."

Momma sniffed and tears filled her eyes. "I love those kids. I loved having grandchildren. I know what you are doing is for Ty's good, but I'm sure going to miss those kids." She pulled her hanky from her pocket and wiped her eyes.

So that's what was bothering her. I hoped and prayed our relationship with Skye and Glen was strong enough to weather this storm. For all of our sakes.

Chapter Twenty

Love never fails. Hope never gives up.
~Tyler Jackson

Ty stared at his laptop screen for the hundredth time trying to understand exactly what had happened. He wrote with incredible news and she broke off their engagement? And now she wasn't talking to him. Here he was a half-world away. He couldn't just jump in his car and go fix it.

Cadence waited in the hotel lobby for him to go with her on a shoot, but he couldn't think. He flopped back on the bed. The pain was too much.

Someone tapped on his door. Cadence called from the other side, "Ty? Are you ready?"

He stood, wandered over, and opened it.

Cadence drew her eyebrows together. "Ty? What's wrong? You look awful."

He felt his eyes grow warm and turned away. He wanted to answer and say nothing was wrong, but he couldn't get the lie out of his mouth. He walked to the desk and sagged in the chair. The words wouldn't come. Only tears.

"Ty?" She strode across the room. "What happened?"

He handed her his tablet. She silently read and then tossed it on the bed. Kneeling down beside him, she said, "Oh honey, I'm so sorry."

"Can you make sense of," he flung his hand toward Avalee's email, "of that?"

"I think so." Her voice barely above a whisper. "Yes, I think I can."

He wiped his face with his palms. "Then explain it to me."

"She is getting out of your way." She stared up at him. "And I think it is beautiful."

"Beautiful?" He shook his head. "Then why do I feel like I've been whacked by a baseball bat?"

"Because you thought you could have both. But you can't. I know." She rose and stepped to the bathroom where she wet a cloth. "Here." He took the cool rag and buried his face in it. "But sometimes these things work out for the best."

"What good could possibly come from this?"

A slight smile formed on her lips. "Time will tell."

****

Ty channeled his hurt and longing for Avalee into his shoots. She was true to her word. She hadn't answered her phone or contacted him in four weeks. He spoke with her friends, even Scott, but they offered no hope. Instead, they advised him to focus on this amazing opportunity, and *didn't he know how hard some people worked all their life and never caught a break?* Clearly, Avalee had coached them, but Scott had proved to be a real ally. He kept reminding Ty to give her time, for him to work hard, and prove she wasn't a barrier to his success. Sounded good. Now if only he could get a grip on his heart. He still felt like his feet had been knocked out from under him. Since the day he'd received Avalee's email, Cadence had been very understanding and attentive. He enjoyed the platonic evenings they spent in his room or in hers discussing the next day's work. She often brought a bottle of wine and appetizers. The wine helped soothe his shattered nerves and helped him to think, plus he enjoyed her company.

He had an important shoot to organize and thought about Cadence. They needed to discuss it. But the real truth of the matter was he needed her to soothe the ache he felt after listening to Avalee's voice on her voicemail. He dialed Cadence.

"Hello, Ty."

"Hey."

"Is anything wrong? You sound kinda down."

"Same old stuff. Hey listen, how about supper tonight? We can talk about tomorrow."

A few seconds passed before she spoke. "I have a better idea. Come to my room. I'll have something to eat here. It is always so loud in a public place."

"Okay, sounds good. I'll bring wine."

"No, I have plenty. Just be here in say, thirty minutes?"

"Thirty minutes then." He disconnected the call and tried Avalee once more. And once again, he listened to her voicemail recording. This time it made him angry. Didn't she know what she was doing to him? All this nonsense about this being for his own good was crap. He was dying inside. And she didn't even have the decency to talk to him about it. Sure, he'd told her over and over in emails, which she never answered. He threw his phone on the bed and went into the bathroom to shower.

Thirty minutes later, he knocked on Cadence's

door.

"Come in. It's open."

He stepped in and froze. His brain lost communication with his feet. He couldn't move. Every particle of his awareness stared at the sight before him. Cadence stood before him like a Venus dressed in a thin white satin gown. The dress's low cut neck exposed more of her breasts than it covered. Her thick blonde hair cascaded over one shoulder in waves. "Don't just stand there, Tyler. Come on in." She step back, causing a slit up the side of her dress to reveal her thigh and hip.

He knew he should turn and walk away. Cadence's intentions were clear. He couldn't do this to Avalee. A slow burn rose inside him. *On the other hand, why couldn't he? After all,* she'd dumped him. Even worse, she continued to give him the silent treatment. Well what about him? Why was he concerned about her? He walked in.

Cadence turned and swayed to the bar. He swallowed as he fixed his gaze on her backless dress, cut down past her waist. She glanced over her shoulder and smiled. "Red or white?"

"Red. Thanks."

She took her time pouring, then casually turned around giving him time to ogle her every curve, the swell of her breasts, her full lips and the desire burning in her eyes.

"Here." She glided to his side. "This will relax you."

"But…what's…I?"

She pushed the glass to his lips. "Shhhh. It's okay. Drink."

He swallowed the cabernet. Its smooth, earthy,

liquid soon anesthetized the thoughts swarming his mind. Cadence linked her fingers with his and led him to a table where supper waited. "Sit." She took his glass and filled it again. "Here you go. Now drink up. You'll feel much better. She sat across from him and leaned forward, giving an amazing view of her perfumed cleavage. "Ty, you have been so unhappy. It is breaking my heart." She watched him as she sipped from her glass. "You are an amazing man, and you do not deserve to be treated the way Avalee has treated you."

He finished his second glass. No he didn't.

Cadence rose like smoke curls from a fire, then walked behind him and massaged his shoulders. She leaned over and whispered in his ear, "You are so tense." Her breath against his skin was hot and moist. Ty felt every muscle in his body respond to her touch.

She stepped around in front of him and held out her hands. He took them and stood as she pulled him into an embrace. He ran his hands over the clinging silky material, feeling her curvaceous body. He wanted her. In a fevered movement, he kissed her, over and over, hard and deep. Each kiss fueled by his anger, his pain, his longing.

Cadence held him tight against her and pulled him down on the bed. He slipped her dress off one shoulder and admired her body. She lifted her face to his. "Make love to me."

He closed his eyes and covered her mouth with his. Passion and desire throbbed through his body just like it had on the swinging bridge with...Avalee? What was he doing? He loved Avalee. He didn't want Cadence. He wanted Avalee. Pushing off of Cadence, he bolted to his feet and ran his hands though his hair. "I can't do this. Cadence, god, I'm sorry."

She propped up on her elbow and watched him. Then in a raspy voice said, "I understand. Really, I do. But I'm here, baby, ready, when you need me."

Ty watched as she languidly drew her dress back on her shoulder. His heart pounded and his body ached. She stood and ran her finger down his jaw line. "Hungry?"

That was the understatement of the century. He had to get out of there. "No. Listen, I'll draw up some ideas, and we will discuss them over breakfast." He turned and strode out. That was close, too close. When he got to his room, he collapsed on the bed and pressed his fingers against his temples. Why him? What did Cadence see in him when she could have any famous, sophisticated, rich man she wanted? He was a nobody and couldn't offer her anything unless she had a fondness for boxed wine, take-out food, and noshing on popcorn while watching *I Love Lucy* reruns. Like Avalee. The very thought of her name sent a stab of pain through him.

He got to his feet, plodded to the bathroom, and splashed his face in the sink. Cat and mouse. That had to be it. She liked the game of pursuit and should she succeed, he'd be history in no time. Avalee had saved him—again—and she didn't even know it.

****

The following two months Cadence didn't let up and wasn't covert in her intentions. When he was tired or the loneliness showed in his eyes, she was there with wine, a seductive voice, fleeting touches, and offers of comfort. At times, her offers sounded pretty darned good. He knew there was only one way to end the barrage of constant enticement, especially while they were taking a break in Greece. He had fulfilled his obligation to her and decided against her following him on his National Geographic assignments. When he made this decision, the memory of his email to Avalee about Cadence following them on their honeymoon flashed through his mind. On their *honeymoon* for crying out loud. He slapped his forehead with the palm of his hand. *Stupid*—slap—*stupid*—slap—*stupid!*

Cadence took his leaving her behind very pleasantly. She said she understood and gently kissed him. "Goodbye, Tyler Jackson. Avalee is a fool. And should you ever change your mind, you have my number." He nodded, turned, and left.

Late in the evening, he packed to leave Santorini and fly to Florence, Italy. He hoped to connect with Levi and Jema while there. He needed the feeling of being home. When he finished, he slouched in the chair, took a bottle of Ouzo, a potent anise-flavored liquor he'd come to appreciate during his stay in Greece and poured it in a glass. After a couple of drinks, he mulled over his idiocy through the haze of the aperitif. He ruminated over the past months and remembered Scott's advice, *give her time, focus on your jobs, and prove she isn't a barrier to your success.* Hadn't he given her time? He'd focused and *National Geographic* was happy with his work. Being *without* her was more of a barrier to his success than being *with* her.

He set his glass on the table and wandered to his hotel room balcony. Leaning on the rail, he stared at the Mediterranean Sea and pictured Avalee's face. "Ava, I'll prove myself to you."

When he returned inside, he wanted to journal his

thoughts from the evening, but true to his habits, he'd already packed and had everything ready to go. He rummaged around the room and found a sheet of paper to write his thoughts and then transfer them to his computer after he arrived in Florence. He finished his entry with, *Please, baby, don't give up on us.*

That would be his prayer, his chant, his mantra.

****

Ty arrived in Florence and strolled through the airport. He bought a coffee and found a place to sit. Searching though his wallet, he pulled the scrap of paper with Jema's number on it. Scott had done some sleuthing for him to get Jema and Levi's cell numbers, without Avalee knowing why. The last thing Ty wanted was for her to know he was seeking help from her friends. He tried Levi's number first.

"Hello? Levi Abrams speaking."

Relief washed over him. "Hey, Levi. Ty Jackson here. I'm in Florence and I was wondering if I might crash with you guys a few days?"

"Why of course. That would be great. Jema's out shopping, but she will be thrilled you are here. Where are you?"

"I'm at the airport. If you'll give me an address, I'll find a taxi. Hopefully, the driver will understand me."

"No need for a taxi. I've been running a few errands and I'm a few minutes from there. Just wait outside for me.

"Thanks, man. I really appreciate this."

"It is providential you are here. Jema and I were just talking about you and Avalee's situation. It'll be good to get your perspective."

"That's just the problem." Ty ran his hand over his

272

forehead. "I don't have a clue on perspective."

"No worries. We have some thoughts about it. Tonight we will talk over supper and drink the most excellent wine you have ever tasted."

"You don't know how good that sounds. Thanks." And it did sound good. It sounded like hope.

****

Ty almost didn't recognize Levi when he got out of the car. He stuck out his hand. "Hey man, you look good. Life in Italy agrees with you."

Levi's smile was broad and honest. "I've put on a few pounds, eh? Looks like I've found what you lost."

"All I know is you look like a happy man. Happier than I've ever seen you."

"That I am." Levi hefted Ty's duffel. "Jema is anxious to see you. She's ordered you an Italian feast from our cook, Lilliana. I hope you are hungry."

"Oh, believe me, I could eat." The hope Ty felt had bolstered his appetite. Something he'd lost a long time ago.

They settled in Levi's Ferrari and sped off. The countryside sliding past the passenger-side window made Ty want to grab his camera and ask Levi to stop. The vineyards, olive groves, and ancient stone buildings on the hillsides peeking between the lush greenery flecked with fall colors were a photographer's dream. He had to work hard at paying attention to Levi's conversation.

Levi turned onto a steep, private drive. He glanced over and smiled. "We're almost home."

Ty tore himself away from the scenery. "This country is amazing. I can't quit staring."

"That it is. We love it here."

"Do you plan on returning to Moonlight?"

"Oh yes, we have some ideas for that town. However, we'll stay here more often than we had originally thought. But not to worry, we will arrange for our friends to come here as often as they would like."

He drove through a tree-lined portion of the drive. The fall leaves made it feel like a golden tunnel, which opened to a magnificent stone house with terra cotta roof tiles.

Levi pulled to a stop on the circular drive by a massive wooden double-door. "There she is. Home sweet home."

"Wow." Ty faced Levi. "How old is this place?"

"It was built in the sixteen hundreds. Jema and I are working on restoring it to its former glory, but it is livable for now. We've finished the wing you will stay in. And we are finished with the exterior."

Ty opened the door and stepped out for a better look. They had done an excellent job. Even though the outside had been renovated, it still maintained the patina of age. Stone pots with some sort of shrub lined the circle drive. Tall clay pots with all sorts of plants were grouped here and there in front of the house.

"Let's go in. Jema is anxious to see you again." Levi extended his arm to pat Ty on the back. "Don't worry about your things; I'll have them taken to your room."

"I'll take my camera bag with me. I hardly let it out of my sight. You never know when inspiration will hit."

"Then you had better keep it close." Levi reached to open the door, but a tiny woman with thin red, no, orange—kumquat orange—hair piled on her head pulled it open and smiled, "Afternoon, Mr. Abrams."

Levi stepped in and wrapped his arm around her. "This is Carina, our housekeeper. Carina, this is our friend Ty Jackson."

"Hello, Mr. Jackson." She reached for Ty's bag.

"Hi there Carina. Nice to meet you." He shouldered the bag closer to his body. "I'll take this though, it's pretty heavy." Not to mention extremely expensive. "I'm glad you speak English."

She nodded. "I speak three languages."

"I speak one, well maybe two. He patted his bag. I speak in pictures."

Carina nodded even though she was clearly confused.

"Ty!" Jema jogged down an elegant curved staircase. "It's so good to see you." She rushed to him and enveloped him in a tight hug.

Ty hugged back just as tight. She had no idea how good it was to see her. Maybe she could help him know how to convince Avalee to come back to him. When she released him and stepped back, Ty studied her face. She looked so young and like her husband, she'd gained a few pounds, but they looked good on her. They both looked alive and vibrant—a love makeover.

Jema studied his face, too. "Honey, at the risk of sounding like Cladie Mae, you look like a starving feral. There is nothing left of you."

"I lost my appetite a couple months ago."

A tender sadness shaded her eyes. "I know. But Levi and I have some ideas." She gestured to Carina. "Look at this skinny man. We must fatten him up."

Carina clapped her hands. "I'll tell Lilliana."

Jema wrapped her arm around Ty's. "I'll show you to your room and you can freshen up then meet us in the sun terrace which is right over there." She pointed to a stone arch leading into a room of glass walls giving a panoramic view of the orchards and vineyards. Curling her finger, she said, "This way."

He followed her across the foyer's marble floor and up the staircase. At the top of the stairs, she stopped in front of a heavy wood door and pushed it open. "These doors are so heavy, but they are original so we kept them."

"They're amazing." He ran his hand over them touching the centuries.

"I chose this room especially for you. It has a great view of the park and woodlands. The colors are so pretty this time of year." She took his hand. "It is so good to have you here. See you downstairs. Lilliana has a beautiful antipasti waiting for you."

"Sounds great. I'll be down in a sec."

After Jema left, Ty set his camera on the marble top of a gilt-wood table positioned between two gilt-wood armchairs. Hand-painted frescos donned each wall except the one made of stone, which had an arched window that opened to a magnificent view of the mountains. Massive exposed chestnut beams drew his gaze upward. *Astounding.* He sank on the canopied iron bed, and the mattress almost claimed him then and there. He could use a nap. However, knowing a feast waited for him motivated Ty to freshen up and hurry downstairs.

He grabbed his travel bag and went into the bathroom and again his mind was blown. The same massive beams crossing the ceiling and the stone walls were the same as in the bedroom, making it feel true to its ancient history. But that is where it ended. The black marble floor was heated. The freestanding tub, the toilet, sink, urinal, and bidet were ultra-modern with a sleek design in white and chrome. Jema and Levi had certainly been busy in the short amount of time they'd lived here.

His stomach started growling even before he made it to the sun terrace. The aroma of fresh baked bread, garlic, rosemary, oregano, teased his nose. If he'd known what was waiting for him downstairs, he wouldn't have spent so much time gawking at his room. Platters of food covered the buffet table that stood under the large tone arch between the dining room and the sun terrace. Prosciutto, pork shoulder, salami, wild mushrooms, truffles, pickled vegetables, chunks of cheeses, bruschetta, focaccia, and several bottles of wine.

Jema poured a glass and brought it to him. "Come and enjoy the first course of your supper."

"First course? You're kidding right?" The wine was amazing. Levi tipped his glass toward Ty. "And now you can understand our expanding girths, eh?" He pulled Jema close and kissed her. While gazing at her he said, "And we don't mind it a bit, do we, darling?"

A smile spread across her face. "No. We don't."

Ty took a drink of his wine. Watching them—their happiness—renewed his ache, his longing for Avalee.

Jema must have noticed. "Honey, have a seat over in the terrace by the fireplace. Let's eat in there so we can relax by the fire and talk."

That sounded good to Ty. He sank onto the deep leather couch and watched from across the room as Jema filled his plate.

She soon joined him and handed him a pile of food.

"Have you spoken with Avalee lately?"

"No, she still won't answer her phone or my emails." He bit into the butter and garlic goodness on the bruschetta. Around the bite of bread he mumbled, "I still have no idea what happened." He swallowed. "Well, actually I do, sort of."

Levi pondered before asking, "I don't have to ask you if you love her because I know you do. But what have you learned during the time you've been overseas, cut off from all communication with her?"

Ty sipped his wine and mulled over Levi's question. The sun had lowered behind the yellow and scarlet woods, sending orange and golden rays above and through the leafed branches. "I always thought I wanted to be somebody. I felt I had to prove myself, especially to my parents. And then, through a miracle named Avalee, I got that chance. My talent was finally recognized and media outlets from all over the world are contacting me. It is, and I have to use this overdone word but nothing else fits, it's *surreal.* To be where I am in this short space of time is beyond my wildest hopes and dreams."

He paused before continuing. "And yet, it means nothing to me without Avalee. To be honest, once we got together, I didn't really care about being a successful photographer. She was all I wanted. I joined Cadence because of Avalee. I didn't want to disappoint her after all she'd done for me."

Levi nodded and set his glass on the table beside his chair. He leaned back and crossed his leg over the other while looking Ty in the eyes. "Would you give all this up for her?"

He didn't even have to think about his answer. "In

a millisecond."

Levi looked at Jema, then back at Ty. "That's all I needed to hear."

Jema grabbed a tissue and dabbed the corners of her eyes. "Avalee and I have spoken almost every day this past month. Ty, she broke up with you because she felt she'd be an encumbrance. She knows how many hours it takes to be successful and how you have to be ready to pick up and leave at a moment's notice. She didn't want you to always have to make a choice between her and your job. Avalee knows the guilt of choosing one over the other. She doesn't stay in contact with you, because she's afraid she will lose her resolve and beg you to come home. Cladie says she has wasted away to a string, like you, and frankly I think it is time to do something about it."

Ty clenched his jaw at the thought of Avalee suffering for his sake. What woman would do that? None he'd ever known, that is until Avalee. "What can I do, Jema? How can I prove to her that none of this means anything to me without her? She won't answer her freaking phone, my texts, or my emails."

Jema sat forward and propped her arms on her lap. "Sugar, Levi and I have a plan."

When Ty returned to his room, he felt more encouraged than he had since leaving Moonlight. He pulled the scrap of paper he'd written on the night before and transferred his thoughts to his computer. When he finished he walked to the window and searched the inky Tuscan sky as he tore the paper into pieces before tossing them into the trash. He contemplated the fingernail moon and sighed. "Baby, don't give up on us."

Chapter Twenty-One

Want some cheese with that whine? Yes, please, and make it Italian.

~*Avalee Preston*

I stared out at the open field after the last of the Moonlight Market tents had been hauled away until next spring. Today marked the last event for the season. Mom's and my venture proved to be a glittering success. We worked hard and frankly, the market kept my mind off my troubles. The old adage, time heals, is a lie.

Skye, bless her, visited often. We had developed a deep friendship apart from Ty and Nathan. At first, I thought she sought me out just to get close to Nate; however, she hardly ever mentioned him. She's smart enough to want to make it on her own and not be a namedropper in order to get ahead. Even so, I made myself a promise to help her, and keep my involvement in the background. That girl has what it takes to be a better investigative reporter than even Nathan, and I'll do all I can to see her successful. Her visits, along with Glen's, helped ease Momma's sense of loss as well. As far as she was concerned, she was still their grandma, their Big Momma. They felt the same way.

The downside to my deepening relationship with Ty's children was it deepened my longing for him. I read somewhere that love was not the briefly blooming rosebud; rather it was the thorny stem that protected the flower and provided nourishment. That was exactly how I loved Tyler Jackson.

I had not spoken with Mrs. Jackson since he left. When we notice each other in town, we both pretend we hadn't seen the other. Each time I pretended not seeing her, something stirred inside me. I knew I could not go on hating her much longer. It was time to free myself and let it go. I just had to figure out how.

"Hey girl."

I turned to see Lexi. "Hi Lex."

She wrapped her arms around my waist from behind and whispered, "You okay? I declare you are thinner than when you came home last summer."

I pressed my hands against hers and leaned back. "Sort of, but not really. I've lost my appetite for food. I'm beginning to lose my appetite for life. Now that the market is over, I'm wondering how to fill my days, fill my mind. This will be the first year I've ever in my life dreaded Christmas."

"I understand, sugar. I do." Lexi turned me around and hugged me.

"Oh, Lexi." I rested my head on her shoulder. "I thought this Christmas would be Ty's and my first together as a married couple."

"We all did, hon." She turned me around in a big hug and patted me as if I were her child weeping over not getting asked to the prom. "Hey, I have a great idea."

Stepping back, I sniffed and rubbed my face with my palms. "What?"

"A double-fat, salted-caramel mocha, with extra

whipped cream at Molly's. She held her finger up. "Plus an iced cinnamon scone."

That Lex. She always knew what to say. "Let's go."

"Want to take my car?"

"No, I want to walk."

Lexi lifted her eyebrows. "Walk?" She crossed her arms. "If I'm walking, don't give me none of that 'let's split a scone' nonsense. I want a whole one to myself."

"Deal." I entwined my arm with hers. Have I mentioned how much I loved my friends?

****

Molly Kate's bakery, buzzed with business, as usual. I readied myself to wait for a seat but when I got in line to make my order, MK waved at me and pointed to a table with a reserved sign. Lexi waved back and headed over to it.

"What's with this?" I pulled out a chair and sat. "Reserved table? We didn't even order."

"No worries. I texted her our order and 'A911'."

"A911?"

"Avalee emergency." Lexi pointed her finger at me. She was in bad need of a nail appointment with Tryna. "We've all gone our separate ways the past few months and things are falling apart. Especially you." She glanced at her finger. "I need to see Tryna."

Molly Kate bustled over with our drinks and scones. "Serotonin lifters at your service." She set the tray down and joined us. "Now, before we dig in, I have a suggestion."

I couldn't wait. I picked up my latte and took a sip of the creamy hot coffee. It made me feel better immediately. "You better hurry. That scone is calling out to me."

MK lowered her chin and stared up at me. "The whole thing or only half of it?"

"The whole thing and maybe half of yours."

"Whoa." Molly glanced at Lexi. "This is serious serotonin depletion we are dealing with here. I'm glad I came up with such an amazing idea."

Lexi grabbed a scone and her coffee. "So, what already?" Biting into the corner of her pasty, she rolled her eyes upward. "Oh my. Just out of the oven. Yum."

Molly patted the table. "We need a Whine Wednesday and today is Wednesday. How about it? We can Skype Jema in, too."

Lexi lifted her cup to her lips. "What's she got to whine about for heaven's sake?"

"It would just be good to be together again. We could have a Martini Monday." Molly cast a sympathetic look at me. "But I don't think it is the time for that."

I thought about it a minute. "I like it. Let's do it."

"Me, too." Lexi spread some cinnamon butter on her scone. "My place?"

"Perfect. Now don't y'all worry about food. I'll bring that." Molly turned to me. "So keep your little wagon at home. But you can bring Miss Cladie." I opened my mouth to say something, but Molly held her hand up. "I know. *Wheel of Fortune.* Does that little lady realize all the fun she misses out on?"

I nudged the last bite of scone in my mouth and mumbled, "She wonders the same thing about us."

Lexi grinned. "That woman is a hoot. She's returning to her old self, isn't she? Only, I think she's improved."

"She is. But I still worry. I'm always sneaking around going through the trash and her bedroom looking for candy wrappers."

"Well," said Molly Kate, "that weight didn't come off from a diet of Snickers and pecan pie."

"One could dream." Lexi closed her eyes relishing the idea, then opened them. "Okay, my place, 6:30. MK is bringing food, I'll have the wine, Avalee, you bring the whine. You will have a sympathetic audience and maybe one of us might actually be helpful."

"Being with you girls is helpful. But I'm afraid my whine is hopeless."

Lexi got her, *I have a secret,* look in her eyes. "Miracles happen."

"And just what is that supposed to mean?" I looked from Lex to MK.

Both of them spoke at the same time. "Nothing."

I'll bet.

****

When I got home from my tête-à-tête with the girls, I found an email from Ty waiting. I eased into my chair and held my finger over the mouse. His messages were still so raw, which did nothing for my heart. I wanted to call him, to hear his voice. I wanted to be wrapped in his arms, listening to his soft breathing. Would this longing—this needing—ever ease? I clicked on the message.

Hi Ava,

I have news. Cadence's agent notified National Geographic about her water project work in Africa and sent my photos. Seems the magazine had to kill an article and needed something in its place and chose my pictures. They will be in the December magazine, in case you want to pick one up. That makes two major magazines in a year. And all because of you, the only one who believed in me.

I'm surprised Cadence didn't trash my photographs after I left her project. She wasn't happy about my leaving. But it was time. Speaking of C. I have news on her, too. She has hooked up with some country and western singer. I wish her luck.

I miss my friend. Would you please consider at least answering my email? Sending an occasional text? Please?

Love,
Ty

I traced my finger over his name on the screen. *He did it. He is living his dream.* I had done the right thing, so why didn't I feel better? Tears threatened, but I refused to cry. It was time to renew my focus. On what, I wasn't sure.

My book was finished, the market was set, Momma was healthy, Ty was a success. I wasn't really sure where I fit into life any longer. Even so, I always seemed to find my way. I'd done it before, I could do it again.

I reread Ty's email. He sounded so lonely. It was time. Time for me to pull up my big girl britches and write him. But what would I say? I hit reply and stared at the screen.

Hi Ty,

I'm sorry that I have not written you. Perhaps it has been selfish of me, but I know my limits. So, let's write back and forth, only not about us, okay?

I can't wait to get my copy of the December edition of National Geographic. I'll give Skye a copy to give to your parents. Speaking of Skye and Glen, they come and visit at least twice a month. We've enjoyed them so much. You have fabulous children. But how could they help it? They have a fabulous dad. And now, a famous one. I'm so thrilled for you.

We've closed the Market for the season, so now I need to figure out what to do next. Molly Kate and I are going to Lexi's tonight. Maybe we can come up with something.

Where are you now, and where is your next assignment? Somewhere exotic, I hope. I want detailed descriptions.

Take care dearest,

Ava

There. I did it. And I didn't even feel like crying. Perhaps time is healing me.

A quarter past six, I left the house and jogged to Lexi's. By the time I reached her porch, I was sucking air. Pitiful. I trudged inside. "Hey, you really ought to lock this door. Anybody could just walk in."

Lexi called from the kitchen. "Not to worry. I have two friends who protect me."

"Well, Molly Kate and I do not live with you."

"I'm talking about Smith and Wesson."

"Oh." Deputy Barney Fife came to my mind. I could see her waving her gun all over the place with trembling hands, frightened to death. "All the same, you need to lock your door."

"Don't lock it until I get all this food inside." Molly Kate lugged an armful of stacked boxes.

"Here, let me help." I took the top two and the delicious aroma of cheddar and gruyere cheese baked into crispy straws hit me square in the face. My stomach got the telegram and groaned.

"Girl, I don't know what you brought." Lexi rifled through Molly Kate's offerings. "But chocolate better be in one of them."

"How about brown butter and chocolate chunk cookies? She picked one up, broke it in half, and pulled the creamy chocolate chunks apart leaving a molten curl on either side. "These just came out of the oven."

"Gimme that." Lexi snatched one of the halves from Molly Kate's hands. "Or I'll have to call my buds, Smith and Wesson."

Molly furrowed her eyebrows at me.

"Don't ask," I said as I grabbed the other half. While munching the cookie, I inspected the other containers. Just as I hoped, cheese straws. She also brought baked brie with fig preserves. Bacon wrapped dates stuffed with Gorgonzola, grilled flat bread, and boiled shrimp with cocktail sauce. "Girl, your outdid yourself tonight."

We arranged the food on the coffee table and poured our wine in extra-large wine glasses. Lexi must have felt our whine time was going to be a big one. She held up her hand. "Now y'all sit down and start nibbling while I get this Skype going. Jema said she'd have a snack and wine at her place, too."

While Lex fiddled with the call, I dove into the cheese straws. All of a sudden, I was starving. The comforting, familiar feel of abiding friendship and good food wrapped me in a warm blanket of peace. Soon the sound of Jema's gentle voice filled the room.

"Ciao y'all."

Jema was proof you could take a southern gal to Italy, but you couldn't take the southern out of the gal. I knew this from personal experience. I moved in front of the screen and waved. "Hi, Jema. We miss you."

"Not as much as I miss you all." She held up her wine. "Toast?"

We held up our glasses and chanted, "To forever friends."

"So," said Jema, "what are we whining about tonight?"

Lexi held up her hand. "I'll start. Nate wants me to stay with him in New York for a few weeks after the first of the year."

Jema cocked her head. "And that is a whine? How?"

Molly Kate sat on the couch with one leg under her. She kicked Lexi with her free leg. "And why haven't I heard about this?"

"Yeah, me neither. You sure are one for keeping secrets." Truthfully, I did know about it because Nathan discussed it with me. He had several events he'd been invited to and thought Lex would make some good contacts, not to mention his *other* motives.

"It's a whine because I'm not in his league or anyone he hangs around with. I'm the poor country mouse visiting the city mouse."

"Country cat is more like it." I made a claw with my hand. "Rawr."

"Oh, hush up." Lexi tossed a pillow at me. "Anyway, as I was saying, I'll be around people who talk different, use big sophisticated words, and of course are a lot more fashionable than me."

"Well, Avalee can help you with the fashion part," said Molly Kate. "And I have a lot of *Reader's Digests* lying around the B & B. They have those word power thingies in them. That might help.

"So, there you go," said Jema. "Go for it girl."

Lexi grabbed a cheese straw. "I just might do that. Thanks."

"Okay, everyone take a gulp for Lexi." We all took a drink. Lexi's whine was answered.

"Next whine. Go MK." Jema smiled from the screen. Lord, I missed her.

Molly thought a minute. "Well, I think Stan is sneaking behind my back."

"What?" Lex shot to her feet. "Are you kidding me? Why I'll—"

Molly Kate put her hand up. "Not that kind of sneaking."

"Don't do that to us." Lex stomped over to the wine bottles and brought one back. "We need refills anyway."

"So, what kind of sneaking?" Jema showed us she was refilling her glass, too.

"I think he has taken to smoking a pipe and trying to cover the smell with peppermints."

"Stan? Smoking?" I had to admit I personally loved the smell of pipe tobacco. What was the real harm, and why would he feel the need to conceal it?

"I only smell it in the library. Stan insists he isn't smoking, even though I tell him it is okay with me. He says it must be a guest. But I smell it when there are no guests. I don't understand why he feels the need to lie about it."

"You know? I smelled it on my wedding night while I waited in there for Levi. The peppermint, too."

"I don't know. It is all so strange. I never smell it on him or his clothes, just in the library."

"I have an idea. Felix likes to hunt maybe he has a game camera. I'll check. He can set it up in the library and we can see who is smoking. If it is Stan, he will have all of us to deal with for lying to you." I smiled. "Problem solved, everyone take a drink."

Lexi tilted her head in my direction. "Okay, Ava. Your turn."

The tears I refused to shed earlier pushed their way between my lashes. "I miss Ty. I know I did the right thing, but it feels so wrong. I just can't seem to get past this." I shook my head. "Of course, this time of year doesn't help one little bit. And I have nothing to do to fill my time or my mind, so the memories are eating away at me."

Jema broke in. "Well, I have a whine and it might just be the solution you need, Ava. I miss my sister-friends. So I propose y'all come here for a couple of days next week. We will send our jet to Memphis, and a limo to pick you all up and bring you to the airport. That ought to divert you a little, right, Avalee?"

I stared at the screen. "Next week?"

"Italy? Whoa! I can get a couple of days off." Lexi fist pumped the air. "All I have to do is mention Nathan and Vince gives me anything I want."

"Wow, I'm in. Stan can handle things for two days." Molly looked expectedly at me.

"It all sounds great, but I'm worried about Mom." This was all happening so fast.

"Oh, Cladie will be fine with it. You know that. Whattya say?" Jema held up her glass, "Problem solved?"

I lifted my wine. "Problem solved." For a little while anyway.

Lexi held up her glass. "Whoo hoo. We are going to Italy. Two problems solved, two gulps."

And with that, we finished our wine and our whines.

Chapter Twenty-Two

Flying to Italy to plan Jema's first anniversary. It's good to have rich friends.

~Avalee Preston

The limo arrived before dawn to take us to the Memphis airport. I used my smallest piece of luggage and duffel. So, you can imagine my surprise when we got to Lexi's and she dragged out two large bags and a carry-on.

"Girl, we aren't staying there a month."

Molly Kate stuck her head out the limo window. "That is exactly what I told her."

"Oh, hush up." Lexi waited for the driver to open the door. "Now get in, Avalee. We can't keep this man waiting."

Before the driver closed our door, he leaned in and pointed to the bar across from the seats. "Ladies, there is coffee and pastries on the bar. Enjoy."

Lexi put her hands to her heart. "Let me just say, it is a good thing when one of your besties marries a rich man." She leaned forward. "And I need coffee. Hope he made enough for the rest of you."

"Well," Molly Kate pulled a thermos out of her bag. "If I'd known there was a coffee bar in this car I wouldn't have brought this. But, at least we have a backup in case we run out before Memphis."

I put my arm around MK. "Let me just add, it is a good thing when one of your besties owns a coffee shop."

On the way to Memphis, we chatted and enjoyed the luxurious limo. Little did we know what we had waiting on us. The driver stopped at a hanger with the name Abrams over the door. We walked into what looked like a lush suite. With all of our ogling, we didn't notice the steward until he spoke. "*Buongiorno belle signore.*"

We turned and…. Oh. My. Goodness. Standing before us had to be a former Chippendale dancer, only with clothes on. "In case you do not understand Italian: Good morning, beautiful ladies." Even though he had a shirt on, it still could not hide his magnificent muscles. His eyes were bottle-glass green, clear, and beautiful against his olive skin. His hair looked as if the curls had been carelessly raked back with his fingers. "My name is Luca."

Lexi grabbed our hands and squeezed hard while whispering, "Don't let me go." That girl had a better grip than Skye.

Another equally gorgeous steward came forward. "And I am Sal." He had a look that beckoned you to come to him with his deep-brown eyes. His Roman nose and chiseled jaw suggested strength. He pulled his black hair back into a ponytail.

"I love men with ponytails," murmured Lexi. She almost broke every bone in my hand.

Luca and Sal led us to the waiting jet. Nothing prepared me for what I was about to see. This wasn't a jet. It was a penthouse. The seating area had sleek leather recliners, a sectional sofa, a large screen television, and an electric fireplace of all things.

"Ladies, if you are tired," Sal pointed to a door at the far end of the jet, "in there is a king-sized bed. After we take off, you are welcome to rest in there. There is also a bathroom in the bedroom and another," he pointed to a door just before the bedroom, "over there."

"We are about to take off." Luca swept his hand toward the seating area. "Please have a seat and buckle your belts. When we are in the air, I'll bring something to refresh you."

Lexi turned her head toward me with a wicked grin and mumbled, "I can think of something, and it doesn't involve food or drink."

"Shame on you. What would Nathan think?"

"He'd never know." She released my hand; thank the Lord. I noticed a similar look of relief on Molly Kate's face.

The flight to Italy was like a vacation on a resort complete with Italian gods serving whatever we wanted to eat or drink. So when Luca asked us to put on our seat belts for the landing, Lexi shot him a look. "You mean we are there? Already?"

"Yes. Already."

"Shoot." She snapped her belt closed then looked dreamily at Luca. "This flight wasn't near long enough."

Jema and Levi met us as we deplaned. Jema looked amazing. They both did. She'd finally grown out her bangs, which she'd fought for over a year. She'd gained weight, but she looked more beautiful than before she'd left. I guessed the reason for the transformation was true love and contentment in their relationship. Whatever it was, it worked for her.

"Girls!" Jema held her arms open and we all joined in a group hug. "Finally, we are together again as we always should be."

Tears flowed, but this time they were joyful tears.

"Hey." Levi joined the hug. "I'm happy to see you, too."

"Let's get you home." Jema picked up one of Lexi's bags. "I'm sure you are exhausted after that long flight."

"Are you kidding me." Lexi nudged Jema with her elbow. "With attendants like that, I could have flown around the world. Three times."

Jema beamed. "I thought y'all would like Luca and Sal. They were given strict orders to take good care of you and make your trip memorable."

Lexi fanned herself. "Oh, they were memorable all right. I'll dream about those boys for months."

Ty's face flashed in my mind. Not even the Italian stallions compared with him. The thought caused a definite drop in my internal excitement meter.

We piled into the car and while everyone chatted, I sat by the window noting the blend of modern and old world architecture passing by my window. Soon we were out of the town and I sat mesmerized as the landscape unfolded before my eager eyes. I wanted to open the window and stick my head out like a dog. Oh, the vineyards, the olive groves, the mountains with pops of fall color, the leafless branches reaching like sculptures to an electric blue sky and the evergreens adding punches of verdant color. Lexi could have her Adonises. I preferred the scenery.

Levi pulled onto their entrance at the bottom of a hill and wound up the long, steepdriveway, which opened to a tree-lined avenue, like a tunnel of golden leaves. Soon a breath-taking mansion came into view with double doors so large, Levi could have driven this car through them.

"Quick, everyone." We all snapped our attention on Lexi. "Did my face just turn green?"

"Oh you." I slapped her arm.

Levi pulled onto the circular drive in front of their palatial villa. Molly Kate gathered her purse and opened the door. "If y'all are waiting on me, you're backing up."

We all scrambled out before Levi had the chance to do the gentlemanly thing and open the doors for us. I stood, enchanted, by the villa's powerful stone walls and the beautiful grounds surrounding it. A silky breeze played through my hair as I took in the loveliness surrounding me. All along the drive were huge stone pots with shrubs. Clay pots in all sizes and shapes filled with ornamental trees, orange, red and gold chrysanthemums, and flowing vines. Benches were nestled among the pots providing inviting places to sit and soak in the exquisite surroundings and bask in the golden light.

"Avalee, quit your gawking and let's go inside." Molly Kate was never one for landscapes.

"I'm coming." I wasn't prepared for what I'd see past those enormous ancient wood doors. The marble floor foyer was the size of our family room, kitchen, and dining room. The staircase with its ornate ironwork balusters flowed in a graceful curve from the top floor to the main floor. The marble steps had decorative inlays on the risers making each one a piece of art.

Lexi opened her mouth when she saw the walls.

"Did you paint those designs on there, Jema?"

"Heaven's no. These are original frescos. So, when we were renovating this portion of the house, and the rooms you all are staying in, we just had them restored to their original beauty.

A tiny lady with orange, and I do mean orange, hair pulled in a topknot approached us. Jema put her arm around her and said, "Girls, this is Carina, our housekeeper and major general." Jema gave her an affectionate squeeze. "She keeps us in line."

Carina spread her arms open. "Welcome. Our cook, Lillianna, has prepared a feast for you. I hope you are hungry."

"Now you're talking." Molly Kate looped her arm around Jema's. "I haven't eaten since we landed." Carina smiled then nodded before hustling off.

"Okay, girlfriends, come with me to your rooms." Levi will have your luggage brought to you in a jiff. We followed her up those amazing stairs. Jema pointed to the room at the top of the stairs. "This one is for you Avalee." She pointed down the hall. "And Molly Kate, yours is the second on the right; Lexi, yours is first on the left. Freshen up but don't take too long. The food is ready."

I pushed through the large wooden door and stepped in. It was as if I had stepped back in time. This space was a piece of history. Goosebumps ran up my arms. Three of the walls were plaster, I guessed, with soft frescos adorning them. The outside wall was stone and it had a large arched window giving a beautiful view of the gardens below and mountains in the distance. The room had terra cotta tiled floors with large rugs under the bed and sitting area. In the wall across from the iron-canopied bed was a fireplace with a marble hearth and mantel. The wood was set and ready to be set to flame.

As much as I wanted to stay and explore further, I knew Jema waited for us downstairs. I hurried to the bathroom to freshen up. When I entered the room I was riveted on the spot. The mixture of ancient and modern was like a beautiful symphony. One harmonized with the other. The outside walls were the same stone as the room. The floors were heated black marble, so I assumed they were new. As were the fixtures, sleek and white, like something out of *Architectural Digest*. The freestanding tub had everything I needed for a hot bubble bath, which sounded really good. I'd be sure and take advantage of that before bed.

Lexi knocked on my door. "Hey, we are going down. Are you ready?"

I hurried to the door and stepped out in the hall. "Yep. How are your rooms?"

Molly Kate grabbed her heart. "There are no words."

Lexi pointed to her face. "Is it green?"

We found Jema and Levi on the sun terrace, which was yet another amazing space. Three walls were made of glass giving a panoramic view of the hills and valleys. The wall adjoining the house was stone with arched openings. Some led to what I assumed were different areas of the villa. Others were simply decorative lighted nooks to display pieces of art.

"Well," Lexi took the wine Levi offered her. "All I have to say is I'm going to be extra nice to any homeless man I meet from now on. Jema, this place leaves me speechless."

"Not possible, Lex." Molly Kate took her wine. "Thank you, Levi."

"Oh hush up, MK."

A tall, jolly woman wearing a white apron strode into the room pushing a cart laden with trays of food.

"Girls, this is our cook, Lillianna." Jema patted her thighs. "And she is responsible for my extra padding."

Lillianna bobbed her head in welcome causing some mousey-brown curls to fall on her forehead. She had ruddy cheeks and a wide smile. I liked her immediately. While she worked setting the food on the buffet table, I sauntered to the window and admired the view. The Chianti I sipped was warm and fruity, possibly the most delicious I'd ever tasted.

"*Per favore goda.*"

Levi nodded to Lillianna. "*Ti ringrazio tanto.*"

Lilliana bobbed her head and hustled out of the room.

"What did y'all just say?" Lexi grinned. "I might want to say that to Luca and Sal.

Levi shook his head. "Lillianna said please enjoy, and I said thank you so much."

"Perfect." Lexi turned to Jema. "Got a scrap of paper somewhere? I need to write that down."

"I think not." Jema cocked an eyebrow. "Both Luca and Sal are married."

"They are? Shoot." Lexi sighed. "Oh well, I suppose that's just the way the mop flops." She eyed the elaborate spread on the table at the end of the room. "Guess I'll console myself with this fabulous-smelling food."

"So, is this home?" I hoped not but couldn't blame them if it were.

Levi sat back on the couch next to Jema and crossed his foot over his other knee. "It will be for a while, but of course we will move back to Moonlight. For now, my Jem is getting caught up on her dreams of Italy."

Lexi pressed her finger to the side of her head. "Oh, that's right. I remember now. Jema said she is going to let her three closest friends vacation here. Namely, the ones in this room."

"But," Molly Kate lowered her voice to a whisper. "When you leave, what about Lillianna and Carina?"

"We will keep them on to maintain the villa. Both of them have a house on the property. And we have gardeners who will keep the grounds up as well as the vineyards and orchards." Levi rose to refill our glasses. "And when Jema's best friends come to visit, Lillianna and Carina will have everything ready for you."

After he refilled our glasses he said, "Now, I will leave you ladies to yourselves so you can talk as long and late as you like." He bent, kissed Jema and winked. "But not too late."

****

Lexi nestled into the pillows on an overstuffed chair and drew her knees up under her chin. "Girl, if I didn't love you so much, I'd hate you right now."

Jema waved her off. "Oh pfff. This house is beautiful, but it is the love inside that makes it wonderful. If I had this without Levi, it would be a cavernous waste of space."

"Do we get to see Florence tomorrow?" I had never been to Italy and was anxious to experience it.

"Absolutely. But we won't get to see it all, since y'all are only staying a couple of days. I suggest we go shopping. It is fabulous here. Wait until you see the Ponte Vecchio. There is shop after shop where you can buy gold jewelry.

"Well that lets me out." Lexi picked up a piece of cheese from the platter in front of her and nibbled it. "Oh, this is so good. So creamy."

"It's Caprino. Made from goat's milk." Jema also took a piece. "And don't worry, they do not charge you to look. Ponte Vecchio is the oldest bridge in Florence and is worth seeing." Florence is also the birthplace of the Renaissance. I hate we won't have time for the museums, so y'all will have to come back and stay at least a month." Jema paused. "Let's fix our plates and eat. And afterwards, I have something I want to discuss with you—a special favor."

That got my attention. "What?"

Jema shook her head. "We eat first."

Lillianna had indeed prepared a feast. Only I didn't know what any of it was, so I decided to try a little of it all. We followed Jema through one of the arches to the dining room. Once again, I found myself gawking. A long walnut table stood between four arched columns with a crystal chandelier hanging above it. A massive fireplace was at one end of the room. The walls were painted a warm terra cotta and on the ceiling were pastoral scenes.

While we ate, Jema didn't bring up her special favor. Instead, we talked about the room and the food.

"Jema," said Molly Kate. "Do you think Lillianna would share her recipes?"

"Oh absolutely, that is, if you will give her your orange roll recipe."

"Consider it done."

"I don't know if I could go back to Moonlight if I were you." Lexi leaned back in her chair and held her stomach. "I want to stay myself." She sat up. "Hey, Jema, why don't I move in here? You've got enough room." Lexi grinned. "If wishes were horses…"

"Well, that kinda brings me to the favor I wanted to ask y'all. Could you all come back the week after Christmas for New Year's Eve? My daughters are coming then. Levi and I thought, since they missed the wedding, that we would say our vows again. I'd love you being here in your bridesmaids dresses, and I will fly Tryna and David here, too, if they are free."

Lexi laughed out loud. "If Tryna wasn't free, she'd move heaven and hell to be free."

"I don't think you'll have a problem with David either." Molly Kate thought a moment. "The B & B will be closed, but I can't leave Stan."

"Of course Stan is invited. Just think of it as a second honeymoon. I'll have Carina make up an Italian love nest for you in the room overlooking the lake." She rose from her chair. "Why don't we go back to the terrace for dessert? I'm sure Carina has the fire going for us."

We settled in the four chairs in front of the fire, nibbling on chocolates and sipping a beautiful chianti.

"So," said Molly Kate, "is Italy what you had imagined?"

Jema smiled. "Well, it isn't what I expected. But all I knew of it was from movies. It does have it's beautiful scenery, and the small villages are lovely. But Florence and Rome are so busy. Oh, the traffic! Scooters flying all over the place. The center line in the road is just a suggestion. I don't know how Levi drives in it. It gets really crowded too with all the tourists. Still, nothing can spoil the gorgeous architecture and amazing art. Statues everywhere. Why I declare, my mind goes numb from all the beauty."

"Is Florence your favorite place in Italy?" I said.

"Actually, I think I prefer Rome. But we found this villa just outside of Florence and fell in love with it."

"I can see why." Molly Kate bobbed her eyebrows. "I might tell Stan we need to come here and open a B & B."

Lexi shoved another chocolate in her mouth and chased it with wine. "Let's talk about this party."

I listened to my friends excited chatting about Jema's first anniversary party. I hadn't said much. To be honest, this conversation was almost more than I could bear.

After a while, Jema looked at me. "You haven't said much, Ava. Will you be able to come? And of course bring Cladie Mae."

I wanted to say no. But how could I? Without taking my eyes off the fire, I simply nodded. Here I was, alone again, by my own doing. I really didn't even have an excuse to feel sorry for myself, but I did anyway.

Jema frowned. "Are you not feeling well?"

I forced a smile. "No, I'm fine. I'm just tired. I think I'll go take advantage of that fabulous tub and then go on to bed if that's okay with y'all."

Molly Kate nodded. "Sure it is, honey. Go get your rest."

"Night, everyone." I stood and walked out, feeling their watchful stares follow me. I felt bad, but honestly, I just couldn't listen to anniversary talk any more.

Maybe tomorrow. All I wanted was a hot bath and a soft bed.

Carina had a fire going in the fireplace giving my room a warm, comforting ambience. I stepped into the bathroom, relishing the heated floors. When the hot water worked its way to the spigot, I pushed the stopper down and liberally poured in eucalyptus and spearmint bubble bath. The label said it was for stress relief. When the tub was full of soothing scented bubbles, I got in and sank deep. Heaven. I dozed off and on until I decided, reluctantly, it was time to get out. After I toweled off and put on my PJs, I surrendered myself to the soft, deep mattress. As soon as I slid between the soft sheets, I fell asleep and dreamed of Ty.

****

A soft knock woke me from deep slumber. Sunlight streamed between the drapes. I sat up and blinked. "Come in."

The aroma of coffee preceded Jema when she opened the door. "Hello, sleepyhead."

"What time is it?" I had to restrain myself from snatching the coffee.

"Almost noon."

"Oh, no. The girls must be champing at the bit to go into town. I'm sorry."

"No worries. I sent them on with Levi. We can go later." She poured my coffee in a large mug, handed it to me, and then poured some for herself. "Actually, I'm glad you slept in. You needed it, and I wanted some time alone with you."

I lifted the cup to my lips. If heaven had a flavor, it would be the coffee in my cup. "If you are worried about me, don't be. I'm okay now that I'm rested. I was just tired, that's all."

Jema wasn't fooled. "It's Ty, isn't it?"

No sense in trying to lie. "Yes. I just can't convince my heart I did the right thing."

"I don't have to ask you if you are still in love with him. That's obvious. But answer me this. If he were to propose to you again, would you accept?"

When I didn't answer immediately, she tilted her head. "Look, Ava, you did what you considered the right thing. You stepped out of the way for Ty to be successful. Well, now he is well on his way. There is no reason to be apart now."

I held my mug against my chin and thought about what Jema had said. "I think, perhaps, I've put a nail in that coffin. His emails have gotten more and more friendship like."

"I have an idea he is protecting himself. You pushed him away. You know that, right?"

"Yes, that is exactly what I did." I set the mug on the tray and dropped my face in my hands. "Lord, I've made such a mess of my life—all my life." With a rueful laugh, I looked up at Jema. "With the same family, no less. And no doubt the only ones who are happy about my breaking up with Ty are his parents."

Jema's voice grew soft. "I think Ty still loves you."

"I don't know why he would. I don't love me."

"Call him. Talk to him."

"I'll think about it, okay?"

"Fair enough. Now, get dressed and we will meet them somewhere."

"Can we take a to-go coffee? This is delicious."

"Of course. Oh, and layer your clothes. It's pretty chilly today."

"Will do." When she left the room, I went to the bathroom and splashed my face. The woman in the mirror looked pitiful. Gaunt and hollow-eyed. If Ty saw me now, he'd run away screaming for Cadence. And I wouldn't blame him one little bit.

Jema waited at the bottom of the stairs with coffees in hand. "Let's go. They are waiting for us to join them for lunch."

"Good, I'm famished."

We met up with Levi and the girls at the Panini Toscani. There, we did a tasting of four cheeses and three meats. Then we were given choices of breads, meats, and cheeses. I wanted it all. By far, that was the absolute best sandwich I ever ate in my life, and even though it was enormous, I ate every bite.

After lunch, Lexi had to stop in every shop, but she didn't buy a thing. I thought about the extra luggage she brought. "Lex, you better buy something to justify all that luggage."

She shot a smile at Jema. "Oh, don't you worry about those. I'll find a use for them." Looking around she asked, "Where's MK?"

"Oh, she's with Levi in the pasticceria. He's translating for her while she picks the baker's brain." Jema shrugged her shoulders. "That girl is always working."

The sun sank behind the hills sending out dazzling red and gold rays. I pulled my coat closer. "I hope she gets her information soon. It's getting chilly."

Jema squinted down the street. "I think I see them."

Just as Molly Kate stepped off the sidewalk to cross the street a bus rambled by and a scooter darted past it. MK jumped back on the walk before trying to cross again. When she reached us she said, "Lord. These streets are no wider than my hips. How on earth can those folks drive like that and not kill themselves?"

"I've wondered the same thing—many times." Jema turned her coat collar against her neck. "I don't know about you, but I'm ready for some wine around a roaring fire. "

"Sign me up." Lexi huddled closer to me. "Wish I'd brought a heavier jacket."

"I tried to tell you." Jema pulled her scarf from her neck. "Here."

Lexi grabbed it. "Thanks."

On the way home, I promised myself another bubble bath before bed. However, once we girls were in front of the fire, sipping wine, and nibbling on the platters of meats, cheeses, breads, spreads and fruit Lillianna prepared for us, all my plans changed. Like yesterday, Levi escaped to his library.

Way into the evening, we had talked ourselves out. But none of us were ready to go to our rooms. It just felt good sitting together, staring at the flames licking the huge logs. After a while, Jema left the room, then returned and settled back into her chair. "Avalee? How do you think I should decorate for my anniversary party? I want it to be beautiful for my girls, but I doubt I can replicate what you did in Moonlight."

"I'm not sure? What is available here?" I finished my wine and tipped my glass at Lexi. She jumped up and poured another.

"Well," said Jema. "We can get almost anything. Just go wild. Think about a perfect wedding." She leaned her head to one side. "What would be a perfect wedding to you?"

Normally, this question would have brought me to my knees, seeing how I had planned so many for myself, none of which came to fruition. But the anesthesia of wine and the warmth from the fire protected my heart and opened my mind. "Well, if it were me, I'd have it right here in this villa—at night. I would float down that beautiful staircase. There would be groupings of candles of all sizes on each step. Then I'd come into this room." I moved my hand in the direction of the three walls of windows. "So I could see the stars. You girls would wear black and carry red roses. The men would wear black tuxedos with red cummerbunds. I'd carry a bouquet of ivory spider mums, tiny white sweet heart roses, white ranunculus, with green herb fillers.

Lexi interrupted. "But you've always loved tulips."

"Not anymore. Tulips must be bad luck." I grinned and took a drink. "There would be no flower arrangements around the room. Only candles. And the cake. It would be the *pièce de résistance*. Six tiers, each a different flavor, all my favorites. Carrot cake with cream cheese filling, German chocolate with coconut-pecan filling, Italian cream with buttercream filling, coconut with coconut cream filling, lemon mousse with lemon filling, and cheesecake, all frosted with buttercream icing and decorated to look as if it is draped in lace and pearls."

Molly Kate set her glass down. "Stop. I'm getting a sugar rush just listening to you."

I rested my glass against my lips and thought some more. "The only light I'd have would be this fireplace and, of course, the candles. Then, at the moment of the announcement of being husband and wife, there would be fireworks right outside those windows. Then everyone would dance to Frank Sinatra, Nat King Cole, and Dean Martin." I snapped my fingers. "And while I'm dreaming, I want snow. Like what you had, Jema. Not a storm, just a kiss of downy flakes."

Lexi moaned. "That sounds so wonderful."

"It does." Jema reached for a cannoli. "It really does."

The bubble bath memory rose to my mind. "Well, girls. I have a date with the bathtub." I stood and stretched. "See you in the morning bright and early. Jema? What time do we leave for the airport?"

"Six o'clock" She rose from her chair. "I guess we should all get a few hours in."

Molly Kate and Lexi started picking up dishes, but Jema spoke up. "Don't bother with all of this. I'll give Carina a nice bonus for her extra trouble. Y'all head on to bed and get some rest."

"Okay. Night, everyone." I blew a kiss and trudged up the stairs to my date with the bubbles.

****

My phone alarm drew me from a deep sleep. Groaning, I rolled over to check the time. Five. The bed held me like a lover, and I couldn't gather enough will to pull myself from its warm embrace. However, fifteen minutes later, I extracted myself from the soft sheets. The room was dark and chilly. Yet something about it brought about a sense of peace. I stepped to the window to view the blue precursor of dawn backlighting the mountains. Stars still glittered in the lapis sky high above the earth. The windowsill was deep and I leaned against it to take in the quiet beauty of the morning. When I laid my hand on the cold stone, I felt something. A scrap of paper with something written on it. The room was too dark to read the writing, but I was curious. In the bathroom, I flipped on the light and read, *Don't give up on us.*

Strange. I wondered who could have written this. Did someone write to Carina? As far as I knew, she was the only one who would have been in here. Surely, Jema and Levi weren't having trouble. I tossed the scrap in the trash and hoped that whomever this was written to would not give up.

The promise of the luscious coffee I had the previous morning helped me dress and pack in a hurry. I padded down the marble staircase, feeling like a princess, and left my bags at the door. The terrace room had a roaring fire, pots of coffee on a cart along with apple-raisin strudel, ciabatta with mascarpone, and brioche with honeyed butter.

"Would you look at that?" Lexi strode into the room. "Lord, I'd weigh five-hundred pounds if I lived here." She stood next to me and poured her coffee. "Where's MK? Are we leaving soon?"

"I don't know. I just walked in here myself." I bit into the brioche and groaned. Nothing I had ever tasted in the states could even come close to comparing with this. I broke it in half and slathered it with butter. "She is probably badgering poor Lillianna for her recipes. I hope she gets the one for this brioche."

"Morning." Jema entered the room followed by Molly Kate.

"Sleep well, Molly Kate?" I buttered the other half of my brioche.

"If my bed had been any more comfortable, I would have been tempted to leave Stan and move here."

Jema forced a smile, but a sheen shimmered in her eyes. "Lord, I'm going to miss you girls."

Lexi was the first to bundle Jema in a tight squeeze. "We'll be right back, sugar, so get ready, you hear?" And be sure to send Sal and Luca. They may be married, but they are mighty fine to look at."

"Oh, they are flying with you back to the states, so look all you want."

We took turns loving on Jema, when I noticed the driver picking up our bags. "Where's your other bag, Lex?"

"I didn't need it after all. But, since I'm coming back, I might want to shop and actually buy something. So I'm leaving it here."

I smirked. "Told ya you wouldn't need it."

"Oh, hush." Lexi finished her coffee. "Jems, do you have to-go cups?"

"Waiting for you in the car." She hugged each of us then stepped back. "Levi said to tell you goodbye. He's still asleep."

"Tell him the same." I hugged her once more, then walked to the car. As promised, three cups of hot coffee waited on us. Once settled, I glanced out the window at Jema. She dabbed her eyes with a napkin. God love her. Even in the best surroundings, we girls still needed each other.

Chapter Twenty-Three

The dungeon of bitterness and unforgiveness only shackles the bearer.

~Avalee Preston

Leave it to Lexi to distract me from dark thoughts. During our flight home, we were all entertained watching her flirt with Luca and Sal. How did she do it? Even if I weren't struggling over my loss of Ty, I still wouldn't have the ability to tease like that little redheaded vixen. The fellows seemed to enjoy her as much as she did them. But enough was enough, and I was ready for the peace of my home to gather my thoughts, make a plan, and get on with life—again.

When I walked through the door I found Momma in the kitchen. She had turnip greens cooking, fried chicken in the warming tray, and banana pudding cooling on the counter. It all smelled delicious, and it sent a message. Welcome home.

"Hi, Momma." I set my bag down and hurried to her for a hug.

"Glad you are home, baby. Now sit yourself down and have some supper."

"I'm not really hungry. All we did while we were there was eat."

"Uh huh," Momma mumbled while she fixed my plate. "Then eat what you can."

I took a bite of turnip greens cooked with bits of ham. Luscious. Before I knew it, my hunger blossomed and I ate with what we call a *coming appetite.*

While we ate, she caught me up on the past two days. Then, as nonchalantly as if she were speaking of the weather, said, "Ty stopped by."

I set my fork down. "He's home?"

"He came back for a day. He's gone now. I can't remember where he said he was going." She shook her head. "I vow I can't remember a thing these days."

"Why did he come home?"

"Emma. She developed a nasty cough and went to the doctor last week. He saw a new spot on her lung. She called Glen and he contacted Ty. So I guess the day you flew to Italy, he flew here." Momma stood. "Banana pudding?"

"Yes, that sounds good. I wonder why he didn't stay longer?"

"He said something about having the assignment of a lifetime, and he had to get ready for it."

The assignment of a lifetime. So he finally realized his career had to take first place in his life. I was right after all. Momma set a heaping bowl of pudding in front of me, and I ate every bite.

"By the way." Momma pointed her spoon at me. "Emma wants you to call her."

"Oh, great." Emma Jackson was the last person I wanted to see. I didn't want to endure her catty triumph.

"Now, baby. Have some compassion. The woman is sick and wants to see you."

"I don't think she has a compassionate bone in her body."

"Don't be that way, sugar. Give her a call and go

see her." Momma's chair scraped the floor when she stood. "Now go in the family room and I'll bring coffee. I want to hear all about Jema and Levi."

"That I can do. But let me help you in the kitchen first."

"Nope. My domain. Now get your fanny out of here."

I didn't argue. It was good to hear her say that. She was returning to her old self, except now she was healthy. Momma was on the mend.

****

It took me two weeks to work up a grain of compassion for Emma and call her. Everything inside me screamed to forget her. To leave things as they were. To not wake the slumbering beast. But I'd made Mom a promise.

After the first ring, Emma's housekeeper, Doris, answered the phone.

"Jackson residence."

"Hi, Doris. It's Avalee."

"Hello, dear. How are you?"

"Fine. I'm calling because I was told Emma wants to see me."

"That's right. She does."

I hesitated. "So, Doris, do you know anything about this?"

"This afternoon will be fine."

"Excuse me?"

"An hour? All righty then. We will see you in an hour."

"Doris?"

The next thing I heard was a click. That was a strange conversation. Emma must have been listening.

An hour? I needed more time to emotionally prepare myself. But, on the other hand, I might as well get this over instead of worrying about it. I decided I'd walk to the Jackson home. At least I could clear my head a bit. Momma was somewhere with Felix, so I scribbled a note before I left.

The cool fall air bordered on cold, but it felt exhilarating. I fell into an easy stride and began pondering on how to handle Ty's mother. Momma said to have compassion. Only problem is Emma Jackson ate compassion like my pet hamster used to eat her young.

Memories of how she treated me when I dated Marc, her lambasting me at his funeral, and the beyond hurtful things she said to me while Ty and I were engaged fueled my anger. Before I knew it, my pace had picked up and my hands tightened into fists as I swung them back and forth propelling my body. And then, before I knew it, my foot rolled on a rock and I face-planted in someone's yard. Embarrassed, I scrambled up and spit grass out of my mouth while looking around to see if anyone had seen me. I ran my hand over my face to check for scratches and didn't feel anything. The only thing hurt was my ankle. I hobbled on. Each painful step reminded me I was no better than Emma. The only difference was I had a filter and she didn't. I could hide my emotions; she chose to show them. But the same thoughts, the same anger, the same unforgiveness resided in us both.

How was I any better? I thought about a blog I'd recently read where the author wrote about his childhood. He was raised in poverty and yet even as a small child he had great ambition for his future. He had a teacher who shamed his aspirations and often humiliated him in front of his classmates. When this man was grown, and very successful, he had an amazing observation about people like his teacher. He realized we all carry burdens and advised patience because no one knows the burdens others carry. Sad thing was, I knew about Emma Jackson's burdens. She had plenty and I had no compassion or patience.

I stopped at a nearby bench to rub my ankle. While I rested, I made peace in my mind with Emma and myself. It was time to let it go. When I stood to walk, my ankle throbbed. A painful reminder of how bitterness affects the soul. Agony must have etched my face, because when Doris answered the door she put her hand to her breast. "My dear, what happened?"

"Oh, silly me. I decided to walk and twisted my ankle on the way."

She took my arm and placed it over her shoulder. "You walked?" Encircling her arm around my waist, she led me to a chair and picked my foot up to set it on the coffee table.

I jerked my leg back. "Don't do that. Mrs. Jackson will have a fit."

"No, she won't." Emma had walked up behind me. "What happened here?"

"Miss Preston twisted her ankle." Doris straightened.

"Go get Mr. Jackson. He will know what to do."

"Yes, ma'am." Doris winked at me and hurried off.

Without a word Emma sat in the chair beside me. An uncomfortable silence hung between us. Then Emma shifted around in her chair and faced me.. "Avalee, I owe you an apology. In fact, I owe you numerous apologies. Too many to count." A fit of coughing overtook her. She pulled a hanky from her pocket and covered her mouth until it subsided.

I couldn't speak. Only stare.

"Would you forgive this old woman for the years of pain I brought you and the hateful foolishness I've spewed?"

Who was this woman sitting next to me? Her short-cropped white hair framed a softly folded face. Her blue eyes had lost their sharpness; now they were like reflecting pools.

"Only on one condition."

Emma held her head erect. "What would that condition be?"

"If you will also forgive me."

She lowered her chin and gazed up at me. "Oh my dear, there is little to forgive. But yes." Laying her hand on mine, she leaned forward and her voice dropped to an earnest plea. "Let's start anew. Shall we?"

Mr. Jackson entered the room. "Where's the patient?" He carried a pillow and ice pack.

"She's right here." Mrs. Jackson signaled Doris. "How about a pot of tea and some of those lovely shortbread cookies you made this morning?"

"Coming right up." Doris' delight was unmistakable. What had brought about this amazing transformation?

When Mr. Jackson finished with my ankle, he walked to the bookshelf. When he returned, he laid several magazines on my lap with bright adhesive strips flagging something inside them. "These magazines have our son's photos in them."

Emma picked one of them up and opened it to a

touching scene of African children dancing around a new well. Tears shimmered in her eyes as she handed it to me. "I had no idea our son was so talented or involved with something so important. I must have gone through his entire life blind."

Mr. Jackson beamed as he held up a copy of *The New Yorker.* "The boys at the club were certainly impressed. There are even pictures of our town in this." He shook his head. "Who would have thought our boy would put Moonlight on the map?"

The phrase, *mission accomplished*, came to my mind. Finally, Ty was his own man in his parents' eyes. "He has amazing talent. But even more so, he is an amazing person."

Mrs. Jackson covered her mouth, and then let her hand drop. "Avalee, honey, we owe all of this to you. You were the only one who understood his potential."

Mr. Jackson cleared his throat. "And, our son told us the reason you broke up with him was to get out of his way." He looked down at his lap and cleared his throat again, then peered at me over his wire-framed glasses. "You, my dear, are also an amazing person."

I was flabbergasted. I opened my mouth to speak, but the words stuck in my throat. Finally, I whispered, "Thank you."

Doris brought our tea and cookies and quickly left. No doubt, she was around the corner listening to every word.

Emma poured our tea and then lifted her cup to her lips. When she set it back on the saucer in her lap, she said in a quiet voice, "I suppose you know about my recurrence."

I nodded.

"Ah've decided against treatment. Only comfort care." When I opened my mouth to speak, she held her hand up. "Glen called Tyler because I wanted to talk with him about my decision face-to-face. When he came home, he brought us these magazines. And that was when I realized what I had done to that boy. He was so timid. Almost afraid to show me." She ran her finger under her eye. "I saw my little boy trying to win my approval. All these years ah'd hardened myself, because I couldn't face loss again. And in doing so, I nearly lost my other child anyway. And then...."

She ran her hand over the magazine in her lap. "And then I saw his work. Important work. Something that will touch millions of hearts, I finally grasped what he'd been trying to tell me for so many years." Without looking up, she said in a trembling voice, "And now that we've finally found each other, ah'm dying." She brought her hanky to her nose and looked up. "But at least we made our peace before he left."

Mr. Jackson rose and stepped behind Emma's chair. "He has invited us on a Christmas cruise. He said it is his gift to us."

"That's wonderful." And it was, sort of. Momma and I would spend a quiet holiday at home where I could disappear until it passed and not have to feign happiness. I set my cup down. "Thank you both so much. And I want you to know I'm here for you." I pulled myself up to a wobbly stand. "I guess I'd better be on my way for now."

"Not on that foot you aren't." Mr. Jackson walked to the coat closet. "I'm taking you home."

I didn't even try to argue. "Thank you. I appreciate it."

He helped me to the door and Mrs. Jackson followed. She patted me on the cheek. "We appreciate you, Avalee."

On the way home, I wondered why Ty hadn't written me about this change of heart in his parents? After all, it was monumental. Further proof he had moved on. Now I truly understood the feeling of bittersweet.

****

I didn't mean to be a Scrooge, but I was relieved when Molly Kate decided against hosting a Christmas party. The B & B's guests had left and since MK and Stan were going to Italy, they decided to take her daughter and granddaughters to visit his kids for the holidays.

Ty finally emailed me about his visit home with his parents. I wrote back, and he replied. We were back to our familiar and friendly communication, if not loving. He looked forward to the cruise and spending quality time with them. No doubt he dreaded being home this time of year as much as I did. He had booked a Caribbean cruise for three weeks. The warmth would be good for Emma and I was happy for all of them.

Even though this Christmas left me a little blue, Momma was exhilarated. Mrs. Armstrong, Lexi, Felix, AJ, and Junie were joining us for Christmas dinner. She was thrilled a child would be celebrating the holiday with us. Presents for Junie spilled out from under our tree. Mom had gone crazy shopping for her.

"Avalee, sugar, run to Pigg's for me and buy more eggnog. We have one more coming to dinner."

"Who?"

"Mayor Campbell."

"Why is Sid coming?"

"Lexi called and asked if he could come. They were working on a tourist campaign and he mentioned he'd be alone this year."

"Where are his boys going?"

"To his wife's mother's house."

"And he wasn't invited?"

"Lexi said his mother-in-law was apologetic, but offered no explanation for not inviting him this year."

I grabbed my purse and walked to the door. "Need anything else?"

"No, that should do it."

"Well, if you think of something, text me."

"I don't text. I talk. Now run along. They close early on Christmas Eve."

When I pulled off the driveway, I admired Jema's house. It was like a bright star in the neighborhood. AJ had strung lights on the house, around the trees, and on the bushes. In the yard were lighted reindeer. One had a red nose. All the other houses along Washington Avenue had trees shining from the windows, but other than that, the street was dark. It was good to have a child in the neighborhood.

Christmas morning dawned cloudy and cold which was fine by me. If I couldn't have a white Christmas, at least I wouldn't have to put up with a bright Christmas. I could fool myself the clouds teased with the possibility of snow...like last year.

Momma was upstairs getting ready, so I had the whole downstairs to myself to be quiet and mentally prepare for the day. I poured a mug of coffee, sliced a piece of cinnamon pecan loaf, and settled in front of the fire. Everything felt strange. Off. Last year I was so busy I couldn't think. The girls and I were laughing, crying, all up in each other's business. Ty and I sat here, in front of the fire....

In my mind's eye, I pictured Ty with his parents. They were probably sitting around a beautifully decorated table getting caught up on the past thirty years, laughing and crying. Making memories. I missed him. Really missed him.

The Grandfather clock tolled eleven times. Everyone was due to arrive at eleven-thirty. We had just enough time to pour our naughty and nice eggnog into the punch bowls and set out the appetizers. When the clock chimed the half-hour, Felix had Mrs. Armstrong on his arm at the door. Momma opened it and Mrs. Armstrong said, "Naughty. I'm getting too old to be nice."

AJ and Junie were the next to arrive. Momma took the little girl's hand, "Come with me, sugar, I have something to show you." She led the child to the tree. "All of these are for you, baby."

Junie's coffee-brown eyes opened wide with delight. She grabbed Momma's hand. "All those presents are mine, Big Momma?"

"Yes, baby. They are all for you, and you can open them after we eat."

Junie turned and grabbed Mom's legs in a hug. "I love you, Big Momma."

Momma looked up at me. "We've adopted each other."

AJ watched with a huge smile. I couldn't imagine how wonderful it must have felt to see his little daughter so happy.

Mrs. Armstrong hobbled on her cane and put

another package under the tree. "This one is for you, too, Junie."

Mom's eyes rounded and she looked at me. I got her message clearly. *Will wonders never cease?*

Junie danced around the tree clapping her little hands. "Thank you, Miz Strong."

"You are welcome, little lady." Pearly looked to AJ. "I really appreciate you bringing Junie to visit me in the evenings. I get right lonely at times."

Junie kept dancing. "When do we eat? When do we eat?"

"Well, we are all here, so we might as well go to the dining room and commence." Momma bent over Junie. "And then, we'll open presents."

When we were all seated, Momma spoke to Felix. "Sugar, would you ask the blessing for us?"

"Yes, ma'am, it'd be my pleasure." We all joined hands and I listened to Felix's rich bass voice intone a prayer. "Lord, we are joined at this table by a common thread. Your love. While we are all so different, we all have you within."

I looked over at Mrs. Armstrong. Her eyes were shut tight, and she was nodding her head. Indeed a wonder. Closing my eyes, I turned my attention back to Felix.

"You are the golden thread that weaves our lives together, and I'm grateful to you Lord. Today and always may we honor you by honoring each other. May we be grateful and show gratitude to others. May we give as we receive. Keep us close, Father, and on your path. Thank you for everyone here today, and especially for our Miss Cladie. Amen."

We all repeated together, "Amen."

In no time, the food was passed around and eaten. Junie's feet barely hit the floor on her way to the family room. It is uncanny how the first ripping of paper really livened things up. Her delighted squeals and prancing around the room holding up the gift she'd just opened had us in stitches. It felt so good to laugh. By the time she finished, there was a mountain of paper, empty boxes, and bows.

While Momma and AJ cleaned up the mess, she noticed Pearly hobble off to the bathroom and took the opportunity to ask him about how they had come to know Pearly. He told us about how their dog Chewy had run off and hid under Pearly's porch. When they finally retrieved the puppy, he noticed some sagging boards and offered to fix them. Of course, Pearly showed him other things that needed fixing and of course, he was happy to help. All this time, Junie entertained the old woman. And now she embraced them like family. A true Christmas miracle. A child had led her from prejudice to respect.

I made a pot of coffee to go with one or more of the four desserts Mom had made, which she promised she had barely tasted. Acid reflux was already threatening, so I ran upstairs to my room for an antacid. When I walked in the room, I found a startled Junie. She backed up with her hands behind her. "Honey, what are you doing up here?"

"Nothing." She started easing out the door.

"What's that behind your back?"

"Nothing."

She looked so small and frightened. I had no idea what to do about whatever she was hiding. "Just a minute. I need to get something in here and then we will go down together."

She nodded. But when I came back to my room she'd already gone downstairs. I scanned the room. Everything looked to be in the right place. I really had nothing of value anyway, except…my engagement ring. When Ty insisted I keep it, I slipped it off my finger and put it in the velvet box and stuck it in my lingerie drawer. I felt silly checking, but I did anyway. For several seconds I rifled through my things growing more and more panicked. It was gone. I knew the child wasn't a thief. She probably just saw something pretty and wanted to play with it. Maybe she dropped it somewhere and thought she'd get in trouble so she was hiding the empty box behind her. I dropped to my knees and looked under the dresser. Nothing.

When I returned to the family room, Junie sat by the tree playing on her tablet while everyone laughed and visited. I hated to spoil the jovial atmosphere with accusations, but I wanted my ring back before she really lost it.

"Ava, honey, would you help me bring the desserts out?"

Perfect. Mom would know what to do. As we walked, I told her what had happened. Momma drew her eyebrows together and said in a low voice. "That baby didn't take your ring."

"But it's gone and I caught her snooping in my room. And, when she saw me she threw her hands behind her. I'm not saying she is a bad child, just curious. What should I do?"

Momma stuck her hand in her pocket and pulled out a pecan made to look like a mouse. It had pink paper ears, black bead eyes, a pink bead nose, and string for its whiskers and tail. On the back of the pecan was a piece of looped yarn for hanging the ornament on the tree. "She was putting this in your room as a surprise. She made them for us.

"Oh." Now I felt like a jerk. But where was that ring?

Momma thought a minute and snapped her fingers. "You put that ring in the lockbox. Remember?"

"No?"

"Yes. Yes you did. I remember it as clear as a bell." She patted my shoulder. "You are too young to be forgetting things like that. Now take this cake to the family room and put it beside the punch."

I felt somewhat relieved. The last few weeks had been a mental battle, so it was no wonder I'd forgotten. But just in case, I decided to check the lockbox as soon as the bank opened. Just to be sure. And if it was there, I needed to make an appointment with a psychologist. It was time to get a grip.

****

The next morning I dressed early and hurried down the stairs hoping Mom wouldn't see me trying to sneak the lockbox key from the desk. I didn't want it to look like I didn't believe her, but the more I thought about it, I didn't. I may have been distracted these past several weeks, but I'd remember what I had done with something so precious to me.

She kept the key in the secretary in her sitting room. I slid open the drawer and scrounged around. No key. I checked the other drawers. Nothing. Where did she put it?

"Morning, baby."

I whirled around. "Morning, Momma."

"Looking for something?"

Think, Avalee. Think. "Lozenges. My throat is getting scratchy."

"I keep those in the kitchen cabinet. You know that." She eyed me. "You are dressed mighty early. Going somewhere?"

"Errands. We leave for Italy tomorrow, and I had a few things I needed to do." I hadn't fooled her one bit.

Her lips turned up at the corners like the cat that caught the mouse. "Okay then, while you are out, would you get me some BC Powders? I'm sure they don't have those in Italy."

"Sure." When she left, I did one last search. Where did she put that darned key?

Momma called from the kitchen. "That baby didn't take your ring. It is in the lockbox."

"Then where is the key?"

She reappeared in the door. "In the desk there."

"No, it isn't." *Oops.*

"I figured that was what you were after." She sighed. "I'll tell you what. You run your errands, and I'll look for the key if it will make you feel any better. And when you see your ring, you will owe my Junie girl a huge apology."

I felt my cheeks burn. "Does she know I suspect her?"

"No, but I do."

And with that burden of guilt, I left to buy the BC Powders, because that was the only errand I really had to do.

****

On the way home, I passed our house and drove to the playground where Ty had given me my ring. I stepped out of the car and slipped my gloved hands in the pocket of my quilted black coat, the same one I wore while playing in the snow with Ty last Christmas. The grounds looked so different. It was different. Last year everything was covered with snow. Last year I was with Ty. Now everything is brown and ugly. Now I am alone. I closed my eyes and imagined snow, and my footsteps crunching deep in its surface. I tried to imagine Ty with me, but I couldn't. I had given up my relationship with Ty, but why did life demand more from me? Why my ring?

Chapter Twenty-Four

If this is a dream, then never wake me up.
                                ~Avalee Preston

The excitement of D-day—departure day—helped me to stop worrying about my ring, at least temporarily. David, Tryna, Molly Kate, Stan, and Lexi were supposed to meet me here at the house. I checked the clock. They'd better hurry. The limo was due in half an hour. Minutes later, I heard car doors slamming. Someone jogged up the porch steps and then knocked. When I answered, a blast of arctic air hit me in the face. Tryna stood there hugging herself. "Get in here, girl."

She traipsed in. "I can't believe this. I'm going to Italy. On a private jet." She held her hands together and bounced up and down on her toes. "I can't believe it."

"Believe it." David sauntered in with a Cheshire cat smile. "Hi Avalee."

"Hi David." I crossed my arms and nodded toward Tryna. "What are we going to do with her?"

"Got any Ambien?"

Tryna slapped David on the shoulder. "Oh, stop. You know you are excited, too."

"I am." David scrunched up his nose. "I'm just not much of a flyer."

"Oh, just you wait. A whole new world of flight is about to open up before you when you see Levi's jet."

"Oh, oh, what?" Tryna started bouncing on her toes again. "Is it amazing?"

"Beyond amazing."

Lexi called up the steps. "Hey, everyone, limo's here. Get the lead out. Let's go."

Tryna flashed a smile at me. "And you talk about me being excited."

"It probably has something to do with Luca and Sal." I couldn't wait until Tryna got an eyeful of them.

"Who are they?"

"I'm not saying. You are wound up enough."

While the driver loaded the bags, we climbed inside. In no time, we enjoyed coffee, ham biscuits, oatmeal-raisin muffins, and champagne while speeding to Memphis.

I tasted the muffins. They were delicious. I offered one to Lexi.

"No thanks, I hate raisins."

"Really? I love them."

"Pfff, they are a tragic waste of a grape that could have been wine." Lexi grabbed a ham biscuit and turned to give Tryna the low-down on Luca and Sal. "Girl, those boys are fine." She looked up, dropped her head back, and shrugged up her shoulders. "They make the trip way too short."

Tryna's smile couldn't have grown any broader. "I can't wait."

David poked her. "Hey, you're married."

"So?" She winked at Lexi. "Just because I'm on a diet doesn't mean I can't look in the refrigerator."

Lexi high-fived her. "You got that right. Besides, they are married, too. No matter, they are charming and eye-candy to boot."

David rolled his eyes and said to Stan who sat next to him. "See what I have to put up with?"

"Hey." Tryna nudged him. "I heard that."

With mischievous brown eyes David said, "I know."

David and Tryna's banter went on like that the entire way, thoroughly entertaining us. I could hardly wait for them to see the jet and I wasn't disappointed. For a millisecond, they were speechless. Their mouths hung open like a baby's waiting for the next spoonful of pureed bananas.

"This is a living room." David scanned the seats and made a beeline to the recliner next to the electric fireplace. He lifted his eyebrows and gave us his famous innocent grin. "I found my chair."

Tryna looked around and then at Lex. "Where are they?"

"I'll check. You sit there on the sectional." Lexi disappeared through the galley door then returned with Luca on one arm and Sal on the other. Tryna sucked in a quick breath.

"Here." David waved a tissue at her. "This is to wipe up the drool."

Lexi clearly enjoyed showing off her boys. "Tryna, this is Luca and Sal."

"Hi, nice to meet you." Tryna stuck out her hand and gasped when Luca fixed his clear green eyes on her, bent, and kissed it.

"The pleasure is all mine."

Under her breath, Tryna whispered, "Not by a long shot."

Sal gazed down at Lexi with his sultry eyes. "What can we get for you? Coffee? Juice? Wine?"

"A room?" David lowered one eyebrow and smirked at Lexi.

"Oh, hush up, David."

"Well," said Momma. "Since you boys are asking, I'll have coffee."

Both men turned to her and their demeanor immediately changed from playboys to little boys seeing their grandmother. Sal spoke first. "Ah, Nonnina."

Luca took her hand. "Come. Sit here. It is the most comfortable."

In nine little words, my mother had turned the Chippendales into little grandsons competing for her attention, much to Tryna's and Lexi's disappointment. I might also add to David's great amusement. Molly Kate didn't notice any of this because she only had eyes for Stan as they snuggled at the far end of the sectional. Watching them made me think of Ty, which made me think of my ring and again, I wondered where it could be. I had a feeling it was most likely at the bottom of Junie's toy box.

****

Since there were so many of us, Levi sent a limo to pick us up. No one spoke on the way except for oohs and ahhs. Italy in winter had a beauty all its own. When we pulled up to the mansion, David said, "No way." He stared at me. "This is where they live?"

"Tryna covered her mouth. "Oh my. Why I'd never move back to Moonlight."

Momma had tears in her eyes. "God love her. The child deserves this."

Jema came running out the door waving her hand. We piled out of the car hugging like we hadn't just been there less than two months earlier. Levi followed with Jema's daughters, Amanda and Olivia. Momma hustled over to them with her arms held high. "Levi, my boy! Amanda! Olivia! How are my girls? Oh, I've missed you all so much!"

"Y'all come in, we will have your luggage brought in."

Carina stood by the door and greeted each of us as we walked in. When she greeted David, he stared at her kumquat hair and tried to smile through his grimace.

Tryna kicked his foot and murmured, "Quit staring. You look like you just put your hand in a messy diaper."

Fortunately, Carina seemed oblivious to David's silent scream. "Welcome, everybody. Follow me, and I will show you to your rooms."

Mom and I started to follow her, but Jema held us back. "I put y'all in the same room. Is that okay? We haven't finished refurbishing the other wing yet."

"I don't mind. That bed is large enough for three people." I turned to Mom. "Just don't snore."

"Mercy, child. Have you heard yourself lately? Now get on up them stairs and show me our room."

"When y'all have unpacked and freshened up, come downstairs to the library, just past the kitchen. Lillianna has our antipasti in there already.

"Antipasti?" Momma frowned.

"I'll tell you all about it, Momma. Now, let's go upstairs."

When Mom walked through the doorway, she stopped short and looked around. "Mercy, Lord, what a room."

"Pretty amazing, isn't it?" I pointed to the

bathroom. "Take a look in there."

"Why, fathers. I'll need a ladder to get in that tub."

"There's a shower over there." I pointed to the stone enclosure.

"There's no curtain. Won't the floor get all wet?"

"No. It's all good, Momma." I dug in her purse. "Now check your blood sugar and then we will head downstairs. You are going to love the food here."

Levi and Jema waited for us in the library. The space felt smaller and more intimate than the sun terrace room. Firelight cast a warm glow against the stone walls, terra cotta tile floors, and buttery-soft leather sofa and chairs. The surface of the enormous walnut sideboard was barely visible beneath all the platters of meats, cheeses, breads, fruits, spreads, and olives. A bar had been built into an arched opening where several varieties of wines and liquors were arranged.

"Come in, Cladie Mae." Jema held up her hands. "What do you think?"

Momma tuned up again. "I'm so happy, darling. So very happy for you and Levi." Jema rose from her chair and enveloped Mom in a long, swaying, embrace.

I could hear Lexi long before she got to the library. "Come on, y'all. You aren't going to believe the spread Lillianna puts on." She paraded into the room and straight to the bar with Tryna following close behind.

Tryna picked up a glass and said to Jema, "I hope this helps my jaw."

Jema lowered her eyebrows. "What's wrong with your jaw?"

"It's hit the floor so many times it's sore." She raised the glass to her lips. "This place is breathtaking."

David sat beside Avalee. "I think she really hurt it on the jet."

Jema grinned with understanding. "Luca and Sal?"

Lexi spritzed seltzer in her bourbon. "Yeah, at first. Until we discovered they were such momma's boys. All the zing went out of the experience." She nodded toward Mom. "Thanks a lot, Miss Cladie."

"Italian men do love their mommas and grandmommas." The flickering light played on Jema's face as she considered what she wanted to put on her plate. "Now eat up. But save room. This is just the first course."

"There's more?" David looked as if he'd fallen into a roomful of diamonds.

"Oh, yea." Molly Kate piled her plate high. "A lot more."

Lillianna had outdone herself again. After the antipasti, we moved to the dining room for seafood soup, pumpkin ravioli, pork spareribs with polenta, and roast pepper salad. While we ate, she cleared out what was left of the antipasti, and replaced it with several desserts and coffee.

We returned to the library gorged. I didn't think I could eat another bite until I spied the cannoli. I prayed for forgiveness for the sin I was about to commit. While we nibbled on our sweets and drank espresso, the mood changed from excitement to satiated weariness. Even the fire rested in an orange radiance.

Jema yawned and said, "I don't know about you all, but I'm bushed."

"My bed is calling me," said Lexi. "In fact, it has been calling me ever since I left it the first time."

"I hear the bathtub." I stood and set my plate on the

table.

Momma started picking dishes up. "Where is the kitchen?"

"Oh no, Cladie. Lillianna is as possessive of her kitchen as you are yours. She will take care of it. We make sure she is paid well." Jema turned to all of us. We have a big day tomorrow. Oh, I forgot to mention, at the suggestion of Avalee we have decided to have our New Year's Eve anniversary celebration in the foyer and sun terrace room. I have workers setting everything up, so please use the back stairs and stay in this wing of the house, okay?"

"Sounds good by me." Stan stood and helped Molly Kate up. "I think we need to put that romantic honeymoon room to good use."

"Oh, puleeze." Lexi put her fingers in her ears. "Lalalalalaa."

Levi chuckled and put his arm around Jema's shoulders. "Night, everyone."

****

I did it again. Momma came in the room with coffee and breakfast. "Are you going to sleep all day?"

Stretching, I looked at the clock. "I can't believe I've slept past noon again. There is something magical about this bed."

"Baby, you're just worn slap out. Here, drink your coffee and eat something. You need your strength."

I bit into a croissant. "Where is everyone?"

"The girls went shopping and the guys are sightseeing."

"Oh, Momma, you should have gone."

"I don't care anything about shopping. But I have enjoyed visiting with Carina. You know, she can take in your bridesmaid dress. So, I told her to come up around one. She will have it ready for you in just a few hours."

"That's nice of her."

"David's befriended her. He asked her to help him set up his station. So, she's been busy with helping him all morning. Tryna, too."

I sipped my coffee. "David's up to something. I just feel it."

"Well, you finish up here and get dressed. She'll be here soon. I think I'm going to bundle up and take a look at the grounds."

"Okay Mom." I lay back on my pillow, finished my roll, and thought about tonight. Frankly, I'd be glad when it was all over. I decided that at the stroke of midnight I'd sneak back to my room and take another long soak. I loved Jema, but I just didn't feel like celebrating.

At one on the dot, a knock came at my door. "Come in."

A woman I didn't recognize walked in. She had auburn hair cut in a blunt bob. "Miss Avalee. I've come to take in your gown."

"Carina? You look incredible."

"You like? Mr. David did it."

"I knew he was up to something. He's the best. We call him our perfect ten."

"Thank you, now, if you would, please put on your dress."

I slipped it on and Carina got to work. In no time, she had it pinned and ready to sew. "I'll bring it back to you in a few hours."

"Thank you." Since the girls were in town, I decided to relax in my room and read. The night was going to be a long one and I wanted to be mentally prepared to celebrate Jema and Levi.

By the time the girls returned to the villa, it was dark. Tryna and David hurried to set up for hair and nails. Once again, the fun began. The only weird thing was Jema insisted we all have red nail polish. That didn't seem to go with our color scheme, but oh well; it was her party.

Within a couple of hours, we all looked like we had stepped back in time exactly one year ago. Carina slipped in and said, "Miss Avalee's dress is on her bed. Would you like to try it on?"

I waved her off. "I'm sure it's fine."

Jema said, "Go ahead and try it on, hon, just in case it needs tweaking."

Just as I thought, it fit perfectly.

"Avalee?" Jema put out her hands. "I need to get ready. Would you mind checking downstairs to make sure everything is right? I don't want to see it until the ceremony."

"Sure." I left my room and walked to the staircase. When I saw it my breath caught in my throat. It was just as I had imagined. There was no light except for candles in varying heights and sizes grouped on each tread. They cast an ethereal glow on the marble surface. I ran my fingers along the banister, admiring the effect as I reverently walked down each step. When I neared the bottom, I looked up and there was…Ty? I gripped the rail. Our eyes locked. He didn't move or speak. I couldn't. My heart began to pound.

The candlelight played against his sexy stubble-shadowed cheeks. He stared up at me and with his intense dark eyes spoke with them what he couldn't say.

They revealed love and loss, pain and hope, fear and joy. All these emotions pooled and emanated from his gaze. I put my hand to my mouth, unable to speak. He never took his eyes off mine as he knelt on one knee and held out a black velvet box with…my ring? The flickering light glinted off the tears collecting in the corners of his eyes. "Avalee, we go through life believing in a dream of our own making. Some of us never achieve it and live in regret. Those of us who achieve that dream, may find it didn't fulfill us as we had hoped. We still live in regret for the things we lost or ignored." His tears fell. "I only want you. Please, don't leave me to live a life of regret. Marry me? Please?"

"Yes" I hurried down the remaining steps and fell into his arms. He swung me around and held me tight. "Oh yes. I love you. I always have and always will."

He kissed me as a man who would never be put off again.

"Hey, down there. Don't mess up her hair."

David? We both looked up to see everyone watching and wiping their eyes before breaking out in thunderous applause. Ty slipped the ring on my finger and then wrapped me in a kiss again.

Jema called down. "Listen up, if you two are going to get married, Avalee had better get up here and change her dress."

"Married?" I frowned up at her. "Now? How? What dress?"

"The one I lugged in that extra suitcase half-way around the world," hollered Lexi. "Now get on up here."

Ty pecked me on the lips. "I'll see you in a few."

Obviously, the confusion was still all over my face. While Lexi helped me out of my bridesmaid gown and David restyled my hair, they all explained.

"Ty came to see us in October," said Jema. The poor guy was wasting away with grief. So, Levi and I came up with this plan to bring you here and after we felt certain you'd marry him, Levi went to work getting the license. He worked a major miracle getting it this fast."

"How did he do it?"

"I don't know. All he said to me was, 'Don't ask.'"

Then the evening before you left, you planned your own wedding. Levi stayed out of sight and took notes for me.

Lexi continued. "I came up with the idea to bring your dress just in case. Brilliant, huh?"

Molly Kate sashayed in wearing her black bridesmaid dress. "And I'm the one who said you looked like a bean pole and suggested we use your bridesmaid dress as a pattern so Carina could take up your gown."

Momma wore a black mother-of-the-bride dress. "And I gave Ty the ring when he dropped by." She put her hand on her hip. "So you see? My baby Junie didn't take it."

David finished and turned me to the mirror. My hair fell in soft waves just as I had wanted. I truly did look like a star from old Hollywood. "You like it?"

"I love it. It's perfect."

David grinned at Tryna. She rolled her eyes. "Oh brother."

The girls helped me slip on my dress and then stepped back to admire. Momma held her hanky to her mouth. I wish your daddy could see you now. You are a vision my dear."

"Exquisite," added Jema.

Molly Kate walked over to me and took my hands. "You are stunning."

"You are drop-dead gorgeous." Lexi stood beside Molly Kate. "I can't quit looking at you."

"She needs just one more thing." Tryna handed me a tube of lipstick. "You need red lips."

Jema took me by the hand and led me to a full-length mirror. I stared at the bride looking back at me. In all my years of dreaming about my wedding, this surpassed them all.

"Here." Jema held out a diamond drop necklace and earrings. "Something new."

Molly Kate gave me a lace handkerchief. "Something borrowed."

"And something blue." Lexi handed me a note written in blue ink. "Wait until later to read it, okay?"

A rap came at the door, then it cracked open and someone thrust in an enormous bouquet of ivory spider mums, tiny white sweet heart roses, white ranunculus, with lacy dill tucked in among the blooms.

"Someone ordered these?"

"Scott." I held my arms out to him. "Scott, I can't believe this."

He tried his usual greeting. "Girrll, you look"—his voice cracked and he swallowed hard—"amazing. Tears streamed down his face. He wiped his eyes with the back of his hand as he stared at me. "You are so beautiful, my southern princess."

Jema handed the girls a red rose, and then they slipped out. Soon an orchestra began to play. Another knock. Oh Lord, I didn't think I could take one more surprise. My heart was already so full I thought it would burst. "Come in."

Felix stepped in.

"Felix? Oh, Felix. You came."

"You don't think I would miss your wedding do you?" He whistled. "My, but you are a sight to behold." He crooked his arm. "Come on, child, it's time. Old Felix is giving you away."

As the music played, Levi escorted Momma, followed by Jema, then Molly Kate, then Lexi. I watched them glide down the stairs and the crowd at the bottom move aside for them to pass. Who were all those people?

The orchestra began to play Bach's Minuet in G Major. Ty walked to the bottom step and held his hand out to me. Felix patted my arm. "Ready, little missy?"

The descent was dreamlike. When we reached the last step, Felix took my hand and placed it in Ty's. When we passed through the crowd, they followed us into the terrace room and took their seats.

Pastor Dixon rose and took his place in front. My mind reeled. Even he was here. I didn't think my smile could stretch any larger. As he spoke, I studied Ty's face and burned this moment in my mind. In the candlelight surrounded by my dearest friends, Ty and I entered into the rest of our lives together. When we kissed, sealing our vows, fireworks exploded outside against the ebony sky. I gazed into the eyes of my husband when a recording of Etta James, "At Last", began to play. That had to be Lexi's idea. I smiled and nuzzled Ty's chest. Yes indeed. At last.

****

During the reception, the lights were raised, and I could see the guests. It was absolutely overwhelming. Friends from all over had come. Nathan stood next to Lexi and gave me a little wave. Skye and Glen nearly tackled us. "This was all so romantic, so beautiful. I can't believe y'all married in Italy." Skye kissed her father and hugged me. Glen punched Ty on the arm. "Way to go, old man." He kissed me and said, "Welcome to the family, Mom." He looked around. "Where's my Big Momma?"

I glanced around the room and saw her standing with…Emma and Marcus? "Ty look."

"I know." He smiled down at me. "Let's go talk to them."

Emma looked up from Momma and smiled. "The ceremony was lovely." She took my hands. "Avalee, dear, you make a beautiful bride." Then she placed a small box on my palm. "I had hoped to get this to Cladie for her to give to you before the wedding. It belonged to my mother."

Inside was a diamond broach. "This is magnificent. But—"

"No, you must take it. This broach has been passed down with each generation. I didn't give it to Ty's first wife because…well, never mind the reason. I know you will take good care of it as you have my Tyler."

"Thank you, Emma." I pinned the broach on my gown and kissed her crepey cheek. "I'll treasure it always and when Skye marries, I will pass it along to her."

"Emma Jackson," Mom handed her a glass of champagne. "Looks like you and I are related now. That calls for a toast to the mothers-in-law."

Emma raised her glass. "A toast indeed."

After they had taken their sip, Momma said, "I'm tickled to death to have a son and grandchildren."

"And I'm happy to have Avalee." Emma paused a few moments. "I may not have much time left. But I want to spend it getting to know my new daughter."

"I feel the same way, Emma." And I did.

Jema called, "Ava, Ty, come cut the cake." We strolled over to where she stood. On a round table in the center of the room rose a six-tier cake, and I had no doubt about the flavors.

The night grew more and more magical. Frank Sinatra crooned over the speakers. Some guests hovered around the food stations and bar. Ty and I swayed on the dance floor in the foyer and others soon joined us. It was exactly as I had described to the girls. Except the snow. But, of course, I didn't expect that. Ty nuzzled my neck. "Hey, let's go upstairs. We have a room to ourselves in the other wing of the house. I hear Scott outdid himself getting it ready for us."

Every nerve in my body tingled in anticipation. I found Jema. "Ty and I are going upstairs."

She grinned. "Wait for a second. Go back to the foyer." Then she nodded at Levi.

He held his hands up and addressed the crowd. "And now for the last request of our lovely bride. Everyone gather for a last dance in the foyer."

When we all had gathered, the orchestra began playing "Winter Wonderland". Something cold dotted my arms. I looked up into the cavernous darkness of the foyer's high ceiling only to see snow falling. Inside. Feathery flakes. Just enough to create an enchanted scene.

I looked at Levi. "How?"

He winked. "Don't ask."

I lifted my face to Ty's and we kissed among the soft flakes. I'd given him up for love, and love had brought him back to me.

Epilogue

Love never fails.

~Mr. and Mrs. Tyler Jackson

Life is truly strange—both unfair and beyond generous. I've learned I will not always understand its ebbs and flows. The key to a good life is to treasure it, to handle it with respect and honor. Not only my life, but the lives of others as well.

Everyone is fighting a private battle, some more difficult than others. I know this by experience—when I lost Marc, and when I walked away from Ty for his good. And Emma. I didn't want to forgive her. I wanted justice. She was a hard lesson for me to learn about compassion and forgiveness. But I learned. And thank goodness, because now Ty and I do not have the ghost of bitterness overshadowing our lives. I realize there will always be highs and lows, but we now have the strength and freedom that forgiveness brings.

With Momma's improved health and AJ across the street, I feel more comfortable traveling with Ty on his assignments, and I enjoy collaborating with him on shoots. He enjoys working the Market with me. This has truly been a draw for tourists. We have people come from all over the county just to attend our first Saturday events. Mayor Sid Campbell is beyond thrilled. Even cantankerous Mr. Fleming attends.

Jema is so happy in Italy. I wonder if she will ever return to Moonlight? I know they both have big plans for Life Source and the people the organization serves. Surely, they will come home. At least I can hope.

Molly Kate and Stan's business is receiving great reviews and they are booked up for the entire spring, summer, and fall seasons. She is toying with the idea of New Year's Eve parties. I wonder why? And what's with the pipe tobacco and peppermint in the library?

And then there is Lexi, my redheaded, fireball friend. She and Nathan are still an item, and I don't know why. He is handsome, but he is also a dedicated career man. I don't ever see him settling down. Her ex who is still in prison has been contacting her, asking her to give him another chance. I won't repeat what she says about that. But maybe he has truly changed. And then there is Sid. He has appointed Lexi to head all the publicity for the Department of Tourism. This throws them together a lot. Life is just the way Lexi likes it. For the first time in her life, she has choices. And knowing her like I do, she will squeeze every bit of pleasure out of her new circumstances she can. But that's a story for another time.

Miss Cladie's Fried Green Tomatoes

Ingredients

Green tomatoes (at least one per person)

White Corn Meal mix (about a cup, but keep the bag
close by in case you need more)

Salt & Pepper (to taste)

Oil (Canola or something with high smoking point. Use
enough to cover the bottom of the skillet)

Directions

1. Slice green tomatoes, oh, about ¼" thick
2. Lay slices on a piece of parchment or a cookie sheet.
3. Lightly salt them. (This causes them to sweat a bit,
   giving a firmer bite and helps cornmeal adhere
   better. I never use egg.)
4. Dump cornmeal mix in a pie plate, salt and pepper to
   taste.
5. Press slices of tomato into the cornmeal mixture on
   both sides and replace on the parchment or cookie
   sheet.
6. Let them dry a bit.
7. Heat oil in the skillet. (I use my cast iron skillet if
   I'm only frying up a few. However, when cooking
   for a crowd, I use my electric skillet. Be sure to
   remove the bits of cornmeal left in the pan that
   start to burn. This will ruin your last tomato slices.)
8. Before easing the slices in the oil, give them one last
   dusting of cornmeal mixture.
9. Fry until golden brown on one side and flip them
   over.
10. Drain slices on paper towel or a rack.

A Note from Miss Cladie:

These yummy jewels are not only good as a meal side, but they make dandy appetizers! Felix even has me make him sandwiches with them. Enjoy!

Molly Kate's Cheese Straws

Ingredients

2 C extra sharp cheddar cheese, grated
½ C Gruyere cheese, grated
½ C butter, softened (real butter y'all, not that fake stuff)
1 ½ C all-purpose flour
1t salt
¼ t cayenne pepper
¼ t garlic powder

Directions

1. Preheat oven to 375 degrees.
2. Mix cheeses-all but one cup of the cheddar- into a bowl (Best if you have a stand mixer or electric hand mixer).
3. Add butter.
4. Cream butter and cheese to a smooth consistency (about 5-10 min).
5. In another bowl, sift together the last four ingredients.
6. Gradually add flour mixture to butter & cheese and mix until completely incorporated and smooth.
7. Add saved cup of grated cheddar cheese.
8. Spoon portions of mixture in either a cookie press or piping bag fitted with a large star tip.
9. Slowly pipe long strands of the dough on parchment-covered cookie sheets about 1 inch apart.
10. Cut these strips into 6" pieces.
11. Bake 10-12 minutes or until edges turn golden brown.
12. Remove from oven and let cool.

A Note from Avalee:

Okay, so I don't cook. But this is one of my favorites from Molly Kate. I think these are the best cheese straws you'll ever taste! I like them with Lexi's martinis. These keep for three days in an airtight container, but they are best eaten the day they were made. Careful, they crumble easy. But this crispy texture is what makes them so yummy!

Molly Kate's Orange Rolls

Ingredients:

Rolls:
½ C warm water
2 pkg yeast
1 ¼ C scalded milk
¾ C sugar
1 t salt
2 eggs, well beaten
5 C flour—more or less

Filling:
1 stick butter, softened
8 T orange marmalade
1 C lightly packed brown sugar

Icing:
2 C confectioner's sugar
4 oz cream cheese, softened
3T butter, softened
3T orange juice—tad more if you need to thin it
1T orange zest

Directions:

Rolls:
1. Soak yeast in warm water.
2. Combine milk and butter. Add sugar and salt.
3 Add yeast mixture and stir in eggs.
4. Add flour until it forms a stiff batter. Cover and let it rise until double. (about one hour)
5. Punch down, roll out very thin.
6. Spread with softened butter and marmalade (add more if needed). Sprinkle brown sugar on top.

7. Gradually roll the dough toward you into a tight log with the seam side down.

8. Slice into ½ to ¾-inch pieces. Place cut side up in a buttered baking dish (there will hardly be any space between them) and allow them to rise until doubled.

9. Bake at 375° for 20-25 minutes until lightly browned. Watch them closely. You don't want them hard as bricks.

10. Icing: Beat confectioner's sugar, cream cheese, butter, orange juice, and orange zest together until smooth. Spread on warm rolls and let it melt into the rolls.

A Note from Molly Kate:

Okay y'all. I got talked into sharing my secret recipe for Orange Rolls. But, let's just keep this between you and me, okay? Enjoy!

Hint: I make an extra half recipe of the icing to drizzle on the rolls after they are cooled. That is, if there are any left to cool!

Lexi's Chocolate Espresso Martini

Ingredients:
1 ½ oz Godiva original chocolate liqueur
1 ½ oz Crème de Cacao
½ oz vanilla vodka
2 ½ oz Half & Half
1T cooled espresso
chocolate syrup for decorating

Directions:
1. Mix the first five ingredients in a cocktail shaker filled with ice and shake.
2. Drizzle martini glass with syrup inside and around rim.
3. Pour martini in glass.

A Tip from Lexi:
For that extra decadent and sinful treat, garnish with a small piece of fudge on a toothpick. Great for stirring and nibbling.

A word about the author...

Linda Apple writes from her soul and speaks from her heart.

She is the author of *Writing Life~Your Stories Matter, Connect! A Simple Guide to Public Speaking for Writers,* and *POW~Promises Kept, the Inspiring Stories of Walter "Boots" Mayberry.* She has been published in sixteen of the *Chicken Soup for the Soul* books.

Her Moonlight Mississippi Series is born from years of living in the South, loving southern culture, its people, and of course, the deep friendships she has forged over the years.

She speaks and teaches workshops for writers' conferences nationwide. Besides writing, her passion is to help others succeed in their writing goals.

Linda and her husband, Neal, live in Fayetteville, Arkansas, close to their five children, five children-in-law, and thirteen grandchildren. (Linda is a very young grandmother!)

lindacapple@gmail.com
lindaapple.com
facebook.com/lindacapple

Thank you for purchasing
this publication of The Wild Rose Press, Inc.

If you enjoyed the story, we would appreciate your
letting others know by leaving a review.

For other wonderful stories,
please visit our on-line bookstore at
www.thewildrosepress.com.

For questions or more information
contact us at
info@thewildrosepress.com.

The Wild Rose Press, Inc.
www.thewildrosepress.com

Stay current with The Wild Rose Press, Inc.

Like us on Facebook

https://www.facebook.com/TheWildRosePress

And Follow us on Twitter
https://twitter.com/WildRosePress

www.ingramcontent.com/pod-product-compliance
Lightning Source LLC
Chambersburg PA
CBHW071511260626

47170CB00002B/338